*New York Times* bestselling author Yasm

**More praise for Yasmine Galenorn:**

'Yasmine Galenorn's imagination is a beautiful thing' *Fresh Fiction*

'Galenorn's gallery of rogues is an imaginative delight' *Publishers Weekly*

'Pulls no punches . . . [and] leaves you begging for more' *Bitten by Books*

'[Yasmine Galenorn's] books are always enchanting, full of life and emotion as well as twists and turns that keep you reading long into the night' *Romance Reviews Today*

'Explore this fascinating world' *TwoLips Reviews*

'As always, [Galenorn] delivers intriguing characters, intricate plot layers, and kick-butt action' *Romantic Times*

*By Yasmine Galenorn*

*Whisper Hollow Series*
Autumn Thorns

# AUTUMN THORNS

## YASMINE GALENORN

**headline**
ETERNAL

Quotation from *The Ingoldsby Legends; Or, Mirth and Marvels*
© 1907 Thomas Ingoldsby

Crow image © basel101658/Shutterstock

Published by arrangement with Jove,
A division of Penguin Group (USA) LLC,
A Penguin Random House Company

First published in Great Britain in 2015
by HEADLINE ETERNAL
An imprint of HEADLINE PUBLISHING GROUP

1

Cataloguing in Publication Data is available from the British Library

ISBN 978 1 4722 3619 7

Offset in 11.8/13 pt Times LT Std by Jouve (UK)

Printed and bound in Great Britain by CPI Group (UK) Ltd, Croydon, CR0 4YY

MIX
Paper from
responsible sources
FSC
www.fsc.org
FSC® C104740

Headl                                                        recyclable
prod                                                         nd other
contr                                                        e expected
to                                                           origin.

*To my mother, Helen, and my sister, Claudia.*
*Both long gone, and yet both still visiting through the Veil . . .*

## ACKNOWLEDGMENTS

I have a usual list of suspects to whom I owe a great deal when I'm writing a book. To my editor, Kate Seaver, and agent, Meredith Bernstein, for encouraging my vision and supporting it. To my husband, Samwise, who is one of the most supportive men I've ever met. To Andria and Jenn, my assistants who help make it possible for me to write three books a year and stay sane. To my readers, who buy the books and support my fan base—without enough readers buying the books, authors wouldn't be getting contracts. And lastly, to Ukko, Rauni, Mielikki, and Tapio—my spiritual foundation.

You can find me on the web at galenorn.com, and all the links to my newsletter and my social networks can be found there. If you want to contact me, please e-mail me through my contact page on my website, or send snail mail through my publisher. Please include a self-addressed stamped envelope if you want a reply.

*Dear Reader:*

*I welcome you to my new Whisper Hollow series. This world, when I first envisioned it, began to haunt my dreams and waking life, and I knew I had to write about it. The characters and world came to life and are firmly established in my head and keyboard now! I hope that you enjoy your time spent in Whisper Hollow, and that you'll be back for Kerris's next adventure.* Dreaming Death, *the next book in the series, will be out in October 2016.*

*Next up, in February 2016, will be* Darkness Raging. *This will be the last Otherworld book from Berkley, but rest assured, I plan on continuing the series on my own after that. After* Darkness Raging *will be* Flight from Mayhem, *the second Fly by Night book, in August 2016.*

*For those of you new to my books, I hope you enjoy your first foray into my worlds. For those of you who have followed me for a while, I want to thank you for taking a chance on my new series. Check my website, galenorn.com, for information on my newsletter, short stories, release info, and links to where you can find me on the Internet.*

*Bright Blessings,*
*The Painted Panther*
*Yasmine Galenorn*

'Twas now the very witching time of night,
When churchyards groan, and graves give up their dead . . .

THOMAS INGOLDSBY

## Advice for Visitors to Whisper Hollow

1. If you hear someone call your name from the forest, don't answer.

2. Never interrupt Ellia when she's playing to the dead.

3. If you see the Girl in the Window, set your affairs in order.

4. Try not to end up in the hospital.

5. If the Crow Man summons you, follow him.

6. Remember: Sometimes the foul are actually fair.

7. And most important: Don't drive down by the lake at night.

### Whisper Hollow:
*Where spirits walk among the living,
and the lake never gives up her dead.*

# THE MORRÍGAN

*The Morrígan, Night Mare Queen, and Goddess of Sover-*
*eignty, Queen of Shapeshifters and Mother of the Fae, culls*
*the dead from the battlefield and gathers them to her, under*
*the embrace of her feathered cloak. She is mother to the Bean*
*Nighe and the Bean Sidhe, the sirens of the spirit world, who*
*warn of death to come by vision and by song. She is mother*
*to the Crow Man, who haunts the woodlands, surrounded by*
*a murder of crows, carrying her messages to those to whom*
*she would speak. The Crow Man walks before the goddess,*
*announcing her appearance. He speaks through the raven*
*and the crow, and to ignore his summons is to ignore the gods.*
*Do so at your own risk.*

*But not all dead wish to stay in their shadowed realm,*
*and not all dead understand the reality of their situation.*
*And in some lands, the energy of the Veil is so strong that*
*spirits can walk freely between the worlds. So it was that*
*the Goddess of Crows engendered nine great families—the*
*bloodline passing through the maternal side—of women*
*born to drive the wandering ghosts back into their graves,*
*to stand between the dead and the living as protectors. The*
*Morrígan's daughters, known as the spirit shamans, are*
*charged with these duties.*

*To each spirit shaman, a match is born—a shapeshifter*
*by birth. He will be her protector and guardian. They will be*
*forever bound. And to each spirit shaman, a lament singer*

*will be assigned—a daughter of the Bean Sidhes. She will bring her magical songs to complete the triad. Together, these triads will protect the portals of the world that lead into the realm of Spirit, and keep the dead from flooding the land of the living.*

# CHAPTER 1

━━━❦━━━

The road twisted, curving through a series of S turns as my Honda CR-V wound along Highway 101. To my left, the forest breathed softly, looming thick and black even though it was still early afternoon. Brilliant maple and birch leaves—in shades of autumn bronze and yellow—dappled the unending stands of fir and cedar. With each gust of wind, they went whirling off the branches to litter the ground with sodden debris. October in western Washington was a windy, volatile month. The fact that I was making this trip on a Sunday evening worked for me, though. There weren't many cars on the road, especially not where I was going.

To my right, waves frothed across Lake Crescent as the wind whipped against the darkened surface. The rain shower turned into a drenching downpour, and I eased off on the accelerator, lowering my speed to thirty-five miles per hour, and then to thirty. The drops were pelting so hard against the asphalt that all I could see was a blur of silver on black. These winding back roads were dangerous. All it took was one skid toward the guardrail, one wrong turn of the wheel, and the

Lady would claim another victim, dragging them down into her secreted recesses.

It had been fifteen years since I had made this drive . . . fifteen years, a ferry ride, and about 120 miles. I grabbed the ferry in Seattle over to Kingston and then wound through Highway 104 up the interior of the peninsula, till I hit Highway 101, which took me through Port Townsend and past Port Angeles. Now, three hours after I had left the city, I neared the western end of Lake Crescent. The junction that would take me onto Cairn Street was coming up. From there, a twenty-minute drive around the other side of the lake would lead me through the forest, back to Whisper Hollow.

As I neared the exit, I veered off the road, onto the shoulder, and turned off the ignition. This was it. My last chance to drive past, loop around the Olympic Peninsula. My last chance to turn my back on all of the signs. But I knew I was just procrastinating against the inevitable. My life in Seattle had never really been my own, and this past month, when the Crow Man sent me three signs, I realized I was headed home. Then, last week, my grandmother died. Her death sealed the deal because, like it or not, it was my duty to step up and fill her shoes.

I slowly opened the door, making sure I was far enough off the road to avoid being hit, and emerged into the rain-soaked evening. Shoving my hands in my pockets, I stared at the lake through the trees. The wind was whipping up currents on the water, the dark surface promising an icy bath to anything or anybody unlucky enough to go tumbling in. The rising fog caught in my lungs and I coughed, the noise sending a murder of crows into the air from where they'd been resting in a tall fir. They circled over me, cawing, then headed north, toward Whisper Hollow.

*Crows.* I pulled my jacket tighter against a sudden gust of wind that caught me from the side. Crows were messengers. In fact, the Crow Man had reached out all the way to Seattle, where he summoned me with three omens. The first sign had been the arrival of his flock in Seattle—they followed me everywhere, and I could feel his shadow walking behind them, looming down through the clouds.

The second sign had been a recurring nightmare, for three nights running. Each night, I found myself walking along a dark and shrouded path through the Whisper Hollow cemetery, as the Blood Moon gleamed full and ripe overhead. As I came to the center of the graveyard, I saw—standing next to a headstone—Grandma Lila. Dripping wet and smelling of lake water and decay, she opened her arms and pulled me in, kissing me on both cheeks. Then she lit into me, tearing me up one side and down the other.

*"You've turned your back on your gift—on your heritage. Face it, girl, it's time to accept what you are. Whisper Hollow is waiting. It's time you came home to carry on with my duties. It won't be long now, and you'll be needed. You were born a spirit shaman, and you'll die one—there's no walking away from this. Something big is coming, and the town will need your help. Don't let me down. Don't let Whisper Hollow down."* Each of those three nights, I woke up crying, afraid to call her in case there was no answer on the other end of the line.

The third sign came last week, a day or two after I had the last dream. Signs always go in threes. Always have. Third time's the charm, true. But bad things happen in threes, as well. I was walking home from a morning gig at work, deep in thought, when I glanced at the store next to me. There, staring from behind the storefront, was the Girl in the Window. A cold sweat broke over me, but when I looked again, she was gone. It *couldn't* have been her, could it? The Girl in the Window belonged to Whisper Hollow and she was never seen outside the borders of the town. Squinting, I craned my neck, moving close to the pane. *Blink* . . . it was only a mannequin. But mannequin or not, my gut told me that I had been visited by the sloe-eyed Bean Nidhe, dripping wet and beckoning to me.

One of the rules of Whisper Hollow echoed back to haunt me. *If you see the Girl in the Window, set your affairs in order.* This was all the proof I needed. I went home and began to sort through my things. The next day, an express letter from Ellia arrived, informing me that my grandparents had gone off the road, claimed by the Lady of Crescent Lake. She was a hungry bitch, that one, and neither age nor status mattered in her selection of victims. The car hadn't surfaced, and neither had my grandfather's body—no shock there. But Grandma Lila had been found on the shore, hands placed gently over her chest in a sign of respect. Even the Lady knew better than to get the Morrígan's nose out of joint by disrespecting her emissaries.

And now, a week later, I was on my way home to take Lila's place before the dead started to walk. I sucked in a deep breath, took one last look at the lake, and returned to the car.

"What do you think, guys?" A glance into the backseat showed Agent H, Gabby, and Daphne all glaring at me from their carriers. They weren't at all happy with me, but the ride would be over soon.

*"Purp."* Gabby was the first to speak. She stared at me with golden eyes, her fur a glorious black, plush and thick. The tufts on her ears gave her an odd, feathered look, standard Maine Coon regalia. She let out another squeak and shifted in her carrier. Not to be outdone, Agent H—a huge brown tabby and also a Maine Coon—let out a short, loud yowl. He was always vocal, and right now he was letting me know that he was not amused. Daphne, a tortoiseshell, just snorted and gave me a look that said, *Really, can we just get this over with?* They were littermates, three years old, and I had taken them in from a shelter after they were rescued from an animal hoarder. They had been three tiny balls of fluff when I brought them home. Now they were huge, and— along with Peggin—they were my closest friends.

Frowning, I squinted at them. "You're sure about this? You might not like living in Whisper Hollow, you know. It's a strange town, and the people there are all . . . *like me*."

I stopped. That was the crux of it. The people in Whisper Hollow—they were *my* people. Even though I hadn't been home in fifteen years I knew that both they, and the town, were waiting for me.

Gabby pawed her face, cleaning her ears, and let out another squeak.

"Okay. Final answer. Head home, it is." With a deep breath, I pulled back onto the road, turning right as I eased onto Cairn Street. We were on our way back to Whisper Hollow, where the ghosts of the past were waiting to weave me into their world as seamlessly as the forest claimed the land, and the lake claimed her conquests.

I'm Kerris Fellwater and I'm a spirit shaman by birth, which means I connect with the dead. I can talk to them, see them, and drive them back to their graves if they get out of hand. At least, that's the goal and job description, if you want to think of it as a profession. The gift is my birthright, from the day I was born until the day I die. My training's incomplete, of course, but instinct takes me a long way. And I've always been a rule breaker, so doing things *my* way seems the natural order of things.

As my grandmother was, and her mother before her, I'm a daughter of the Morrígan. Our matriarchal line stretches back into the mists, as do the spirit shamans. I can feel and see energy, and I can manipulate it—to a degree. Some people might call me a witch, but the truth is, most magic I can cast is minor, except when it comes to the world of spirits and the dead. There, my power truly blossoms out.

When I turned eighteen, after a major blowout with my grandfather, I decided to ditch my past, the town, and anything resembling family, so I took my high school diploma and the two hundred dollars I had saved and headed for Seattle. I found a room for rent in the basement of a house and a job at Zigfree's Café Latte. Over the years, I moved into a high-rise, and I worked my way up from barista to managing the store, but it was just something I did to pay the rent on my shiny new apartment.

At night, I slipped out into the rainy streets to take on my second gig—one that made very little money but kept me sane. A few months after I arrived in Seattle, the headaches started. I knew what they were from, and the only way to stop them. If spirit shamans don't use their powers, the energy can build up and implode—not a pretty future, to say the least. At best, ignoring the power can drive one mad. At worst, it can kill from an energy overload.

So I hunted around till I found a gig for a penny paper that later turned into an online webzine as the Internet grew into something more than an oddity. I investigated haunted houses and paranormal activity. On the side, I evicted a number of ghosts. The job didn't pay much, but that didn't matter to me. The coffee shop kept me in rent and food money, but the ghost hunting? That was what kept the headaches at bay. I spent all my spare time tromping through haunted buildings, looking for the ghosts who were troublemakers—the dead who were too focused on the world of the living to do anybody any good.

When I found them, I'd drop a hint to the owner, and about fifty percent asked me to come in and deal with the spirits. And kicking their astral butts, so to speak, is what kept me from falling over the edge of the cliff into La-La Land. I began to create my own rites and rituals from the training Lila had given me before I left home, and for the most part they worked. There were a few missteps, some of them embarrassing and a few downright dangerous, but overall, I managed.

In my personal life, I kept to myself. I had met a few friends but no one I felt like I could trust, other than keeping in touch with Peggin. Mostly, I read a lot, and I'm a speed reader and I have a photographic memory when it comes to what I read in books.

I have a lot of time to pursue my hobby. See, once people find out that I hang with spirits . . . well . . . it goes one of two ways: Either they're afraid of me, or they glom on to me in hopes of gaining tomorrow's lottery numbers or finding out if old Uncle Joe had actually squirreled away money somewhere and forgot to leave a note about it in his will. Being a spirit shaman doesn't make for easy dates, either. When guys find out that I can chat up their dead sisters or friends and get the lowdown on what they're *really* like, that usually ends the date. At first, their fear—couched as "It's not you, it's me"— bothered me. After all, the boys in Whisper Hollow had

accepted me for who I was, quirks and all. So it seemed like
a pale excuse. After a while, though, I learned to ignore the
brush-offs and eventually, I stopped dating, for the most part.

But now I was going home, where everybody in Whisper
Hollow is eccentric, in one way or another. Everybody's just
a little bit mad. And I realized that I was actually looking
forward to it. Especially since my grandfather was dead and
could never bother me again. At least . . . that was my hope.
Because in Whisper Hollow, the dead don't always stay put
where you plant them.

I yawned, blinking. As I struggled to sit up, I wondered
where I was, then it hit me over the head. *Home.* I was
home. Stretching my neck, I realized that, for the first time
in a long while, I had slept soundly. The master bedroom
was on the main floor, but when I'd pulled into town it had
been past seven. After stopping to grab a burger and fries
and a few things at the local convenience store, I reached
the house around quarter past eight.

I'd been exhausted, more emotionally than anything else,
so I had set up the litter boxes in the utility room and locked
the cats in there for the night. After I called Peggin—my best
friend from high school and the one person I'd kept actively
in touch with while I was in Seattle—to let her know I was
back in town, I dropped on the sofa to think over my next step.
The next thing I knew, I was waking up, still dressed, and
morning was pouring through the partially opened curtains.

Stumbling to the bathroom, I showered, then sat at the
vanity. As I leaned in, trying for a decent makeup day, I
grimaced. My face looked as tired as I felt. Circles under-
scored my eyes, but that would clear up with enough water
and another good night's sleep. My eyes were dark today—
they varied from almost golden to a deep brown depending
on my mood. Right now, they were mostly bloodshot.

I brushed out my hair and braided the long, brunette
strands to keep them out of my face while they dried. At
thirty-three, I had yet to see a gray hair, for which I was

grateful. As I shifted, looking for my bra and panties, I caught the reflection of the mark on my back and paused. *A reminder of who I was. Of what I was.* It was a birthmark, though it looked like a tattoo—and it was in the center of my back, right above my butt. If it had been actual ink, they would have called it a tramp stamp. But I had been born with it, as had my mother and grandmother. It was the shape of a crow standing on a crescent moon, and it was jet black. It was the mark of a spirit shaman.

I slid into my underwear and then fastened my bra, shimmying to position my breasts in the cups. At a solid size eight and a 38F cup, I was happy enough with myself. I liked my curves—and I had plenty of them, in the classic hourglass shape. I hurried into my jeans and a snug V-neck sweater and patted my stomach. I did need to find a gym, though. I worked out a *lot*. I tended to favor weights and the stationary bike, though mostly for health and strength. Unlike so many of the women I met, I wasn't on a diet and I ate what I liked, preferring meat and vegetables and the occasional pasta dish. I ate my junk food, too, but tried to keep it to a few times a week.

Finally, I was ready to face the day.

*You mean, face a new way of life, don't you?*

*Fine . . . face a new life. Happy now?*

*Yeah, I guess so.*

Snorting—I usually won most of the arguments I held with myself in my head—I wandered into the kitchen. Next order of the day: Secure caffeine. Life always looked better after a pot of coffee, and as a former barista, I made a mean cup of java.

Early light filtered through the kitchen window, silvery and gray with the overcast sky. The room was spacious, with an eat-in nook, and a large window by the table that overlooked the backyard. I ran my hands along the smooth, cool countertops. My grandparents had renovated during the time I'd been gone. The laminate had been replaced by granite; the white cabinets had been switched out for dark. All the appliances were now stainless steel, and tile on the floor had replaced the checkerboard linoleum. But the walls were still the same warm gold color they had always been—although the paint looked fresh—and the kitchen had the same cozy feel.

On the counter stood a shiny stainless steel espresso machine. Spotting a grinder and a container of beans next to the machine, I smiled. Grandma had loved her caffeine and I'd inherited her addiction. Grandpa Duvall had preferred tea— strong and black and bitter. I opened a cupboard at random to find neat, tidy shelves of packaged foods. The refrigerator, however, was empty and spotless. A few days ago, when I told her I was coming home, Peggin had promised to come in and clean it out for me. Apparently, she had managed to do so before she left on vacation. I breathed a sigh of relief. One less task I'd have to deal with.

I pulled a couple of shots of espresso and added some of the creamer I had picked up at the store the night before. As I carried my mug over to the table, the phone on the kitchen wall rang, startling me out of my thoughts. Who could be calling me? Peggin was out of town till Monday night, and she was the only other person who knew I had come home, besides my lawyer.

Hesitating, almost hoping it was a telemarketer, I picked up the receiver. "Hello?"

"Kerris . . . you're really back. Peggin called me. You got my letter, then? I'm sorry about your grandparents, my dear."

*Ellia.* She sounded shaky, but no matter how many years it had been, I would never forget the lilting sound of her voice. When I was little, I'd clutch my grandmother's hand as we followed Ellia into the graveyard. She would sing, leading the way, her violin in hand. I had been mesmerized by her songs.

I propped the receiver on my shoulder, shrugging to hold it up to my ear as I peeked in the various drawers, looking to see what might be there. "I was going to call you, but figured it would be easier to talk in person. I suppose we'd better meet. Grandma Lila came to me in a dream; she told me there were things happening in town. What's going on?" I knew I sounded abrupt, but Ellia had never been aces in the diplomatic department either, and she didn't expect it from anybody else.

"There have been stirrings in the forest for several years. The Lady has been more active over the past couple of years, as well. Spirits are on edge, Kerris. Lila noticed this before she died and told me. We think Penelope's having a hard time keeping them over on her side." Down to business, all right.

The news didn't bode well. First, Penelope was usually pretty good at keeping the Veil closed. That she was having problems was a bad sign. And second, that the Lady of the Lake was hungrier than usual meant nobody was safe.

"What changed? Has Veronica been at it again?" Veronica could be friend or foe depending on her mood, though mostly she was interested in her own agenda and tended to ignore the living. But if she got her mind set to an idea and had to turn the town on its ear to achieve her goals, she wouldn't hesitate. We had seen that when I was thirteen and Veronica decided to throw a grand ball for the dead.

A pause. Then—"No. I have my suspicions, but I don't want to discuss them over the phone. Let's just say that over the past few months, things have begun to escalate with more Haunts, more Unliving. Your grandmother started to investigate, but then . . . Anyway, since her death, the dead have been walking more. I've been doing my best to play the shadows to sleep, but my songs won't work right without a spirit shaman to lead the rites for me."

I was nodding, though she couldn't see me. The night of every new moon, the lament singers and spirit shamans went out to the graveyards to calm the dead who had not yet passed beyond the Veil.

The Veil was a world between the worlds—it was a transit station for the dead, in a sense. A nebulous place of mist and fire and ice, where spirits wandered, not fully detached from the world of the living, and not yet ready to cross the threshold and move on to the Beyond. In most cities and places on the planet, the line between worlds was highly defined and it was easy for the Gatekeepers to guard the dead and keep them reined in, but in Whisper Hollow, things were different. The Veil was strong here, and so were the ghosts.

And now, with Grandma Lila dead—without a spirit

shaman to perform the rites and escort spirits into the Veil to begin with—the lament singers' songs would not work. And while Penelope held the ghosts at bay as much as she could, until she was able to persuade them to cross the threshold and leave behind all they had once been, the dead were still able to return and walk the earth.

Grandma Lila had been a strong woman—a stronger spirit shaman than I could ever hope to be, though Grandfather fought her every step of the way. I never knew why, but I knew that he wasn't her protector. In fact, unlike most spirit shamans, Grandma Lila had not been paired with a shapeshifter to watch over her. I wondered if that would be my fate, as well. She had never broached the subject during my training, and I had been too nervous to ask.

Shaking off my thoughts, I tried to push away my self-doubt. "When can we meet?"

"Tonight at my house? At six P.M. You remember where I live, don't you?"

I let out a slow breath. This was my job now, my heritage. I owed it to the town. "Fogwhistle Way. I don't remember the number, but I remember your house."

"That's right. Three Thirty-seven Fogwhistle Way. I'll be waiting for you. It's good to have you back, Kerris. I'm sorry about your grandmother. We needed her. And now, we need you." With that, she hung up.

I glanced out the kitchen window as a flock of crows rose into the sky from the maple in the backyard. They circled the house once, then headed out to the south. A storm was coming in from the north, off the Strait of Juan de Fuca. My gut said that it would barrel through the forest and hit us by afternoon.

Deciding I needed more caffeine, I pulled another couple of shots, then checked on the cats, setting down fresh food and water for them. They were freaked, of course, but they were safe and I'd let them out of their prison once I returned from shopping. I wanted to go through the house first to make certain there was nothing that would hurt them—no open windows, no rat traps.

With one last glance at the kitchen, I reached for my jacket and purse. As I paused, my hand on the doorknob, a wave of shadow rolled through. It reached out to examine me, cold and clammy as it tickled over my skin. Then, as I blinked, shivering, it vanished. Whirling, I glanced around the room, searching the corners. But the kitchen was empty.

Something was looming in the town, all right, and whatever it was, it knew I was back.

"I'm home, Grandma Lila," I whispered. "I just hope you'll be around when I need you."

And right then, I knew that—before whatever this was had ended—I was going to need all the help I could get . . . from *both* sides of the grave.

# CHAPTER 2

~

I pulled into the driveway and eased the car into park. As I stared at the stone house, I wasn't sure just what I had expected. I had been to Ellia's house before, but I remembered it as cold and looming. I was expecting to see a broken-down house, covered in moss, behind an overgrown tangle of weeds. But there it stood, pristine and tidy. The house was old, that much was true. Built of stone, it looked like it was from out of another era and it probably was. Whisper Hollow had been founded in the mid-1800s, when it was barely a settlement of ramshackle houses in the woods.

As I gathered my purse and slipped out of the CR-V, I took a deep breath as I looked around the yard. The gardens were neat and tidy, with a hint of overgrown wildness. Ellia liked mums—a row of mums lined the pavers that ran up to the front of the house. The lot, like my own, was thick with trees looming up and over the yard. Where Ellia lived on Fog-whistle Way wasn't far from my own house, and close enough to the cemetery that she could walk there if need be.

It had stopped raining and the clouds had scattered for the moment, letting the stars shine through. In late October, the night came early, especially out in the outlying areas without the incessant glow of the big city to light the area. Finally, I decided to face the inevitable. Somehow, the thought of facing Ellia made everything real—once I walked through her door, my grandmother was truly dead, I was committed, and both thoughts scared the hell out of me. But my time to run was over. Slinging my purse over my shoulder, I took a deep breath and headed up the stone steps to the front door, slipping on my gloves as I did so. The last thing I wanted to do was to touch Ellia's hands. That was one rabbit hole I knew I didn't want to fall down.

The bell was shaped like an ornate brass flower. I pressed the center and waited. Another moment and then the door opened, and there she stood, pretty much the way I remembered her. A little older, a little grayer. An ethereal smile stole across her lips, and she stood back, ushering me in.

She smiled at my hands, not offering me her hand or a hug. "Gloves. You remembered."

Her voice took me back and I flashed her a shy grin. "How could I forget? Are things the same? Do you still . . ."

"Oh yes . . . these old hands of mine can still drag you down to hell." She laughed, then sobered and held up her hands. She was wearing long cream-colored opera gloves that disappeared up her sleeves. "If I could wear gloves and play the violin, I would, but unfortunately, I'm not quite that dexterous. I hate causing unnecessary pain, so I just make sure I carry them with me wherever I go."

She stood aside as I entered the hallway. A sharp bark came from behind her, and a dog peered around from behind her, gorgeous and white as snow, looking suspiciously like a wolf.

"Don't mind Viktor. He knows friend from foe." She ushered me into the foyer and shut the door behind me. The dog gave me a long look, sizing me up. He was either going to eat me for dinner or—he pranced forward, leaned down toward the ground with his head against his front feet, and then did a little wiggle and barked. A lick to my hand and he bobbed his head, then abruptly turned and padded down the hallway, out of sight.

"His name is Viktor?"

"Yes, and you guess correctly if you are thinking he looks like a wolf. He's an Arctic wolf–Siberian husky mix. Apparently he's decided you're nothing to worry about." But she said it with a laugh.

As she led me toward the living room, she glanced back at me, as if reassuring herself I was really there. Ellia was a tall woman, at least five eleven. Her hair flowed in shimmering waves down her shoulders to her lower back, and it had shifted color only slightly in the fifteen years I'd been gone, transitioning from spun platinum to silver. But her face remained unlined; her lips were a little more pursed, her eyes still blue and crackling with flashes of white heat. She was a lean woman, but not gaunt, and tonight she was wearing caramel-colored slacks with a green plaid blazer. She had always struck me as elegant, and when she spoke, her voice registered with a regal, yet ephemeral tone.

"Come now, Oriel and Ivy are waiting."

Oriel, I vaguely remembered. But Ivy? I wasn't familiar with anyone named Ivy. As we entered the living room, the décor looked the same as it had the week I left Whisper Hollow. Sparse, but refined, in neutral shades of camel and rust and tan, contrasting greatly with the outside of the house, which looked like it belonged in the middle of a dark forest.

Two women waited on the sofa. One was round and stout, with a cheery smile and golden hair wrapped up into a braid around her head. Oriel. She would have been around my mother's age, if my mother had stuck around. I remembered that she had taken over the boardinghouse or something, but I had never really had a reason to speak with her when I was a teenager. She was dressed in a green jersey dress, with a brown leather belt that wrapped around her ample belly.

The other woman looked closer to my own age. In her late thirties or early forties, I'd guess, with shoulder-length black hair, streaked with white like a skunk. It was cut in a fashionable bob. Her eyes were a deep brown, and for some reason, she reminded me of someone, though I couldn't figure out who. She was wearing a denim pantsuit, though, that looked oddly out of place on her, though she seemed comfortable enough in it.

Ellia motioned me to a chair off the side of the sofa and I sat on the edge. A tray of cookies and hot cocoa rested on the coffee table.

I sniffed appreciatively. "Cookies and cocoa? Whatever we're going to talk about must be bad if you're already bribing me with food." I turned to the woman I didn't recognize. "I'm sorry, but I don't remember you. I'm—"

"Kerris Fellwater. I know who you are. I've watched you since you were a baby."

At my startled look, she smiled. "I'm not a stalker, I promise. There's a reason I've kept watch. We're kinfolk, though you don't know it."

I stared at the woman for a moment, not sure what to say. Finally, I settled for, "How could you have known me when I was born? You can't be that much older than me." Then the second part of her statement hit me. "*Kinfolk?* We're related?"

She leaned forward, holding out her hand. "I'm Ivy Primrose. I've wanted to meet you since you were born, but your grandmother was always the voice of reason—she insisted it wasn't the right time yet. I live down the street from you."

Either she had the best plastic surgeon around, or there was some hidden secret about her that I didn't know. Still uncertain of what to say but figuring she'd get around to it in her own time, I slowly reached for a cookie and a mug of hot cocoa. Over the years I'd learned that I found out more by being observant than barging in with a slew of questions. Sometimes, being taciturn was a tactical maneuver.

I decided to stick to my life as a topic. "I wasn't going to come back, you know. I swore up and down I'd never set foot in this town again. But you know how well that works." With a laugh, I settled back in the chair and put my feet up on the ottoman. "So yes, I'm back, and here to stay. The Crow Man came to me, and so did my grandmother. The week before she died, she came to me three nights running in a dream. And I saw the Girl in the Window. Well, it was a mannequin in a window, but the Bean Nighe was superimposed over her. I know better than to ignore the summons."

Oriel shook her head. "So many try to leave, yet almost everybody born here stays. Or returns." She cocked her head to the side. "I tried once, you know. Long ago. I got as far south as Portland before the town insisted I come back." She let out a sigh. "I want to state up front that we tried to persuade Duvall to lighten up on you. We didn't want you running away. But the old bastard wouldn't listen. Except for at the end . . ."

Something in her voice caught me short. "What?"

With a glance at Ellia, Oriel cleared her throat on a sip of hot chocolate. "Your grandmother wanted us all to meet her the night that she died. She said she had something important we needed to know, and that Duvall would be there with her. That he wanted to tell us something before—" A slight shift told me that she was debating whether to continue.

"Go on. I want to hear this."

"Your grandfather was dying. About three years ago, he developed idiopathic pulmonary fibrosis. There is no cure, and Doc Wallace gave him two years—three at the most. About a year back, something changed in his nature . . . I think the fear of what waited for him on the other side of the Veil took hold. He started doing his best to turn things around." She stopped, waiting for me to digest the information.

A pit opened in my stomach. Five months ago, I'd received a letter from him—one I had never opened. I had burned it without reading it. "Crap." They looked at me, but I shook my head. This realization was one I'd have to take to my grave with me. "So . . . Lila and Duvall were supposed to meet with you the night they died? And he wanted to tell you something?"

She nodded. "That's right. And whatever it was, was important. Your grandmother stressed that we needed to talk to him now—all three of us. She was crying . . . her voice shaky. When I asked her what was wrong, she told me that her world had just been shattered . . . but she wouldn't talk about it over the phone. Two hours later, the Lady took them. They went off the road."

So the Lady had taken them before Duvall could reveal whatever it was that had apparently caused a change of heart. I stared at my cup. "I wish I'd come home in time to see my grandmother before she died. But I was too stubborn." I paused, then glanced over at Ellia. "Did you . . . did you play for her? For my grandmother?" A sudden hitch caught in my throat. What if she said no? What if . . .

Ellia reached out and almost touched my arm, then paused and ducked her head, pulling her fingers back. "Yes, I did. You'll have to lead the rites over her grave, of course. But I think she heard me, and so far, she rests easy. I doubt she'll be walking any time soon."

Relieved, I let out a long sigh. The thought of Grandma Lila up and prowling the city felt like heresy. I didn't really want to ask but decided I'd better. "Still no sign of my grandfather's body?"

Ellia slowly shook her head. "We haven't been able to find him. Their car went over the edge at the Lady's Finger mile marker, down near Juniper Creek. That seems to be one of the prime places lately for the Lady to drag them in."

I frowned. The fact that she had kept his body could turn out to be a serious problem, but there was nothing we could do about it right now. "Do you have any idea what Duvall wanted to tell you?"

Oriel shook her head. Ellia followed suit, but more slowly.

Ivy, however, toyed with her cookies. "I'm not sure, but I think it might relate to your father, Kerris. And maybe . . . your mother."

My father? My father had taken off, abandoned my mother when he found out she was pregnant. I hadn't thought about him in years—not really. I had no idea who he was, other than his first name and a picture my grandmother had given me.

"What do you mean . . . You think he knew where to find him?" Not sure why that was the first thing out of my mouth, I stopped. I wasn't looking to meet Avery, the man who had decided his life was better off without my mother and me.

"I think . . . perhaps that might be the case." There was still something she wasn't telling me, and I felt like I was tiptoeing around in the dark, cautiously skirting a can of worms that—once I opened it up—I'd never be able to close again. Sipping the steaming drink, I tried not to think about my grandfather, somewhere under the dark surface of the lake, dancing with the Lady. She reached out for those she wanted. Not even the spirit shamans could counter her desires in that regard.

Desperately trying to stall, I said, "It's true that I don't have the full training I should, but as I said, I think I've learned enough to tackle the job. But I need to find my grandmother's tools. Do any of you know offhand where she might have kept them?"

The three of them looked simultaneously relieved and worried.

Ellia shook her head, a somber look crossing her face. "Your grandmother kept them hidden. Through most of his life, Duvall fought her calling. He hated what she was. They're probably still hidden away somewhere in the house."

"Then, first order is to find them because normally, she would have helped me to gather my own, and gifted me a few of hers. If I can find her kit, so much the better." I worried my lip. "You said the dead have been walking more, even while Lila was alive?"

"Yes. Even though we worked together to persuade as many families as we could to perform the rituals over their dead, we were still noticing a rise in spirit activity. And that from more than just those who went to their graves unprepared. The dead are returning from the Veil. Haunts . . . Mournfuls . . . the Wandering Ones. I fear that next, we'll see a rise in the Unliving crossing back over. And only a spirit shaman can take on the Haunts and the Unliving."

And *this* was why the Crow Man had summoned me. But there was one little problem. "Over the years, I have developed some rites and rituals but I don't know how they'll work here in Whisper Hollow. And Lila was the only one who could teach me."

Oriel spoke up. "We can guide you. We can't *teach* you—the spirit shamans keep their secrets—but we'll do our best." She reached across the coffee table to give me a gentle pat on the hand. She cocked her head to one side. "Penelope might be able to help us out." She paused, then continued. "Kerris, you know I guard this town. That's part of my job—to keep Whisper Hollow and its secrets safe. I worked with your grandmother on occasion, when the need arose. Her gifts ranged beyond merely turning the dead back to their graves—she was a very strong spirit shaman. So are you, but you just don't realize it yet."

So Oriel was more of an interested bystander. I glanced over at Ellia. I knew how *she* fit into the equation. But Ivy . . . There was something about her. I finally quit evading the subject. "How do you play into all of this?"

She paused, staring into her cocoa mug. After a moment, she sat back, crossing her legs smoothly. Regarding me quietly, she finally said, "I'm your grandmother. Your father was my son."

Cue a dozen bombs going off one after another.

Ellia caught my cup as I let go of it. As hot chocolate splashed across the knees of my jeans, as well as all over the floor, she set the cup on the table, then handed me a napkin before returning to her seat. As I dabbed at the liquid, the room plunged into a deep silence, freezing us all.

*Your father* . . . The words echoed inside me, ricocheting like bullets. *Your father was my son* . . . words I never thought I'd hear. Especially from a woman who looked like she could be my older sister, rather than my grandmother.

"I'm a shapeshifter. Your father was one, too—he was matched to your mother."

*Of course* . . . shapeshifters were very long lived, aging normally till they reached their twenties, and then the process drastically slowed. That was why she looked so young.

My world shifting with every breath, I searched for something to say. I didn't know how to respond. I'd long ago given up hoping to ever find out about my father, and now the opportunity was sitting right here in front of me. I thought about just getting up and leaving—this was all far more than I had expected to face and I had no clue how to react. Finally, I cleared my throat and looked over at her, into those clear brown eyes. No wonder she had seemed familiar to me—she was my blood kin.

"I suppose . . . you'd better tell me everything." Though I spoke calmly, inside I was screaming, pounding on the walls in a tantrum born out of both frustration and joy. I'd given up hope long ago of ever knowing about my father and why he had left before I was born, and all along, the answer had been living right down the street.

When I was three, my mother disappeared. Tamil just vanished one day, never to be heard from again. For a long time, I thought I saw her—she'd be there, around the corner. Or I'd turn to find her standing behind me, watching me with worried eyes. But I'd blink and she'd be gone and eventually, I stopped seeing her. I told myself she ran off to find my father, and that someday, they'd come back to get me. *Someday* never came.

My father was gone before I was born. When I was old enough to realize that other kids had fathers and I didn't, I asked Grandma Lila why. She just shushed me, telling me he had gone away for a long time and that he was very important and was on a secret mission for the government. Being a highly imaginative child, I bought her story. And later, when I asked her if my mother was with my father— hiding like spies in some foreign country—she just murmured a soft answer that could have been yes or no. What I *didn't* realize was that her stories were a source of wicked arguments between her and Grandpa Duvall. I learned the hard way when I was eleven. On that day, I asked him when Daddy would be allowed to come home.

Grandpa Duvall, who was well over six feet, long and lanky with eyebrows the color of ink, and thin, and scary as hell, glared down at me. "Never. Your grandmother's been feeding you a pack of lies about him, and you're old enough to know the truth. Your father skipped town when he found out your mother was pregnant with you. He disappeared, leaving her in the lurch. That's why she ran off, you know— she couldn't handle raising you alone. So let that be a lesson to you, young lady. Don't go getting yourself knocked up without a ring on that finger."

I stared up at him, assessing his answer. Grandpa didn't sugarcoat anything, and he was always a little too eager to squash any joy or enthusiasm. The gleam in his eye told me he had enjoyed destroying my dreams. And right then, I realized just how much I hated him. He was a hard man, and I'd learned to stay away from him when he was in one of his moods. He never hurt me, not physically, but I knew the hard way that he enjoyed tormenting people.

As I stood there, staring right back at him, he never wavered. Without a word, I turned and walked out of the room. Ten minutes later, I was sobbing into Grandma Lila's skirts. Half an hour later, I knew little more than I had before, except that he—like my mother—had simply vanished. There was no secret government job, no mission, no romantic liaison half a world away. Just two people who had loved each other, gone missing three years apart.

Lila had given me a picture of them, though she warned me not to tell Grandpa Duvall about it. Tamil and Avery were standing together, he behind her with his arms wrapped around her shoulders. They looked happy—my mother's eyes were smiling. But Avery looked distant, almost frightened. I tucked the picture away behind a book on my shelf to hide it should Duvall come searching my room one day. I still had it, in my jewelry box.

The one thing I *did* realize on that day was that I would never love my grandfather. Our relationship was tenuous to begin with, and after that—no matter how polite he was, no matter what he said—I kept my feelings protected from him. He was a stranger to me from that day on.

*   *   *

Y ou're sure that *you're* Avery's mother?" The questions barraged my brain, but I managed to keep my mouth shut. It wouldn't do any good to swamp her.

"Yes, your *other* grandmother." She paused, glancing at Oriel and then Ellia. "This is so not the way I wanted you to find out. I tried to get Duvall to let me tell you when you were young, but the old bas—" She paused.

I held her gaze, shrugging. "Call him whatever you like. I fell out with him when I was young, and my only regret is that our feud separated Grandma Lila and me."

Ivy nodded. "Yes, he was a bitter man. Duvall wouldn't let me near you, not even when your grandmother tried to intervene. He threatened me, and . . . when your grandfather made threats, he followed through. Lila kept me updated on your progress. She gave me pictures of you." This was said almost shyly, and as I gazed into the softened face, I realized that none of this had been Ivy's fault.

"Grandma Lila could handle Duvall to a point, but he had a nasty temper. He never struck her, not that I knew, but he was cold and bitter and a poor excuse for a human being. I never understood why she married him. Spirit shamans are supposed to have guardians—a shapeshifter born to each of us. But she didn't. At least, not that I know of." I ducked my head, wishing that Lila could be sitting here with us, free from him. "Tell me about my father, please. Did he really run out on my mother like Duvall told me?"

Ivy let out a soft sigh. "Avery loved your mother. One morning, shortly after Tamil announced she was pregnant, Avery went out to go buy supplies, and then he was supposed to head up to Timber Peak to go hunting. He never returned. My ex-husband—Roger—came back to Whisper Hollow as soon as I called him. He led a group of searchers, but they found no evidence Avery had ever walked into those woods. The store he normally bought his gear from hadn't seen him that day. Roger stayed for two months before finally giving up and returning to the city. It almost pulled us back together, but Whisper Hollow is a dangerous place for him, so I told him to leave. He wasn't born here, and . . . the town doesn't like him. His clan is . . . different. If he stayed, Whisper Hollow would offer him up to the Lady, I fear."

I frowned. "My grandfather told me that my father just up and left during the middle of the night. He never said anything about Avery disappearing in the woods." My disgust for my grandfather was rapidly escalating, even more than I thought it could. Still . . . what secret had he wanted to tell these women? And if he was truly trying to change, had impending mortality been the only reason for the shift?

"Duvall hated my son. He was furious when he found out that Tamil had gotten pregnant and that she wanted to marry Avery and have the baby. When Tamil announced they were engaged and why, well . . . the blowup was epic." Ivy snorted, shaking her head. "The shot heard round the world, so to speak."

Ellia nodded. "Tamil showed up at my doorstep, begging me to let her stay here. I had been helping her learn how to use her gifts. Lila had asked me to take part in Tamil's training—lessons that I could show her. I took her in, but Duvall insisted she come home the next week, and neither Tamil nor I dared go against his wishes. Lila did her best to intervene, but he insisted."

My ears perked up. *Training?* "You helped my mother with her training? I thought only another spirit shaman could do that."

"We did what we could, child." Oriel laughed. She always looked like the cat who'd swallowed the canary, but she managed to make it appealing instead of a threat. "Your mother's gifts were incredibly strong. She would have taken over from your grandmother if all had gone as planned. But the minute we found out she was pregnant, we had to stop. Working with the spirits while pregnant is not the best idea. To be honest, we don't know if what she was doing affected you or not, since she was four months gone by the time she let anybody know."

*Four months.* I frowned. "Why did she wait so long to say anything?"

Ivy glanced over at Ellia, who nodded. "We think she and Avery kept it a secret so your grandfather couldn't force her to have an abortion, and when they did reveal that you were on the way, they told a lot of people all at once so the word got around. Duvall would have made her get rid of you, you know."

Stunned, I sat back and mulled over everything that I had learned in the past ten minutes. The three women waited quietly, and I was grateful to them for that.

One: I had a grandmother I never knew about. A grandmother who looked close to my age and was a shapeshifter.

Two: My father may not have run out on my mother—he seemed to have disappeared as silently and abruptly as Tamil. Which brought to mind the question: If they *had* left town, had she caught up with him? Had they intended to come back for me, but been unable to?

Three: My grandfather had a secret he felt he could no longer keep hidden, and had died hours before he was to reveal it.

Four: My mother was incredibly talented with her gifts. And on top of that, her training may have affected me, since she had been pregnant with me while she was learning. I let the information settle in, then glanced over at Ivy.

Suddenly hungry for answers, I decided to put to rest some of the questions that I'd been carrying around my entire life. I slowly let out a long breath. "What else can you tell me about my father? My grandmother didn't want to talk about him, and I didn't dare mention him in front of my grandfather. What was he like?"

"My son loved your mother, Kerris. Please know that. His last name was Forrester. When I left his father, I went back to my maiden name of Primrose, but I left Avery with his father's name. Avery liked to cook. He loved rockabilly music, he drove an old pickup truck. His favorite color was green, and he loved hot dogs and pizza and lasagna. He was a smart man and had planned on going to college until Tamil got pregnant, but he adjusted quickly. In fact, the day they broke the news, he went over to the newspaper and secured himself a job with Earl—the publisher of the *Whisper Hollow Gazette*. He also asked me if he could have his grandmother's wedding ring to give to Tamil. He had already proposed, I gather, but hadn't been able to give her a ring." Her smile faded away. "I don't know if he ever got the chance. I never saw the ring again after that evening."

I paused, then asked one more question. "You said he was a shapeshifter. So he was her guardian? And how does that affect me? I've never even had a whiff of that ability."

"Yes, he was. And as for you, when shapeshifters mate with spirit shamans, the daughters come out with the spirit shaman ability—not the shapeshifting one. You would only be able to shift your shape if your mother hadn't been a spirit shaman. If she had just been . . . well . . . a *typical* human, you would have had the ability. The shapeshifting gene is dominant. We can talk more about that later," Ivy said.

And that was enough for the night. There were a million other things I wanted to know, but they would keep. I slid over to her side and hesitantly wrapped my arms around her. "Thank you. Thank you for telling me. Thank you for . . . being here."

She looked startled, but hugged me back, kissing me on the forehead. "Kerris, you don't know how many times over the years I almost sent you a note, or stopped you on the way home from school. But Duvall . . ." With a shudder, she shook her head. "He was a dangerous man."

I shook my hair out of my eyes and gave Ivy a soft smile. "What did the ring look like? Your mother's ring? If I happen to find it somewhere when I go through the trunks and things in the house, I can at least give it back to you." I wanted to comfort her—to do something to make up for the way my grandfather had treated her and her son.

Ivy let out a slow sigh as she sat back. "If you find it, I want you to keep it, because it will have meant that he actually got a chance to give it to Tamil. Duvall never let me talk to her again after the news came out. The ring was a rose gold fili-gree setting, with a half-carat diamond in the center. My father had it made for my mother when they got engaged."

I nodded. Not sure what else to say—I felt as wrung out as a limp, wet towel—I leaned back against the sofa and glanced over at Oriel and Ellia. Both had somber looks on their faces.

"So, where should I start?"

Ellia stood. "I suppose we can start by going out to the cemetery . . . let you get a feel for what's going on and what is to come. That seems the best plan. You've been gone so long, I don't know how much you remember from your time here." She motioned to the others. "Do you all want to come? It's not necessary, not tonight, but you're welcome if you do. I'll take my violin and play for the dead for a while."

"Don't take her to the Pest House graveyard, though. Even *your* music can't calm the spirits who walk there, Ellia. And we're heading into a new moon—the dead love this time of the month." Oriel opened her bag and pulled out a pendant on a chain. She handed it to me. "Here, this was your grandmother's. I took it from her body for safekeeping till you came home. You'll need it. Wear it at all times, even in the shower. It has been charmed to help protect you."

The pendant weighed heavy in my hands. A silver five-pointed star in a circle, it hung on a chain that also looked to be silver. *A pentacle.* But atop the pentacle rested a skull. Not a screaming, Halloween skull, but a somber skull, carved from crystal, affixed firmly to the metal.

"Magical, isn't it?" A vague memory stirred—I remembered seeing Grandma Lila wear it, though she usually kept it beneath her shirt or dress.

Oriel laughed and the room lightened with her cheer. "Dear Kerris, it's *all* magic, isn't it? The world is a magical place, if people only were to open their eyes. Except the clouded can't always feel it surrounding them, so they think it doesn't exist. Magic runs through these ancient woods. The rain forest is primeval, so deep and thick that you'd have to be blind to not know it was here. Now put on your pendant, then Ellia will show you the graveyard, and you will begin to understand why we need you so very much."

With that, she and Ivy headed for the door. I asked Ivy if I could come over later in the week—get to know her better—and she said yes before she and Oriel left. Alone in the hallway with Ellia, I shrugged into my jacket and slung my purse over my shoulder. Ellia opened the hall closet and withdrew her violin case. She settled a long cloak around her shoulders, fastening it with a Celtic knotwork brooch. With her long skirts and flowing gray-streaked hair, she looked like she'd stepped right out of the pages of some historical romance.

"Do you remember the rules?" she asked me.

I nodded. Once you had lived in Whisper Hollow, you never forgot the rules. In fact, they were printed on a sign at the entrance to the town.

"Recite them, then."

I let out a slow breath. "Okay . . ." I felt like I was in grade school again. We had recited them every day, a lot like the Pledge of Allegiance.

> "One.   If you hear someone call your name from the forest, don't answer.
> "Two.   Never interrupt Ellia when she's playing to the dead.
> "Three. If you see the Girl in the Window, set your affairs in order.
> "Four.   Try not to end up in the hospital.
> "Five.   If the Crow Man summons you, follow him.
> "Six.     Remember: Sometimes the foul are actually fair.
> "Seven. And most important: Don't drive down by the lake at night."

Ellia nodded. "You remember. Good. All right then, put on your necklace and let's head to the cemetery. It's time you met the dead."

# CHAPTER 3

The cemetery wasn't far from Ellia's house, or my own. It suddenly occurred to me that the fact that we both lived near it was most likely more than by accident. Ellia rode with me. She lived close enough to walk home if she wanted to, though I told her I would happily give her a ride if need be. The thought of her prowling through the streets after dark didn't set well with me. Not in Whisper Hollow.

The cemetery was on the appropriately named Cemetery Avenue, at the end of an L-shaped intersection that connected with Bramblewood Way, the road running past my house. In turn, Bramblewood Way bordered Bramblewood Thicket, a dense patch of forest on the western side of Whisper Hollow that was rumored to be home to a spirit called the Grey Man. It was also the home to the Tree of Skulls, a very gruesome little patch of woods.

The fog was rising as we pulled into the circular parking lot. Here, you could either park and walk into the gated graveyard or take a narrow access road to reach the areas farthest away. Ellia directed me to drive down the access road until we were overlooking the shore of Lake Crescent, where we turned right and followed the narrow street to the end of the marked graves. I parked in a small turnoff and killed the ignition.

"Who's the undertaker now?" The undertaker was also the caretaker of the cemetery. When I had been young, a very old man had been in charge of the dead, but I couldn't remember his name and he had no doubt died during the intervening years.

"Jonah Westwood, the nephew of old Elijah. You probably remember Elijah as the undertaker. He held the job for sixty years. About seven years back, he died and his nephew moved to Whisper Hollow and took over." She paused, then added, "I played for Elijah, and Penelope had an easy time escorting him through to the Veil. He deserved to rest after giving so many years of service to the dead. His nephew is an odd duck, though. We have to work together, but I steer clear of him during the rest of the time."

That didn't sound promising. "What's the matter with him?"

She shook her head. "Just a feeling. I'm not sure, to be honest. Maybe nothing, but I'll tell you this: I hope, by the time it's *my* turn to leave this world, that he's not the one presiding over my interment."

"Well, that makes me feel *ever so* much better." Laughing softly, I locked the car and followed her down one of the narrow walkways. The air was damp, and even my jacket couldn't keep the moisture from seeping into my lungs. Unlike in graveyards in other towns, families didn't come to the cemetery to picnic, and most of the teenagers stayed away, saving their dares for other, safer areas.

One glance at the headstones and a barrage of whispering hit me. Shadows—misty forms—were moving through the graveyard. I caught them out of the corner of my eye, watching as they moved and swirled in the damp night air.

"What's stirring them up? I don't remember things being this uneasy when I left."

Ellia started to say something, then shook her head. "I can't tell you . . . not yet. I think I know, but I'd rather be certain before saying anything. Maybe they sense that Lila died and the town's been without a spirit shaman for a week or so. A few of the rites and rituals haven't been performed like they're supposed to be. But to be honest? Something else is going on." She paused, then let out a long breath. "What I will say is this: There's a force moving against the town. The signs are all there, and the Crow Man has been calling those of us with power. The Walker in the Woods has been spotted five times in the past two months. The Girl in the Window appeared to Douglas McPhearson and he died the next week. And the Lady's appetite is growing."

I grimaced. Those were signs, all right, and not good omens. "Do you think it's out of the forest, or pulled in by the town itself?"

The Hoh rain forest held its own spirits—Sasquatch, for one, and a number of other creatures out of Native American lore. They were real, never let anybody tell you otherwise, but they bordered the edge of my work with the dead, and while I knew about them and had seen evidence of their existence, I tried to steer clear because spirit shamans weren't geared toward dealing with elementals out of their world.

"Oh, Sasquatch is around and active lately, but I don't think he has anything to do with whatever's going on. Though a hunter was attacked three months ago up on Timber Peak. A handful of mutilated deer have been found, so yes, he's awake." She stopped along the path, pointing toward a pair of graves. They looked well established. "Watch."

"What are we looking at—" I started to ask but quieted down when two figures shimmered fully into sight next to the graves. A man and woman—teenagers, actually—appeared, facing each other. The girl was wearing an A-line skirt and a blouse, a sweater tied around her shoulders. Her hair was pulled back in a tight, bouncy ponytail and she had on loafers. The boy wore a leather jacket and skinny blue jeans. His hair was slicked back. Both looked soaking wet, and their faces were bruised so badly it was hard to tell what they had looked like when they were alive. I thought I could hear a song playing in the background. I strained to hear what it was, and the whispers of Fats Domino's "I Want To Walk You Home" echoed from around them.

The boy reached out his hand and the girl took it, bringing it to her lips where she kissed it. Then, her eyes burning fiery red, she glanced over at us and laughed. The boy let out a snort, they stood, and then—in a blur of speed—they were standing directly in front of us, defiant grins on their faces. They gave Ellia the once-over, then turned to me.

I stared coolly at them, though inside my stomach was churning. Were they simply Haunts, out to cause havoc? Or were they Unliving, in which case we were in serious trouble? The girl met my gaze.

Without thinking, I reached up to clasp the pendant Oriel had given me with my left hand, then focused my energy and plunged my right fist into the girl's misty form. "Don't even think about it!" It felt like I had rammed my hand into an ice bath. I grinned, pleased to see I still had what it took. I'd used the maneuver on a few frisky spirits in Seattle, and it worked ten times better than the rituals I'd read about in books.

The girl shrieked and stumbled back. The boy hissed at me, his eyes narrowing, but he, too, cautiously stepped back. They stared at me for another moment, then, huffing like spoiled brats, joined hands and—in a blur—they were gone, racing out of the cemetery so fast I could barely follow their movements.

I let out a long sigh. "Well, that was special. I gather they're out to wreak some havoc."

Ellia snorted. "You think so? Well, you certainly ticked them off. What did you do? I never saw Lila do that."

"Yeah, they didn't look overjoyed, did they? That's a technique I developed to deal with spirits who like to get too touchy-feely. It's kind of like . . . think of using your energy like an electronic bug zapper. I assume that pair are Haunts? It works on Haunts the best. And Joanie and Chachi don't seem to have enough strength to classify them as members of the Unliving."

She shook her head. "Thankfully, no, they aren't Unliving.

That pair has been stirring up trouble for a while now. Lila and I were having trouble with them before she passed. Kerris, your grandmother was the most powerful spirit shaman I've ever met, but . . . she couldn't drive them back across the Veil. The ley lines are active, and the dead are restless."

I nodded slowly. If Grandma Lila had been having trouble corralling them, then I was in for one hell of a ride. But what I had done to the girl wasn't exactly textbook, nor was it easy, and it shocked me just about as much as it shocked the ghost. I had some other tricks up my sleeve, so maybe they wouldn't be prepared for me next time, either. "I'm glad I decided to try that out. At least we know it works. I wasn't sure what part of my repertoire would actually be viable here, but I suppose ghosts are ghosts, the world 'round."

"Blood wins out. Spirit shamans are born to interact with the dead—and to destroy them, when necessary. You come from a long line of women who walk between the worlds. It's your birthright. Spirit shamans affect the ghosts—all varieties—in ways that *no one* else can. Not lament singers, not witches, not necromancers. And I don't think it's so much the precise rituals that matter, but the energy you put behind it. But as to *what* it was you did to them, besides tick them off, I'm not certain."

"Yeah . . . well, usually that tends to send spirits running for cover, but I think I just gave them a nasty shock and pissed them off. So, what are we going to do about those two? Who are they? Unless ghosts have a retro fashion sense, they didn't exactly look freshly buried."

Ellia let out a little laugh. "You're very observant. And correct. That pair . . . when they were alive, they were Betty Jean Daniels and Tommy Freeman. They went to high school in the 1950s, they were a few years behind Lila and Ivy and me. Betty was the daughter of one of the town bankers, and Tommy . . . he was just trouble. They took up together and he brought out her inner Bonnie to his Clyde."

"What happened to them? Did they die at the same time?"

She jerked her head toward the lake. "1960 . . . they were headed out to her grandma's one frosty November evening.

Rumor has it they were on their way to steal her money. Before they could get there, the Lady took them. Car skidded off the road. Witnesses said that for once, they were actually driving the speed limit, not speeding. It was chilly but the road was dry. One moment they were on the road, the next, they broke through the guardrail and went into the lake. The car sank so deep they never recovered it—or the bodies." She paused.

I closed my eyes, thinking about my grandparents. About the Lady, dragging them down to drown in her icy arms. A slow burn rose in my heart and I sucked in a deep breath, trying to shake off the mix of emotions. Because as angry as I was that the lake had claimed Lila, the truth was—you live in Whisper Hollow, and you had to accept that there was always the chance that she would drag you down.

"What did the cops say?"

"Not much. You know how it goes here. They officially listed it as a murder-suicide, but everybody knew the truth."

I stared at the gravestones. Empty graves, then. But you couldn't very well stick a headstone on the surface of the lake. "So they're still out there . . . whatever might be left of them."

"Along with who knows how many other souls. Along with your grandfather." Ellia shook her head softly as she rested her hand on my arm. "At least the Lady had the respect to give you back your grandmother's body. But here's the thing: Tommy and Betty? Not once have they ever walked . . . not before the past few months. I played for them at their funeral, and they were at rest. I was younger then, but I was more than able to work with your great-grandmother. Betty and Tommy started rising about three months back, and nothing Lila and I could do would send them back to the Veil, back to Penelope. When you think about it, they should have long gone through the Veil itself and moved on, so even there—something is amiss. Regardless of why, we need to banish them before they take it into their heads to unleash their anger on the town, because after all these years, they're still a volatile pair. Whatever they learned after their death, well, if it was any good, it sure didn't return with them."

"So you and Lila tried to send them back?"

She nodded. "Several times. I've played over their graves twice a week since they were first spotted, but it doesn't seem to do any good. And the magic Lila used . . . something was countering it, Kerris. *Someone*." She stared down at the violin case. "At first, I was worried that I was losing my touch. That it was time to train someone new."

I nodded, cautiously sitting on one of the gravestones. "That's not it, though, is it? Ellia, you've been playing for the dead since long before I was born. You won't lose your touch till you cross over."

She smiled, then. "Thank you. Yes, I have the gift and it will stay with me till the end. And you're right—I may be seventy-five, but I still have a lot of good years in me. My family is . . . long lived." Squinting, she scanned the grave-yard. "Without your grandmother, it's only going to get worse. We need you to take over immediately, and then we need to sort out what's infiltrating the town before . . ."

She gazed off toward the lake, her voice falling silent. The wind swept through and sent a cold line of fear down my back. There was something riding it, some night hag laughing in her joy. The bare branches gleamed against the dim lights of the cemetery as smoke from the chimneys of the town drifted past, a pale hex against the cold chill of the autumn night.

Ellia shivered and rubbed her hands together, slowly pulling off her gloves. "There's not much more we can do tonight. I'll walk home after I play a few songs to try to quiet the evening. You go ahead and head out."

Not wanting to leave her there, I argued. "It's dangerous on the roads. I know you don't live far, but . . ."

She laughed, her voice ricocheting off the gravestones. "Kerris, this is my symphony hall. I come here to play both under the moonlight and in the dark of the moon. This is my home away from home, and soon it will be yours, as well.

Don't worry about me—I'll be fine. I want to try out a new ballad I learned last week to see if I can keep anybody else from walking. Meanwhile, you go home. Search for your grandmother's Shadow Journal. She'll have a notebook that she kept as spirit shaman. You'll need to find it and read it because it will tell you more than the rest of us can."

I nodded, and then with a sigh, I added, "Right. There's a lot to do, isn't there?"

"More than you want to know." And with that, she draped her gloves over a gravestone and sat down on the bench next to it. She opened her case and lifted out her violin. As she struck bow to strings, a mournful echo of notes filled the air.

"A lament song for the dead," she said as I gazed at the quivering strings. "But as good as I am, without your powers in conjunction? I might as well put down my bow." And with that, she closed her eyes, and her song echoed out, weaving through the graveyard like a net of silver light, spinning a mournful lullaby to calm the restive dead. A whirl of leaves gusted up, caught by the wind, and fluttered past us, swirling to the rhythm of her song.

I flashed back, through the years, to the nights with my Grandma Lila. A sudden memory of her and Ellia dancing through the graveyard, weaving magic to quiet the spirits, filled my thoughts and I could almost reach out to touch the web they had been spinning. And then, as quickly as it had come, the image vanished.

Shaking off the haunting strains, I headed back to my car. Ellia could handle herself. She was right. She was as much a part of the cemetery as were the headstones and markers. She belonged here, and soon, so would I. Resting secure that she would be safe for the evening, I fastened my seat belt and then, hands on the steering wheel, I stared into the darkness. Within the space of twenty-four hours, fifteen years had slipped away and I was back in a world I'd sworn to leave behind. But it felt so natural, so right, that I wondered—just with the littlest part of my heart—why I had ever left in the beginning. Pushing aside the jumble of thoughts crowding my mind, I started the ignition and headed for home.

* * *

As I turned onto Bramblewood Way, the fog rose thick and fast to surround the car. It smothered the road in one quick swoop. I slammed on the brakes as a dark figure vaulted out from the trees on the side of the road, loping into the street. It looked for all the world like a huge wolf, hunched and misshapen. Another figure followed—this one human—and I skidded to the side as I tried to avoid hitting him. As I brought my CR-V to a halt, I lurched forward against the seat belt, almost hitting the steering wheel.

My ribs felt bruised and I was panting but otherwise unharmed. I gripped the wheel with one hand as I fumbled to shift the SUV into park.

*What the hell had just happened?*

Hands shaking, I slowly unfastened my seat belt, then reached beneath the seat for the crowbar I kept stashed there. Being a single woman in a big city, I had learned how to defend myself with whatever I had at hand. After a moment, I also grabbed the switchblade I kept hidden in my glove box and shoved it into my jacket pocket. Hesitating another moment—there could be anything out there from a coyote to a serial killer—finally, I opened the door and stepped out of the car.

I stood there, scanning the road around me, the crowbar clutched in one hand, while I kept the other free and near the knife in my jacket. I knew how to throw a punch, and I could use a baseball bat with decent effectiveness, but it all depended on who was on the receiving end.

The road was silent, a hush of fog. My house was a block and a half away, but right now it felt as good as a mile. As my breath coalesced into a cloud of white vapor, I tried to sort out whether I had actually hit anyone. No body in the road—check. No sign of what dog . . . wolf . . . whatever had launched itself in my path—check.

"Are you all right?"

Startled, I whirled around, raising the crowbar. To my left stood a man, around five eleven. He was lean and fit, and so close he could have grabbed my arm. I took one deliberate step back.

What the hell? I hadn't seen any sign of him—or anybody else—when I'd stepped out of the car. Nor had I heard him approach, and I had good ears. "Where did you come from? Who are you?"

He held up his hands, gesturing to the raised crowbar. "I promise, you won't need that. I'm not going to hurt you." He took a step back and kept his hands out in plain sight.

As I slowly lowered the makeshift weapon, I looked him over. His wheat-colored hair was in a casually tousled shag, reaching his collar in back and on the sides. A well-trimmed beard and mustache shrouded his face. But something about his eyes caught my attention. I realized that, even this close, under the streetlamps, I couldn't tell what color they were. And yet his gaze pierced through the fog. I frowned. There was something familiar about him . . . but I knew we hadn't met.

He ventured a smile, still holding his hands where I could see them. "Allow me to introduce myself—and apologize for startling you." His voice was soft but firm. I had the feeling he could sing with that voice. "My name is Bryan Tierney. I'm your neighbor."

*Neighbor?* When I'd left Whisper Hollow, the estate next door had been empty, and I hadn't realized somebody lived there now.

I gazed at him calmly, but inside, alarm bells were going off—but I couldn't tell what they were warning me about. I wasn't afraid of him, not really. I didn't sense danger from him, and he most definitely wasn't a spirit—but something was tugging at the edges of my consciousness.

"Neighbor? Really?"

"*Really.* Don't worry, I'm not hiding a second head anywhere." He laughed again, and I realized I had been staring.

I blushed but found it hard to drag my eyes away. He was an arresting man. His black leather jacket looked vaguely European in style—the sleeves were pushed up to show what looked like, in the dim light, a line of Japanese kanji on his inner arm. The jacket's collar shrouded his chin and neck. Tight-fitting jeans hugged his ass, and a pair of knee-high boots with three straps that buckled across the lacings, and chains that jangled above and below the straps completed his outfit.

Suddenly aware that I was standing there like an idiot, I cleared my throat. "So, Bryan Tierney, where did you come from?" I glanced around. "I don't see a car."

He gave me a long look. "I was out for a walk."

Realizing that he wasn't going to elaborate, I debated continuing the conversation.

"Are you going to tell me your name, or do I have to guess?" His smile was irritating—it wasn't smug, but it did feel a little too familiar.

I let out a faint huff—the chill was damp on my lungs and I was rapidly becoming disenchanted with the entire evening. "Kerris Fellwater. I just took possession of my grandparents' home, so you must live in the estate next door?"

A large mansion sat on the double lot next to my house. When I was a child, it had been empty and I had thrown rocks at the windows until my grandmother caught me and spanked me.

"Right." He glanced at my car. "I thought I saw your SUV this morning as I drove past. So, I was right. You are Duvall and Lila's granddaughter." The way he said it could mean that he thought that was a good thing or a bad thing. There was definitely something about him that struck me as odd, but try as I might, I couldn't put my finger on it. Well, other than the fact that he had run right in front of my car. Normal people generally didn't plaster a *road kill* target on their backs.

"Yes, I am. *Was.* Did you know them?" I wondered just how chummy he had gotten with my grandmother . . . and with Duvall. If he was a friend of my grandfather's, I'd have to be cautious.

He flashed me a subdued smile. "Your grandmother was

very sweet to me. Your grandfather, on the other hand . . ." He trailed off, a frown crossing his face. "You lived with them when you were younger, didn't you? Lila said you left as soon as you graduated."

I wondered what else my grandmother had told him about me. I was about to ask when a gust of wind wailed past, hurting my ears with its howling. The mist had grown thicker, creeping through treetops to shroud the road. Shivering, I realized I needed to get inside *now*. There was something out here in the night that was dangerous to me, and until I knew what it was, I needed to get inside and lock the door against the night.

"I left when I was eighteen." I glanced back at my truck, debating one last question. I wanted to know what he'd been chasing. But something held me back. For one thing, I wasn't sure how much I *really* wanted to know. Every person in Whisper Hollow had secrets tucked away. Sometimes it was better to just pretend they didn't exist. And second: I wasn't at all sure whether he'd tell me the truth.

I stowed the crowbar back under the seat. "If you're sure you're okay, I'd better get home. My cats are waiting for me." At his look, I laughed. "Yeah, it sounds like a cliché, but I *am* the crazy cat lady. I have three Maine Coons—two sisters and their brother, and it's past their dinnertime. They're not happy campers when I give them their dinner late, so I'd better get my ass in the house and feed them."

The somber look fell away and he smiled back with his eyes. Giving my car a nod, he said, "Go on with you, then. Have a safe evening."

As I started to get back in the car, he added, "Maybe we can . . . grab a cup of coffee some time? We're neighbors, we should get to know each other. Just in case . . . you know. *Emergencies*."

That made me laugh. After all . . . I was standing with a handsome, mysterious stranger in the middle of a dark road as the mist rose around us and he had just suggested a coffee date. Who could resist that?

"Maybe we can. After all . . . *emergencies* do happen. And

it's always good to know one's neighbors." I popped into the car, and as I eased back onto the road, I called out the window, "You know where to find me. Drop over whenever you like."

Long after I was home and cuddling with the cats, the strange figure bounding across the road, and my altogether too intriguing neighbor, preyed on my mind.

# CHAPTER 4

⟡

The next morning, I had just turned the espresso machine on when there was a knock at the front door. Sighing, I put down my mug and headed to answer it.

"Kerris Fellwater, you beautiful bitch! Welcome home!" Peggin was leaning against the door frame. A little taller than me—she was about five seven—she was luxuriously padded in all the right places like I was. The epitome of an opulent, plump pinup girl. Her hair was a deep copper and she was wearing a retro fifties dress that cinched in at her waist to flare into a full skirt, a cropped blazer, and chunky heeled pumps. She lit up my front porch like a bottle of fireflies.

All of a sudden, coming home seemed like the best idea ever.

"Peggin! You're back! Get in here." Unable to control the smile that spread across my face, I grabbed her hand and yanked her inside. We had been best friends in high school, and she was one of the few people I had kept in contact with all through the intervening years. We'd met for an occasional lunch in Seattle, called at least once every couple of weeks, texted off and on. "How was your vacation?"

She shrugged. "Not bad, but I don't think I'm cut out for California weather. Or the lifestyle. I was only there for a few days, but I'm glad to be home, to be honest." She shimmied out of her jacket. The woman was basically sex-on-legs, with a damned good brain to go along for the ride. "Coffee first, then talk." She had her priorities straight, that was for sure.

I headed to the espresso machine. "Three shots espresso, a little milk, and a lot of sugar, right?"

"You remembered." She grinned. "I rushed out the door without grabbing a drop, but I couldn't wait to see you. I would have come over last night but my flight got in late and by the time I got home, I wasn't sure if you'd still be up."

"Yeah, I crashed pretty early. Yesterday was . . . a lot happened. I learned more in one afternoon than I did my entire eighteen years here before I ran off." I fitted the mesh cup in the filter and spooned in ground coffee, then gave it a turn to lock it into position. I flipped the switch and a stream of creamy brown espresso flowed into the shot glasses. "I can't believe I'm really back here, Peggin. Back in Whisper Hollow. The intervening years vanished like smoke when I drove back into this town."

She nodded. "I hear that happens. I've never tried leaving . . . not for good . . . so I don't know. But I'm glad you're home, if only for my sake. I missed you." She leaned against the counter, the satin finish of her dress brushing against the granite with a soft sound. The style fit her perfectly. Peggin also wore glasses—horn-rimmed frames that fit her personality perfectly. Even when I knew her in high school, she had been the odd one out, always setting her own style.

"You have to go to work today, or can you stay? I wanted to ask you about some things that I learned." I pulled the rest of our espresso and carried the cups to the table. Peggin carried the creamer and sugar bowl. She poured a dollop of cream into her coffee cup, then added two spoons of sugar.

"No. I took today off so I could catch up on my errands. I *wish* I could just hang out, but I have to do laundry and go grocery shopping and pick up Frith and Folly at the kennel before I head back to work tomorrow." Peggin owned ferrets.

They were more of a handful than Maine Coons, into everything and as curious as cats. As she stared into the cup, a soft smile crossed her lips. "Corbin's a good boss, but he's sure an odd duck. Remember him?"

I nodded, though I mostly remembered that he had been tall, with skin the color of espresso, and his eyes had been odd. They reminded me of a snake's eyes. "He was a few years older than us, right?"

"Right. He was a senior when we were freshmen. He's the only one I'd trust as a doctor. He got married and they have a thirteen-year-old daughter. She's following in his steps, I think." Peggin lifted her espresso, cupping the china in her hands as she inhaled the rising steam with a grateful sigh.

"I've missed you so much." She stared into her cup. "Whisper Hollow is changing, Kerris. Something's going on, and it isn't good. It's always been dangerous to live here, but when you're brought up here like we were, you learn the ropes. Now, I'm not so sure. Everything seems off-kilter and even people who should be safe, aren't so much. Don't trust anybody blindly."

Her concern unnerved me. Peggin had always been able to home right in on potential problems. When we were fifteen, she kept me from dating Danny Tremain, a boy I'd had a crush on. She warned me that he was trouble waiting to boil over. Sure enough, after I turned him down, he took up with a girl named Wendy and she ended up with two black eyes, a broken nose, and a broken rib. And Danny hightailed it out of town before Wendy's brothers could catch hold of him.

I mulled over her words. "Yeah, I got the gist of that yesterday from Ellia, Oriel . . . and Ivy. Peggin, do you know Ivy Primrose?"

She frowned. "Yeah, I know her. Not well, but she comes in for her physicals every year and I see her at the farmer's market now and then. What's going on?"

I hesitated, then told her everything that had gone on, asking—at last—"Did *you* know that Ivy was my grandmother? Did anybody ever tell you?" If she said yes, it was going to be hard to navigate that point. Peggin and I had never lied to each other, or withheld anything important.

She stared at me, her eyes wide. "Well, if that isn't a tangled mess. And to answer your question, no. I had no clue." Pausing, she stirred another spoon of sugar into her espresso. "No wonder the woman never aged. I guess I never even thought about it—so many odd people live here in Whisper Hollow." She paused, then added, "There's more to Ellia than meets the eye, Kerris. Rule number six keeps popping up in my head . . . You remember the rules, right? *Sometimes the foul are actually fair.* The converse can be true, as well. What seems fair, might just be foul. Lately, I've found myself being very aware of just who I tell anything to."

I listened to the subtext below the words. Peggin often spoke in riddles. It was her nature and I had realized over the years growing up that she was like an unwitting oracle. And right now, she was warning me not to trust anybody at face value.

"What about Bryan? My neighbor? Got anything on him?"

"Bryan Tierney. He keeps to himself a lot but I've met him a time or two. He's an odd sort, not rude but he definitely isn't forthcoming with information about himself. Handsome man, though." She smiled then, and shook her head. "You're intrigued."

"Yeah, I am. There's something about him that I can't shake off. A feeling . . . that I know him even though I know full well we've never met before last night." The image of those piercing eyes flashed into my mind again, and I found myself unsettled all over. "I wish I knew what secret my grandfather had wanted to tell them. It's almost as if the Lady didn't want him talking . . ."

Peggin shivered. "The Lady is a force unto herself, but I know—in my bones, I know—that she will work with others if supplicated enough. I just . . ." Her voice trailed off for a moment, and then she said—almost squeaked—"I feel you're in a lot of danger. I don't want to see you end up at the bottom of the lake, too. Promise me you'll be careful?"

I finished my espresso and, staring at my cup, nodded.

"I promise." Trying to lighten the cloud of gloom that had enveloped the both of us, I added, "Today I'm on a hunt to find Lila's Shadow Journal. I can learn a lot more from that than anything or anybody except Lila herself. Are you sure you don't want to hang around and help?"

Reluctantly, she stood. "I wish I could, but I really do need to run some errands. And Frith and Folly are waiting for me. But what about getting together for dinner? I can bring chicken."

The cloud suddenly lifted as a sense of nostalgic joy swept through me. How many dinners had Peggin and I shared over the years when we were young? How many confidences had we shared? And now, I was going to have that back again. I realized how keenly I had missed having my best friend by my side . . . any friends, really. The cats were great, but sometimes I needed somebody who could talk back to me in actual words. But, not wanting to sound maudlin, I just said, "Sounds good. I'll make a salad and bake some potatoes."

I saw her to the door, hugging her once more before she left. In an odd way, I had my life back. The past couple of days, even given everything I'd learned, I felt more at home than I had all the years I'd been away. I shut the door and started hunting for Grandma Lila's Shadow Journal.

The Fellwater house resembled a castle en miniature. The central area—the living room and kitchen, were single story, but the two wings off to either side rose two floors high. They weren't connected—you couldn't get to one side of the second story from the other without going downstairs first.

To the left of the kitchen and living room were my grandfather's den, a bathroom, a pantry-utility room, and a staircase leading up to what had been two bedrooms and a bath. The bathroom was a Jack-and-Jill between my old bedroom and the guest room, though my room had been the more spacious of the two. Still furnished with my bed and some of the things I'd left behind, it was waiting like an old friend.

Grandma Lila hadn't changed the brilliant purples and pale gold I had chosen the last time we'd painted. The guest room, however, had been redone in shades of pale gray and light blue, with a vivid royal comforter on the bed, and the furniture had been painted white.

To the right of the kitchen and living room, the hallway led to the master suite where my grandparents had slept and another staircase, leading up to an attic and a spare room that my grandmother had used for her sewing.

As I stood in the doorway to their bedroom, I realized just how much I'd been dreading this. Everywhere I looked were reminders. The air was tinged with the lingering scent of Grandma Lila's favorite perfume: Lilac Orchard, a spicy floral scent. It mingled with the stale scent of Grandpa Duvall's cigars and the acidic note of the aftershave he had used.

I hesitated for another moment, then resolutely marched into the room. Gabby, Daphne, and Agent H sashayed their way behind me, curiosity lighting up their faces.

"Don't get into trouble, you three." I frowned as they ignored me and promptly began to sniff their way into the closet and under the bed. I let them have at it. The bed was barely far enough off the ground for Agent H to slide under, but when I got down on my hands and knees and peeked, he seemed to be getting around okay. I just didn't want him stuck. Maine Coons were big, and he was a good twenty-four pounds. Gabby opted for the closet, and the sound of shifting boxes and shoes told me she was working her way to the back. Daphne, however, decided she wanted to sprawl out on top of the bed, where she rolled over on her back, tufted feet hovering in the air. The blending of orange and black fur didn't extend to her stomach, which was a blaze of white. She squirmed happily. Laughing, I leaned over and rubbed her tummy with my nose. She purped and bounced away.

Refocusing, I headed for the bathroom. Though I'd taken my showers in there, I hadn't really poked around yet. It was an en suite and, like the kitchen, had been renovated since I'd left. A sunken tub had replaced the claw-footed one, and a walk-in shower had been installed, along with marble countertops on the vanities and a new linen closet. I went through the vanity drawers, but it was easy enough to see that Lila hadn't kept her journal in there.

No, the bedroom was the logical place to start. And while I was at it, now was as good a time as any to begin packing up some of their things. The thought left me melancholy, but it had to be done. I couldn't live in the middle of what had been their lives. I had to make the house my own, even though moving in and taking over meant my grandmother was really dead.

With a long sigh, I trucked myself back into the kitchen and then out to the back porch, where I'd left a stack of cardboard boxes and a couple of boxes of large trash bags. Clothing would go in the bags, other items in the boxes. I added a roll of strapping tape to my supplies, along with a flashlight and a pair of scissors, and carted everything into the bedroom.

I decided to start with the dressers. Clothing was easy. There were a few scarves of my grandmother's that I wanted to keep, and maybe a hat or two, but most of the clothes could be donated. I quickly worked through my grandmother's dresser, then my grandfather's. But when I reached the last drawer, though, it seemed to stick. I pulled, hard, and the drawer gave way, coming all the way out. A flurry of handkerchiefs covered the floor as everything went flying.

Probably needed some oil on the sliders, I thought. But as I stuffed the handkerchiefs into the bag and went to replace the drawer, I saw something in the space between the bottom and the floor. There was a little box there. Cautiously, I flashed the light into the space. No spiders, no vermin. I reached in and lifted the box out, forgetting all about the drawer.

The case was silver, with a moon and stars embossed on it in a cloisonné design and the box felt . . . *sparkly* . . . when I touched it. Some sort of energy was attached to it. I held it up, looking for a lock, but there was only a fastener. I carefully eased it open. Inside, a small key nestled on a pillow of black velvet.

"What have we here?" I picked the key up, turning it over in my hand. It was long and ornate, embellished with scrollwork, and reminded me of a skeleton key, though the shaft was shorter than usual. It had obviously been important enough to my grandfather to keep safely hidden away. My guess was that my grandmother hadn't even known it was there.

A loud shriek startled me and I glanced over at the window. A crow was perched in the great maple overshadowing this wing of the house, and as I watched, the bird swooped off the branch and toward the house, aiming directly at the bedroom window. At the last moment, it pulled a sharp left and disappeared.

*The Crow Man.* He was still watching me, which meant that just returning to Whisper Hollow wasn't the whole of his message.

Seeing nothing that might be unlocked by the key, I tucked it back in the box and slipped the box into my pocket. Replacing the drawer, I moved on to the vanity. Most of Lila's creams and perfumes I kept—they were still good and I liked their scents. When I came to her jewelry box, I slowly opened it. Her wedding ring had been on her finger when they found her, and that I had in my possession. But here were her daily-wear items. Some things were obviously costume; others I wasn't so sure about. As I stared at the jumble, I decided that I'd just take the whole lot in and have it all appraised. I didn't want to give away anything without knowing exactly what was there first. I searched for any sign of Avery's ring, but there was nothing in sight that matched Ivy's description.

After that, I fell into a rhythm and the rest of the room went quickly. Soon, I was lugging bag after bag of clothing out to the car. I also stripped the bed, washed all the sheets, and packed up the linens. I kept the handmade quilts that were family heirlooms, and some of the tea towels, but as much as I had loved my grandmother, we had vastly different style and color choices, so I decided just to start fresh and give most everything away. All through clearing out the bedroom and bath, I kept an eye out for her journal but only came across notepads with to-do lists written on them. Careful ticks showed completed tasks to the point of making me feel like a slacker.

After I was done, I took a break for lunch. I made myself an omelet and sat at the table, staring at the box with the key in it, and wondering where Lila's journal was. Maybe she kept it in the desk in the living room? Grandpa Duvall's den had been off-limits to everybody, so I doubted that I'd find it there, but I'd have to go through the room anyway. Another day for that, though.

As I nibbled on a slice of toast, my mind a million miles away, I was startled by the sound of a door closing. It hadn't been the front door, but I had heard it loud and clear. I quietly set down the bread. If somebody was in the house, I didn't want them to know I knew.

Slowly, I eased my way out of my chair, remaining by the table as I listened for any further sound. *Nothing.* The cats weren't door-closers, though I knew of a few who could—and did—push doors shut. No, this had come from the direction of Lila's bedroom. My heart beating rapidly, I cautiously turned toward the hall leading to the master suite. I had barely gotten to the edge of the kitchen when a door on one of the bottom cupboards next to me opened, slowly but deliberately.

"Well, then, you want me to know you're here." I paused. I could see spirits fairly easily, but they had to want to be seen or conditions had to be right. I held out my hand, palm facing the cupboard door. Sure enough, the energy was strong enough to make my skin tingle.

I closed my eyes, reaching out. Making contact with spirits could be dangerous, but Lila had taught me early on how to protect myself from being jumped, so I wasn't worried about possession—I always kept my shields up. But once contact was made, it could be difficult to push them out, if need be. It was almost like in the vampire novels where, once you invited the vampire in, it was hard to stop them until you rescinded the invitation.

* * *

There are six categories of the dead, Kerris." Grandma Lila had taken me out to the graveyard one lovely spring afternoon. We were sitting on a bench. I was holding a candy bar. "You need to remember this, because it can mean the difference between putting yourself in danger and keeping yourself protected. The dead can be harmless, or harmful. Do you understand?"

I was seven years old, but I already knew that one day I'd take my grandmother's place. I had her gift, and even though I didn't say much about it, inside I was proud of the fact that I'd grow up to be a spirit shaman. It felt like continuity—and ever since my mother had vanished, the fear had been there that, at any day, at any time, I could lose everything important to me.

I nodded. "Yes, I'll remember. What are they?"

My grandmother smiled. "The first type, the *Resting*, we don't have to worry about. They have passed into the Veil, though they haven't passed through the other side yet. But after they go through the Veil, they aren't our responsibility, unless they try to come back. And the Resting are content with knowing they're moving on to the next cycle in their existence."

"Penelope helps them, then, right?" I squinted, staring at the graves. Old bones and bodies filled the ground here, but they weren't what we had to worry about. *Bones* didn't walk. *Spirits* did.

"Yes, Penelope lives in the Veil and she helps them cross to their next destination. The second type of spirit is called a *Mournful*. They mourn their loss of life, and sometimes you see them repeat their deaths, but they don't usually bother us. They know we're here, but they don't really care unless they want us to help them. Think of them . . . like a TV show—a rerun of what happens."

"Do they move through the Veil to the other side, too?"

My grandmother shaded her eyes, tipping her hat so it reflected the light. "Yes, if Penelope or one of the other

Gatekeepers can help them. Sometimes a spirit shaman will help jog them free from being stuck. That's part of our job at times, too."

I frowned. "I don't think I want to become a Mournful when I die. It sounds lonely."

"It is, love. It is. Now, the third type of spirit is known as a *Wandering One*. Do you know what they are?" She crossed her legs and leaned back, handing me a handkerchief to catch the dribble of ice cream running down my chin.

I wiped my face, thinking. I had heard about the different categories of the dead, but Grandma had never made it one of our actual lessons before. I thought about the name. *Wandering Ones* . . . that meant they weren't tied to one spot—not that most ghosts were trapped in an area. But there had to be a deeper meaning. After a moment, I shook my head.

"I'm not sure. They walk around a lot?"

"The Wandering Ones travel and are seldom found near their graves or the places where they died. They don't really pay attention to us, like the Mournful, but the Wandering Ones don't repeat their deaths over and over. They just wander the earth, lost. A lot of times they don't even realize they're dead. They tend to be confused. We also try to help them, when we can. If we can guide them into the Veil, we can help them realize that they have died and that it's time to move on."

I processed the information, feeling rather sad. "It must be awful to die and not realize it."

Grandma patted my shoulder. "Don't worry, Kerris. Spirit shamans *never* join the ranks of the Wandering Ones. Now, the fourth kind of dead can be dangerous. They're called *Haunts*—"

I finished my chocolate. "I know what a Haunt is. They scare us—they're Halloween ghosts."

Lila laughed. "Yes, they are Halloween-type ghosts. They enjoy scaring people. Sometimes they can cause physical harm to us, and sometimes they can possess people. Poltergeists usually fall under this category. They're angry ghosts, and they don't want to go into the Veil. Sometimes, they've gone over but are able to break free and return. So we have to drive them back before they cause too much havoc. Now, the fifth kind, the *Guides*, are helpful. They come to tell us things we need to know, or they come back to check on those they loved. They've gone through the Veil, and they . . . well . . . they act like guardians for a while before going on to their next destination."

I'd heard my grandmother talk about the spirits who helped her out all my life. "We leave them alone, right? Unless we need their help?"

"Right. We can talk to them if the need arises, and we can ask for help, but yes—we don't interfere with their activities. Now, what's the last type of dead?" She waited.

I bit my lip. I knew the answer, but the very name scared me.

"Kerris, you have to learn how to talk about them. If you fear them, you give them too much power. So tell me, what's the last type of dead?" She leaned down to take my hands. "I know you're afraid, and truly—they can be terrifying— but you have to gain mastery over your fear. Fear strips your power, fear leaves you vulnerable. Always respect the power of the dead, but never give them power over you."

Sucking in a deep breath, I nodded. "All right. The sixth form of dead are the *Unliving*, like Veronica."

Veronica was a queen among the Unliving, and she had a lair near the cemetery. She seldom interacted with the town, but she occasionally brought spirits back from the Veil to serve her. The Unliving were corporeal, but they weren't solid. They formed bodies from sheer will—from the energy they commanded—and they couldn't be physically attacked. Dangerous and unpredictable, they were the most powerful form of the dead. They crossed back from the Veil filled with agendas that the living knew very little about. And they were able to manipulate physical objects, often harming the living. They could also affect the living on a mental level. The Unliving could control the environment around them, and they did so with general contempt for the living.

My grandmother slowly inclined her head. "Yes, the Unliving, like Veronica. And these spirits, Kerris, usually hate spirit shamans, because we are among the few who can harm them."

# CHAPTER 5

～

I waited, hand on the counter. The next moment, a soft laughter tickled my ear. Jumping, I searched the room. I knew that voice. There, standing beside me, was my grandmother. She was dressed in a violet pantsuit—her favorite color. She looked healthy, although I could see through her. I was used to seeing the dead the way they had died, which wasn't always a pleasant sight. Grandma Lila, however, looked happy and whole and not at all like a drowning victim.

"Grandma!" I was so happy to see her that—for a moment—all my common sense flew out the window. Then, I pulled back, logic taking over again. "Are you really Lila?" I scanned her energy and she stood there, waiting, arms out at her sides. Moving into *soft focus*, the technique she had taught me to see the truth behind illusion, I examined her. As far as I could tell, there was nothing hidden behind the image. No façade or assumed persona. Breathing easier, I relaxed.

A lot of people didn't seem to realize that spirits could—and did—lie. In fact, Haunts often used that tactic to raise havoc, pretending to be Guides. That was another reason spirit shamans urged the average person to talk to a professional. It was all too human to trust that your loved one would never, ever try to harm you. But some of the dead—especially Haunts and the Unliving—were able to disguise themselves as somebody else. Not every spirit was happy about being dead, and some of those spirits wanted to share the misery.

My grandmother raised her hand and a mist began to rise in the room. I caught my breath and could smell the scent of mildew and wet cedar, of water dripping off tall timber into the forest detritus below. The faint sound of lake water lapping against the shore whispered past as mist began to whirl around me in spirals, like fog creatures dancing in the air.

Lila motioned for me to follow her. Leading me toward the staircase, she headed upstairs. As we passed out of the natural light in the kitchen, her figure began to glow softly with a pale blue light. Neon . . . I thought. A soft bluish-white neon glow. A sense of familiarity rushed back.

When I was six, I had walked in on my grandmother once to find her glowing like this. The memory swept back like crows on the wing. She had been in her sewing room, sitting at a small desk, writing in a leather journal. She was so intent on what she was doing that she didn't see me standing there. As I watched, the energy around her swirled, wafting off her body in spiraling curls. I stayed in the shadows and watched as she knelt by the desk to open a cubbyhole on the floor hiding beneath the throw rug. She slipped the journal inside, then closed the panel and covered it with the rug once more. I slipped away before she could catch me, aware that I had been intruding on a private moment.

Like bricks from a crumbling wall, it hit me. *The leather journal* . . . that was her Shadow Journal, the book I was looking for! I caught my breath and stopped, halfway up the stairs. "You meant for me to remember that—you showed me what I'm looking for. I had forgotten all about that time! I didn't even know you realized I was there."

Grandma Lila didn't turn around, but she gestured for me to continue. I followed her into the sewing room. A sewing table and ironing board were the central focus. Along two of the walls were sturdy built-ins, shelves and cabinets for supplies. Grandma's walnut writing desk was against another wall, looking out through a window into the side yard and right into Bryan's property. Beside the desk was the throw rug. The room was exactly the way I remembered it.

Lila stood back, waiting. I knelt beside the pigeon-holed desk and reached for the rug, looking at her. She nodded and I slowly lifted the woven throw. There was the panel, with a small silver handle. I reached for it, and the metal sparked against my skin as I lifted it open. I scooched back so that I could see inside the cubbyhole as light from the room illuminated its interior.

There were two objects in there: an old-fashioned doctor's bag upholstered in a blue-patterned jacquard, and something wrapped in ice blue satin. I lifted both of them out, and my fingers tingled as I touched them. Making sure the cubbyhole was empty, I closed the panel again.

Sprawling on the floor, I stared at the bag. Grandma Lila stood, unmoving, watching me as I pushed aside the satin to reveal a leather-bound book. The size of notebook paper, it was black leather and a good two inches thick. The leather was worn but still strong and supple and smelled of neatsfoot oil. Embossed on the cover was a sigil—that of a crow sitting on a crescent moon. A leather tongue with a snap on it kept the journal shut. My skin rippled, goose bumps rising as I stared at the rune—it was the same mark as on my back. The same my grandmother had also had. *The Crow Man* . . .

I slowly opened the Shadow Journal and thought I heard a long sigh escape from it. The journal was about half full, my grandmother's writing neat and even. I turned to the end and found a loose page inserted there. To my surprise, it was a letter to me. It was dated the morning of her last day alive.

*Dear Kerris,*

*I hope you never see this, but if you do, it means that I am dead and you have finally returned. I have a premonition that something huge and dark and cold is waiting in front of me, so I decided to write this . . . just in case.*

*I wish I could have trained you fully, but if wishes were pennies, we'd all be rich. Within the pages of this journal you will find all the spells and rituals I know that you will need in order to perform your duties as spirit shaman, along with the history of our tradition. I have also made notes on the spirits who wander Whisper Hollow. This town is a magical place and, like all faerie lands, can be deadly to the unwary and the unwise. I cannot write everything here that you need to know, but you will find your way. You are strong and I know you can do the job.*

*Look to the caretakers for help. Penelope waits on the other side. She is your other half, the Gatekeeper of the dead from the land of spirits. Trust in your instincts. Friends and colleagues may be true, but there is danger in the forest, a deep cunning desire to corrupt the powers of Whisper Hollow. These lands are ancient, and they rest on the crossroads of ley lines. Whisper Hollow is a vortex of power, attracting those who would take control. And our people—the sons and daughters of the Morrígan—have enemies who would seek to stop us in their anger from so long ago.*

*I will help you as I can, but my powers from the other side will be handicapped by those enemies who have sought to stop my work in life. Look to my past in order to move on with your future. By now, you know the truth about your grandfather—as will Ellia, Oriel, and Ivy after we talk to them this afternoon, if we are allowed to make it that far. My sense tells me we may run into trouble. Please, don't let hatred cloud your sight . . . I don't know if I can ever move beyond this, but I have to, for everyone's sake. And you need to be strong, and open to help from where you least expect it.*

*All my love in death, as well as in life,*
*Grandma Lila*

I closed the book. The truth about my grandfather? There it was again. Secrets and hidden agendas. I turned to ask my grandmother's spirit what was so damned important that she couldn't write it down in her journal, but she shook her head before I could speak and pointed to the bag.

All right then, I'd play by her rules. As I opened it, the scent of lilac and dusky rose swirled up. Inside the satchel, I found a leather sheath containing a silver dagger. The blade was a good eight inches long, and the hilt had two wings wrapped around it, the pommel being the head of a crow. The blade was etched with symbols. I flicked my finger along the edge and it quickly drew a thin line of blood. *Sharp.*

Licking the blood off my thumb, I replaced the blade in the sheath and moved on. Along with the blade, I found a quartz crystal skull four inches in diameter. Fractures within the crystal formed prisms and rainbows, and it was hard to drag my gaze away. There were several bottles of powders—each labeled neatly, a thin silver wand fitted with quartz crystals, and a black velvet bag of crystal runes—though they weren't any symbols that I recognized.

Another bag, purple satin, caught my attention. I shook out several large teeth into my hand. There were nine, each inscribed with some sort of sigil. They resonated in my palm with a heartbeat that was so deep and thundering it made me dizzy. I quickly slid them back into the bag, not wanting to stir up anything until I knew what I was doing. The last item in the doctor's bag was a black velvet case. Inside, on a bed of blue satin, rested a fan made out of what looked like crow feathers. I unfurled it and swept it around and the sound of crows shrieking filled the air. Startled, I quickly slipped it back into the case.

The pentacle around my neck was humming and I realized it was reacting to the items in the case. Slowly, a million thoughts racing through my head, I replaced everything in the case, including the journal, which fit snugly alongside the other items. Then, pushing myself to my feet, I dusted off my jeans and set the bag on the desk.

Lila didn't seem finished with me, though. She motioned for me to follow her. I picked up the case and followed her over to the other room—the attic. When I opened the door, it felt like I was walking into the hidden heart of the house. Attics were reservoirs, where old memories came to rest, lurking in the shadows. One large room, the attic was illuminated by a single bare lightbulb hanging from the ceiling. Everything was coated with a layer of dust, and I could see several old trunks, a rocking chair, and a few odd assorted pieces of furniture. Lila stood to one side, only the look on her face had suddenly shifted from smiling to bleak. She gave me another nod.

Wondering why she had brought me here, I began to look through the trunks. There were several filled with miscellaneous china and bric-a-brac, but one in the corner caught my eye. Drawn to the box, I skirted the rocking chair and a small table and knelt down to examine it.

The chest was square, like a footlocker, carved from cedar. When I cleared the dust away, I saw that it had been polished to a warm golden glow. Three initials were carved across the top: TEF.

*Tamil Eileen Fellwater* . . . my mother. This had been her chest.

I glanced at Lila. She shrugged, gently, a sad look on her face. It hit me then. Lila had died without my mother ever coming home again. I wondered if she had ever heard from Tamil but never told Duvall. But surely she would have told me? Surely she would have put me in touch with her—and Avery, if the pair had really run away together? Squatting back on my heels, I thought about my mother's disappearance. Where had she gone? Even after this long, I couldn't help but wonder . . . had she loved me? And if so, why had she run away? Why hadn't she come back for me?

A vague memory flared—my mother and I were in the front yard, and she grabbed my hands and spun me around under the summer sun, laughing as I laughed. We went faster and faster, and then suddenly, we toppled over onto the grass and she pulled me into her arms and brushed my hair back.

"I love you, Kerris. Don't you ever forget that. No matter what happens, you remember I love you. Promise me?" She was forcing me to look at her, to hear her. I suddenly remembered that her eyes had been filled with tears. She had been crying, though until now I hadn't remembered.

A week later, she vanished. And I had pushed that day out of my mind because it hurt too much to remember how happy I was and how much I loved her.

Sighing, I pulled my focus back to the present. "This was my mother's, wasn't it?"

Lila nodded, still silent. I knew that the dead could speak, but Grandma wasn't saying a word to me. She was merely acting as a tour guide right now. Hesitantly, I tried to open the chest, only to realize that it was locked. I examined the lock. The moment I touched it, I knew that the key I had found in my grandfather's drawer belonged to this trunk.

I tried to lift the chest but it was too heavy for me. I'd have to bring the key to it.

I glanced up to say something but the attic was empty. Lila had vanished.

"Grandma? Grandma!" I quickly scanned the room, but there was no one there except for me. Wishing I had told her how much I loved her when I had the chance, I slowly made my way over to the staircase. If I was lucky, she'd come back.

I reached the kitchen and was about to pocket the key and head back upstairs when the front doorbell rang. That couldn't be Peggin—it wasn't anywhere near dinnertime yet. Frowning, I answered the door to find Bryan standing there, leaning against the wall. He was carrying a bouquet of flowers—autumn zinnias that looked freshly picked.

"Hey, neighbor. I decided to play welcome wagon." He thrust the flowers at me. As I accepted them, he caught my gaze and once again, I had the feeling that he was full of hidden secrets.

I tried to discern whether there were any spirits hanging around him. I could almost always catch a few if I looked, but when I tried, all I could see was a flare of energy rising around him. There was something . . . I sought for the words to pin down the feeling.

*Too much to contain in one body . . . there's more of him*

*that you can't see—more than appears on the surface. This man has secrets and they run swift and deep.*

Where the hell had *that* come from? Startled, I moved back a step. "Come in."

Taking the flowers, I carried them over to the sink. They were obviously fresh-picked, not from a store. "You have a garden over there behind the castle gate?" Flashing him a smile, I pulled a vase out of the cupboard and filled it with water. Bryan's house was more like a mansion, and his yard more of an estate, with a high stone fence that surrounded the huge lot. There were at least two gates in the fence—the front one, and one dividing his yard from mine.

He settled into a chair at the table and leaned back. "Yes, I do. A rather extensive series of gardens, actually. I have a green thumb and it relaxes me." With a glance around the kitchen, he added, "You haven't changed much around here."

"Not yet. Remember, I've only been back for a few days. The reality of how much I have to do is just starting to set in. I've uprooted my entire life for the second time, and coming back . . . it's going to take some adjustment to figure out how I fit into this town again."

Readjustments like . . . what was I going to do with my days? Would I find a job or—perhaps—start my own business? Being spirit shaman might be a heavy responsibility, but last I looked it didn't come with a monthly salary. I had money thanks to my grandparents' inheritance, and the house was long paid off, but I didn't like the idea of just sitting on my ass doing nothing.

"I imagine it's not going to be easy. Your grandmother had heavy responsibilities on her shoulders. You will, too."

So he knew. Not that Lila being a spirit shaman was any secret. The whole town knew, just like they would know why I had returned. It was only a matter of time before the word got around, and then I expected to have a string of people at my door, asking for help. It had been like that when I'd been growing up. Lila had constantly been intervening with the dead for people.

I set the vase on the table and leaned over to inhale deeply. The zinnias were brilliant colors—the colors of autumn: yellow and gold and copper. The flowers were full and lush, and the heads had a faint but rich floral scent that played on my nose.

As I fingered one of the velvet soft petals, I let out a soft sigh. "You're very sweet to bring these over. They're beautiful. I haven't had a chance to garden over the past fifteen years. I lived in an apartment in Seattle, and my cats eat indoor plants, so I never kept any around. And speak of the devil . . ." I paused as Daphne padded in softly. She was the socialite of the group. Gabby and Agent H were friendly but it took them a while to warm up to strangers. Daphne, however, was a flirt.

Bryan paused, eyeing her cautiously. He had that look of someone who wasn't sure of cats—and that, in itself, bothered me. I had discovered that people who didn't like cats tended not to like me.

"You allergic?" It was the easiest opening into the question.

He shook his head. "No, but I'm not used to cats. I used to have a dog, though, when I was young. He made it to fourteen, a good span for dogs. I've . . . been on the road a lot over the years, so I decided to wait until I was ready to settle into one place for a while before getting another pet." Hesitantly, he leaned down and held out his hand—slowly so that he didn't spook her. Daphne cautiously edged forward. She sniffed his fingers, took another look up at his face, and then leaped into his lap.

Well, *that* was a surprise. She started to purr, rubbing her chin along the sleeve of his jacket.

"She's friendly but she seldom warms up so fast." Some people thought I was nuts, but I let my cats guide me in terms of trusting people who came over to the house. Inevitably they shied away from the ones who had issues or who were hiding a mean streak. Which meant, whatever else he might be, Bryan was safe enough to have inside my home.

Relaxing, I moved to the counter. "Would you like some coffee? A latte? A cappuccino? I've got the goods and I used to be a barista."

A whisper of a smile flickered across his face. "You're a caffeine freak like your grandma, aren't you? And sure—I was going to ask you out to the Broom and Thistle, but this works fine."

"The Broom and Thistle?" I turned on the espresso machine. "What do you want and how many shots? And yes, my grandmother taught me when I was fourteen how to appreciate the benefits of a good caffeine buzz." I didn't add that she told me it helped her focus on her work.

"The Broom and Thistle Coffee Shop. It's on the corner of Fifth and Cedar streets, and Michael and Nelly Brannon own the joint. Nice place. I'll have a triple latte, thank you." He was softly stroking Daphne's fur. She turned to gaze up at him and then, satisfied, bounced down and ran off into the living room.

As I pulled the shots, I sought for something to say, feeling awkward. I wasn't good with small talk—not unless it was somebody like Peggin. Bryan made me nervous, mostly because I couldn't get a good read on him.

*Oh, be honest with yourself, woman. He makes you nervous because he's so ruggedly handsome and totally the type you go for. Quit kidding yourself. You're interested and you know it.* Irritated—sometimes facing reality sucked—I searched for something to say while the machine was heating. But I had no clue where to take the conversation, and he certainly wasn't filling the awkward silence. I turned slightly, so he couldn't see me, closed my eyes, and reached out to see what else I could sense about him.

A rush of mist surrounded me, and I caught a glimpse of the rain forest, towering firs swaying in the night against a raging windstorm. I could smell the rain, thick and chill, and even though I could not see her, I knew the moon was dark and hiding. A rustle in the bushes told me something was near—something dangerous, with sharp teeth and a vicious nature. Something like what he'd been chasing when we met on the road. As a swift sense of self-preservation raced over me, my eyes flew open.

The light on the espresso maker flicked to ready and

without thinking, I began to pull the shots, but my hands were shaking. Whatever had been hiding in the bushes was dangerous, and I could still feel the hunger behind the shadow. It wasn't a ghost . . . and I didn't think it was one of the Unliving. But whatever was there had a gnawing ache in its belly and whatever it was, it was trailing Bryan—that much I knew. It shadowed him, like a lurker, or maybe . . . they were stalking each other. As I prepared our drinks, I tried to calm my nerves, reminding myself that Daphne liked him.

At that moment, Bryan joined me. "Need any help? Milk from the refrigerator?"

"Thanks, yes. I have creamer in there." Grateful for something to say, I added, "And there are cookies in the cupboard. Several varieties, actually." I blushed. "I like sweets. Choose your favorite and set it on the table."

He laughed. "I don't usually eat sugar, but who doesn't like cookies?" And then the shadow around him lifted and he was just my neighbor again. Wondering if I had been imagining things, I carried our cups to the table as he opened the bag of cookies. He had chosen Oreos and I melted just a little bit more. Truly, a man after my own heart.

"So, what are you up to on this blustery afternoon?" He sipped his drink and let out a satisfied sound. "You really are good at this."

"Told you." I grinned. Then a thought hit me. "Actually, I was about to head back upstairs to the attic when you knocked on the door. I found a trunk that I need to get into, but I can't carry it down by myself and I'd rather not open it up there. Would you mind giving me a hand after we finish our drinks?"

He arched one eyebrow. "Sure thing. I'd be happy to."

I glanced at the clock. It was two P.M.—plenty of time before Peggin was due back. As much as I was embarrassed to admit it, and as much as I liked Peggin, I wanted to get to know Bryan a bit before introducing them. She mesmerized men without trying. I usually turned them off because I was so blunt, and because I could see through them so easily. Actually, I had the same effect on women, too, which was probably why I had so few friends.

"So, Bryan, what do you do? And hand me one of those cookies, please."

He passed me the tray. "I dabble in this and that. I own a couple of international businesses. Boring stuff, really."

"Oh, I'm easily amused. Try me." I was horrible at flirting, really, but I gave it a try.

He shifted, looking uncomfortable. "Antiquities . . . trips . . . nothing I feel like discussing right now." He wasn't encouraging follow-up questions—that much was obvious.

I regrouped. "When did you move to Whisper Hollow?"

He toyed with his cup. "Let me think . . . five years back? Six? But I had visited a few times before that. I liked it so much that I decided to make this my home."

I shook my head. "Why on earth would you choose to live in this town when you don't have to?"

"You ask a lot of questions." His tone of voice was friendly enough, but I caught the edge beneath it.

"I was just curious," I started to say, then stopped. I wasn't going to defend myself when I had just been trying to be friendly. So, he didn't give out information easily and he didn't like people asking questions. That alone raised questions. I understood the need for privacy, but if he wanted to talk, he had to give me something to work with.

Another awkward pause while he finished his drink. "Come on, let me help you with that trunk."

Feeling a little less friendly now, I considered telling him not to bother. But before I could speak, he was on his feet and waiting. If I said anything at this point, he would object and then I'd counter and it would devolve into something far more awkward than it already was. Plus the truth was, even with Peggin's help, I doubted she and I could lug that trunk down the stairs without denting it or ourselves. The wood was heavy and solid, and we just didn't have the muscles that he did.

"Follow me, please." I didn't smile, didn't say much of anything as I led him up to the attic. All business, I pointed to my mother's trunk. "Here . . . this one."

Bryan knelt down, running his fingers over the top. "This is beautiful workmanship." His voice was soft, almost awed.

The shift in tone threw me. I frowned. "It was my mother's. I never knew about it till now."

He glanced up, meeting my gaze. A flicker in his eyes and the wariness seemed to back away. "I'm sorry I sounded so brusque. I'm afraid I don't get out much and I'm not one for small talk. I'm not used to being diplomatic and the truth is, I don't like talking about myself all that much. I'm a private person and like to take my time getting to know someone before I give away all my secrets."

Once again, I could sense the shadow behind him. Whatever it was, it was definitely stalking him. I wanted to ask him about it, but after the way he had responded to my other questions, I decided to leave well enough alone. However, his apology went a long way toward easing my irritation, especially since I understood exactly how he felt.

"I'm pretty closemouthed myself. Here, let me take one end of that." As I reached to pick up one of the handles, he motioned me back.

"I've got it. Don't strain your back. Just make certain there's nothing on the stairs for me to trip on, please." As he followed me down out of the attic, with me guiding him to the bottom, my attention returned to the trunk. Bryan Tierney was handsome, but this trunk had belonged to my mother, and now all I could think about was what I might find inside. Maybe Avery's ring? Or some clue as to where she had gone.

"Now I have a question for you," he said as he lifted it onto the table. "And if you don't want to answer, feel free to bitch-slap me. I deserve it." He was laughing with his eyes again, their blue intensifying.

"Ask, then." I pulled the key out of my pocket, suddenly feeling a bit shy.

"Why did your mother run away? Your grandmother told me a little about her—that she disappeared, leaving you behind." He was standing close enough for me to feel the warmth radiating off his body and it sent a tingle up my spine . . . a good one that made it hard to think about anything else.

I stared at the key in my hand. "I don't know. I'm hoping

to find something in this trunk that will tell me what happened. Why she abandoned me. My father vanished before I was born. His mother told me that he went out to Timber Peak on a hunting trip and was never seen again. He wanted to marry my mother, but . . ."

Bryan motioned to the table. "Do you want me to step away while you open that? Or leave? I can understand this might be a private affair."

I considered his question. There was always the chance something in the trunk would make me burst into tears. Or maybe . . . maybe it was just garbage, or old memories that I wouldn't relate to. After a moment I said, "No, stay. I barely knew her. I was three when she left."

As I fitted the key into the lock and turned it, the air grew thick. Mist began to rise around me—the kind that always signaled some spirit near—and I opened myself up, searching for where it came from. As I creaked back the lid, I saw a light jacket, folded and sitting on the top of whatever else was in the trunk. I recognized it—my mother had worn it the day when she spun me around in the grass. As I slowly pulled it out of the trunk I noticed there was something on it. Spread across both sides of the chest was a reddish brown stain surrounding what looked like a bullet hole. As I stared at it, a faint cry rose up and I glanced over to see a young woman squatting beside the table. She was weeping, her hands raised to ward off something. Bryan was watching her, too.

"Who is that, Kerris?" His voice was so soft I could barely hear it.

Horrified, I watched the cowering ghost. "My mother. That's my mother, Tamil. And that means . . . that she never ran away. She's dead, and I think the blood on this jacket is hers." I turned to him, stammering out the words. "I think my mother was murdered."

# CHAPTER 6

~

M y breath caught in my chest as I leaned close to my mother's spirit, surprised that Bryan could see her, too. I wasn't sure what to do—was she a Haunt? Or a Mournful? I reached for the pentacle around my neck and ran my fingers over the crystal skull. I didn't have an itch to punch through her like I had with Betty's spirit, nor did I get a sense of danger. Instead, I let instinct guide me.

I approached Tamil's spirit cautiously, praying that she wasn't affecting her sorrow. Haunts also could do that—get you feeling sorry for them and then when you let down your guard, they'd move in and either try to scare you, possess you, or just fuck with your mind. I didn't know enough about my mother to be able to place her, yet.

Tamil suddenly jerked her head toward me and her eyes grew wide. She looked at the jacket in my hands and a confused expression slid across her face. Then, once again, she turned as if seeing someone behind her and cowered down. At that moment, I saw the blood covering her chest, right over her heart. I caught what looked like a bullet wound before she vanished.

Bryan cleared his throat. "Did she say anything? I could see her but not hear her."

I shook my head. "No, I couldn't hear her, either. I think . . . she's a Mournful. And I think she may have only now realized she's dead, though I can't be sure about that. The look on her face when she saw me holding the jacket was one of recognition, but also . . . realization."

I froze, abruptly sitting down in the nearest chair. It suddenly hit me—I had just seen my mother's *ghost*. That meant Tamil was really, truly, never coming back. It also meant she hadn't run away, hadn't deliberately abandoned me. It meant that she hadn't met up with Avery. The world began to spin as all of the jigsaw puzzle pieces went flying and tried to rearrange themselves into a new picture.

After a moment, I looked around, hoping Lila would be there, but she was nowhere in sight and I couldn't feel her around. I didn't want to take a chance on summoning her, in case I screwed things up from being so startled. It was quite one thing to reach out to talk to ghosts when you were prepared, quite another to do so right after a shock.

Bryan handed me a glass of water. I hadn't even noticed him pouring it. Gratefully, I accepted it. He pulled a chair over to my side. "Are you okay? Should I call someone?"

I took a long drink of the water, trying to clear my head. After a moment, I shrugged. "I have no one to call, really. Peggin will be here for dinner, but otherwise . . . I'm pretty much alone." Then I thought of Ivy, but Peggin's warning stuck in my head. I didn't know Ivy well enough yet. Given it had been fifteen years since I'd been in Whisper Hollow, truth was I didn't know *anybody* here that well.

"What about the police? Your mother vanished what . . . how many years ago?"

"Thirty."

"There are no statutes of limitations on murder."

I stared at the jacket in my hands, realizing I was probably holding the last thing my mother had worn. Then it hit me—if it was in the trunk and my grandfather had the key, he had to have known Tamil was dead. And that led to some very unsettling thoughts. Very slowly, I set the jacket on the table, unable to take my eyes off it.

"Kerris? You've just turned a scary shade of green. Is there anything I can do? Anything at all?"

I was moderating my breath, trying not to spin into a dark place. After all, as much as I hated my grandfather, maybe he hadn't found out about her death till after I left. But what about the secret he wanted to talk about? Could it have had anything to do with the jacket? With my mother being dead? Maybe . . . maybe . . . there were a hundred maybes.

"I don't know what's worse," I finally said. "Not knowing if she'll ever come home, or knowing she never will. Not knowing why she left, or knowing that she was murdered."

Bryan let out a long sigh and leaned back. "I know what you're going through. My father was murdered. Except . . ." He paused, looking as though he was trying to figure out just how much to say. After a moment, he leaned forward, elbows on the table, resting his chin on his hands. "I saw my father die. I was . . . very young, but I still remember every detail of that night. Not the day, not even the general time around that period. I don't remember much of anything except every single detail of those moments."

Startled out of my thoughts, I stared at him. That could go a long way toward explaining his reclusive nature. I started to say *I'm sorry* but it seemed far too little, far too late. I wanted to ask him more about what had happened, but *that* seemed too intrusive. Finally, deciding he'd tell me more when he felt comfortable talking about it, I just nodded.

Bryan pushed the plate of cookies my way, but I shook my head. My appetite had vanished.

I debated what to do. Ellia and the others had said Duvall had been furious when Tamil showed up pregnant, and then Avery had disappeared. Now I wondered about my father's disappearance. If Duvall was so angry at Tamil that he might have killed his own daughter, what would he do to the man who'd impregnated her? And why would my grandfather even think of killing Tamil, instead of turning her out?

I tried to compose myself. If I was on the right track, there might be other people involved. Whoever they were, they could still be living in Whisper Hollow. Another thought occurred to me. If there were, did they know my grandfather had Tamil's jacket with the bloodstains? Was that somehow tied into the Lady of the Lake taking him down before he could reveal his secrets to Ivy, Oriel, and Ellia?

A thousand questions whirled in my head as I realized that I had been staring at the water glass for over five minutes. Bryan hadn't interrupted, and by now Gabby had meandered into the kitchen to nose around. She jumped up on the table and, ignoring the cookies, wound her way through the cups and saucers till she was standing in front of me. With a loud mew, she rubbed her head against my face and I brushed the soft black fur with my lips, kissing her gently. She began to purr and flopped down in front of me.

I snuggled her, looking over at Bryan. "I suppose I should examine what's in the rest of the trunk."

He shrugged. "It might help. Here, let me get a bag for that jacket, though. In case you give it to the police to examine, you don't want it contaminated any more than it already has been. Where do you keep your garbage sacks? Plastic would be best, I imagine."

I pointed him to the cupboard the trash bags were in, and he brought me one, unfolding it and holding it open while I eased the jacket in. I was lost in thought. Why wasn't I crying? I had just found out my mother was dead. If that didn't warrant tears, I wanted to know what did. I examined my feelings, but mostly, I just felt at a loss for words and a little numb.

Bryan gently set the bag aside and then squatted down beside me, bracing himself on the table. "Kerris . . . I know this is a big shock. Even though you haven't seen your mother in so many years, I can tell this has really shaken you. Are you *sure* you don't want me to call someone?"

All of a sudden, I didn't want to be alone. My grandfather had known my mother was dead and he never told me. And Grandma Lila, she was a spirit shaman—how could she not know? And if she had known, she had kept quiet about it. If she hadn't known, then she knew now. My entire childhood felt on shaky ground.

I reached for Bryan's hand without thinking. "Please, don't go. Not till Peggin gets here, at least. I don't really want to sit here thinking about this alone. My mind can be a scary place and I'm not so sure I want to listen to what's going on up there right now. We can . . . I should go through the rest of the trunk, I guess."

Bryan stared at my fingers, then flashed me a gentle smile. "Only if you let me make you some more coffee. And only if you promise to eat a few of those cookies. Shock drains energy and the food will do you good."

I nodded, and he headed over to the espresso machine. "Do you know how to use that thing?"

"I've got a similar setup at home, only it's a little more . . . advanced." By the tone of his voice I knew he meant *expensive*, but he laughed and pulled out the beans, starting to grind them.

Meanwhile, I forced my attention back to the trunk. Beneath the jacket were several journals—including a leather one like my grandmother's. I gently lifted it out of the trunk and opened it. Sure enough, it had been the Shadow Journal belonging to my mother. I realized I needed one of these for myself. I flipped through the pages and saw that it had several entries, but nothing much. Setting the journal aside, I began to dig through the pile of papers and trinkets below it. There was a small jewelry box with a few items in it, which I put to one side. I gave a quick glance through it but saw no sign of Avery's ring.

My mother's high school yearbook was in there from her junior year. I also found a few pictures. I recognized my mother as one of the girls in a group photo of four teenagers standing on the lakeshore. They were laughing, arms around each other's shoulders, and in the background I saw the sign for the Katega Campground, near the swimming hole. I had no clue who the others were, but flipped over the picture to find the names: Caroline, Tamil, Eversong, and Tracy. None of the others looked familiar to me, so I set it aside for the moment.

The rest of the items were odds and ends—a porcelain cat, a flower-pressing book with pressed rose petals in it, and lastly, I picked up what looked like a very small X-ray. As I held it up to the light, I realized it was a sonogram. *Me . . . that had to be me.* Feeling unaccountably sad, I stared at the debris of my mother's life. So little. She had been so young, and had so little time in which to figure out her life before it was snatched away.

"Here you go." Bryan sat a piping hot cup in front of me, complete with foam, which he'd managed to shape into the form of a cat's face, whiskers and all.

I laughed. "Really? You can do coffee art? I never could master it, but so cool!"

"Did you eat any of those cookies or do I need to force-feed them to you?" He cocked his head to one side, hands on his hips.

I was struck with a sudden urge to reach and take one of those hands again, only this time I wanted to rub it against my face. Blushing, I quickly turned my head before he could catch on to the direction my thoughts had taken. I didn't need distractions, and I certainly didn't need any more complications in my life right now. Instead, I nibbled on a cookie. Bryan was right—the sugar began to revive me a little.

"You know, when I was little, I used to dream that my mother would come rushing back with some story about being kidnapped by aliens or foreign spies or something . . . anything that would prove she hadn't just run off and abandoned me. I even thought she ran away to meet my father and to protect me, they had to keep hidden. Now that all seems so terribly sad." I decided to chance a question. "You don't have to answer if you don't want to, but . . . how . . . why was your father killed? And how is it that you were there?"

Bryan's face clouded over, but then he let out a soft sigh. "I don't talk about this much, but . . . for you, I will. My father had enemies—rivals who didn't appreciate him. One night, we were at home, alone. My mother had gone out for the evening—to some women's meeting or something. We lived out in the forest, away from the center of town. Three men showed up at the door. They broke in and went after him. Father pushed me into the closet before they could see me— we were in his bedroom. He had been reading to me. He ordered me to keep quiet—to not breathe a word or make a sound. I was brought up to obey his orders, and so I huddled there. But I lay down and peeked under the crack at the bottom of the door."

Without thinking, I asked, "What was he reading to you?"

"*Around the World in Eighty Days*, by Jules Verne."

I didn't know why but his answer surprised me. I just nodded, though, and he continued, his voice oddly calm.

"I watched as the men cornered my father. He didn't have . . . well, he wasn't armed and he couldn't reach the gun rack. I wasn't sure what they wanted, but he couldn't reason with them, and so they fought—he fought tooth and nail, but they overpowered him. At the end, they decapitated him. But I obeyed his last order. I didn't make a sound. They left after that. I suppose they figured that my mother had taken me with her when she went out. I stayed in the closet till she got home. I watched her find him . . . saw her walk in the room all cheerful and happy and then . . . she saw his body. They took his head with them."

Bryan leaned forward, folding his arms on the table. He cocked his head, his expression unreadable. "I'm a private person. I seldom talk about my past. Maybe you'll understand why I was so . . . abrupt, earlier. I still apologize. I was rude, but I do have my reasons."

I glanced around him, looking for some sign of his father's spirit. Usually when people were witness to violent crimes, the energy would linger in their auras until they had it cleared. But once again, I was only able to see the faint wisps coming off him. The man was a closed book. But his story had punched me in the gut. Regardless of his collected exterior, an ocean of seething emotion lurked below the surface. He was a ticking bomb, given the right circumstances and the right people.

"Did they ever catch the men who did it? If you saw them . . ."

"Yes, they did. They were . . . taken care of. Our clan handles things in a different way. My people don't leave loose ends, and we never forget a blood grudge. We clean up our own."

*Clan? People?* Who was he? Just what background did Bryan come from? And what kind of enemies came in and decapitated a man? A brief thought that he might have ties to the mafia ran through my head, but somehow it didn't fit. The questions were piling up, but I had the feeling I needed to walk cautiously. Not to mention, the trauma of seeing your parent's head cut off wasn't exactly a memory I wanted to stir up. Bryan was being nice to me and I had no desire to make his story worse by dredging through the details.

"Are you of Irish descent? The name sounds like it might be."

He bobbed his head. "Gaelic. Originally the Ó Tighearnaigh of Brega. Tierney means 'lord' or 'master,' and my ancestors were born near the Hill of Tara."

I cocked my head. "I'm Irish, as well. The origins of the spirit shamans are from Ireland—we're considered daughters of the Morrígan. She's—"

"I know who she is." His gaze was cool and collected. "Trust me, I know more about the Morrígan than I think even you do." But the way he said it held no hint of arrogance . . . a simple statement of fact and one that was probably true.

"I know some . . . what Lila taught me before I left. I should have studied into it on my own, but I wanted to put the world between me and Whisper Hollow when I left. I tried to use my abilities in other ways, so they wouldn't overwhelm me, but I kept as far away from my heritage as I could without driving myself nuts. I need to read my grandmother's Shadow Journal. I know some of our history will be found in there. Hell, I couldn't even tell you the origins of my family at this point, though she could have talked your ear off, I'm sure. For all I know, she did?" I glanced over at him, wondering just how much Lila had told Bryan.

He shook his head. "I know she was a spirit shaman. I watched her leave in the evenings, heading out to the cemetery with the lament singer. Your grandfather didn't seem extremely pleased—I heard them arguing several times when I was working in my garden. Either they were outside or they had the windows open, I'm not sure which." Pausing, he added softly, "You left because of him, didn't you?"

I caught his gaze, wondering how much to say. After a moment, I nodded. "Yeah . . . he never hit me—nothing like that—but he was a vicious old man. He had absolutely no respect for my grandmother and he didn't love me, I knew that much. I have no idea why my grandmother married him, or stayed with him. I don't think I ever asked, to be honest." Actually, it had never crossed my mind to ask—Grandma had been loving and kind to me, but I had always known that she would defend my grandfather, though I had no clue why when he was so abrupt with her.

After another cookie, I was starting to feel like the color was coming back into my cheeks. I finished my coffee, then pushed my chair back and stood up. "I guess . . . my next step is to figure out what I want to do about this. My mother disappeared thirty years ago—that's a long time."

"Murder shouldn't be allowed to go unpunished. Or unreported." Bryan cleared our cups away from the table and put the cookies back in the cupboard. "Seriously, Kerris. I know it's your decision and I respect that, but if I were you, I'd call the cops."

I thought for a moment. "Who's the chief of police now?" If it was somebody who might have been Duvall's friend, I wasn't sure I wanted them to know.

Bryan finished rinsing the cups and upended them in a drainer on the counter. "Sophia Castillo. I've seen her around the town." He seemed to sense where I was going. "I doubt if she and your grandfather were pals."

The name sounded familiar. I glanced at the clock. Peggin would be here within half an hour. "I need to start the baked potatoes and make a salad. Listen . . . would you like to stay to dinner? My friend Peggin's coming over—"

"I've met her. Don't know her very well, but she seems nice enough. And dinner sounds good, thank you. Put me to work, woman. Whatever you need doing." Bryan gave me a long look, and I had the feeling that I'd passed some sort of test with him, though for the life of me, I had no clue what.

An odd flicker ran through me. I frowned. "She's my best friend—we were best friends in high school and she's the one person I stayed in contact with while I lived in Seattle. So, you've met her, then?" Even as I asked the question, I blushed. Damn it, I hated the flicker of jealousy that flared up when he said he knew her.

He gave me a side glance, an annoying smile tilting the corner of his lips. "Yes, while I was at the doctor's office. She's nice."

I had absolutely no right to, but I wanted to ask him if he thought she was pretty. *Get a grip, woman. You so don't need to be acting like you're fifteen and back in high school. Peggin's your friend, not a rival.* Irritated with myself, I gathered up my mother's things, sans the jacket, and gently replaced them in the trunk. "Can you lift this off the table—it can sit over there in the corner next to the archway."

Bryan obliged. "I have some peaches and nectarines over at my place. Why don't I go grab them and we can have an old-fashioned dessert. I've even got whipping cream and a pound cake to go with them."

That sounded good . . . plus it would give me time to regroup after everything that had gone on this afternoon. "I think that would be lovely. Thanks, Bryan—and . . . thanks for everything. I'll see you in a little bit."

"You're sure you'll be okay while I run home?" He hesitated at the door.

Touched, I waved him on. "Go. I'll be fine. By the time you get back, Peggin should be here."

As the door closed behind him, I shivered. Now that I was alone in the house again, a brooding sense came over me and I paced the kitchen nervously. I wanted to see my grandmother. I wanted some sort of reassurance, but I had no sense that she was around. Instead, it was as if something else lurked in the shadows. At that moment, Agent H came running in. He took one look around the kitchen, let out a yowl, and then raced back into the living room. That was all it took. With a glance over my shoulder, I hustled after him.

Once I was in the living room, the mood seemed to lighten and I breathed easier. I decided that hearing somebody else's voice would be a very good idea right now, so I flipped on the TV and turned it to the Cooking Channel. As I settled on the sofa, draping a throw over my knees, the cats all converged on me. Agent H took up his place on the back of the sofa, right where he had perched back in Seattle. Daphne crawled into my lap, and Gabby sat beside my feet.

The comforting glow of the Tiffany-style lamps warmed the room, and the bustle of Andrea Ceres—one of the newest stars in the kitchen—took my mind off the trunk in the kitchen. Andrea was preparing a chicken in mandarin sauce and I focused my attention on her every move, keeping my mind on a narrow track away from my mother and her death. Or at least, I tried. It worked after a fashion, though the stray edges of my thoughts kept creeping back to the jacket, the blood, and what I had seen.

Finally, the bell rang. I jumped, scaring the cats, and as they went shooting out of the room, I draped the throw over the side of the sofa and answered the door. It was Peggin, carrying a bag. My stomach rumbled as the inviting smell of fried chicken wafted up from it.

"Thank God you're here." I pulled her in and shut the door, locking it.

She handed me the bag—which had not one, but two buckets of chicken inside—and shrugged out of her coat, hanging it on the coat rack by the door. "What's going on? You look way too pale. What happened since this morning?"

"Come on in the kitchen with me, please. By the way, Bryan is coming to dinner. I wouldn't have asked him but . . . after today . . ." Setting the bag on the counter, I pulled the chicken out and arranged it on the table. "The potatoes will be done in about fifteen minutes. I hope you don't mind going without salad. I forgot to make one. Bryan's bringing peaches and pound cake for dessert, though."

"I'm not a rabbit, so no salad is fine. And peaches and pound cake sound good." With a worried look on her face, Peggin slid into a chair. "Tell me what happened. You seem all shaken up."

I let out a weak sigh and slumped in the chair next to her. "You see that trunk? It was my mother's. I found it in the attic when I was hunting around up there."

"Oh, pretty! What's in it?"

"Some things of hers. Peggin, I found a jacket in the trunk that's covered in blood. When I pulled it out, my mother . . . her spirit showed up here. I'm pretty sure she was murdered." Saying it to Bryan had been different than saying it to Peggin. Saying it to Peggin made it far more real.

She let out a little squeak, then walked over to the trunk and knelt down by it. "Are you sure it was hers? You haven't seen her since you were three."

"I'm sure. I remember what she looked like right before she left. And the jacket was the one she was wearing the day before she vanished. I think somebody killed her. And my grandfather knew because the key to that trunk was in his dresser drawer. Which makes me wonder if my grandmother knew, too. Was she hiding it from me all these years, like Duvall?"

Peggin set her glasses on the table and rubbed the bridge of her nose, looking frazzled. "I have to tell you, this looks pretty bad for your grandfather. Didn't you tell me that Ellia said he was really bent out of shape over her getting pregnant?"

"Yeah. I wish I knew why. That might answer some questions. And then, there's whatever secret he was hiding that he never got to tell. Oh, Peggin, what do I do now? Bryan thinks I should go to the police. I was thinking about it, but . . ." A crow cawed loudly from the bush near the kitchen window.

Peggin shook her head. "Not yet."

"Yeah, I'm not certain what I want the cops to know. At least, not yet. What do you know about Sophia Castillo?"

Peggin let out a slow breath. "She's a good sort. Steady, levelheaded. Her family seems fairly popular. She isn't power hungry, but she's no pushover, either. She was in the sophomore class when we were seniors, so she's about two years younger than we are. The only reason I know who she is, is because we met in a store a year or so back and she reminded me that we used to have the same piano teacher. Her lessons were always right after mine, so she would be waiting whenever I got done at Miss Helen's. She has a husband and a daughter. Her daughter, Maria, is best friends with my boss's daughter, Kimberly."

"Do you think I should talk to her?" I still didn't want to. I didn't want to do anything until I knew more about what I was dealing with.

"I think you need to trust your instincts." Peggin looked up as a knock sounded on the kitchen door. I answered, escorting Bryan in.

"Hey, you." Peggin gave him a coy smile, but I could tell she was holding her energy back. Whether it was for my benefit, or whether she was preoccupied with what I had just told her, I didn't know. Either way, I was grateful because when Peggin turned it on, she *turned it on*.

Bryan gave her a two-fingered salute. "Hey, how's your boss? I haven't had a chance to play racquetball with him in a while."

"He's been busy helping out at the community theater. His daughter has a part in . . . what the hell is it?" Pausing, she squinted and put her glasses back on. "I think better with them on," she said at my look. "Oh, right! They're doing an adaptation of *Alice in Wonderland*."

We set out dinner. The potatoes were ready, and Bryan had not only pre-sliced the peaches and nectarines, but he had whipped the cream and also brought over the pound cake to go with them. I set the table with Lila's china—my china now—and my fingers slid smoothly around the plates. They had belonged to Mae, my great-grandmother. The edges were gilt, and the pattern was ornate. A scrollwork of pale green leaves and pink roses encircled the rim. I wasn't certain of the exact name of the design, but it was beautiful and I remembered eating off these dishes every night when I was a child. I added water goblets and dessert plates.

When we were seated, I took a moment to savor the food. None of us seemed to be in a talkative mood, but finally when we were full enough to think straight, I set down my fork. "I've decided that yes, I will talk to Sophia. I think it's the best way. I'm not a detective, and neither are you two. I want to do some poking around into my mother's case, but if I talk to her, maybe they can come up with the leads we won't be able to find. And maybe I can get her to keep it out of the papers. If anybody else besides Duvall was involved in her death and they're still alive, I don't want them to know what we've found. Not yet."

Peggin polished off her fourth piece of chicken. "You're probably right. That's the best bet. But, Kerris, what *are* you going to do if they find out your grandfather killed her? He's dead, at the bottom of the lake. Other than making sure his spirit stays over in the Veil, there isn't much you can do."

"I know. But as I said, I believe that if he did hurt her, then he had help. And that person—or persons—may still be alive. If so, I want them to go down for this, too. All I know is that I need to find out the truth about this situation, and as soon as I can."

When we were done with our meal, Bryan dished up the cake, fruit, and whipped cream, then dusted a little cinnamon over the top. He handed it to us and we polished off every speck.

"The fruit tastes remarkably good for it being October."

Bryan nodded. "I know. A local farmer has an orchard. He keeps some in cold storage for a few select clients." With a grin, he added, "Like me."

The front doorbell rang.

"Excuse me." Feeling a bit braver now that I had company in the house, I headed to the door. Outside, a rush of wind and rain rattled at the windows. Wondering who was out in this mess, I opened the door to see Ellia standing there, violin in hand. She was soaking wet—she must have walked all the way from her house.

"Kerris, I need you. Time to saddle up and take on your first job with me. Diago's on the move, stirring up trouble. He was spotted in the Katega Campground, near the lake." Her expression told me there was more to it than that.

"Hell, let me grab my grandmother's tools."

She blinked away the water streaming on her eyelids. "Gareth was on his rounds when he spotted him. He called me fifteen minutes ago. We've got to get a move on because we know Diago's on the way back to the hospital."

And with that, the peace of the evening disintegrated.

# CHAPTER 7

⌒

"Hell . . . okay, let me grab whatever I can. Diago's worse than one of the Unliving." I motioned her in. Peggin and Bryan were standing by the kitchen arch, watching.

Ellia glanced at them. "We have to go before he makes it to the hospital. Do you think you're up for this?"

"Yeah, though I'm not sure what to do." I shivered, giving her a pleading glance. "You're *sure* Diago isn't one of the Unliving?" It was a futile question; I already knew the answer.

In a soft voice, she said, "You know as well as I do what Diago is, and what he can do."

"As I expected you would say. I was just hoping I was wrong." I licked my lips.

"I was hoping we wouldn't have to take on one of Whisper Hollow's resident spirits until you were more acclimated, but Diago will eat when he's hungry. He hasn't walked in a few months, so he must be starving." Ellia passed by on her way to Bryan. She gazed at him for a moment, then whispered something to him that I couldn't catch. "Am I right?" Her voice was low, but insistent.

He regarded her for another moment, then turned away without answering. "Do you need help?" He posited the question to me.

"It's going to be dangerous. Diago—"

"I know what Diago can do. I've dealt with worse, Kerris." He was back to cool and aloof, but beneath the surface, I could hear the catch in his voice. He gave a quick sideways glance at Ellia, then refocused on me.

"If you want to come, yes." Surprised to see Ellia looking relieved at my decision, I wondered what she had asked him, but there wasn't time to play twenty questions.

Peggin jumped up. "I'm going, too. I can't fight the dead, but I can play sidekick. Plus, I know the hospital, and the people there know me and can smooth possible obstacles. Don't even try to talk me out of it." She shoved her glasses up—they were always sliding down—a dare to challenge her.

"You aren't dressed for it, love."

"Bullshit. I can run a block in these shoes and I can run even faster if I take them off. Dresses don't slow me down." She folded her arms across her chest, glaring at me.

Ellia let out a soft laugh. "Let them come. Allies are allies, whether they hold a flashlight or a sword. But we have to move. Gather your things—whatever you think you might need. You'll have to run on instinct, Kerris. I know you haven't had time to study your grandmother's Shadow Journal."

I asked them to wait while I ran upstairs to fetch the bag. I withdrew the journal and set it aside, not wanting to chance losing it or destroying it while out in the field. I honestly had no clue what I was going to do, but I'd figure out a way to wing it. I'd faced some nasty ghosts during my stint in Seattle.

I paused, "Grandma Lila, if you're around, I really hope you can have my back tonight. I don't expect you to help—I doubt you can—but even if you were just there for moral support, it would give me a really big boost."

Still nothing. I'd have to do this on my own, apparently.

I hoisted the bag and headed downstairs, pausing next to my suitcases to haul out a pair of boots. I loved my boots. Since we were headed into a campground in the dark, I decided on my Dingoes, a pair of black microsuedes that came to midcalf. They had a chain around the ankle that hooked onto a silver circle, then looped snugly under the arch. With the two-inch heel, the chain was nowhere near the ground and snug enough not to get caught on anything. And their polished steel toes were handy in case I had to kick anybody. The campground was relatively flat, but it was wet out and I didn't want to be stepping into any puddles. I shrugged into my green denim jacket and grabbed my keys and wallet out of my purse, sliding them, along with my phone, into my pockets.

"I'm ready. Let's go. Get your asses into my car." I beeped the car locks even as I made sure the front door was firmly secured.

Ellia rode shotgun. Bryan and Peggin piled in the back. As I eased out of the driveway, I wondered just what the hell I was going to do. Diago was a dangerous spirit—unclassified among the six categories. Some spirits were so strong we had no way to categorize them. They were highly individual, almost gods among the spirit world. And Whisper Hollow had its share of them. I had no hope of sending him through to the Veil, but I *could* thwart whatever he was up to. However, it wasn't going to be easy, given how long Diago had been around the town and that I was new to the business.

"I assume we head to the campground first, since that's where Gareth spotted him. And who *is* this Gareth, by the way? You mentioned him several times."

Peggin spoke up. "He's . . . he's a biker. He hangs out at the Fogwhistle Pub a lot." The way she said it made me think there was more to his story than just a barfly.

*The biker . . . the biker . . .* I shook my head. "I don't remember him. Was he in our class?"

"No, he's in his late forties, I think."

"What she's trying to say is that Gareth is trouble. He's always been on the wrong side of the law . . . at least on the surface."

"And yet he tells you when spirits are walking?" I cocked my head, waiting.

Ellia cleared her throat. "What I tell you must not leave this car. Do you all agree?"

I nodded. Peggin mumbled an "okay" and Bryan, after a moment, shrugged a noncommittal yes. Apparently that was good enough for Ellia.

"Gareth Zimmer is part of the Crescent Moon Society, and he also works—on a strictly *unofficial* level—for Sophia Castillo. He . . . fixes things the police can't officially touch." She let out a little cackle. "Gareth is one of the most feared men in this town, but more people owe their safety to him than will ever know."

I blinked. "The Crescent Moon Society?" The name sounded familiar but I couldn't place it. "What's that? And are you talking supernatural fixes . . . or . . . outside-the-book fixes when it comes to his dealings with the police?"

Ellia gave a little shrug. "With regard to Gareth, I would say it's six of one, half dozen of the other. As for the Society . . . we are a group of individuals dedicated to protecting Whisper Hollow from the malign creatures who run through these parts. While the Society can't chase back the dead— that's our job, yours and mine—they investigate whether deaths and disappearances are due to natural causes or to something that the police can't touch. Sophia isn't part of the Society—as chief of police, she can't be. But one of her officers is, and she works hand in hand with the CMS. Gareth is an integral part of the group."

I strained to think back. "I think . . . my grandmother must have mentioned it. The name is familiar. Was she part of it?"

"Yes, and so you will also be. I'm to bring you to the next meeting. Since you're the spirit shaman, part of your job will be to work with these people. As I do." She glanced in the backseat at Peggin and Bryan. "Anything you hear about the CMS *must* be kept quiet. Too much hangs in the balance. Breathe a word and I will have no trouble setting my hands on you. Peggin, you know what that means."

Peggin let out a strangled sound. "I know. Trust me, I like you, Ellia, but I don't ever want your hands on me. I remember Toby Voit."

"Toby was . . . an unfortunate incident. He is one of the few things in my life that I regret, but there was nothing else I could do." Ellia let out a soft sigh. "Is he still institutionalized?"

"Yeah. Corbin checks on him now and then. He won't ever recover."

"No, it's not likely. I sent him too deep, too far." Ellia shook her head and turned to Bryan. "My adjuration to silence goes for you, too. These old hands can set even *you* to spinning, my friend. I don't like ultimatums, but so much depends on secrecy and I will not fly on the wings of hope— too often they're clipped and fail."

Bryan snorted. "I am sure I could handle it, *lament singer* . . . but your secrets are safe with me. I have no use for the politics of the town. Nor any interest."

I glanced sideways. Ellia had turned around in her seat and she was staring at Bryan, a cunning smile on her face. Something unspoken passed between them. As much as I wanted to know what the hell was going on, I decided to leave it for later.

"You will soon *develop* an interest. Trust me, the politics of the Crescent Moon Society will reach even *your* doorstep, and you know why I predict that. There are powers out there that are working against Whisper Hollow and you have the ability to help turn the tide. I expect you won't turn your back when the time comes, and I suspect that time is coming soon." Then, before I could ask, she added, "As to the other members, Kerris, you will meet them soon."

Not sure what to think about the interaction, and wondering who Toby was, I drove on in silence. We were headed to the Katega Campground, past the Storm King Lodge on the edge of Lake Crescent. The Katega Campground had a guardian spirit, and it suddenly occurred to me that Diago shouldn't have been able to enter the boundaries.

"How is it that Diago made it through the borders of the campground? The Lightning Spirit should have repelled him."

Almost 150 years back, when the town of Whisper Hollow was first founded, the Katega Campground had been an area where people set up camp while the houses were being built. A young man had wandered outside during a thunderstorm and was hit by a bolt of lightning. His body vaporized, but his spirit had been sucked into the land and air around the area. Ever since then the Lightning Spirit had guarded the campground. Usually, people were safe within the boundaries. It was said the Unliving and Haunts couldn't invade it, nor could Sasquatch, or the Grey Man, or any of the other entities who made these woods their home. It was a safe haven. At least until *now*.

Ellia stared out the window. "That's a good question. Gareth knows what he saw, though. He's smart, and he's observant. If he says he saw Diago wandering into the campground, he did." Her phone jangled and she pulled it out of an inner pocket of her long cape. Brushing the hair back from her ear, she answered. "Yes? All right. We're on the way. We should be there in a few minutes." Sliding the phone back in its case, she glanced over at me. "Change of direction."

"Do I really want to know?"

"Gareth says that Diago's moving quickly. He slipped away before Gareth could trail him and is already at the hospital. Gareth received a call from Corbin. Diago's after one of the patients and he's already attached himself. We have to get over there as soon as we can or he'll drain the man."

I slowed. We were almost at the turnoff to take us to the campground. Instead, I continued on Sherwood Place as it turned into Lakeshore Drive S. and headed north to the center of town. Another couple of minutes and a few more turns, and we pulled into the curved driveway and parking lot of the Underlake Hospital. I slid smoothly into a spot near the door and we tumbled out of the car.

As we bustled into the foyer, I saw Corbin Wallace, and memories came flooding back. He'd been the quarterback on the football team, and he hadn't lost any of that muscle or tone. Tall, with ebony skin and eyes that still reminded me of a snake's—the pupils looked oddly like slits—he had traded his dreads for a shaved head, and his beard and moustache had vanished along with the rest of his hair. But the Vin Diesel look worked for him, and he lit up when he saw Peggin.

"I didn't expect you till tomorrow, girl."

"I told you Kerris was coming back in town. You know she's my best friend and always has been." Peggin laughed softly.

"So you did." He turned to Ellia. "Thank you for coming . . . and . . . Kerris—I'm glad you're here because I doubt if Ellia can handle this herself."

Ellia lifted her violin. "No, but I can help. Who is he after?"

"Mike Sanders. He suffered a serious heart attack three days ago and we thought we had him on the mend, but he took a turn for the worse earlier today. I can get him through the rough spot, but not with Diago after him—and a child from the cancer wing saw Diago slip past a few minutes ago. I knew exactly where he'd be going, and sure enough, he's attached himself to Mike. Follow me." He began to stride down the hall, his long legs propelling him along. I scrambled to keep up with him.

Diago had been around as long as I could remember. He was the Scuffler under the Bed, a spirit creature who leeched off those who were seriously ill. He never went after anyone with just a cold or who was in for a simple operation. No, he fed on the energy of those who were straddled on the crossroads, who were poised to turn toward recovery or turn toward death. Many a parent in Whisper Hollow had used him in place of the bogeyman when trying to get their kids to behave, and it usually worked because everybody knew he was real and not just some nebulous threat.

"Shit . . . Ellia, what do I use on him? What did Lila do?"

"You can't eliminate him. Lila never could. And there's no sending him over to the Veil. So don't think in terms of destroying him. Just focus on driving him back to his haunts. He usually lurks in the woods across the street, and like I said, he hasn't fed for several months."

"*Diago's Copse*. That's right—I remember. I always used to get the creeps because the words *copse* and *corpse* seemed so close together."

"One letter apart, but a world of difference." Bryan's snarky attitude had disappeared, and a worried crease furrowed his brow. He reached out, gently tapping me on the shoulder. "Kerris, may I talk to you for a second?"

I nodded, moving a step away from the others. "What is it?"

"Diago is a dangerous being. You haven't dealt with this kind of spirit, have you?"

I shook my head. "Not really, but I have to start somewhere. Why?"

"I don't know if Ellia has mentioned this. She might think you already know, but be cautious about looking at entities like this straight on. Staring contests never work with them, and a number of them can mesmerize with their gaze. If you aren't aware of what they're doing, they can mesmerize you long enough to attack."

I gave him a quizzical look.

He shrugged. "I've had some interactions with them—enough to be wary."

Wondering just who he'd been hanging out with, I gave him a short nod. "I didn't know, so thank you. If you say they might be able to make me go *Bambi in the headlights*, I'll believe you."

As I caught up to the others, I looked around for a place to get ready. "I need a bench to set my bag on while I prepare myself." I had no clue how to use some of the items Grandma Lila kept in there, but I was hoping instinct would take over.

We stopped outside door number 220. I glanced at it, a cold chill stealing its way down my back. Even from outside the room, I could feel Diago in there. The energy was cold and wet, sticky like a frog's tongue. Peggin had disappeared into a side room, and now she came out, wearing booties over her shoes and a white smock. She handed the rest of us booties and masks.

"If he's as sick as Corbin says, then we don't want to chance exposing him to anything."

"My tools aren't sterilized, Peggin."

She glanced at the doctor.

"Good thought, but I doubt if it matters at this point." He turned to me. "Do what you have to. If we just leave him be, Mike won't last another hour. Diago works that fast."

Ellia set her violin case down and pulled out the instrument. The wood gleamed with a rich luster beneath the stark fluorescent lights. I opened Lila's bag and looked at the jumble. I was wearing the necklace. Rest Easy powder wouldn't work—Diago couldn't be dispelled to the Veil. But the wand spoke to me, as did the crow feather fan. I removed them, then snapped the latch shut on the bag and handed it to Peggin.

"Guard this. Don't let anybody else touch it."

She nodded. "No problem."

"Bryan, you stay here with Peggin and the doctor. Ellia and I will go in alone." I hated taking charge when I didn't know what I was doing, but this was the way a spirit shaman worked. If I gave control to Ellia now, I'd lose confidence. I had to step up and take the reins. It was my place. "Ellia, start your playing." I paused, feeling so out of my league. "What . . . do I tell you what song to play?"

"Normally you would, but don't worry. I'll know the drill with Diago. My song will allow you to see him easier. It's not a song for the dead, but one to help illuminate the dead. These are things you'll learn as we go along. But remember the tunes—it's important that you come to know my melodies."

She lifted the bow and set it to the strings, and began to trill over the notes. They ricocheted off the walls, like drops falling in a waterfall—each one making a soft sound that joined with the others to produce a cascade of sound darting over the rocks.

The energy began to rise around me and I caught my breath—the music was shifting something in the room. My inner sight began to open up like a camera lens as I began to notice a sweep of movement through the halls. Misty shapes wandered back and forth. Spirits walked the halls—spirits I could normally see if I focused my energy but now were just as clear as Peggin and Bryan and Corbin. They took no notice of us. They were the Wandering Ones, the Mournful, those who had died over the years and either had elected to remain in the hospital or had forgotten they were dead and now traversed the spirit world, confused and lost.

I gripped the wand in one hand and the fan in the other as Corbin opened the door for us. I stepped into the room first, Ellia following me, her bow flying over the strings.

The room seemed oddly out of phase—a blur of two worlds colliding.

The man in the bed was hooked up to so many machines that he looked cybernetic. I stared at him, gauging his energy. A swirl of mist seethed around him, exiting his body as Diago drained him. I followed the trail of mist and vapor and found myself turning to the far corner. There, crouched in the shadows, was the Scuffler under the Bed.

He was tall and long, gaunt, like a walking stick insect or a walking skeleton. His skin stretched over the bones, paper thin and flaking, and covered with rashes and sores. Diago's eyes sank into the sockets, dark purple circles bruising his cheeks beneath them. He wore a top hat over long ratty hair that coiled down his back. He wore no shirt, showing his long, jointed arms, and his ribs pushed against his chest. His pants were so loose that they barely stayed up, kept on by a belt cinched to the last hole. Diago's tongue flickered out like a lizard's as he inhaled the stream of energy coming from the man in the bed. He sucked it in with a greedy smile.

Diago suddenly seemed to realize I was watching him. He slowly rose, standing on the tips of his toes, and leaned *backward* from his waist at a ninety-degree angle as he twisted his head to hold my gaze. His gaze was hypnotic and beckoning. As mesmerized as I was repulsed, I found myself stumbling forward a few steps, before Bryan's warning echoed in my head and I managed to stop myself.

"Hold steady"—a whisper behind me. Ellia changed her song and a dark melody poured out of her violin. The music energized me and I could hear the cawing of crows at my shoulder. Averting my eyes from Diago, I focused on the wand and the feathered fan. The crows screeched in my ear. Holding up the fan, I swept it three times. A faint breeze sprang up, crackling around him. I could see pale sparks light the rippling air that had come from the fan. The shriek of crows grew louder.

Diago pulled back with a hiss. *"Spirit shaman . . ."* His words flew by on the crackle of autumn leaves, and he crouched, tiptoeing toward the bed. "Leave me with my prize."

I shook my head. "I will not allow you to claim him. Go back to your thicket. Go back to your nest."

"You cannot destroy me, spirit shaman." Diago's eyes gleamed with the glow of decay and forest mold. A cunning smile crept across his lips.

"No, but I can cut off your supply, you freak of nature." I pocketed the fan and, with my right hand outstretched, I moved forward. I thrust my left arm into the air, holding the wand high. Ellia's music shifted again, her violin emulating a drumbeat.

Diago glared at her. "Old woman, go home. Leave me to my feast or one day I will come for you."

I stepped between them. "Not as long as I stand as spirit shaman in this town. Go home, Diago. Go home to your nest and hide in your lair, nursing your hunger!" The force was building, though I had no clue where I was drawing it from. But, as with Betty's spirit in the cemetery, I could feel the power rising. I jumped toward him as a bolt of energy spiraled down my wand, into my body, and out my other hand. Focusing it squarely at Diago, I let loose a pale mesh of violet light to wind around him like a lasso.

He screamed, struggling as he backed away from the bed. As the light faded, he turned back to the patient and a huge crest of mist rose from Mike's aura. This would finish him off if I didn't stop Diago. Not knowing what else to do, I rushed forward and slammed the tip of my wand against his back.

Instead of passing through him like it would most spirits, the wand hit solid flesh.

*Oh shit.*

Diago roared, spinning to face me. He loomed over me and I cringed, suddenly aware that I was out of options. Grabbing me by my right wrist, he squeezed and I cried out as the bones begin to give under his unnatural strength.

"I will teach you what it means to disrupt me, *girl . . .*" Diago's tongue flicked out, long and snaking. As it touched my cheek, a burning pain knifed through me. I screamed.

Ellia had stepped up her music, and she was moving closer,

attempting to drive him back with her playing, but she wasn't strong enough to take him on by herself.

Just then, the door burst open and Bryan rushed in. I caught sight of him, his eyes blazing, and then—the next moment—a sparkling shower of color surrounded him and a massive wolf stood in his place, growling at Diago as it slowly inched forward, eyes flashing ice blue, rimmed with black, that glowed like polished jewels.

Diago let out a hiss—*"Shapeshifter"*—and let me go in his haste to back away. The wolf bounded past me, his jaws snapping at air as Diago spun into a whirl of dark mist and smoke and vanished. The next moment, Ellia and I were facing the wolf, alone in the room. Shaking, I started to take a step back, but then—another shift in the air, and Bryan was crouched on the floor in front of me.

Ellia set down her violin. "So, shapeshifter, you have decided to introduce your true self and join the fray. I told you the fight would come to your doorstep and so it has, though sooner than I predicted."

I could barely hear her speak, my thoughts were racing so quickly. Bryan was a *shapeshifter*? And then, another thought hit me—was he *my* shapeshifter? My guardian? And *that* thought opened up a whole new batch of questions.

# CHAPTER 8

"You're a shapeshifter?" I started to back away, instinct taking over—after all, he'd been one freaking huge wolf just a moment before. But then I thought, no, he'd also saved my life and helped chase Diago away. I steadied myself.

"We'll discuss that in a bit." He slowly rose to his feet. "First things first. How is the patient?"

I shook my head, bringing my focus back to where it belonged. "I don't know—Ellia, call Corbin, please?"

As she peeked out into the hall, I edged my way over to the corner where Diago had been hiding. The spirit was the reason for Whisper Hollow's rule number four: *Try not to end up in the hospital.* Because the hospital wasn't always the place of recuperation and healing it was supposed to be, thanks to his appetite.

Corbin entered the room and examined Mike. After a moment, he pulled the stethoscope out of his ears and straightened up. "He took some damage, but I think we will be able to pull him through now. I wish there were a way of keeping Diago from returning. He's got a taste for Mike's life force now. Do either of you know of a good warding sigil or spell?" He turned to Ellia and me. "Security sure as hell can't do anything about him."

"I'll look through my grandmother's Shadow Journal, but offhand, I don't know what to tell you." I shook my head. "I'm still new at this, Corbin—very new. While I worked the ghost hunting circuit in Seattle, mostly I cleansed houses of the Mournful or the occasional Haunt. I have never had dealings with spirits like this before."

"But you have, child." Ellia spoke softly. "When you were little . . . don't you remember the Shadow Man?"

I froze as a cold snake of fear wrapped around my throat. *Something* . . . the Shadow Man had been dangerous and terrifying . . . but I couldn't place him. "It won't come back— I know the name and I feel fear, but . . . What about him?"

"I can't tell you, because your grandmother only mentioned it in passing, but I remember her mentioning that you met a Shadow Man and how terrified she was for you. I'm afraid this is one of those memories you'll have to unearth on your own. I can only be the catalyst." She lifted her violin. "Doctor, I can play a song to protect the room for the rest of the night. Tomorrow, I'll have Ivy come over and set some wards. She's good at that. They will help, though against a spirit like Diago, it's impossible to have any permanent effect."

"Thanks . . . until then, your song will have to do. And I will have a nurse watch over him the rest of the night. Can you be on call for a while, in case the Scuffler returns?" He jotted down a notation on the man's file.

"I have no problem with that. Kerris?" Ellia turned to me.

"I'm good with being on call." As we walked out of the room, I gave one last look toward Mike. He was breathing easier and his energy was secure again—there was none being siphoned off, as far as I could tell.

"I'll just help Corbin a moment," Peggin said. "I'll be out in a minute."

When we were in the hall, I dropped to the bench. I was exhausted, wrung out like a wet rag. "What should we do next?"

"Let me call Gareth to keep him in the loop. I can't use

a cell phone in the hospital, so I'm going to ask the desk to let me use their guest phone. Wait here till I return." She strode off down the hall. How she had so much energy after what we'd gone through eluded me.

Speaking of . . . I glanced at Bryan, who was regarding me quietly. "Shapeshifter, huh?" So that was why he had used the word *clan* when talking about his father.

"You have a problem with that?" He stood beside me, leaning against the wall, arms crossed.

I considered his question. I'd been brought up to fear Skinwalkers, Native American shapeshifters. And I knew that various forms of shape changers existed—under one name or another. Truth was, shapeshifters were a worldwide phenomenon. And there were differing tribes and clans of them, all with their own unique abilities. Some were as evil as they came, others not at all. My immediate reaction was concern, but I pushed it aside as I remembered him jumping between Diago and me, knocking the spirit aside.

*And then . . . there are the shapeshifters who guard the spirit shamans . . .* The thought wouldn't quit running through my mind.

"You saved my life, Bryan." I gazed up at him, my voice soft. "You could have let him attack me . . . feed off me, but you didn't. You exposed what you are in order to save me. And for that, I will forever be grateful. So, no, I don't have a problem with it. I'd like to know more, though. I'd like to understand you better."

He was suddenly sitting beside me, searching my face with a question I couldn't quite place. But the energy had thickened between us, and I couldn't look away from him.

"If you understand me better, it means you let me step into your world, Kerris. It means you open the door, knowing that once I come in, I won't be leaving. There are consequences for that, and not all of my own making." His voice was husky and I realized his face was mere inches away from mine.

As if in a dream, feeling like I was falling over the edge of a cliff willingly, I whispered, "I think I've already dragged you in."

Who moved first, I don't know. But the next moment his lips were on mine and he was holding me, one arm around my waist, the other holding the back of my head as he explored my mouth. His chest pressed against mine, warm and strong and muscled, and his arms held me firmly. I inhaled a deep, rich scent off him—the smell of cinnamon and cedar, of the mist rolling through the trees and strong rum and power.

My lips parted and he gently slid his tongue between them, and then the kiss exploded into a frenzy and all I could think about was that only the thin material of my shirt stood between his fingers and my bare skin, and how much I wished that barrier weren't there. The chasm between us blurred and I felt myself melt into him as he entered my psyche. There was no separation, no division between us as our connection buoyed us up, darker and deeper with every passing second. Shaking, we pulled apart. He looked as dazed as I felt. I'd never felt such passion in a kiss before—never this much intensity.

"What was that?" His voice trembled. "Did you . . . I just . . . Kerris . . ." He cupped my chin with his hands and gazed into my eyes.

"Is it always like this with your people?" I could barely contain my breath. I was still panting and I tried not to shift on the bench, I was so wet and hungry for him.

He shook his head. "No. It's passionate, yes, but I've never . . . Kerris, I've never felt myself merging like that with anybody. *Ever*."

"What are you two up to?" Peggin emerged from the hospital room, slipping out of her white coat. She looked tired.

I gently disentangled myself from Bryan, not sure what to say.

He stroked my arm, then turned to her with a smile. "Just getting to know each other better, it seems. How's the patient?"

"Mike should be fine if we can keep Diago off him the next few days." She shuddered. "I hate that spirit. He's taken so many over the years. Your grandmother and Ellia would come in and set what wards they could, but we've never been able to keep him out."

I frowned. "If Lila was able to set up wards, there's bound to be something about it in her Shadow Journal. I've got some late-night reading to do." With a sideways glance at Bryan, hungry to see if we could re-create the passion that had ignited between us, I let out a shaky sigh. "I wonder if Ellia's gotten through to Gareth yet. Speak of the devil . . ."

Ellia was striding back from the nurse's station, a somber look on her face. The soft tapping of her boots against the floor and the swish of her cape were the only sounds in the hallway beyond the soft hum of the air conditioner and the static white noise all hospitals seem to have.

"Gareth says it's fairly quiet out. I suppose we're done for the night. Kerris, at some point, you need to go have a talk with both Penelope and Veronica. You'll have to come to terms with them and their subjects at some point. Better sooner than later." She sat on the bench that was against the opposite wall. "Though I'd advise leaving that little chat for another day. At least we took care of tonight's problem."

"I'm not champing at the bit to go hunting around Veronica's lair right now, I'll tell you that for certain. Or Penelope's tomb." I glanced at the clock. I couldn't wear watches; I stopped them cold. I had finally gotten the clue after the fifth watch I bought in six months had died on me.

"Ellia, I need to tell you something we found out today." Not at all sure if I was doing the right thing, I told Ellia about my mother's spirit and the jacket. "I think my grandfather may have had something to do with her death. I think that's what he might have been going to tell you about the day he and Lila died."

Ellia paled. "Then it's true. Your mother is dead."

"Do you know anything about this?" If she'd been holding out on me, I wasn't going to be a happy camper. I was getting awfully tired of pulling the secrets about my life out of the woodwork, one painful nail at a time.

She ducked her head. "We didn't know . . . not for sure. But Ivy and I suspected your grandfather might have had something to do with her disappearance." Ellia's face fell and she crumpled against the wall. "If he did, then rest easy that your grandmother never knew all of those years. Though, perhaps at the end . . . maybe she knew by the time they were coming to see us. I suppose we should have said something, but . . . Duvall was a powerful man with powerful connections. Making an enemy of him entailed severe consequences."

I glanced around the hall, suddenly uncomfortable discussing the situation in public. "Come on, let's get back to the car if we're done here."

We headed out into the night. The fog had socked in and there was a cold wind blowing off the lake from the north. I squinted into the darkness, wondering just how many spirits were out there right now running around, causing havoc. As I fastened my seat belt and slid the key into the ignition, I realized that I was shivering. Whether it was from the energy expended chasing Diago out, or Bryan's kiss, or voicing the reality that I thought my grandfather might have killed my mother, I didn't know, but one way or another, I felt tapped out. My stomach rumbled.

"I need waffles." I turned to the others. "Does Mary Jane's Diner still serve the late crowd?" Peggin and I had hung around the diner on Saturday nights when we didn't have a date.

Peggin nodded. "Yeah, it does. And the food's still as good as the day you left. But Mary Jane retired and her daughter took over. Now it's called Lindsey's Diner."

"Point me in the right direction. I don't fully remember where everything was in this town." I eased the car out of the parking lot and turned right on Main Street, then left on Oak. One block later, we were there.

The diner was exactly as I remembered it, only updated. It was still a retro fifties joint, but the checkerboard floor looked clean and new, and the booths and counter and stools—while reminiscent of the time period—were obvious upgrades. But the old nickel-soda signs were there, as were the pictures of the drive-in addition the diner had once sported in what was now a new drugstore next door. The smells coming from the kitchen made my mouth water.

The restaurant was nearly empty, with a few stragglers here and there, and we had our choice of booths. I selected one out of earshot of the others, and we settled in, Peggin next to Ellia, and Bryan sitting next to me. I was all too aware of his proximity and had to force myself to stop edging toward him.

The waitress took our orders. I asked for a waffle with plenty of syrup, some chicken strips, and coffee. Bryan and Peggin ordered burgers and fries, and Ellia asked for fish and chips. She had put her gloves on again and sat quietly in the corner next to the window, playing with her coffee mug.

After the waitress left to put in our orders, I let out a long sigh. "Okay, then. I have some questions, and, Ellia—if you know any of the answers, I want it straight. Got it?"

She nodded. "I'll tell you whatever I know."

"Who did my grandfather hang out with? We need to know who his cronies were."

Ellia frowned. "It's been so long . . . let me think. Lila hated his friends, I know that much. Also, while I'm thinking about it, something else I don't think you know is that your grandfather had some sort of information on your grandmother. That's why she never went against him. He blackmailed her with it—if you can call threatening your own wife blackmail. I'm not sure of the legal terminology."

The reality of my grandfather's duplicity was starting to set in. I'd detested him as a child and now it seems like the cruelty I had seen only touched the tip of the iceberg. "He was really a freaking bastard, wasn't he?"

She nodded. "He was also a powerful man in town. Kerris, how much do you know about his beliefs? About the organizations he belonged to?"

I frowned. "Only that he really disliked seeing people happy. Or it seemed that way. He certainly ruled the house with an iron fist, though my grandmother did a lot of subtle undermining . . . she was good at getting her way for the most part."

"Well, your grandmother didn't want to marry him in the first place. She and Ivy and I were in the same class at school. We hung out together when we were teens, after my mother ran off into the woods. I took over the house and managed to keep afloat as best as I could. When I was eighteen, Lila got engaged to Aidan Corcoran, but two months later, she broke up with him and was dating Duvall. She was terribly unhappy. I asked her what had happened, but she wouldn't tell me. She wouldn't say anything to Ivy or me except that she didn't want to see Aidan get hurt, so she made him leave town."

"I knew it. I knew she didn't love Duvall."

"Well, she was so cruel that poor Aidan took off and never came back. And that alone tells you something was wrong. Lila didn't have a mean bone in her body—not against those who didn't deserve it. The night he left, she came over to stay at my place. She was in tears, brokenhearted. But she would never tell me why. Two weeks later, she accepted Duvall's ring and even though their engagement lasted for years before she gave in and set a date, she never mentioned Aidan again, and she never explained why she was marrying a man she didn't love."

I soaked up the information, mulling it over. It made me sad to think of Lila stuck in a loveless marriage. I knew that she'd been leery of my grandfather's temper, but I didn't know she had gone into the marriage with such doubts, or that she'd driven away someone she truly loved.

A thought crossed my mind. "Duvall wasn't her guardian. She didn't have a shapeshifter. Do you think Aidan might have been the one?"

Ellia shrugged. "It's possible. She was good at hiding her secrets. As to Duvall's friends . . . he ran with a group of young men who eventually became the power players in Whisper Hollow's business crowd. There were five of them. Jack Whitman became a lawyer and founded the Whitman-Dyson Agency. He's retired now. Another was old Doctor Benson—long dead. The Lady took him. The third was Elmore Johnson, he was the mayor of Whisper Hollow for a long time. He and his wife retired and moved over to the Quinault area. The fourth was Heathrow Edgewater, and he

owns the Peninsula Hotel, though he was always on the outskirts of the group. And then there was Duvall, and he, of
course, was an architect. The group were buddies before college, and they were even tighter when they returned home
and set up their practices."

I considered what she had said as the waitress brought our
orders. She set a basket containing ketchup, mustard, vinegar,
and other assorted condiments on the table, made sure I had
enough syrup, and then excused herself. We picked at our
food for a moment—or rather, Peggin and Ellia picked at
theirs. Bryan and I set to with what seemed like equal gusto.

"So . . . Duvall and his buddies ruled the roost, so to
speak." After I'd eaten my way through half the waffle and
two of the chicken strips, I sat back. "I don't know why I'm
so hungry. I ate a big dinner."

"The energy you ran in the hospital drained your reserves.
It will get you every time, so be certain you always take
food with you and don't skimp on the meals." Ellia winked
at me, then—after a sip of her coffee—dabbed her lips and
frowned at her plate. "As to your comment, yes, the five of
them were welded together at the hip after college. They
ruled the political and financial interests of Whisper Hollow
and still do, at least those who are still alive. There's more
to this conversation, though, but I don't want to go into it
here. As to which one of them might have helped Duvall
kill Tamil? Any one of them would be capable of it."

I hadn't realized just how much power my grandfather
had wielded in the town. "Ellia, the Crescent Moon
Society—how long has it been in existence?"

She frowned, twirling a French fry between her fingers.
"Since before I was born—I think it was probably founded
shortly after the town of Whisper Hollow was built."

"Did my grandfather belong to it? You said my grandmother did."

She let out a short laugh. "No, rest assured your grandfather was the last person they would have asked to join
them, and that ties into what I didn't want to bring up here

in public." She paused, as if she were deciding whether to continue.

"If you know something—anything—tell me. I should know if it in any way is going to affect my work as a spirit shaman. Did he piss them off? And how could my grandmother belong to it when they wouldn't invite Duvall in?"

Ellia finally shrugged. "He was a direct threat—he and his friends. Your grandmother had to belong; she was the spirit shaman. But we warned her that she must *never* tell Duvall what went on, and that she had to hide her Shadow Journal and her tools from him. She gave her blood oath on that, pledged on the wings of the Morrígan."

I knew what that meant—if she had betrayed them, the Morrígan would have exacted punishment. You couldn't be a daughter of the Morrígan and break your vows. But there was more . . . something she wasn't telling me. I decided to let it rest for now. We had way too much to think about as it was.

Peggin had been silently listening, but now she spoke up. "What about his other cronies? Were any of them members?"

Ellia shook her head. "No. I really can't say much more about this subject. Not till you're a member, Kerris. Then we'll fill you in on everything that we know about Duvall and his group. And, Bryan and Peggin, even though you're Kerris's friends, I shouldn't be talking in front of you. The only reason I'm doing so is that Whisper Hollow is facing a threat from the outside and we're going to need to change the ways we've been doing things. We need people willing to help keep the town from being swallowed up."

Her phone rang at that moment and she answered, mouthing *Gareth again.* As she moved away from the booth to speak to him, the three of us sat there, mulling over what we knew.

"So, we need to find what we can about your grandfather's buddies."

"Yeah . . . where they were near the time Tamil died. Maybe if anything suspicious happened to them at that time—if my mother tried to fight them off, maybe she hurt somebody? If she managed to fight back, wouldn't that be in the medical records if she hurt one of them bad enough, Peggin? If there's any way we could get a look at them."

Peggin squinted. "To be honest, that would take some doing, but I might be able to swing it. Your grandfather's records are in our office—Lila managed to persuade him to start going to Corbin when Corbin bought out Doc Benson's practice ten years ago." She paused. "Doc Benson—Doctor Benson . . . Duvall's buddy. So the records might be in the archives. I can hunt around, though I'll have to be discreet."

Bryan shook his head. "I didn't move here till about five or six years ago. Your grandmother talked to me a lot. Your grandfather didn't. I never told them what I was, but I think Duvall had a sense that I could be a dangerous enemy and he chose to avoid any confrontation. Lila skirted any questions that dealt with my nature, though she was always pleasant. In turn, I never asked her about the work she did as a spirit shaman except when she volunteered information."

"Here's the thing." I glanced over at Ellia, who was still on the phone, out of earshot. "I don't know how much I can rely on Ellia and her friends, beyond helping me take care of the spirits. I have a strong sense there are politics flowing like a wild river under the surface, and I'm not sure at all what to expect when it comes to the Crescent Moon Society."

Peggin finished her burger. "I think you're wise. Remember what I told you. Things are changing in Whisper Hollow, and I'm not sure how much you can trust anybody here."

"Will you two help me? I want to find out who killed my mother. I'm going to turn her jacket over to the police, but you know as well as I do how many cold cases actually end up resolved."

"Not many." Peggin sighed. She glanced over at Ellia, then held a warning finger to her lips. Another moment and Ellia was back, sliding into the booth again.

"What did Gareth say?" I asked.

"Diago seems to have quieted down and there's been no further trouble at the hospital. So I think we can safely go home." She reached out, stopping short of patting my hand. With her skin gloved, I'd be safe, but years of constant reinforcement seemed to have imprinted themselves on her behavior. I had never seen Ellia touch anyone.

"I have to admit, I'm tired." I thought about the house. I hadn't even made up my grandmother's bed yet—it would be another night of sleeping on the sofa till I could move my things into the bedroom the next day.

"I think we all are. And I have work bright and early at eight A.M. tomorrow. Corbin is a good boss, but he doesn't put up with me being late." Peggin picked up her purse and slid into her coat. "Although, given he was there tonight, he might make an exception for me this once."

Bryan tossed a fifty on the table. "My treat, all around." He stopped us before we could protest with "No, no arguments"—and that was that.

We dropped Ellia off at home first before pulling back into my driveway. Peggin declined to come in. She gave me a quick hug, whispering, "I'll see what I can dig up tomorrow. Text me if anything happens or you find out anything."

"Night, and love you." I watched as she got into her car and eased out onto the road. It felt so good to have her back in my life on more than an occasional basis. That left Bryan. I turned to him, thinking about our kiss. He must have been thinking the same, because he swept me into his arms, on the front porch, and leaned his forehead against mine.

"Don't even ask. All I know is that when we were at the hospital, I felt the danger you were in. I had to help. I'm not sure how this will all play out, but I'd like a chance to explore it further," he murmured.

"I would, too . . . but tonight . . . it's too soon, I think." I had slept with several men on the first date—well, with the ones that had passed the ghost-over-the-shoulder routine— but this was different. What I had experienced in that one kiss with Bryan was beyond anything I'd ever felt before. It had taken me out of myself into a whole different realm. As hungry for him as I was, I didn't want to rush this.

Bryan softly pressed his lips against mine and once again, the rush between us buoyed me up, making me rethink my stance. My body felt natural against his, as if it belonged. I fit against him, in a niche that seemed made just for me.

"I think you might be right, though parts of my body are screaming otherwise." He laughed, and I could feel his erection as he pressed against me. It only made me want him more.

"I guess you'd better go home, or the issue is going to be moot." I shifted, burrowing into his arms, wondering again just who this mysterious shapeshifter was. Where had he come from? And the question burning in my heart . . . was he the chosen one to be my guardian? That wasn't something I could just blurt out and ask.

Finally, even though I didn't want to, I pushed him away. "If you don't go home now, I'll drag you inside. And tonight . . ."

"I know, too soon. But it won't be long, Kerris." He softly stroked my cheek. "Do you want me to come in and make certain everything's okay before I go home?"

I shook my head. "No, I'll be fine. But we need to talk—I need . . . I need to know more about you. I need to know what . . ."

"We have time for that, I promise you." But Bryan refused to allow me to go inside before he'd helped me search the house, including every closet and every room. We found no sign of anyone except the cats, who were thrilled to see us. Daphne raced up to Bryan and rubbed against his leg.

"She likes you, too." I grinned as he scooped her up and snuggled his nose into her side.

"She smells soft. I'm glad she likes me, because I have a feeling she'll be seeing a lot of me in the months to come." He set her on the sofa, then paused, hand on the doorknob. "You're sure everything's okay? You good for the night?"

"Yeah, I'm good for the night." Though I'd be better if he would stay and fuck my brains out. But I kept that thought to myself, even though I knew he was riding the same wavelength.

"Dream of me," he joked as he exited the door. I locked it behind him, then leaned back against the door frame, staring at the kitchen. Too many shifts for one day. I was exhausted. Without another thought, I padded to the shower and then—warm and clean—slid beneath the covers on the sofa. There, I fell into a deep sleep . . . until four A.M., when I woke up to see a dark shadow looming over me.

# CHAPTER 9

Daphne let out a yowl loud enough to wake the dead. It certainly woke me up. I opened my eyes, wondering what the hell was going on, and that was when I saw the dark shape at the foot of the sofa. It was a man, tall and broad, and so thoroughly black that all of the ambient light from the dim room seemed to be sucked right into his form. He was a silhouette—like a black hole in man-shape, made of inky fog. When he leaned toward me, the anger that exuded from his presence hit me like a sledgehammer driving through my brain. He leaned down, grabbing my covers. As I scrambled back, he yanked the blankets off me, sending me tumbling. I went sprawling off the sofa, across the coffee table, smashing the glass top.

Several shards pierced my skin. *"Son of a bitch!"* The needles of glass sliced sharply into my right arm. I landed on the floor by the table's side and scrambled back like a crab, using my hands and feet to scoot away from the approaching shadow. It was hard to look away, and the energy surrounding him was so violent that I could barely think over the sound of my heartbeat. I screamed, shattering the silence, then screamed again.

The shadow continued to inch closer—he was almost within distance to reach out and grab my ankle. Breaking out of my fear-induced haze, I forced myself to roll away, which shoved the glass shards in a little deeper. That made me scream again, but it also gave me the wiggle room to come to my feet. Once I was on my feet, I could run.

At that moment, Agent H came racing into the room and interjected himself between me and the Shadow Man. An entirely new fear set me to panicking—that he would hurt my cats. Heedless of my pain or safety, I raced forward, anger raging as I hit the light switch on the wall. The lights flared to life, flooding the room, and the Shadow Man let out a garbled hiss and vanished, shading himself with his hands as if the light were burning him. The next minute he was gone, vanished from sight, and I couldn't feel him around anywhere.

I stared at the living room. The table was destroyed, thanks to my falling on it. A quick glance at my arm showed me that there were at least three bigger cuts, with the glass firmly embedded in my flesh. Wondering why they didn't hurt more than they did, I decided that I must be in shock. Agent H and Daphne came running up to see if I was okay, while Gabby poked her head through the kitchen archway, blinking as if she had just been woken from a sound sleep.

Breathing hard, I dropped into a chair. Damn it to hell . . . it was one thing to go out chasing spirits, but to have them show up in my house was too much. As I gingerly tugged on the glass, attempting to pull it free from my arm, another image rose up, and I realized that Ellia was right—I had met the Shadow Man before, and then it all came flooding back.

L eave the light on, please, Nappa." For the first few years of my life, it was Nanna and Nappa, until Duvall decided I was too old to use those names and he had instituted the more formal Grandfather and Grandmother—at least in his presence.

My grandfather let out a disgusted noise. He was putting

me to bed because Grandma Lila was busy in the kitchen. "You're six years old, Kerris. It's time you got over your fear of the dark. You aren't a baby anymore. There's nothing to be afraid of and you know it." He stood at the door, his hand on the light switch. I had gotten tucked in, but no story and only a cold peck on the forehead. Nappa didn't believe in excessive displays of affection.

I knew damned well he was wrong—there were things in the dark that nobody in their right mind wanted to meet. I'd seen a few on my excursions with Nanna, but she had kept them at bay, telling me that I'd grow up to learn how to do what she did. But I wasn't grown up yet, and if one of those creatures came after me in the dark, I wasn't sure she'd be able to get to me in time to stop it. When my mother vanished, I realized that anybody, at any time, could fail you.

"Please, Nappa . . . please leave it on." I knew better than to cry—if I cried when he was irritated, he spanked me. Not hard, but firmly. Or worse, he made the punishment fit the fear. I'd been locked in closets for half an hour several times when I cried about the dark. Not when Nanna was home to know—and he'd warned me sternly against tattling.

"Enough of this nonsense. You lie back down in that bed and quit your whimpering right now, if you know what's good for you, young lady." And with that, he slammed the door.

The darkness took over and I slowly inched back against the headboard, sitting as straight as I could as I bent my knees, pulling the covers up to chase away the night chill. Charlie, my stuffed bear, was sitting next to me, and I rested him against the tops of my thighs, trying to make out his sunny smile in the gloom that filled my room.

I wasn't afraid of spiders or snakes, or even of clowns, though I had no idea why other kids thought they were funny. But the dark . . . I knew what lurked in the dark. And until I learned how to protect myself, I'd taken on the approach that it was better to avoid a conflict than engage it. But avoiding the dark meant turning on the light.

For a moment, I contemplated doing just that—getting out of bed and flipping the light switch. But Grandpa's study was right downstairs, and if he had a notion to check on me before he turned in for the night and found my light on, the repercussions would be bad. *Very* bad. So I huddled there, on my bed, wishing I could just lie down and go to sleep like most of the other kids I knew.

It started out slow. I was just starting to relax—my six-year-old body wearing out from the day—when a soft *swish* echoed through the room. It was coming from the closet. Freezing, I tried to see through the darkness, but my room was truly dark. The curtains were a heavy forest green and there were no streetlights outside the backyard to shine through my window. I pressed harder against the headboard, wishing I could hide behind it.

Another moment and another *swish*; this time it sounded like the muffled fall of a foot on the braided rug that covered the hardwood floors in my bedroom. I tried to breathe, tried to avoid panicking. If I screamed and Nappa came and turned on the light and there was nothing there, I'd get a paddling. Closing my eyes, I tried counting to five. Count to five and it would be gone.

*One . . . two . . . three . . .* The sound of heavy breathing—low and throaty. I stopped counting and bit my lip, trying not to scream as I opened my eyes.

There, at the bottom of the bed—a huge shadow of . . . a man-thing. It was shaped like a man, but I knew it wasn't really human. It was a living shadow, a dark blotch that sucked in light and hope, and as I stared at it, the creature leaned down and grabbed my covers, tearing them out of my hands.

I screamed as loud as I could, and kept on screaming. He ignored my shrieks and tossed the blankets aside. As he reached for my feet, grabbing me by one ankle, the door slammed open and Nanna stood there, panting. She said something—I couldn't hear what, my heart was racing so loud in my chest—and the Shadow Man vanished with a loud hiss, snarling as she hit the wall and light flooded the room.

"Baby, baby . . . it's okay, he's gone, my little love." Nanna was there, then, gathering me into her arms. I could see an exasperated Nappa standing in the doorway, but he said nothing, just merely puffed on his pipe and turned to go back down the stairs. Nanna held me tight, singing to me as I calmed down and finally dozed off, exhausted by the fear and the day.

After that, I had a night light in my room until the day I turned eleven and decided I didn't need it anymore. I never saw the Shadow Man again, but I knew—I always knew—he was out there in the dark, waiting.

As I stared at the glass still embedded in my arm, I realized I was going to have to do something about protecting the house. Ivy was supposed to be good at warding, so I decided to call her at first light. Meanwhile, I tried to gauge the severity of the cuts on my arms. Should I head toward the hospital? Was there an urgent care facility around? I thought for a moment. I could call Peggin. She wasn't a trained nurse, but as a medical receptionist she had a smattering of knowledge. But the doorbell ringing put a halt to my indecision. Frowning, I cautiously moved to answer it, holding my arm out to one side so I didn't accidentally drive the glass in any deeper.

I flipped on the porch light and squinted out the peephole. *Bryan?*

Never so happy to see anybody in my life, I called out, "Hold on, I'm naked and need to get something on." Then it occurred to me that I wasn't going to be able to slip anything over my arm very easily, so I hurried back to the sofa, where I grabbed a light throw and managed to get it wrapped around me in a vague toga fashion. I shuffled back to the door and fumbled with the locks while trying to keep my blanket up, and he rushed through.

"Are you all right?" He sounded frantic. A second later, he caught sight of my arm. "Fuck . . . what the hell happened to you, Kerris?"

"Nothing I feel like writing home about. Come in and help me and I'll tell you. I was just trying to decide whether to go to the hospital." I held out my arm for him to examine the cuts.

"I can take care of these, though when was your last tetanus shot?"

"Two years ago. I cut myself on a rusty nail."

"You should be okay, then." He motioned toward the kitchen. "Where do you keep your first-aid supplies? Bathroom?"

I wasn't sure of the answer to that. I still hadn't gotten to know the house all that well. "I don't know, to be honest, but I imagine that would be the place to look. Lila was pretty organized."

He vanished into the hall bath and returned with a pair of tweezers, a tube of antibiotic ointment, and some self-stick gauze pads. "Sit down and rest your arm on the table so it's steady. This is going to hurt, Kerris—there's no way I can avoid it."

I nodded. "Go ahead. I can handle it. I've got enough adrenaline coursing through my veins that I probably won't even feel it." I settled onto the chair, my train of blanket providing an ample cushion. As I leaned my arm straight out on the table, resting my head on my other arm, I realized that I felt totally comfortable around him—even though I was in a terribly vulnerable state right now.

Bryan gave me an encouraging smile and set the teakettle on to boil. I was about to say I didn't want any tea, but then stopped. A hot drink might do me some good.

"You know, any other time, I'd be more than happy to see you wrapped up only in a blanket, but right now, I just want to get this goddamn glass out of your skin. So, tell me what happened." He went to work extracting the pieces, including several small shards I hadn't noticed. I winced as he pulled them out, especially when the blood began to flow freely, but none of the pieces had stabbed through any major veins or arteries, so I counted myself lucky for that.

I told him about the Shadow Man—both what had happened that night and when I was a child. "Ellia was right. I don't know why he chose tonight to show himself, but it feels almost too perfect, given her mention of him. Do you think I can trust her?" I hated asking the question, but

Peggin had expressed reservations and now I was second-guessing my dealings with the lament singer.

Bryan frowned. "I don't think it's Ellia you need to worry about, to be honest. I think this is something else. Shadow People . . . they have been known through history." He dabbed at the wounds, then brought a bowl of the boiling water over and began to wash the blood off.

"At least you shouldn't need any stitches. We'll just let the blood flow a bit to clear out the wound." He waited for a few minutes, then slathered the cuts in ointment. There were seven in all, ranging from small punctures to a good half-inch-long cut where the glass had sliced through. After that, he bandaged the biggest ones. Pushing the first-aid supplies back, he let out a long sigh.

"I need to clean up the glass in the living room and make sure the cats didn't get into it."

"You wait here. I'll do it." He wouldn't take no for an answer, so I leaned back in the chair, closing my eyes until he returned.

"All done. And I checked the cats—they're okay." He paused to pour the tea. "Well, you can't take a chance on this happening again. It's five thirty and you must be exhausted."

I sipped the hot raspberry tea. It coursed through me like a healing balm. "Yes, I really am. And I don't mind admitting I'm scared. I don't know anything about the Shadow Man, though first thing I'm doing when I've got my wits about me is reading Lila's journal. She has descriptions of some of the spirits around Whisper Hollow in it, and I'll bet you anything I find mention of him in there." Slumping back, I let my head drop back and stared at the ceiling. Bryan was right, I was exhausted.

The next thing I knew, he was standing behind me. "Lean forward."

"What?"

"Just do it."

Wondering what he was up to, but too tired to argue, I pushed my teacup to the side and leaned forward. The next moment his hands were on my shoulders and he was massaging the muscles, gently, the warmth of his hands tingling against my bare skin. I let out a soft moan as he worked the knots under his fingers, pressing just enough to make them hurt for a brief second and then release their hold.

"You don't have to do this—"

"Shhh . . . quiet. Let me take away the strain and worry." His voice was low—almost rhythmic, and it lulled me into a soft, cushioned place where the fear began to subside and could find no way in. I closed my eyes and let the gentle massage carry me away from all thoughts of the Shadow Man and of ghosts and murders. A few minutes later, I realized he had gathered me up off the chair, blankets and all. I tried to say I hadn't finished my tea but the words wouldn't come, and I rested my head on his shoulder as we entered the living room. He smelled strong and sexy and safe all at the same time—a comforting mix. I let out my breath slowly, content to remain silent.

In the living room, he laid me down on the sofa and, leaning over, kissed me softly on the lips. I tried to pull him down to me, but he disentangled himself and—finding yet another throw—made certain I was covered. The last I knew, he was sitting in the rocking chair, the lights turned low, watching me. As I drifted off to sleep again I knew without a doubt nothing would bother me while he was standing guard.

The second time I opened my eyes, it was to a faint shadow of late-autumn light shimmering through the windows. I blinked, wondering what time it was, and—as I pushed myself up to a sitting position—I realized my arm was sore. Then the events of the night all came tumbling back. I glanced around, hearing a whistling coming from the kitchen, and, with a slight groan, struggled to my feet. There was a sleeveless nightgown next to me—it had come from my suitcase, and I slipped out of the blankets and into the satin gown, grateful for the lack of sleeves. My arm ached and material would be grating against it. I glanced at the clock. It was almost nine.

As I padded into the kitchen, the first thing I saw were the cats—all lined up at their food dishes, chowing down on gushy food. They gave me a look as if to say, *Slacker* . . . and went back to eating. I laughed and turned to find Bryan hovering over the stove, watching what looked to be an omelet puff up in the skillet.

"Not only can you give one hell of a massage, tend to wounds, and feed cats, but you can cook? Too good to be true." I edged my way toward the espresso machine, but he just let out a sharp whistle and pointed to the table. There, a steaming latte with a dollop of foam waited.

"Sit. Breakfast will be on the table in a couple minutes. I have to leave soon—I have business to attend to—but you should be all right for now. I'm pretty sure the Shadow Man only comes out in the darkness." He slid a plate in front of me. Omelet, toast, and sausage.

I stared at the food, my smile fading. "Yeah, I think he's tied to the night. Bryan, thank you. I never managed to ask last night, how did you know I needed help?"

He paused, then sat beside me. "Eat while I talk."

I dutifully dug into the food, which was delicious.

"You're left-handed?" He looked at me. "I didn't notice before."

"Yeah, why?"

"No reason . . . Anyway, last night I was in bed, when I woke up hearing you scream. It was in my head—I couldn't hear anything out the window—but you were screaming for help and I knew you needed me. So I came running." He slowly reached out and placed a hand over my right wrist. "Kerris, I think you know what this means. We're linked."

I set down my fork, knowing what he was going to say. "You're my guardian, aren't you?"

He nodded. "I had a vision about seven years ago. I had returned to Ireland on a buying trip, and while I was there, the Morrígan came to me when I was out at one of the ancient sites. She told me I had been chosen for an important task. My clan is dedicated to her, and so there was no walking away from her decree. I followed my instincts and they led me to Whisper Hollow. And I settled in to wait. When I met Lila and realized what she was, and when she told me about you, I knew that I had to wait for you to come home. So, I did. Last night—in the hospital and then here, when I felt your panic and fear, I knew that everything was true. I'm your guardian. Your protector."

Resting my hand over his, I was all too keenly aware of his proximity, of how one more shift and I could be in his arms. "*To every spirit shaman, a shapeshifter will come, to protect and guard.* Bryan, I didn't come back to Whisper Hollow expecting anything except a lot of adjustment and juggling as I found my place here. I sure as hell didn't expect to meet anybody, especially . . . you. I barely know how this whole gig works. And . . . not every shapeshifter is mated to their spirit shaman."

"Yes, I know. But will you sit here and deny the sparks between us? Kerris, I want you so much. I want to kiss you, and touch you, and make you mine. And I think you want me, too."

"You know I do. It's just . . . this is all so new."

Bryan leaned back, letting out a small sigh. "I won't press it if you don't want me to . . . I promise you that—I'll stand by you, regardless of how things between us evolve. It's my duty and I'm happy to watch over you."

Hesitating, wanting so much to reach out and take his hand, to kiss his fingers, I forced myself to sit very still. "Before anything else happens . . . before we go any further, I need to know—are you seeing anybody? Is there anyone I need to know about? I'm not a player. Hell, I'm not usually even willing to get into the game because so often it's led to disaster when the man finds out about my abilities. I guess what I'm asking is . . ."

"Am I leading you on just so I can fuck you?" The corners of his eyes crinkled, their ice blue frosty and pulling me in like an alpine lake. "Kerris, I have no mate. I was married, a long time ago, but she died. Since then, I've dated, but never seriously. I don't play with people's feelings. Hell, I don't like *most* people. It's not my nature. I won't ever claim to wear a white hat. I'm not one of the good guys. I admit it, I've done my share of things that . . . well . . . leave that for now. But I do have a personal code of honor and I follow it."

As he spoke, a wisp of energy flared around him—like strong tendrils of ivy. The first night, when he ran in front of my car, I had been surprised by how I couldn't read him. Now, I realized it was because of *what* he was. From what little I knew of shapeshifters—regardless of the clan or background—they were a difficult read and had generations of practice cloaking their nature.

So he was a widower. How long ago was "a long time," though, and how had his wife died? "You were married?"

"Yes." His eyes were cool. Not aloof, but masking his emotions. I suddenly realized I needed to learn as much as I could about shapeshifters, so I understood the nuances that were probably escaping me. Different race, different culture, and I didn't want to blindly do something that would offend him.

"Was she a shapeshifter, too?" All of a sudden I was hungry to know about her. I wanted to know what she had been like, what she had looked like. Why she had died.

He hesitated, then—"Yes, she was. She was a good woman, Kerris. I made a mistake marrying her. But I did right by her, as much as I could. She wanted children. Unfortunately, her body wasn't geared toward having them, and the medical technology wasn't as advanced as it is now. She died in childbirth."

Childbirth? Then . . . "You have a child?"

He ducked his head. "Yes. I have a daughter. She's older than you. Kerris, I don't know if you realize it, but shapeshifters live a long time. I told you that I saw my father murdered—that was in 1878. I was born in 1872. I've lived a number of lives—moving around, taking a new name so that people never find out what I am. I've never felt truly safe and keep to myself a lot so that nobody finds out my secret. The other day you asked me why I moved to Whisper Hollow. Now you know. I was drawn here, and now I realize it was because of you. But it's also a place where those who are odd and unusual fit in. I have the feeling there are others here who . . . are not exactly human, so to speak."

I blinked. This was a lot to take in, and I wasn't sure what to think. If I'd been anybody but me, I might have run like hell. But I was a spirit shaman, and the world was filled with strange and mysterious creatures. And I was supposed to be paired with a guardian who had, apparently, dropped right in my lap. Or in front of my car, to be more accurate. I had the sudden urge to know everything I could about him.

"What were you chasing the night we met?"

He glanced at the floor and didn't answer for a moment. "There are creatures in the woods here. You know that. This . . . this is a danger to the town. A *d'yavol-volkov*. A devil-wolf. It's a form of demon. I've dealt with them before, but very few people know how to handle them."

A distant chill echoed through my body. "Devil wolf? What are they?"

"A demon who can shapeshift into a wolf, but they don't really have any connection to wolves. They aren't really shapeshifters, either. They're . . . dangerous and they feed off the living. Leave it at that, love. I don't even like talking about them."

The thought that one lived in the woods near here was far from comforting, but I changed the subject as he asked. "Where were you born? Are you originally from Ireland, then?"

"My parents were. They left there in 1860, during the height of the potato famine, and immigrated to Boston. I was born in a small house on the outskirts—well, what the outskirts were then—of the city. A small group of the Tierney shapeshifter clan came over together. We kept to ourselves, were polite but reclusive. Nobody knew what we were, at least not till a rival clan sniffed us out and murdered my father." He spat out a curse. "I told you that my clan took care of them. My uncle took a handful of our warriors. They tracked them down and . . . well . . . the rest is history."

I forced myself to ask the next question. "What about your wife and daughter?" I leaned back in my chair, then let out a slow, soft sigh. I wanted to hear it all.

He gave me a defeated look. "Katrina and I were promised

to each other by our parents. In my clan, there are traditions we don't question. We just obey. Even though I didn't love her, I finally capitulated and married her in 1950. She was pretty, with a beautiful voice and long blond hair, but the spark just wasn't there. We did the best we could, though, trying to make it work. It was expected we would have children, and so she got pregnant a few years after we married. As I said, she wasn't physically suited to having children—I'm not sure what the doctors would call it, but during childbirth she died."

The reality of all he had been through in his life—and I had a feeling we'd just touched the tip of the iceberg—hit me. "I'm sorry that she never got to see her child grow up." Then another thought hit me. "The baby . . . Did . . ."

A smile spread across Bryan's face. "Yes, as I said, I have a daughter. Juliana survived, and today, she's still living in Boston. She's a lovely woman—looks around twenty if she looks a day, though she'll be sixty-three this year. I occasionally go back to visit her. I've never let her come here because people would assume I was dating her. Shapeshifters age at a different rate than humans, as I said, although we do have an illusion that can age us up, but it's tiring to constantly use. I suppose I could get away with telling people she was my daughter from a liaison I had when I was too young, but we haven't worked out any cover story."

As I digested the information, not knowing what to say next, Bryan tapped me on the arm. He stayed well clear of my injuries. "Now, *I* need to know something. I know why you came back to Whisper Hollow, but are you sure you're willing to dive into the darkness that surrounds this town? Are you here for good? Because if you take up your grandmother's post as spirit shaman, this town will never let you go."

Shaking my thoughts away from his story, I considered his question. He was right—I could already feel the town's spell weaving itself around me. Whisper Hollow was more than just a town on the peninsula in need of protection from the spirits that walked the streets. Whisper Hollow had an energy, a deep and vibrant consciousness, whose heart beat just below the surface of the town and its inhabitants. And once Whisper Hollow got its hooks into you, it wouldn't let go. Some people it spat out like a bad-tasting food . . . but others, it took in and swaddled them with its energy, like bees preserved in amber. Whisper Hollow wanted me . . . No, more than that. The town *needed* me. And for some reason, I had the feeling it needed me more than it had needed my grandmother and that was why she was dead.

"Whisper Hollow has a will and rule of its own, Bryan. I had to come back. There was no choice. There *is* no choice. Not for me." I held his gaze.

He let out a low breath. "Then it seems we are both here for good."

I nodded. He was leaning closer to me and all I could think about was his lips on mine. And then he was out of his chair and he pulled me out of mine, into his arms, as he drew me in for a kiss. His lips were warm and once again, the hunger to have him—all of him—flared. I wanted his skin against mine, his chest pressed against my breasts, I wanted to feel him moving inside me. He sensed my need, because he slipped his fingers beneath the folds of my robe, stroking along the curve of my waist, running his fingers lightly over my ass. I caught my breath, my nipples hardening at his touch.

"I want you . . ." I whispered.

"Later, my love. It will have to be later." He groaned softly, his lips by my ear, and then they were on my neck, licking and sucking the skin. The next moment, he let go— though I could feel his reluctance—and backed away with a rueful smile. "Damn it. Work calls. But will you be all right today? I'll come over tonight."

Flushed, I held up my cell phone and stammered, "I'm going to call Ivy in a little while, to ask her if she has any ideas about the Shadow Man. I also plan on tracking down a few people today, letting them know I'm back in town—if they don't already know. Word travels fast in small towns, and Whisper Hollow's grapevine is a lot more active than most." I grinned then. "The crows have ears, and they also tell secrets."

He sucked in a deep breath, then let it out slowly. "So I gathered. I took the liberty of entering my name and number into your contacts on your phone while you were asleep. If you need me, call, though I'm starting to doubt we're going to be needing a phone at all." And then, he reached out and took my hands. "Kerris, do you know how beautiful you are?"

I held his gaze and—for once—felt truly radiant. I mostly got catcalls from men because of my boobs, but here was a man talking to *me*, not to my chest.

"I really, really don't want to leave, but I have a call coming that I can't miss. I'll check in on you in a while, to make certain everything is all right." And with that, he turned and vanished out the back door.

I stared at the remains of the omelet, so pent up that I could barely stand it. There was only one cure. I marched into the shower and lathered up with my Bath & Body Works Sensual Amber shower gel. Sliding my hands over my body, I began to breathe hard as I slowly reached between my legs, caressing myself with hard, insistent strokes. As the ache in my stomach began to build, I used my other hand to cup my breast, squeezing hard, rubbing, imagining Bryan's hands in place of my own. The image of his face loomed in my mind, and I could hear the soft panting of his breath—as if he were beside me. A moment later and I could see him, in a gray tiled bathroom, leaning against the sink. His jeans were pushed down, and he gripped his erection with one hand, as he used the other to brace himself on the vanity. His fingers slid over his penis, long firm strokes driving him on. I massaged myself harder, my finger swirling around the nub of my sex, as he polished himself. I could feel his passion build, and then—he looked straight at me and I realized he was seeing me just as I was seeing him.

Together we rode the frenzy. I squeezed my breast hard, the pressure shoving me higher as I caressed myself to the edge of orgasm. He clenched his penis and with one final pull, he called out my name as he came, fountaining out into the sink. Seeing him come, I gave myself one last tweak and joined him, coming hard and fast and loud.

As the waves of pleasure surged through me, rippling like breakers on the water, I let out another cry and then, slowly, slid back against the shower wall, the spray of water easing the spasms that ran through my body. I caught one last glimpse of Bryan—he was smiling and he whispered my name again, and then the image faded and I was alone in the shower, both relieved and yet hungrier for him than ever.

Feeling slightly embarrassed—because I was certain that Bryan had picked up on what I'd been doing—I finished my shower, dried my hair, and slipped into clean clothes, taking care to choose a V-neck tank top that wouldn't aggravate the wounds on my arm. The bandages had gotten wet, so I did my best to change them with one hand. The wounds were still red, but they weren't infected and they looked a lot better than they had a few hours ago.

I cleared up the remnants of breakfast and then sat down at the table with my phone. Agent H decided that it was prime time to jump up and get a belly rub, and I absently stroked his fur as I put in a call to Ivy, hoping it wasn't too early. But she answered on the first ring.

"Hey, Ivy . . ." I thought about calling her Grandma, but it seemed too weird for someone I had just met, especially someone who looked barely older than myself. "Kerris here. I have a problem." I told her what had happened the night before. "I could really use some advice on warding, and Ellia said you're good at it."

After a moment's silence, she said, "Can you come over around two P.M. today?"

"Yeah, that would be fine."

"Bring the bag of tools Lila left for you. I'll see you then. I've got to go now—the bread's about ready to come out of the oven and I don't want it to burn." She hung up.

I couldn't tell whether she was happy to hear from me, but she had volunteered to help and if I was going to become some sort of protector for the town, I knew I couldn't do it alone. It was nearing quarter to ten, and I decided that I needed to swing through town for supplies, to drop off all the old clothes, and to pick up some new sheets and a comforter. It was time to put my credit card to good use. Making sure the doors and windows were shut and locked, I grabbed my purse and keys and headed out to reacquaint myself with Whisper Hollow.

# CHAPTER 10

———

Whisper Hollow had evolved from a few rough-in-the-wild homesteads into a very pretty, semi-Victorian small town. Unlike Port Townsend and Port Angeles, however, Whisper Hollow seldom encouraged visitors and most of its money came from the locals. While the economy wasn't exactly thriving, neither had it gone to rack and ruin. Mostly, people did their jobs, few ever moved away—at least not for good—and every now and then the town would lure in somebody new to stay.

Usually, they would come in, needing to stop for gas or a quick bite, and something would take hold of them, and before they knew it, they had settled in. Bought a house. Become part of the background as if they had been born here. The town had built up around a vortex of energy, ley lines crossing every which way. The vortex both cloaked the town from much consideration by the rest of the world and yet drew to it the people who were called to move in and settle down.

A number of the buildings were old brick and stone, with

some Victoriana interspersed among the solemn gray and red. The central downtown area looked a lot like it had when I had left home, though the upkeep had been considerable. Nobody ever let their shops go dank, or get too weathered without slapping on a new coat of paint or fixing the broken boards. A few new shops had gone in since I'd left—the Broom & Thistle Coffee Shop, the Herb & Essence apothecary. Although the latter was kitty-corner from the hospital, it was in no way a modern pharmacy. As I drove past, it occurred to me I might end up frequenting the place depending on what Ivy and my grandmother's journal had in store for me.

Gritting my teeth, I parallel-parked in front of another shop I didn't recognize. Vintage Books was on Cedar Street, one of the main drags downtown. I slipped out of the car and wandered over to check it out. I loved to read and spent a good share of my time with my nose in a book. The shop was open, so I decided to drop in and see what they specialized in.

The shelves were jammed—both new and used books, though housed in two separate sections. The shop had the feel of an old-world library, with tall ceilings and shelves that stretched up higher than arm's reach. Step stools were conveniently located around the shop, though, and as I navigated through the aisles, I began to notice that Vintage Books specialized in nothing, and carried just about everything. Romance, science fiction, fantasy, mystery, cookbooks, travel—they all seemed represented.

The man behind the counter looked to be in his late twenties, and he was Native American. That much was obvious right off the bat. He had long brown hair, smooth and silky, that flowed past his shoulders, nearly to his waist. His eyes were a soft brown, and his smile, genuine and gentle. He was sorting through a pile of what looked like used books—dividing them into sections. As I approached the counter, he glanced up.

"May I help you find something?"

I glanced around, then shook my head. "To be honest, I'm just checking out the shop. I just moved back to town and this wasn't here before. I'm Kerris Fellwater." As I reached out to shake his hand, a flicker of recognition raced across his face.

"Ah, you would be the granddaughter of Lila Fellwater, then? I'm so sorry about her passing." He took my hand, his fingers firm and steady. "I'm Trevor Riverstone, the owner."

As I touched his fingers, a tingle told me he was a little more than he seemed. "What brought you to Whisper Hollow, Trevor?"

He moved a pile of what looked like paranormal romances to one side and began sorting through another stack. "I don't know, to be honest. About five years ago, I lost my father—my mother died when I was twelve. I lived in Aberdeen. So I took what inheritance my father left me and decided to open a bookstore—and the only place I could think of to do it was here." With a shrug, he added, "The town has always intrigued me."

A book slid to the floor and he bent to retrieve it. As he pushed his hair to one side, out of the way, I noticed that on the back of his neck, he had a tattoo—a crescent moon with a raven on it.

*Just like my birthmark. Just like the symbol of the spirit shamans.*

Only, this one was in color, with the raven's eyes brilliant red, and a bit of green foliage coming out from beneath its talons.

"Your tattoo . . . when did you get it?"

He quickly brushed his hair back to cover it, but then, catching my eye, he stopped. "About two years after I moved here. You *would* recognize it, wouldn't you? Being the new spirit shaman."

"Why did you get it?" I wanted to know why he was wearing a symbol I only associated with my grandmother. Was he a spirit shaman, too? The blood ran only in certain families, and usually through the women as I understood. We were few and far between. But that would explain him being drawn to Whisper Hollow.

He glanced around the shop, making certain we were

alone. "I belong to the Crescent Moon Society. We all wear the symbol. I shouldn't tell you that I'm part of the group, but you'll be joining us soon and I'd rather have you find out from me than go asking around town."

"Then you're *not* a spirit shaman?" I *really* needed to read my grandmother's Shadow Journal and decided that as soon as I finished up in town, I'd start.

"No. Not in the least." He pulled up the stool in back of the counter and hopped on it. "Listen, you're going to find out all this sooner or later, and I think you should know now before you go asking too many questions and get us all in trouble. We're your support system—the Society. We are . . . backup, in terms of policing, though our duties range a bit further abroad than yours. And we need to keep our secrets, so don't go asking around. Ellia's supposed to bring you to the next meeting. Together, we all make the town as safe as we can."

I liked his quiet, steady energy, even though I didn't like being told what I should—or shouldn't—do. It made sense that the spirit shaman would need more help than just the lament singer. There was so much that I didn't know, and so much to learn. Damn it, why hadn't I stuck it out . . . I could have found a job and gotten away from my grandfather that way. But something inside told me I'd made the right decision—that if I had stayed, I might have ended up just like my mother.

I gave him a soft nod. "Yeah, I get that. Okay, then. I won't ask you any more until the meeting. I don't want to get you in trouble for spilling secrets, though I wish to hell I could just get on with it. I'm tired of being the last to know. Tell me, though, how did you join them if it's a secret society and you were new in town?"

"They came to me. And, Kerris, this town is a hotbed of secrets. We aren't the only ones around—and there are those who really don't like the Crescent Moon Society or the spirit shamans. There are those who would love to see the town fall to the forces we work against. There's power here . . .

my people have known about it for years. And power attracts those who would use it—be they for the light, or the shadow world."

*"Sometimes the foul are actually fair."* I grinned at him. "Thank you, Trevor."

"For what?" He looked confused.

"For being straight with me. Now, if you'd preorder a couple books for me, I'd appreciate it."

He laughed. "Not using BookShopStop.com? You can get anything on there and usually cheaper."

"Ah, but then I'd miss the chance to come in and browse around when they get here." I wrote down the names of a couple of books I was eagerly awaiting, then sashayed out the door, feeling oddly lighthearted. Trevor had a way about him, and it occurred to me that he put a smile on a number of his customers' faces just by existing.

After Vintage Books, I wandered up to the Broom & Thistle for my second latte of the day. I had developed a high caffeine tolerance while managing Zigfree's Café Latte and had no intention of scaling it back. I didn't drink much, never smoked, and kept my consumption of junk food to a reasonably low amount, so I figured that coffee was my one vice and damned be the person who tried to convince me otherwise.

The owners—Nelly and Michael Brannon—I recognized from school. I hadn't known them very well, but they'd been nice enough and even back then, you could tell they belonged together. He had been the star of the fencing team and she had always landed the lead in whatever musical the school theater department was producing. Now, Michael sported a smooth ponytail and what looked like just as good a build as he'd had in high school, if not better. Nelly had long black hair to her midshoulders, with razor-straight bangs across the front. They moved behind the counter like well-oiled cogs, darting around each other with ease.

I glanced at the menu. They had all the regular sizes—short, medium, and tall, but had added "Bigfoot"—a sixteen-ounce quad-shot drink, and Landa—after the lake monster—a twenty-ounce quad-shot drink.

"I'll have a Bigfoot mocha, and hello . . . it's been a long time." I waited to see if they'd recognize me.

Michael gave me a vaguely familiar look, but Nelly—after a moment—let out a gasp. "Kerris Fellwater, as I live and breathe, you're back in town." Her surprise was real, with no affectation. She really hadn't known.

I nodded. "To stay, it seems." As Michael made my drink, I chatted with Nelly for a few minutes, catching up and accepting the usual sympathies about my grandmother. I was trying to think of a polite way to ask who the town gossip was. "Hey, if I wanted to catch up on everything that's happened since I left, who would I talk to? You know, get all the news in one fell swoop, so to speak."

Nelly snorted. "You mean, who dishes the juiciest gossip and keeps their nose in everybody's business, don't you?"

Blushing, even though I really wasn't that embarrassed, I nodded. "Yeah, so to speak."

"That would be Clinton Brady—the owner of the Fog-whistle Pub. You remember him, right?"

I blinked. Clinton had been the owner of the pub when I was younger—he was my mother's age and had taken it over from his father when the old man had a heart attack. I had forgotten all about him—and the pub. "That old place is still standing?"

"*That old place* was brought over brick by brick from Ireland." Michael, who had been listening, joined us as he wiped down the espresso machine. "Clinton's great-grandfather had it dismantled from the shores of Eire and sent here via cargo ship. They rebuilt it exactly as it had stood in the old country. The pub is at least four hundred years old." He straightened his shoulders. "The pub is older than any building in the United States, barring those that were here when the colonials came over."

The pride in his voice was evident and then I remembered, Michael Brannon was second-generation Irish himself. His parents had come over from Ireland and settled in Whisper Hollow when they were young, and while that wasn't all that unusual nowadays, he acted like they had entered via Ellis Island with the great wave at the turn of the nineteenth century.

"I suppose I should mosey over there and reacquaint myself with it. When I left town, I wasn't legally able to go inside." Even though I had sneaked in a couple times. Clinton had pretty much ignored Peggin and me, never carding us because we almost always bought one drink and stopped right there. I had my doubts that he would have sold us any more if we had asked.

Michael slung his bar rag over his shoulder and glanced up—another customer had come in. "Welcome back, Kerris. Excuse me, I've got my work to do. So do you, Nelly."

She stuck her tongue out at him but gave me a wink. "He's right. Busy morning ahead. A couple of the local groups always come in here on Wednesdays for their meetings—one in the afternoon, and one in the evening. I need to make certain we have plenty of pastries and supplies on hand."

As she moved off, I took my drink and headed to a table by the window. As I settled in, I pulled out my iPad and began to make notes about Trevor and Clinton and what I'd found out. It was nearing ten thirty, and I needed to do my shopping, then head home so I could start reading up in the journal before my appointment with Ivy. Staring at the overcast sky—a storm was moving in from the north, it looked like—I sipped my drink, trying to make sense of the whirlwind my life had suddenly become.

After stopping at Carter's Market—the main grocery store in town—and also a quick visit to the Whisper Hollow Town Square, where there was a Bed Bath & Beyond, I headed home with my spoils. I'd found a comforter set in shades of dusky green and blue, and matching sheets, and I had stocked up on staples and coffee beans and cat food, along with a good selection of produce and meats. I had enough to keep me for a week or so. At the last minute, I'd added a garlic braid to the cart. Something told me I was going to need it, even though I didn't like garlic all that much. I remembered that Grandma Lila used it for protection, and it seemed to me that it wouldn't be a bad idea to hang it up in the kitchen.

I arrived home by eleven thirty, quickly stowed the groceries in the kitchen, and hung up the braid on the wall that separated the kitchen from the living room. Touching it lightly, I whispered, "Do your work." Then I tossed the new sheets in the washing machine and carted the comforter set into the main bedroom. I carried my suitcases in, too, and decided that I would start putting away clothes after I returned from Ivy's. I was determined to sleep in an actual bed tonight, and unless Ivy could teach me everything in one go, I had the feeling I'd be keeping the lights on.

My stomach rumbled and I glanced at the clock. Noon, meaning lunchtime and meaning I had almost two hours before dashing over to Ivy's. She lived close enough I could walk there in ten minutes. As I popped a premade pizza in the oven, it once again struck me how, all those years, I'd lived within a stone's throw of my paternal grandmother's house, but had never known.

While the pizza baked, I settled down at the kitchen table with Lila's journal and opened the first page. In her meticulous hand, she had written:

*Traditions & History of the Spirit Shamans*
*Generation 48: Lila Fellwater*
*Daughter of Mae Edgewater*
*Daughter of the Morrígan*

I stared at the writing for a moment. If my mother was the forty-ninth generation, that made me . . . the fiftieth. When I started my own journal, how would I account for Tamil's absence? Where were the other journals from the other spirit shamans in my family? And how far back did fifty generations span? With a score of questions racing through my mind, I turned the page and began the journey into my lineage.

### Our History

*With every lifetime, there is a start. And with every sacred office, there is the initial calling. So it was that the spirit shamans began. The original versions of the stories are lost to time, but the retellings continue and so most of the following has been pieced together throughout the years and translated when need be. The following translation comes from my great-grandmother, who learned English later in her life, and who sent her daughters to America in search of a more fruitful life.*

*I leave this journal to my granddaughter, Kerris, since my daughter, Tamil, the forty-ninth generation, has vanished. Take up your post and keep it sacred and honor your word and work.*

*Kerris, I am certain you will meet your guardian— the Morrígan has promised me that. My own protector was driven off when I was young, and to keep him safe, I was forced to marry a disciple of the Night Mare's enemy—a son of Cú Chulainn. As to why and how this happened, this journal is not the place for that telling. I have secreted information about it away in my private diary—find it and read it, for you will need to know these things for your own safety.*

*—Lila Fellwater*

I stared at the page, trembling. So many answers within those few paragraphs, and so many more questions. I pushed the journal away, a gazillion thoughts racing through my head as I waited for my lunch. Finally, the welcome ding of the timer shook me out of my head and I retrieved my pizza.

Who was Cú Chulainn? The name sounded vaguely familiar. Why was he the Morrígan's enemy? And, if Duvall was the disciple of the Morrígan's enemy, then how had this happened? Why had he forced Lila to marry him and how had he brought it about?

As I bit into the pepperoni, it occurred to me that I didn't know much about my ancestors—on either side. I knew very little about my history and before now, I'd never thought much of it, except for wondering what happened to my mother and father. I'd been so wrapped up in worrying about why they both abandoned me that I'd totally ignored any family history before that.

If Lila had only been able to confide in her shapeshifter and her lament singer, and she had to drive away her guardian, that meant that the only one who might have a clue about my lineage was Ellia. The only other option I'd have would be to dive into genealogy and trace back my roots. But even then, I had a feeling it wasn't going to be as easy as just showing up and saying, "Hey, I'm your long-lost cousin, tell me about the family."

As I ate, the food settling the butterflies in my stomach, I forced myself to return to the journal. I could skim through, pick and choose what to read, but I needed to know the history. I needed to understand the dynamics. Because I had my lament singer, and I was pretty sure I had found my shapeshifter, and I had a nasty premonition that once the three of us came together to work the way we were supposed to, more than one force would creep out of the woodwork to try to stop us. My grandmother had been a strong spirit shaman, but she had been hampered by her lack of a protector and by being married to someone who was apparently an enemy of the Morrígan. Without those limitations, just how far down the rabbit hole would this journey take me? And what would I find there?

The next few pages talked about things I already knew—
the six forms of the dead, the fact that Penelope was the
Gatekeeper on the other side of the Veil for this area, that
Veronica was one of the Queens of the Unliving. But then
I found an entry that scared the hell out of me.

### January 22, 1959

*My mother and I were out training in the graveyard—
she says it's time I started learning how to face the spirits in the Pest House Cemetery. Ellia came with us, of
course, but she was upset. Mother asked her what was
wrong, rather sharply it seemed to me. Ellia said that
she had been out in the woods earlier, near the Tree of
Skulls, and that someone tried to snatch her up. It wasn't
a spirit, she said—or the Grey Man, or anything like
that. She was so upset that Mother finally said we
weren't going to train today, and instead, we went to
Mary Jane's Diner. There, we were able to pry out what
happened to her.*

    *Ellia had driven out over past Galaxy Drive, and
decided to stop for a while and take a walk along one
of the trails there. She was deep into the woods, singing,
when a man jumped out of the bushes behind her—he
must have been following her. He grabbed her and she
screamed, but nobody was around to hear her. She managed to get one of her gloves off and slapped him on the
face. He let go of her, shrieking, and pulled back. She
grabbed him around the wrist and held on. He begged
her to stop and she said she would only if he told her
who sent him. He said it was Magda . . . that she had
hired him to kidnap her daughter and carry her off into
the woods to wherever it is she's living. Ellia was so*

*shocked that she held on until the man went into a sei-*
*zure, and then she let go and ran.*

*Well, that certainly made both Mother and me stop*
*short. Here we all thought Magda was long dead and now*
*we find out she's still alive? She's got to be getting up*
*there—Ellia said that as far as she knows, her mother was*
*born in 1900. When the old Kerston house burned down,*
*we were all certain Magda was caught in the fire. But*
*Mother said that she never asked Penelope, and Penelope*
*never volunteered any information. You'd think that if she*
*knew her mother was still alive, she would tell us so Ellia*
*would know—since they're sisters, and Magda was respon-*
*sible for Penelope's death. But then again, the dead have*
*their own agendas and we aren't always aware of them.*

*I don't know what to think now . . . Magda's alive.*
*Ellia's afraid. And Mother's pissed off. I was supposed*
*to go on a date with Aidan tonight, but Duvall Fellwater*
*asked me to stop in and talk to him first. I didn't want*
*to go—he has a foul feel to him, no matter how good-*
*looking he is—but he insisted that it's important, so I*
*agreed to meet him after my lessons tonight and told*
*Aidan I'd see him tomorrow.*

*But with what has happened to Ellia, I think I'll can-*
*cel and she can stay with me tonight. We have to protect*
*her. She's our lament singer, and if her mother really is*
*alive and after her, then we need to figure out what the*
*hell is going on.*

I glanced at the clock. Another fifteen minutes and I'd
head out for Ivy's. I also realized that I had eaten my way
through the entire pizza. So much for moderation. I puzzled
over the entry. So Ellia and Penelope were sisters? And
Ellia's mother was born in 1900 . . . which meant Ellia had

come along later in Magda's life. I knew Penelope had been the Gatekeeper of the dead for a long time, but this meant that she had to have taken the position at some point well after 1900.

Sighing, I realized that I had better write up a list of questions so that I wouldn't forget any. I hunted around till I found a blank notebook and decided to transfer all my notes from my iPad—technology was wonderful, but you couldn't always depend on it.

I decided to start with the questions roaming around my head first; that way I wouldn't forget them while transcribing the others. I quickly dated the page and began making a list:

- *Did Duvall kill my mother?*

- *Which of his friends might have helped him?*

- *Since Duvall wasn't my grandmother's shape-shifter, then was it Aidan? Why had she broken off their engagement and married Duvall? What could he have possibly held over her head to force her to give up the love of her life?*

- *Who is in the Crescent Moon Society, and how are they connected to the spirit shamans and the Morrígan?*

- *Magda . . . Could she possibly still be alive? It seems ridiculous to think so, but then again, considering the year Bryan was born in—maybe not so ridiculous.*

- *Ellia had mentioned a force moving against the town—find out more about that.*

- *Find out more about Cú Chulainn and his followers.*

As I finished, I pushed out of my chair, made sure the oven was off, transferred the sheets to the dryer, and then slipped back into my jacket. Ivy lived about a five-minute walk away, and although it was raining, I decided it was worth getting a little damp in order to get some fresh air and think about everything I'd found out. Everything was spinning like a whirl of leaves in my head, and I had no idea how they'd fall out.

I locked the door and headed out to the road. Now that I knew what Bryan was, it made me even more curious to find out more about him. I thought about what he had been chasing—the *d'yavol-volkov*. The very name set off a warning alarm. And just what else was hiding out in these woods? Whisper Hollow attracted the strange and obscure—they were drawn by the security of being a stranger in an even stranger land. When you're the odd one out, and you move to the kingdom of misfits, you're no longer one of the freaks in the sideshow.

Trying to shake off the kaleidoscope of questions and thoughts, I came to Ivy's house. As I stood there by the garden gate, it occurred to me that I had passed this house hundreds of times during my childhood. I vaguely remembered seeing Ivy a few times, working in her garden or sitting on her front porch as I'd ridden my bike or walked right past my grandmother's house, unaware of who she was.

I had barely rung the bell before the door opened. There she was, in a pair of gray jeans and a blue sweater. The raven tones of her hair and her porcelain skin made her look like an ice figure. As I looked at her, I could see the faintest resemblance between us. Our noses were similar, long and narrow, and I had her coloring—pale as frost, as Grandma Lila used to say.

She ushered me in. "Let's get you out of that rain. I put on a pot of tea, though I know you prefer coffee, so I could make you some . . ." And then she stopped, staring at me. "Kerris, I can't believe you're finally in my house. At last, I can talk to you." A flutter of lashes, and then—tears, trickling down her cheeks. Her hunger for connection, for contact, surrounded and embraced me. "I can't believe this is real . . . that it isn't a dream."

I opened my arms. "Give me a hug, Ivy. You've waited a long time . . . and so have I."

As her arms wrapped around me, I felt oddly safe, and for the first time in a long while, I felt that I had family on my side. Grandma Lila had always stood by me, but always—always there had been Duvall looming in the background and when push came to shove, she took his side. But Ivy? She was unencumbered. Duvall was dead. He couldn't scare her into submission anymore. I had the freedom to finally learn about my father.

After a minute, she stood back, wiping her eyes with the back of her hand. "I'm sorry—I don't mean to be so emotional."

"Don't apologize. Ivy . . . you know, I want to but I can't call you Grandma . . ." I flashed her a grin. "You just don't look old enough to be my grandmother! Please don't be offended, though."

She laughed then. "Offended? No, girl, not at all. Ivy suits me just fine. So, come in, have some tea and tell me everything that's happened."

And so, as I slid out of my coat and followed her through the cozy living room into her kitchen, I told her about the Shadow Man.

# CHAPTER 11

~

I remember when Lila told me about the Shadow Man.
That's when I started working protection magic for you.
You never knew, but some of the toys in your room? I
enchanted them on Lila's request. They were there to watch
over you and keep him away." Ivy refilled our cups.

"I wonder, is that why he never came back? I can't remember him coming back after that."

"Most likely. I looked after you from a distance, sort of
a fairy godmother. In fact, Lila made me promise that if
anything happened to her before you were grown, that I
would secret you away from Duvall and get you out of here.
I'm just grateful that I never had to attempt that." The look
on her face told me her gratitude was for herself as much as
me. I was beginning to see just how afraid people had been
of Duvall.

"I'm beginning to understand just how much sway my
grandfather held in this community."

"Your grandfather had a tremendous amount of power
within a certain sector of Whisper Hollow. They were all
old money, Ivy League graduates, from long-established

families, and your grandfather—while he didn't have the highest pedigree among them—was the strongest in personality and greed."

I had never heard my grandfather talk about wanting to be rich and said so.

"Oh, I'm not talking money, Kerris. Your grandfather craved power over other people. He loved to make the rules and watch people squirm. He was a bit of a sadist at heart. In some ways, he would have made a good military commander. He never seemed to be fettered by emotion. Other people's suffering didn't affect him." She frowned. "In fact, Duvall missed the Vietnam draft by a couple of years—he was . . . oh . . . I think about twenty-six when they started heavy-duty conscription of boys, and while he could have been called up, by the time they were drafting everybody, he was past the age."

I frowned. "He was an architect . . . I suppose he designed a number of homes."

"He did, and he was a good one. He joined a firm—I don't remember the name of it now—back after he returned from college. Within two years, he managed to make partner and then it was only a matter of another five years before he took over the firm and pushed the original owner out. Think Scrooge and Fezziwig."

That sounded about right. I frowned. "I wish he had been nicer, and not just to me."

"I don't think the word 'nice' was in his vocabulary. Your grandfather had a real knack for taking the lead. He was good at pretending to be part of the team, until he was ready to strike, and then he would put his plans in action. That's how he got his claws into your grandmother. We've never been sure just why she left Aidan—she even chased him out of Whisper Hollow—but Ellia and I both knew she still loved him as much as she despised Duvall."

"Yet she married Duvall, hating him." Another thing to find out: what Duvall held over Lila's head in order to make her marry him. "So, what was my mother like? I have some memories of her, but they're all rather blurry. I remember she smelled good, like lemon and lilac."

"Tamil was a smart woman. She was also a romantic and a rebel, and those qualities did her in, when it came to your grandfather. They fought constantly. Unlike Lila, your mother refused to keep her mouth shut. She couldn't ignore Duvall's crustiness. She argued back, she mouthed off at him, and Lila used to tell me it was like living in a war zone, being between them. She supported your mother as much as she could, but in the end, Duvall always got his way." Ivy pursed her lips. There was something she wasn't telling me.

"What is it? I know there's more."

Ivy gave me a long look. "There's no way to prove it, so I'm hesitant as to whether I should even bring it up."

"Tell me. I need every piece of the puzzle I can get." I pushed my tea out of the way.

"There's some speculation that your grandfather may not really have been your grandfather. That Lila slipped away to Seattle for a couple weeks and . . ."

I caught my breath. "Got pregnant with my mother there." And then, I read between the lines. "Aidan! Where did he go when he left Whisper Hollow?"

"Seattle." Ivy shrugged, a tight little shrug with her head pressed against her left shoulder. "There's no way to know for sure—not really. Not unless you can track him down and ask him about it. He might know. But . . . here are the facts as I know them. First, Duvall married Lila in 1961. She was twenty. They'd been engaged for several years and she put off the wedding as long as she could. I know she wanted children—she was a spirit shaman and expected to have a daughter to carry on the blood. The power travels through the maternal lineage. We—Ellia and I—knew full well Aidan was her shapeshifter and she rejected him. I can prove this because my clan is connected to his. Mae was *not* in favor of her marrying Duvall, by the way. Your great-grandmother was an extraordinarily powerful spirit shaman. She was pissed as hell when Lila chased Aidan away."

"What happened to her? I never met my great-grandparents."
It seemed odd to me now that Grandma Lila had never talked
much about her mother, and for some reason, I hadn't asked.
Maybe I sensed that Duvall would have been angry.

"Your great-grandfather, Tristan Stonecross, and your
great-grandmother Mae emigrated from Ireland and settled
here in 1936. Mae told us they were in their early twenties
when they arrived here. He was a huge man, burly and strong
and he went into the logging industry. Tristan died in a logging accident when your grandmother Lila was thirty. That
would have been . . ." She calculated for a moment. "Lila
was born in 1941, a few months after I was, so that would
have been in 1971."

I blinked. That made her only a few years older than Bryan's daughter. "You really *are* young, for a shapeshifter."

"Yes, actually—I married young and had Avery right
away. That's tradition in my clan. We mate early and usually
for life. That Roger and I split up is unusual, but we are still
friends."

"Was Tristan Mae's protector? Her guardian?"

Ivy nodded. "Yes. And that made him a shapeshifter, too.
After he died, Mae had no guardian, so she focused on
increasing her power as a spirit shaman to compensate."

I thought about this. My great-grandfather had been a shapeshifter. Lila had been an only child, so there had been no boys
to carry on that side of the line. "What happened to him?"

"Tristan was driving a logging truck down one of the
access roads and for some reason, he put it into park on the
side of the road. Besides the parking brakes, logging trucks
often have wheel chocks—they wedge in around the wheel
on a slope to keep accidents from happening. He must have
thought he had the chocks firmly secured, but nobody really
knows what happened. All they know is that Tristan was
checking something behind the truck when it lurched and
began to roll backward. It caught him under the wheels,
and . . . well . . . cut him in half. Another logger found him
a couple hours after it happened."

I blinked; the image forming in my head was by far more

grisly than anything I'd been thinking might have happened. "That's horrible."

"Unfortunately, it's an occupational hazard when you log up in these hills. But yes, it tore Mae up. They were quite the couple—absolutely in love. So that was ten years after Lila married Duvall. But anyway, Lila wanted children. She told me once that she had been to the doctor, and he said there was no reason she shouldn't get pregnant, but Duvall refused to go in and get himself checked. So we all figured that he couldn't father children."

"Then she turns up pregnant." I was beginning to see how this was playing out.

"Yes, a number of years after they were married. And two or three months before she made the announcement, she took a vacation on her own and went to Seattle. Duvall didn't want her to go, but Mae was still alive, and Mae frightened Duvall."

"I wish I could have met her. How did she die?"

Ivy shifted. "Doc Benson said it was a heart attack."

I sensed an undercurrent there. "But . . . ?"

"But . . . Mae never had a health problem in her life."

I rubbed my forehead. This was getting worse and worse. "I see. I'll just file that fact away with the rest. So what happened?"

"Mae scared Duvall into backing down—I think she threatened him with something, because suddenly he was all in favor of Lila running off to Seattle for a vacation. When she returned, she seemed happier, like she had a new lease on life. She quit arguing with Duvall so much, and he—in turn—grew more imperious. She announced that she was pregnant, and how surprised they were that after all these years somehow . . . You get the picture."

"And Duvall's name went on the birth certificate because there's no way in hell my grandfather would ever admit to being cheated on. Especially if it resulted in a pregnancy. He'd suck it up and claim paternity before that." I knew my grandfather only too well, and that was absolutely what he would have done.

"Yes, that's what we thought, too. Ellia and I discussed it privately and decided not to press Lila. Why push her on an uncomfortable issue when her life was already so disrupted? But we always secretly believed that Tamil was actually Aidan's daughter." She paused to clear the cups off the table and leave me to think about that for a moment.

If so, that would make me Aidan's blood, too. The man my grandmother truly loved. "What did you say his last name was?"

"Corcoran. Irish . . . comes from the word for *purple*. He used to be heavily into genealogy, if I remember. One of those odd facts that stuck in my mind. He was a sweet boy, Aidan was." She leaned over my shoulder, brushing my hair out of my face. "I don't think there would be any harm if you thought to look him up and find out the truth—at least as much as he knows of it."

"If he's still alive . . ." I murmured. All roads were leading back to the Morrígan. But it was time to focus on why I had come. "So, what should I do to protect myself? The Shadow Man was able to grab hold of me physically. Either he's one of the Unliving, or he's some astral entity who's obviously dangerous. I don't want to face him again, not without some sort of protection. And I think that means sleeping with the lights on until I learn how to fight him. He seems to show up during the night, when all the lights are off."

Ivy motioned for me to follow her. "Let's go back in my ritual room. I'll see what I can teach you. Or at least try to find something to protect you until I can piece together what information I can find on him. Shadow People are dangerous."

"Shadow People? You mean there are more than one?" I had dealt with a number of ghosts over the years and had heard the term bandied about, but I'd always been reluctant to delve into any research on them—something held me back, like a restraining belt. The very words made me nervous, and after my experience with the Shadow Man, and remembering my childhood experience, I understood why I'd blocked it all out.

Ivy nodded. "Yes, there are. They are called the Ankou in Celtic lore. They're rogue soldiers of Arawn, the Celtic lord of the Underworld. The Ankou, along with the Black Dogs, are members of the Unliving, but unlike the Unliving who rise from the graves here, they have been assigned specific tasks and they are always dangerous. Rumor has it that they've escaped from the rule of Arawn and wander the Earth rather than staying in the land of *Annwn*—the Underworld—where they belong."

I thought about this. It made sense. "So, technically Unliving, but with stronger powers because they come directly from the Underworld itself."

"Right. Spirit shamans appear to be able to take them on, so there's a natural antipathy. And it's difficult to displace them once they get their hooks into an area. I know Lila had to fight a couple during her time, and it wasn't easy. We even petitioned Veronica at one point, asking her if she could control them since she's Queen of the Unliving, but she said they weren't under her jurisdiction and she seemed frightened of them. And not much frightens her."

I frowned. If they scared Veronica, then the Shadow People weren't anything to take on lightly. "Is there a way to petition Arawn to . . . I don't know . . . corral them up?"

Ivy stared at me, then laughed. "I don't want to be the one to try. Honestly, is that something you would like to do? Call on the god of the dead? It's scary enough petitioning the Morrígan, and you—and most of us in the Crescent Moon Society—have a *connection* to her."

The light wavered. I wrapped my arms around myself. She had a point. Even the thought of attempting to contact the lord of the dead made everything take on a darker note. I tried to shake off the sudden gloom that had risen. Ivy's house was bright and cheerful, filled with living plants that coiled and crept along the walls and up stakes, and whose leaves cascaded down over plant stands to fill what would otherwise be empty corners of the rooms.

"You have a green thumb," I mentioned, musing over the contrast between our surroundings and our conversation.

"I have an understanding with the natural world." She tilted her head to one side. "Plants have a form of consciousness, you know. Not like you and me, but they feel, they calculate . . . they . . . sense. There's far more to the green world than a lot of people realize. That carrot you pull for dinner—it knows it's doomed, as much as any animal you hunt down. Maybe on a different level, with a different type of reaction, but it knows when it's being uprooted."

I wasn't sure how I felt about my salad knowing that it was dinner-in-waiting, but then again, I was no vegetarian. "All life feeds on life. Death is necessary to ensure life continues, whether it be the death of an apple off a tree or a cow for beef, or whether it's us—to keep the world from being overcrowded. We're worm food, Ivy. And that's something I've always known. Lila was extremely good about instilling a strong respect for the cycle of life in me."

"Good, because as a spirit shaman, you need to respect the process. Come, follow me." She opened a door on the right side of the hallway and led me into a large room. It looked like it might have been a master bedroom at one time, or a second sitting room. "Welcome to my temple."

The moment I stepped across the threshold of the room, my body started to tingle. The energy was high in here—active and alive, and curious. It swirled around me, testing and probing, tapping me on the shoulder to let me know it was there. At no time did I feel threatened, but I knew without a doubt that if I had been a threat to Ivy, it would have struck out like a snake, and I had no doubt its fangs were nasty.

"Your guardians are very strong."

"My guardians are very old, Kerris. They go beyond history, beyond the human world." She winked at me. "I am the descendant of a long family line of shapeshifters and witch women. You have my blood in your veins—never forget that. And even though the shapeshifting side won't play through, I have strong magic in my bones. And so do you, though you haven't tapped into it yet."

I sucked in a deep breath. "Does Oriel know you're a shapeshifter? Did she know about Avery?"

"Of course she knows. Oriel's a special breed, by the way. She took over the boardinghouse from her mother, but don't let that cheerful demeanor fool you. Oriel's sole focus is to help the town thrive and continue, regardless of what that means. She can be a ruthless enemy and if you are out to harm the town, you are going to face her anger."

"She's not a shapeshifter, though."

"No, nor is she a spirit shaman, nor does she pledge to the Morrígan. But she . . . her roots go deep into the natural world, and she is the hearth and heart of Whisper Hollow. She was born into a human body, but she's no more human by soul than I am."

I frowned, trying to decide how much to say. "Bryan . . . his father was killed by a rival shapeshifting clan. Are all shapeshifters pledged to the Morrígan?"

"No, not at all." Ivy motioned for me to follow her to the center of the room. "The Morrígan selected several clans of shapeshifters to be her Chosen. The rest? Follow other gods, other ways, and other paths. And trust me, they don't all like each other."

Ivy motioned for me to sit on a bench in front of her altar. There, in the center, was a statue of a woman with a crow on her shoulders, and several at her feet. Without turning my head, I said, "That's a statue of the Morrígan, right?"

"Correct. You, Ellia, me . . . we are all pledged to her service. We are all part of this together."

"Tell me what you know about the spirit shamans—I haven't had a chance to read through Lila's journal yet."

"There are many places in the world like Whisper Hollow, where the dead rise and walk. Each culture has its own form of guardians. Since this town was founded by those of Irish blood—well, we brought our customs with us and that includes the spirit shamans. But you have counterparts all around the world, pledged to different traditions, who all basically do what you do. Protect the living from the restless dead."

"What about the Native tribes here? Don't they resent us? After all, they have their own beliefs and sacred traditions connected to this land." I couldn't take my eyes off the statue. The tall bronze woman was dressed in battle gear, but a circlet with a crescent moon ringed her head, and in one hand, she carried a sword. In her other, she carried a crystal ball.

"The tribes welcomed us when they realized we weren't here to supplant their traditions. The vortex here—the convergence of ley lines—makes it difficult for them, too. They were often plagued by the dead walking and by the creatures that haunt these woodlands. We were able to come in and help control the issue, giving them more freedom. We work with them—at least one member of the Native council belongs to the Crescent Moon Society."

"Trevor Riverstone." I did glance at her then, just in time to see her blink. "I met him earlier today. I saw his tattoo and insisted he tell me what it stood for."

She nodded. "Trevor is a member of the Makah tribe. He reports to them on us, and in return, we have a liaison for when we might need to go into sacred areas to deal with trouble. We've found a way to work together."

I glanced around the room. The main altar was wide and broad and had not only the statue of the Morrígan on it, but another statue of a man. "Who is that?"

"The Dagda. He is her consort."

The table was covered with a cloth the color of the night sky, with hints of blue and purple, and sparkling silver stars in it. In the center, between the two statues, stood a smallish cauldron—copper, by the looks of it. Crystals ringed the altar, and other assorted tools. A wand, gleaming silver, and a dagger—with a hilt made out of bone from what I could tell—rested horizontally in front of the statues. A wand of crow feathers—far bigger than the one I had—leaned against the corner of one wall, resting on a luxurious ivy. Votive candles dotted the surface, all within blue and purple and green mosaic glass holders that shimmered in the dim overhead light. A framed photo of a murder of crows hung to one side of the altar, and in the center, over everything, was a wall statue of a large raven. The altar faced the west.

"Why this direction?" I asked.

"The Underworld—Annwn, the world of the dead—as

well as the lands of the Sidhe both lie across the western seas. So the Morrígan looks to the west." Ivy settled down at a small circular table in the center of the room. It was covered with a jet black cloth. "Come. Sit here."

I glanced at the rest of the room as I joined her. To the north was a small craft table, covered with bits and pieces of bone and fur and a large shelf of oils. Deep drawers lined the sides of the table, and I had the feeling they were jammed full of goodies. To the east, a window overlooked the side lawn and fence that divided Ivy's yard from Bramblewood Way. To the south, a bookcase stretched across the wall, filled from floor to ceiling with books.

Sliding onto the chair opposite her, I gently rested my hands on the table. In the center was a taper candle—black— and a deck of cards. Next to the cards was a crystal ball. It wasn't lead crystal, but quartz, filled with prisms and fractures that pulled me into their designs. She lit the candle, then moved to flick off the light. When she returned to her seat, she was carrying a black lacy veil, which she draped over her head. I could see her features beneath the veil still, but they were masked and muted by the delicate needlework. She placed her hands on either side of the crystal ball.

I wasn't sure what I was supposed to do, so I waited. A moment later, the temperature in the room dropped abruptly and goose bumps rose on my arms, as the hair on the back of my neck began to tickle. I caught my breath and leaned back in the chair, staring at Ivy.

Beneath the veil, she was shifting, her head weaving from side to side. Then, with a slow inhalation that resonated so deep I could feel it ripple through the room, she sat straight and stared at me. Her eyes, barely visible in the dim candle-light and behind the lace, were glowing red.

"You have a question for me?"

I wasn't sure who I was talking to, but whoever it was, her voice was throaty, rich and deeper than Ivy's, and the magic running through it was enough to make me quake in my boots. Ivy had gone bye-bye, that much was obvious, and somebody else had come out to play. Somebody big, and someone who was as ancient as the hills.

Not certain what to say, but realizing I needed to say something, I cleared my throat. "I need to know how to protect myself against the Shadow Man. The Shadow People . . . the Ankou."

A hush fell through the room—a silence that made the quiet before seem loud. The spiral of energy around Ivy began to grow and as I watched, a flutter of crow wings darted past, circling her like pale purple shadows. They spun faster and faster, till I was dizzy with watching them, and then, with a quick swoop, she reached up and lifted the veil from her face.

I wasn't facing Ivy. Who she was, I didn't know yet, but she was brilliant and beautiful, with dark eyes that shimmered red, and her nose had lengthened a bit, and her hair was shining red. Her face was masked in patches of black kohl and creamy white—a patchwork of camouflage. Ruby red lips glistened in the candle's flame as she cocked her head to the side, a curious and coy smile on her face.

"Do you truly not know who I am, Kerris?" The woman reached out one hand to me and without a single hesitation, I took her fingers in mine.

A spark raced up my arm at first, like fire shooting, and then the stinging became a rush of pain. As I opened my lips to scream, the pain shifted and sent me into a massive orgasm. I came hard, bodywide—shaking from the crown of my head to the tips of my toes. It was sexual and yet there was a deeper resonance that rang through it. My spirit had climaxed, too—in a way that I had never before experienced. It was as if the universe had torn me wide open and exposed me to some brilliant light that poured through every vein and capillary of my body.

Gasping, I couldn't find my breath. It had been stripped out of me—ripped from my lungs. I struggled, wondering if I was dying, and then, slowly, my chest rose and fell and I caught the motion, caught the breath and inhaled deeply, filling my lungs with a rich blend of air and energy. The pain subsided and I sat quivering, feeling washed from the inside out, new and whole and shining as brightly as Ivy had been.

The woman sitting opposite me smiled. "Do you know me now?" She was still holding on to my hand.

I felt two inches tall—not in shame, but in stature compared to her. Nodding, I whispered, "Yes, my lady."

"Then you will be able to remember what you need to know. I have just performed the ritual that was to be your initiation rite, from your grandmother. Your powers have been fully activated. Study, and the studying shall be as core to your being as is the energy you feel now. Learn by doing. But, Kerris, a warning." The Morrígan leaned forward, holding my hand so tightly it felt like she could break my fingers with any harder pressure.

I winced against the pain. "Yes? What?"

"To find the key to controlling the Ankou, look to your grandmother's journal. And . . . Kerris?"

"Yes?" I held my breath, wondering what was coming next.

"Ellia and Ivy are correct . . . there is a force that seeks to break this town's spirit. It is an old enemy of mine, and he and his minions appear here and there, looking to avenge himself on my chosen. I fought him in my time, and still he seeks revenge for my triumph. You must find and root out his servants or the town will no longer be safe for the children born under my wings." And then, with a blink, Ivy slumped forward, and the Morrígan vanished.

I slowly let go of her fingers, moving the candle away before the flame could lick against the lace veil, then leaned back. Her children? She couldn't be just talking about the spirit shamans and their triads.

Ivy blinked slowly as she pushed her head up from the table. She shook her head, looking confused. "Did you get your answer?"

I nodded. "Yes, and more questions, but I think . . . I did. Do . . ." I paused, eyeing her carefully. "Do you remember what happened?"

She frowned. "Vaguely . . . kind of." Then, with a winsome

laugh, she said, "Not really. I know that I played the oracle for you and someone came through to answer your question. I can hold against negative spirits, and my warding is intensely strong against being jumped against my will. This is simply one of my duties."

Nodding, I debated on what to tell her. Was I supposed to fill her in on what had happened? Or not? But, as I opened my mouth to ask, no words came out. Maybe not, then. Another question occurred to me, and this one I was able to phrase aloud. "Do you know who the children of the Morrígan are? In general, I mean?"

Ivy folded the veil and set it to the side. She blew out the candle and motioned for me to follow her back into the kitchen. "That depends on who you ask. Technically, if you're talking gods and goddesses—"

"No, not really. I mean in general. Who might be living here." I knew the Morrígan hadn't been talking about legends, but people living here. Humans.

"Oh." Ivy pursed her lips, thinking. "Well, often those who are considered mad—well, would have been considered mad—were seen to be under her influence. But really, when you look at Whisper Hollow, I think you'd be talking about those with psychic powers. About those who see beyond the boundaries of what the world perceives as reality. The seers and the visionaries, the artists, those who have the power to create other worlds that feel as real as this one. Those who can . . . say . . . speak to the dead. Like the spirit shamans. One aspect of the Morrígan was once referred to as Mania . . . the mad."

She paused, then turned back to me. "I don't need to teach you any spells, do I?"

I shook my head. "No, I don't think so. I do need to go hunt through Lila's journal for a reference to protection from the Shadow Man, but I should be able to take it from there. Thanks, though, Ivy. You gave me an incredible gift. Now, it's up to me. I'll talk to you in a bit." I slung my purse over my shoulder, gathered my things, and hurried home as the rain pounded down around my shoulders.

* * *

Once home, I called Peggin and told her what had happened. "So, there's a chance Duvall wasn't my grandfather after all."

Peggin paused, then softly said, "I might be able to shed more light on that."

"How?"

"Just give me an hour or so . . . I'll text you when I'm done. Don't ask me how right now, because if I tell you . . . then I might not have the courage to go through with it." She hung up before I could tell her to wait. I wanted to know what she was planning.

I called her back but she ignored it, letting it go directly to her answering machine. Deciding that I could put the time to good use, I first made my bed, tucking the warm, dry sheets onto the mattress and shaking out the new comforter. Then I curled up on the sofa and skimmed through Lila's journal. Finally, about thirty pages in, I came across an entry about the Shadow Man.

### October 21, 1968

*Last night, I met the Shadow Man. My mother warned me that there were Ankou here in Whisper Hollow—they were summoned by Cú Chulainn's hag. But until now I've been lucky enough never to encounter one. But tonight, all that changed. Duvall was out at some meeting, and I was called out to deal with a Haunt who had come out of the grave, hungry to stir up trouble and unfortunately, she did some serious damage. It was Patty Dryden.*

  *Patty's family had refused to let Ellia play for her at her funeral, and they insisted I stay away from the grave before she was buried. So Patty was never properly prepared for the Veil, and Penelope wasn't able to hold her on the other side. Patty has been rising the past few nights, but we've missed her every time. Tonight, she actually managed to wreak sorrow on the town. Tommy*

*Stanton, Mary's little boy, is only eight. His father, Drake, took him and his ten-year-old brother Jack to the pub with him. While he was in the pub having a couple of beers with the guys, Drake let the boys play outside.*

*Tommy crossed the street, though Jack tried to stop him. Jack followed behind him, when Patty appeared. She got between the boys and chased Tommy out to the end of Fogwhistle Pier. Jack was screaming for her to stop, but Patty ignored him. The last Jack saw, Tommy was crouching on the end of the pier, with Patty screeching at him. Then the Lady rose up out of the water and caught the boy around the waist. She dragged him under the surface. Patty vanished, and Jack raced back to the pub screaming.*

*Drake and the other men were out on the pier in minutes, but they could find no sign of Tommy. Drake was frantic, and before his buddies could restrain him, he dove into the water to search for his son. He didn't surface. Neither of them have been found so far, and considering it was Fogwhistle Pier, we know that the Lady won't let go of them without a fight.*

*So the Society called Ellia and me out, and we managed to track down Patty. Like most Haunts, she seemed pretty pleased with herself, until I managed to drive her back across the Veil. Ellia played the song of sealing, and I took some of Patty's graveyard dust and bound it within my chamber. She shouldn't be able to walk again. I hope Duvall never discovers my hidden room—he could wreak terrible havoc on the work I have done if he should do so.*

*I got home late, exhausted. Thank gods Duvall was still out, so I stowed Patty's dust, then went to bed. I woke up in the middle of the night to a Shadow Man standing over my bed. The Ankou tried to kill me—I know that was his aim. He ripped my covers off and lunged for my throat.*

*I called on the Morrígan and the Crow Man, and the violet flame was there—I grabbed hold of it with my*

*hands, even though it burned so cold that I almost got*
*frostbite. I drew the Void Runes and sent them into his*
*core—not where you'd think the heart is, but directly at*
*his solar plexus, and it dispersed him. I don't know if it*
*permanently dispelled him, but there was no lingering*
*energy around, so that's something at least.*

*I need to find out more about the Ankou and how she*
*is summoning them. Arawn would not concern himself*
*with us—and he has no feud with the Morrígan. So it*
*must be Cú Chulainn's Hounds and their hag who are*
*drawing them from the Underworld. Saturday, Duvall*
*will be at a conference, so I can take that time to secret*
*wards against the Ankou around the property. I'll ring*
*it with the Void Runes to guard against the creatures*
*from the abyss entering.*

The entry stopped there, with a drawing of three runes.
The first looked like a lightning bolt across a vertical line
shaped almost like a hockey stick. The second was an arrow
stabbing through a crescent moon. And the third, a skull on
a cauldron.

I stared at them for a moment, then hurried over to the
counter, where I grabbed my notebook out of my bag, along
with a pen. As I returned to the table and began to copy
the runes, a tingle ran through my fingers. I knew these
symbols—I didn't know from *where*, but I knew them. They
were buried deep in my subconscious and as I sketched them
out, my body began to tingle. Knowing what to do—without
knowing why—I inhaled a long breath and blew onto the
sigils. As my magic transferred into the symbols, I felt myself
falling, and the next moment, I was no longer in my kitchen,
but in a deep, dark valley, back in the thick woodland, and
I was staring at the Crow Man.

# CHAPTER 12

～～

He was brilliant, the Crow Man was, and beautiful and terrifying all at the same time. He was tall—tall as a giant, seven feet or more, and a mist of blue fire surrounded him. His coat of ragged patchwork blue dragged the ground, and over that, a fur throw made from the skin of some animal. His hair was long, black as ink with blue highlights, curling down his shoulders. Atop his head, he wore a headdress of a giant crow's head and feathers. The crow's eyes glowed red, while the Crow Man's own eyes were shining black, with glowing slits of white fire that slashed through them. Beneath the coat, he wore what looked like blue jeans and black leather boots with platforms that raised him another foot taller than he actually was. The Crow Man was carrying a wand in one hand—silver, a good two feet long with a glowing crystal on the top end. The handle was wrapped in a black leather thong.

Unsure, both afraid and fascinated, I leaned back against the nearest tree, waiting. The forest around me was dark and shrouded with fog. Ancient trees rose high in silhouette, conifers that towered a hundred feet above the sloped ravine we were in. I couldn't see the sky, the fog was so thick, nor could I see any colors save blues and blacks and grays and a silvery sheen that lightly frosted everything.

The Crow Man took a step toward me, a curious smile on his lips. He looked cunning and wily, and he reminded me of somebody but I couldn't think of who. Some cartoon figure, perhaps, or someone I met long ago in a dream.

"Pomegranates."

I stared at him, not sure I'd heard him right. "What?"

"Pomegranates. Hidden secrets. Look for the answers buried deep within, like the seeds of a pomegranate. She waits in the ravine, for you to find her. Screaming skulls still lurk beneath long roots that dig deep into the ground." He took another step closer, his taut gaze holding mine. "The shadows that come in the night are very real."

I pressed my back against the trunk of the tree, mesmerized. The Crow Man was beautiful and hypnotic and entirely too deadly for my own good. "The shadows . . . the Shadow Man? The Ankou?"

"The Ankou live between the worlds. While shadows need light in order to be seen and absolute darkness usually gives them no home, the Unliving *do* lurk in the darkness, though they have little truck with daylight." His voice was low, almost growly.

For a moment I thought I saw a coyote standing in his place, and then, in a fraction of a second, he was the Crow Man again. I could almost understand what he was saying, but the meaning fled. I shivered, aware that I was so cold I could barely feel my feet or fingers. And then, before I could say another word, the Crow Man swept his arms out, his cloak suddenly becoming massive, dark wings. He let out a long *caw* and leaped into the air, shimmering in the rolling fog, and vanished. I blinked and . . .

*. . . was back at the table, staring at the runes on the piece of paper.* My skin was covered with goose bumps and my teeth chattered like crazy. My phone chimed and I shook my head, trying to sort myself out, as I picked it up.

Peggin was texting me. Can I come over? I need to talk to you about what I found out. I took the rest of the afternoon off.

Sure, I texted back. I could use a good sounding board. Be there in twenty.

I felt like I'd just been shifting between worlds.

*Maybe because you have been, dork.*

Yeah, yeah, I told myself. I wanted more caffeine but decided to wait until Peggin arrived. Instead, I aimlessly crossed to the kitchen door and stared out the window into the backyard. The gardens were overgrown, yet I knew that Grandma Lila had always kept them neat and tidy, and she hadn't been gone long enough for them to grow into the tangle they were now. Frowning, I moved back to the table, where I jotted down everything the Crow Man had said while I could still remember it. I was just finishing up when the doorbell rang. Peggin was at the door.

She was wearing a pair of capri pants, a button-down V-neck cardigan, and a rain jacket. She had braided her hair back in a French braid, and she was wearing a pair of sneakers, for once. I frowned. The capris and sweater were her to a T, but usually she wore a cute coat and ballerina flats with them.

"What's going on? You look dressed for . . . well . . . what's up?"

She shrugged out of her coat, draping it on the coat rack. "Kerris, I found out the answer to one of your questions, at least." The perkiness had vanished, showing an underpinning of worry and more than a little fear.

I motioned her toward the kitchen. "Want some coffee?"

"Latte, please. Triple, lots of syrupy goodness. Mocha if you can, actually." She let me bundle her into a chair and turned to watch me as I flipped on the espresso machine.

"Which question? And by the way, did Diago ever come back? How's the man we helped last night?"

She shook her head. "Mike's doing fine. No more problems, and we think he'll heal up without incident. He's out of the woods. Kerris, I was in the back room today doing some filing. We keep older files in the storeroom, and the current patients out front in the cabinet. Corbin was out to lunch, so I was the only one there. Anyway, after talking to you, I had a thought. I was supposed to archive your grandparents' files into the inactive cabinets and . . . I got curious. I had a look through them."

"What for?" I frowned. "Couldn't you get in trouble if Corbin found out you did that?"

"Yeah, those files are confidential. I never would have but . . . after what you told me, I knew there was a way I might be able to verify something for you. Otherwise, I never would have done something like this. This is the first time I've ever broken the rules—at least as far as work is concerned." She sounded desperate for me to believe her.

"I believe you—I know you wouldn't have done this if you didn't think you could help me. And . . . they're both dead, so . . . What did you find out?"

"Your grandfather? Duvall? He was sterile. He couldn't father children. The test was done before your mother was born."

"That verifies what Ivy suspected, then." I began jotting down notes as she talked. "Which means . . . that he's not my grandfather."

"Right. I decided to double-check so I took a look at his and Lila's blood types. I cross-matched them against your mother's blood type. Lila was AB, and Duvall was type O. Tamil was type AB."

"And . . . that means?" I didn't know much about blood, other than it was red.

"Just that there's no way those two blood types can pair up to produce an AB child. Duvall *couldn't* have been Tamil's father, even if somehow he regained his fertility."

"Then that proves it. Duvall's not my blood grandfather." I leaned forward, a thought striking me. "Did Aidan Corcoran have a file in the archived section?"

She nodded. "Yes—because Corbin took over Doc Benson's practice and he kept all of the files. I thought of that, too, so I did some digging and found his records. Aidan's blood was type A. He *could* have been Tamil's father."

I stared at my latte, stirring quietly. "So my actual grandfather is quite possibly Lila's guardian. Something else happened today." I told Peggin about my visit to the Crow Man.

"What the hell are you supposed to do next?"

"If I didn't know that it was futile, I'd think about heading back to Seattle. This is all just too weird. But I guess . . . one thing at a time. It would help if I could find my grandmother's private diary. Especially now that we know about Duvall." A thought struck me and I jumped up. "Come with me. I want to check out something. I read something in Lila's Shadow Journal." I motioned for Peggin to follow me upstairs to the sewing room, making sure all the lights were on as we went. I had no desire to face the Ankou again.

"What are we looking for?"

"Lila mentioned a hidden room where she kept vials of graveyard dust. Maybe her diaries are also there." I gazed around the sewing room, then went over to the attic and peeked in. Something wasn't jiving, now that I looked at it. There was a space between the two . . . I hurried over to the wall of the sewing room that flanked the attic and began rapping against it. Peggin followed quietly. The fourth tap on the wall reverberated with a hollow sound. "Here! Look for any sign of a hidden door."

We scoured the wall, and a few minutes later, Peggin drew my attention to a small lever by the floor, snugged up against a bookcase. I told her to wait while I drew the dagger from my tool bag. I wanted some weapon, even a small pointy one. Armed, I motioned for her to go ahead, and she pulled the lever.

A slow hiss sounded as a door—seamless against the wall—slowly opened inward to a dark room. Shivering, I peeked in and to the right of the door, saw a light switch. One flick flooded the secret room with a dim light. As I softly stepped through, Peggin followed me, propping open the door with a step stool she found nearby.

The secret room was small—about eight by eight, and one wall was lined with shelves and cupboards. The other wall had a built-in worktable, with more cupboards above it. The air was musty, but there was no real dust buildup.

"My grandmother must have been in here recently." I nodded to a paper plate with the crusted remains of a peanut butter sandwich. The bread was moldy but it obviously hadn't been here more than a couple of weeks. I slowly moved to the shelves. There, rows of mason jars lined two long shelves—jelly-jar size, each filled with dirt and each bearing a label with a name and date on it. I picked up one and examined it. *Rodger Lyons: December 12, 1989. Mary Lou Singer: September 8, 2010.* The dates went back to 1936, before Lila was born. The handwriting on the jars was different as well, up until the late fifties, when I recognized Lila's entering the mix.

"What are they?" Peggin crept forward, staring at row after row of jars. Another box of empty jars sat on the floor near the shelves.

"Graveyard dirt. From every death my grandmother and great-grandmother presided over." I counted the jars. There were ten deep per row, and they spanned three room-length shelves. "There must be almost two thousand jars here. Two thousand deaths my grandmother and great-grandmother presided over—that they worked their magic on." As I stared at the wall of glass, it hit home that each jar represented someone who had died, who had passed on. A light gone out in this world, looking to move on to the next.

"What does the P stand for?" Peggin pointed to the letter—written in red—on some of the jars. Most were from before the 1950s.

I thought for a moment. "Pest House Cemetery. These were people buried in the Pest House Cemetery before the modern section was added." I frowned. "Ellia never mentioned these bottles. I wonder if she knows that Lila collected graveyard dirt from every person. I have to find out why it's done, and I suppose I better follow suit. Yet another question, but I'm guessing I'll find the answer in her journal."

"Speaking of journals, you were looking for her private diary?" Peggin held up a notebook. It was a composition book, and on the cover was written *2015*. She passed it to me, and I flipped through it while she began to open cupboards and drawers.

I flipped through the pages. Lila's writing. "Yeah, I think this is it. But if this is just for 2015, then where are—"

"Here." Peggin motioned to one of the cupboards.

I peeked inside and saw a stack of notebooks. There was one per year, dating back to 1954, the year my grandmother turned thirteen. Her handwriting was bigger then, with the looping letters and exaggerated dots of most teenagers. "Almost sixty years of journals. Sixty years of records. I've got my reading cut out for me."

"Well, at least you know where they are."

"At least I do, at that."

We explored the rest of the room and found more magical supplies, mostly what I figured were spell components, along with a variety of tools, implements, and books. The books were mostly Irish mythology. I was about to cart all the journals out to the sewing room when a glint in the corner of the cupboard caught my eye. I set down the notebooks and reached for the object. It was a silver box, about the size of a bar of soap. A red ribbon held the top on, tied in a bow. Feeling vaguely like a busybody, I pulled one of the ribbon edges and undid the bow.

The box was silver, all right, with a simple embossed decoration on the surface of a crow and a moon. My birthmark and my grandmother's birthmark. Quietly, as Peggin watched, I lifted the lid. Inside, on a pad of red velvet, was a heart-shaped cloisonné locket. I quietly opened the locket. Inside, I recognized a picture of my mother as a baby—I had seen one like it downstairs on the kitchen wall. On the other side of the locket was the picture of a man. I stared at him for a moment, thinking he looked familiar. And then I noticed the inscription on the back.

*To my darling Tamil. Your loving father, Aidan.*

There it was. Carved into metal. Proof that Aidan was indeed my actual grandfather. I held the locket, running my fingers over it. Peggin glanced over my shoulder at the engraving. I cast a look at her, feeling the weight of a hundred years on my shoulders.

"If Duvall knew he wasn't Tamil's father, do you think

that would make it easier for him to kill her? I want to know, Peggin. I want to put her to rest—to prove to the world that she didn't just run away, that she didn't abandon me. I wish I could figure out where her body is. I know that sounds morbid, but it might give us some answers and it would sure as hell give me closure."

"Why don't you ask Penelope? You don't *need* anybody's permission, you know." Peggin narrowed her eyes, and had hauled out her *don't-sass-me* voice.

I thought about the ramifications of talking to Penelope. I needed to meet her anyway, since I'd be working with her. And maybe, just maybe, I needed to do this on my own rather than having Ellia tag along. If I recalled, my grandmother had done plenty of things on her own without a lament singer there.

"All right. Would you go there with me tonight?"

"Graveyard creeping you out?" Peggin was repressing a smile.

I stuck my tongue out at her. "No. It's just . . ."

"Just that it's creeping you out?" She laughed then, and the mood lightened.

Carrying the locket, and a stack of journals, including the one for 2015, I headed for the door. "Grab another stack of those, please. These will keep me busy for some time. It's a good thing I'm a speed reader."

"You always did ace classes because of that." Peggin obligingly grabbed an armful of the diaries, and then we headed downstairs.

I stacked the journals on one of the side tables and she followed suit, and then we returned to the kitchen, where Peggin crossed to the cupboard. "You keep your junk food in here?"

"I don't eat junk food. Not much."

"Bullshit, what are these?" She held up a bag of potato chips and I gave in with a rueful smile.

"Fine, so I do eat junk food. Yeah, chips are fine. Or cookies. Or whatever." I thought over her question, though. "On a serious note, it's not that the graveyard is creeping me out. It's the idea of actually meeting Penelope. The thought doesn't scare me as much as meeting Veronica, but jeez . . . I've spent years remembering my grandmother talk about the both of them. I run off to Seattle, then come back fifteen years later and boom, here I am, on their doorstep with little more than a *'Hi, I'm back and have taken over?'* I'm not sure how either one will take it."

"Penelope probably won't care. I think it's more Veronica you have to be wary of. Penelope has the same ultimate goal as you do—keep the dead in their place. Veronica likes waking them up." She poured the chips in a bowl and set them on the table, biting into one with a satisfied look. "Yum, salt. I love salt."

"Then you should have no problem coming out to the graveyard with me tonight to knock on Penelope's tombstone." I grinned.

Peggin let out a snort. "Yeah, right. Of course I'll come with you, but damn, woman, you need to think of a better way to show a girl a good time, you know?"

I absently nibbled on a handful of chips. "You know you want to go."

"Yeah, I do. So why would Duvall have it in for your mother? It can't be just because she wasn't his child, unless he was looking to hurt your grandmother. But he would have done that sooner, wouldn't he? And we can't forget your father vanished. Did Duvall have a hand in his disappearance, too? I don't know. I feel like there's something we're missing . . . or a piece of the puzzle we just don't have yet." She swallowed the mouthful of chips she'd just taken, and leaned forward, an excited glow in her eyes.

I nodded. "Right. And if it's something we're missing, there's not much we can do about it for now."

"He obviously knew she wasn't his. He was tested sterile before Lila got pregnant. I wonder if he told her about it, though? Did she know he couldn't father children? Maybe she thought he wouldn't realize he wasn't the father?"

Why hadn't I thought of that? It made sense. "Well, that

makes sense. But why wait until Tamil was an adult? Until I came along? Unless something was tying his hands."

Still puzzling, I wandered over to the fridge and pulled out a box of breaded fish fillets from the freezer. I spread them on a cookie sheet, getting them ready to go in the oven. By the time I was done, Peggin was playing with my laptop. "What are you doing?"

"Checking out the names of his buddies that Ellia gave us. Hmm . . . Here's Heathrow Edgewater. He's done well for himself. He owns the Peninsula Hotel, and his son works there with him. Looks like a shrewd businessman. Besides working together at the hotel, the pair have developed a real estate business that now earns a pretty penny—they cover the entire peninsula area and apparently they're the number one earners in the area. Hmm . . . what's this?"

"What?" I glanced over her shoulder.

"This link? It looks like it leads to a back-end list of names."

"What do you mean?"

"The website that this page is linked to doesn't have a return link to the home page. Let's see where the root link leads." She erased the web address back to the root URL. "Cuchulainnshounds.com. What have we here?" The page that came up was a splash page to what looked like a club. It said very little—*Cú Chulainn's Hounds* and a picture of the Celtic warrior in full battle dress.

I glanced at Peggin. "Crap. Cú Chulainn . . . he's an enemy of the Morrígan. And my grandmother was convinced that Cú Chulainn's hag—whoever she is—is responsible for summoning the Ankou."

"Then we need to find out more about them." Peggin leaned forward, examining the screen. "Before we click on the *Enter Here* sign, are you working through a proxy server?"

I frowned. "What do you mean?"

"I mean, if they log IP addresses, they won't be able to trace the fact that you surfed their site."

"How do I find out if I have one of those?" I wasn't an Internet dunce, by any means, but neither was I terribly savvy.

I knew enough to keep strong virus protection working on my computer, I scanned it regularly, I never opened an .exe program or file unless I knew who it was coming from and what it was, and I was cautious about phishing sites and e-mails. But that seemed pretty basic knowledge to me.

"Let me see what you have here . . ." Peggin's fingers flew over the keys and a moment later, she broke out into a wide smile. "You have a really good antivirus program; it offers a proxy server, a firewall, and safe-surfing options. Let's just enable these and we should be okay, unless they're computer geniuses. Go ahead."

When I clicked on the *Enter Here* link, it brought up a pop-up window in which to enter my name and password. "Definitely members only." I flipped back to the other tab, where the list of names was still visible. There were at least one hundred names, though a D preceded a number of them.

"You know, I don't think that the person who created this website realized that a search on names might bring up the page. I think they meant this to be private, but they didn't understand how search engine spiders work." Peggin frowned.

"Okay, let's copy the names down, in case they get wise to the fact that their organization isn't as protected as they seem to want it to be."

"Let me do a screen shot." She tapped away again, and a moment later said, "I just e-mailed you the screen shot. I also e-mailed it to myself. We can print it out later. Let's see . . . who is listed here . . ."

And then I saw—Duvall Fellwater. "Duvall. Only there's a D after his name. Deceased. The D stands for *deceased*, I'll bet you anything."

Peggin leaned over my shoulder. "Who else is there?"

"Well, Leon and Heathrow Edgewater, for one thing. Hmm . . . the other cronies Duvall hung around with are all here. Some names I recognize from high school, but mostly I don't remember any of them."

"Is Corbin there?"

I scanned through the listings. "No. Neither is Bryan. Wait—Ellia's mother—Magda! Magda Volkov is listed here.

There can't be two of them in the same small town. And no D, which means . . . Magda is still alive and she's connected with this group."

Peggin frowned. "Penelope and Ellia are sisters, right?"

I nodded. "Yeah, that much I figured out through my grandmother's journal. Ellia hasn't bothered to mention that little fact to me yet. I'm not sure if she thinks I already know, or if she just doesn't want to talk about it. She has to know I'll find out sooner or later. But whatever the case . . . yes, Ellia's mother is a member of this organization and appears to still be alive. This listing has to be fairly up-to-date, given Duvall hasn't been dead all that long."

"Cú Chulainn . . . he was a legendary warrior, right?" Peggin jabbed at her glasses. "Celtic?"

I nodded. "I think he may have something to do with the Morrígan. Now, I really want to talk to Aidan Corcoran." A pause—"My *real* grandfather."

"See if he's got a phone number or listing. You said Ivy said he was in Seattle, right?"

So I typed in his name and the city name, and within seconds I was facing a phone number plastered across my screen. "Do I dare call him?"

"I don't see why not. He may be a shapeshifter and long-lived, but, Kerris, you need to find out everything you can before . . . anything else happens." Peggin let out a small squeak. "Do it—and soon. I have a feeling . . ."

"Another feeling, huh? All right."

I pulled out my phone but it was on the last bar, so I plugged it in and reached for the landline. As I dialed the number, I held my breath as it began to ring. A moment later, "Hello?"

"Hi . . . is this Aidan Corcoran?" How the hell was I going to dive into this? I had no clue what the hell to say.

"Speaking. How may I help you?"

I glanced at Peggin, who nodded to me. "You don't know me, but my name is . . . Kerris Fellwater. I live in Whisper Hollow, and I'm the granddaughter of Lila Fellwater. I'm Tamil's daughter."

Silence. Then, "Oh." Another pause. "You know, then?"

And just like that, he knew exactly what I was calling about. It was in his voice; it was hovering in the air between us.

"You're my grandfather, aren't you?"

Aidan cleared his throat. Finally, he spoke. "Yes, I'm your grandfather. If you know that, then . . ."

"Duvall is dead. So is Lila . . . they died in a car crash last week. The Lady took them. I came home to Whisper Hollow to take up my grandmother's work."

More silence. "What about your mother? Tamil? Didn't she follow in Lila's footsteps?" His voice strained as he said their names and right then I understood that he didn't know. He didn't know that Tamil was gone.

I worried my lip, then let out a slow breath. "My mother disappeared when I was three. I think she was murdered."

There was absolute silence for yet another long moment. Then Aidan let out a soft sigh. "I feared something like that might happen. I wanted to go back, I wanted to protect the both of them—it was my job. But Lila refused to allow me to return. I had to abide by her wishes. I never got to meet my daughter." The sorrow in his voice was tangible.

I tried to absorb the fact that I was talking to my true grandfather. That Duvall had been a pale substitute. It was a relief to realize that his blood was not mine. Somehow, it made things easier to handle, knowing that the man who had been so cruel hadn't actually been my own blood.

When Aidan spoke again, his voice contained a whispered urgency. "Kerris, the danger's not over. You'll be their next target, if my guess is right. I'll do my best to fight my way back. I never thought I'd darken the roads of Whisper Hollow again, but now . . . Tamil needed me and I stayed away because I thought it would help her. I was wrong—I should have been there, to guard Lila and my daughter. Maybe . . . maybe I can make up for that."

At first I thought, no—he'd be an old man, too old to help. But then I remembered, he was a shapeshifter. "I left when I was eighteen. I just got back."

He sounded all business now. "I'll contact you shortly. I'm going to drive up and meet you. I need a little while to make arrangements. Just be careful who you trust. The Hounds have eyes everywhere." And with that, he hung up.

I stared at the phone, not knowing what to think or to say. "He's coming back. He sounds worried and told me to be careful who I trust." I looked over at Peggin. "The fact that he's so concerned that he's coming back to Whisper Hollow after all these years frightens me, to be honest. He said that I'm going to be 'their' next target, but he wouldn't say who they were."

Before I could say anything else, my phone rang. I glanced at the caller ID. Bryan. "Hey, how are you?" As I answered, I realized that I sounded like all those women I tended to snicker at. But truth was, I was happy to hear from him.

"Hi there, gorgeous."

I blinked. Not many people called me that, and he sounded like he meant it. "Can you come over? Peggin's here. I have a lot to tell you . . . and a favor to ask you."

"I'll be there in twenty as soon as I clean up. I helped mop up after a nasty accident at a friend's store today. Don't ask—you don't want to know. It just necessitates a lot of soap and water and scrubbing."

Feeling slightly flirty, I asked, "You're a dirty boy, huh?"

He snorted, and then his voice dropped, low and sultry and beckoning. "Kerris, if you knew what was going through my mind all day, after this morning, you'd see just how dirty."

"You promise to tell me later?" Once again, my breath slipped away and I felt a keen ache. Hunger . . . it was actually a hunger to feel his hands on me, to hear his breath—slow and easy—near my ear. My nipples stiffened, brushing against the lace of my bra, and I felt ripe for the picking. "Please, promise me."

A pause, then—"Oh, it's a promise. I want you, and when I get over there, I'm going to take you in my arms and kiss you. And later on, I'm going to explore every inch of you, from head to toe, if you'll invite me in." And with that, he hung up.

I stared at the phone in my hand, my throat dry. My body felt like it was on fire, and all of a sudden I wanted water to put out the heat that slaked through me. I pulled a bottle from the fridge and drank deep, the cool liquid calming my nerves as it raced down my throat.

Peggin stared at me, a grin on her face. "I don't have to ask how it's going between you and Mr. Shapeshifter. That's obvious on your face."

Wiping my mouth, I drank again until I had finished the bottle, then let out a long sigh. I slid the fish fillets into the oven and began fixing a salad to go with them. "Peggin, he's my match. He's my guardian. We figured that out last night, after the Shadow Man attacked me."

She sucked in a slow breath. "I wondered, after that scene in the hospital. So you've found the third part to your triad." A loud thump hit the roof and then skidded across it. "What the hell?"

"Wind's picking up." I glanced outside only to see, over the fence dividing our properties, a large gust whale on one of the trees in Bryan's yard. It bent the maple—a sapling—almost in two before letting the branches go singing back into place. "Another gust or two like that and the limbs will be flying off the trees. We're set up for a blow."

"Yeah. Well, look on the bright side." Peggin shivered. "It's the perfect night to go visit Penelope."

"Yeah, I'd say so." I continued to stare out the window. Something out there was calling to me, and I had no idea what. I slowly moved to the door and opened it. As I edged out onto the cement patio, I realized that I had yet to come out and explore the backyard.

As I glanced around, I saw a tangle of vegetation. Highly unlike Lila to leave it in disarray. Even though she had been gone only a week, it looked like months of growth had overcrowded the yard. The rose arbor, behind a white wooden lattice fence and an overreaching trellis that arched over the entry, was covered with drooping vines—not ivy, but some other plant that had taken over and now lay heavy and sodden across both fence and arch.

A gust of wind hit me full force, nearly blowing me off my feet. Steadying myself on the edge of the patio table, I eased forward, listening with every sense I could muster.

The howl of the wind overshadowed whatever noises might be hiding in the dark, but as my eyes adjusted, I realized that a fine mist was rolling along the backyard.

"This isn't healthy." Peggin had followed me out. She was standing by the screen door, making certain it was closed so the cats wouldn't be able to get out. "The mist—it's tainted."

She was right. The mist boiled along the ground low and thick and had taken on a faint greenish hue—not a healthy growing green, but the green of sickness and disease. I started to close my eyes but stopped. It wasn't safe. I knew it in my gut. I needed to keep all my senses, including sight, on high alert. Instead, I reached out with my mind, tried to intuit what lay beneath the mist and rolling fog.

*Loss . . . and anger. A flash of irritation—it was so much harder now. Why couldn't things work out the way they were supposed to? Why did that goddamn shapeshifter have to move next door? It was an upset in the plan . . . a plan that had already gone awry so many times it curved more than the Elwha River.*

The voices in the mist paused and I realized that I had been listening in on a conversation. They certainly weren't *my* thoughts. The thought crossed my mind that the last thing I wanted was to develop late-blooming telepathy. But my attention was brought back to focus by a darting movement from my right.

"Stay back," I warned Peggin. "Get ready to run inside if something happens."

"You're not making me feel any safer. What the hell are you going to do?"

"I'm going to walk into the tangle over there, where the rose arbor used to be. I think . . . whatever this is, it's emanating from that area and I want to find out what the hell is going on."

"Kerris Fellwater, don't you dare—" But Peggin's warning was cut off by a sudden, sharp cawing from the tree above.

*Stop . . . stop . . .* the crow shrieked. *Go back before it catches you.*

With a sudden burst, the rolling mist churned toward me. It was searching for something, probing my energy. I stumbled back a step. "Who's there? What do you want?"

*You, Kerris Fellwater. We want you, and we're coming for you. Whisper Hollow will be ours. Leave now or we'll make certain you truly follow in your mother's footsteps.* As the mist touched my skin, it began to burn like a cold fire, and I let out a long scream.

# CHAPTER 13

～

A loud growl emerged from the shadows and the next thing I knew, a giant wolf leaped over the fence and knocked me back, sending me out of the mist. The creature was beautiful—a brilliant white wolf with gleaming blue eyes.

*Bryan.* I was able to get a better look at his wolf form than I had at the hospital. He was huge—almost the size of a small pony. And his fur was silky, glowing with a faint blue sheen. His eyes were ice blue, ringed with black—haunting and filled with years of living. He turned back to the mist and snarled.

"Peggin—get my bag, hurry! It's in the kitchen." I took a step back, cautious to stay clear of the toxic fog. Bryan growled again as the mist crept forward, but it had slowed, as if it had suddenly become cautious.

"Here!" Peggin had hold of my bag, panting from her mad dash into the house. She looked petrified but stood her ground as she held it out, opening the clasp for me.

I had no clue what I needed, but as I thrust my hand inside, my fingers lit on the dagger and I instinctively grabbed for it. "Stand back, but near enough in case I need something else."

I unsheathed the dagger and tossed her the leather sheath. She caught it and edged back.

Turning to the mist, I thrust the dagger into the air. I struggled to remember the runes I had drawn that afternoon. What were they? Oh yes . . . first . . . a lightning bolt through a hockey stick. I swept the dagger through the air, drawing the sigil. Then I drew the next—the arrow through the crescent. Lastly, I envisioned the cauldron and drew an outline of it in the air, then an outline of the skull in its center. I realized that I had closed my eyes when I heard Peggin gasp.

"Look!"

I opened them quickly, just in time to see the runes floating in the air in front of me. They were a brilliant blue, and glowing. Focusing on them, I quickly ran over what I remembered. They were the runes of the Void, the runes of the abyss. So maybe they could eat up whatever this was. As I mentally pushed them forward, they began to move toward the mist's direction.

The vapor came to a stop. The runes shot forward, hitting the mist square center, sizzling as they exploded in a bright shower of sparks. With a last *pop*, they vanished, taking the fog along with them.

The patio flooded with light. Blinking, I realized that Peggin had gone inside and hit the light switch. As I turned back to Bryan, he was standing there, tall as life, all signs of his inner wolf gone. The reality of what had just happened hit then, and without a word, I walked over and he wrapped his arms around me, kissing the top of my head as I leaned against him, shaking.

"Watch the dagger, love," he whispered.

I struggled to smile, making certain the point was away from him. "Don't want to stick you with this," I whispered.

He held me tight. "I'll protect you. Trust me, Kerris. I'll watch over you."

My heart beat a staccato tattoo as Bryan nuzzled my ear. "What the hell was that?"

"Dark magic, my love. Someone was trying to hurt you." He lifted my chin to look into my eyes. "I'm here, Kerris."

"I know." I glanced into the gloom. "It's really gone?"

"You appear to have dispelled it. But we have to figure out what's going on. Let's get you inside, you're freezing." As he bundled me into the kitchen, I glanced once more over my shoulder. The wind was still raging and the rain had started up, but the unhealthy mist had vanished from the yard.

I locked the door. Peggin was already heating water for tea—for once she didn't seem to want more coffee and neither did I—and my bag was on the table. I sheathed the dagger, replaced it in the bag, and set it aside. Bryan shrugged out of his jacket and hung it over the back of one of the chairs. Peggin brought three cups, the teapot, and honey and lemon to the table, and then she pulled the fish out of the oven. I silently set three plates on the table, along with silverware, and the salad and then sat down.

We sat there, staring at one another, still speechless.

Finally, Peggin broke the silence. "Who do you know can work magic like that?"

"That's the thing. I don't *know* anybody. I've been gone too long." I stared into my cup, the tea shimmering under the light. I added a little more honey, listening to the sound of the spoon as it clinked delicately against the china. My grandmother had prided herself on her teapots. She had a half dozen: one for every season, one for Christmas, and one matching her good china. Peggin had chosen the autumn one, a delicate shade of tan with whirls of color—orange pumpkins, black cats, and swirling leaves painted along the sides.

"Well, someone knows you're back and isn't happy about it, that much we can assume." Bryan helped himself to the chips that were still on the table.

"We'd better figure it out soon, then." I looked up at Bryan. His expression was one of worry, but in his eyes, I could still see the desire—the heat—flaring in those alpine pools. "Peggin and I had planned to go meet Penelope tonight, to ask her about my mother. I still want to do that. Will you go with us?"

Bryan sighed. "Of course, you know I will. Are you taking Ellia—"

"No!" Peggin was quicker than I was. At Bryan's startled look, she shook her head. "There's something going on, Bryan, and you know it. I can feel it. The whole town's on edge. Till we find out who's involved and what it is, Kerris needs to pick and choose who she tells her secrets to."

"But you trust me?" A smile danced at the corner of his lips.

Peggin blushed. "I know about you. I know who you are. So yes, I trust you. I trust you to watch out for her, especially after . . . well . . . after Diago, and after that mist just now."

He laughed then, a loud, hearty laugh that broke the tension in the room. "As wise as you are pretty." But when he said it, there was nothing attached to it and I smiled softly, happy to see my best friend connecting with the man who was so quickly stealing my heart.

"Do we get to eat first?" Bryan asked. "Or should we head out now?"

"Since dinner's on the table, eat first. It's only five thirty. We have time."

While we ate, I filled Bryan in on the day, including my encounter with the Crow Man, my visit to Ivy's, the hidden room, the journals, the locket, and the Cú Chulainn's Hounds website.

He picked over his salad. "What do you know about Magda? Penelope and Ellia's mother? What kind of powers does she have?"

"I don't know, but it does seem odd that if Ellia is a lament singer and Penelope's a Gatekeeper, Magda is on the side of Cú Chulainn's Hounds. Did she go rogue?" Finishing the last bite of fish, I pushed out of my chair; Agent H ran over and entwined himself through my legs. He let out a squeak. "I'll leave on the lights in every room, so the Shadow Man can't come in," I told him. But truth was, I was nervous about leaving them alone. "I need to ward this house and ward it good tomorrow."

"You should go through your grandfather's study before establishing your wards. In fact, you should comb through every nook and cranny you haven't touched. You have no idea what he—or your grandmother—might have stashed away. Best to know what's here first so you can either strengthen it or get rid of it." Peggin slid into her coat.

"Where are your heels, Miss Priss?" Bryan pointed to her sneakers.

She rolled her eyes. "I had a feeling this night would end in something beyond dinner and dancing. And, given the weather and the knowledge that we might not end up cozying up by the fire all evening, I opted for *easy to navigate* in the footwear department."

I slid into my boots—the Dingoes—and shrugged on a heavy denim jacket. Bryan was dressed for the weather, too. Sliding my wallet and keys into my pocket, I grabbed my bag o' tricks—as I was starting to think of the bag of tools—and we headed out to my car.

Peggin rode shotgun—Bryan graciously insisted. She flashed him a smile as he helped her into the car and then started around to open my door. I waved him back, hopping in without help. Truth was, it was pouring and I didn't want to wait for chivalry when I could easily get into the car on my own and avoid getting totally soaked. As I turned the ignition, the chime started that indicated I hadn't fastened my seat belt.

"That thing drives me crazy." Finally, it stopped as I fumbled the fastener into the clasp. I put the car into gear and backed out of the driveway onto the street. We could walk to the cemetery, but any chance of putting off getting wet and cold appealed to me. Besides the fact that if we had to get out of there fast, I wasn't about to rely on my running speed. I really didn't know track and now wasn't the time to test my endurance, let alone Peggin's. Bryan, I had a feeling, could take care of himself.

We were at the cemetery in no time flat. I glanced around, wondering if Ellia would be here, playing to the dead, but the night seemed so wind-tossed and rain-swept that I doubted she'd be out in the weather if she didn't have to be. I unfastened my seat belt and slid out of the car. I knew where Penelope's tomb was. And that was where my grandmother had told me the entrance to the Veil was. At least—*one* of the entrances to the Veil. There were so many throughout the world.

The cemetery was a-rustle with dripping rain and the ever-present wind. The evergreens keeping watch over the graves were blowing hard, their tops waving like wild dancers in the night sky. As the clouds boiled overhead, the dim streetlamps that lit the paths of the dead cast eerie shadows on the ground behind us. Grateful for the light, but knowing that light itself wouldn't keep back the spirits, I led Bryan and Peggin through the labyrinth of headstones, along the well-worn cobblestone paths that wound through the grass. Finally, in the center of the graveyard, I saw what I was looking for—Penelope's final home.

Unlike most of those buried in the cemetery, Penelope had been buried in a tomb, a mausoleum. It was small, with just enough room inside for a few people plus her sarcophagus. I wondered who had placed her here. If her mother was responsible for her death, surely she wouldn't have gone to the trouble to set up a memorial like this.

The mausoleum was built into the base of a knoll along the edge of the graveyard that led into the Pest House Cemetery. It was built of thick cinder block, and the back half of it vanished beneath the dirt and grass that shrouded it. In the soft glow of the lamps that illuminated the cemetery walkways, the cinder blocks took on a dark, shadowed hue, stained and worn from time. A double door in the center guarded the entrance to the chamber. A plaque to one side of the door read: *Here Lieth the Mortal Remains of Penelope Volkov, Guardian of the Veil, Gatekeeper of the Graveyard. Enter and Despair.*

"Have you ever been here before?" Peggin asked in a hushed voice.

I shook my head. "I've been to the tomb, but never in it. My grandmother wouldn't allow me to go with her when she went in. I don't really know the proper procedure, so we're going to have to wing this, folks." I sucked in a deep breath and put my hand on the round door handles. "Here goes nothing."

As I pulled on the door handle, the hinges let out an unearthly shriek, as if they hadn't moved in a hundred years and now only opened under protest. The blood in my veins turned to ice water. Maybe this wasn't such a good idea? And yet, I didn't have any choice. The spirit shaman had to work with the Gatekeeper of the graveyard. For whatever reason, Penelope had been elected the guardian of the Veil for Whisper Hollow, and sooner or later, we had to meet.

Letting out my breath in a slow steady stream, I stared inside. A single room with a sarcophagus in it, the chamber was illuminated by a diffused light that seemed to emanate from a crystal chalice that sat beneath a glass display box on a plinth near the back.

*There's no going back . . . not now. The day I decided to return to Whisper Hollow, I knew there was no turning back from anything that might happen here. This is it, Kerris. This is your life—this is what it's going to be from now on. Filled with spirits and Ankou and a dark goddess watching over your shoulder.* I stepped inside the tomb.

Peggin followed me, and Bryan brought up the rear. When we were all inside, the door blew shut with a huge gust of wind, slamming defiantly behind us. Peggin jumped, but I forced myself to stand steady. I motioned for them to stay near the door as I crept forward as softly as I could. There was no hiding that we were here, but I wanted to show as much respect as I could. The lighted chalice was glowing so bright now that it filled my vision, and I found myself moving over to stare into it.

Formed of clear crystal, the chalice glimmered from the liquid that churned inside it—crimson and thick like boiling blood, it kept up a continual motion, swirling in a perpetual phantasmagoria within the large goblet. As I stared at the sparkling display, I heard Peggin gasp, and I knew we weren't alone. I turned, slowly, to face the sarcophagus.

There, standing beside it, was a specter so terrifying and beautiful that it was all I could do to stand still. Tall, nearly six feet, the blonde was dressed in a black lace sheer dress beaded with black sequins that shimmered under the light of the chalice. Her golden hair was piled up in a messy chignon, wisps of it tendriling down to kiss her shoulders. Her irises were crimson, bloody against the glowing whites, and her skin pale as porcelain. Dark black shadows accentuated her eyes, setting them off like a raccoon's mask, and delicate black veins trailed out from the inky black to decorate her face. Her lips were black as night, and another trail of veins spread from her lover's pout.

But what transfixed me were the nails jutting from her skin.

From the crown of her forehead, dappling her neck and shoulders, jutting out through the sheer black lace of her clinging dress, all over her body they jabbed from within, as if someone had climbed inside her with a nail gun and gone crazy, shooting them from the inside out. Small pools of dried blood—sparkling like jewels—glistened around each of the nails. One of her hands trailed down, touching the sarcophagus. She cocked her head to the side, staring at me, ignoring the others, and then slowly began to walk forward.

I wasn't sure what to do, but I knew when I was in the presence of royalty, and Penelope felt like royalty. I bowed, steeling myself for what was bound to be the oddest discussion of my life.

She paused when she was about a foot away from me, looking me over. "So you are Lila's grandchild? You claim the title of the new spirit shaman?"

I had the distinct feeling this was a test and all I could do was run on instinct. "I am Kerris Fellwater, granddaughter of Lila Fellwater, the new spirit shaman of Whisper Hollow. I claim the title and come to honor the agreement that binds your office and mine."

She inclined her head. "Seal the agreement, then."

At my confused look, a faint, ironic smile crossed her face. "Your grandmother came to me too soon for you to be properly introduced. I will forgive the breach of the ritual." Gliding as though she were walking about two inches above the ground, she moved to the chalice. "A drop of your blood mingled with my own binds us to work together. Your great-grandmother's blood joined mine when I took over this office, and your grandmother's as well, when she joined her mother as a spirit shaman. Now, the wheel turns and so you will pledge yourself to this ancient bond between the world of the living and the world of spirit."

It felt so right that it scared me. As frightened as I had been when we entered the mausoleum, I had no doubt this was what I needed to do. I set my bag down on a bench and withdrew the dagger, unsheathing it. Peggin and Bryan watched, uncertainty in their eyes, but as I glanced their way, I knew they wouldn't interfere unless I called for them. They had accepted my role—it was written on their faces.

Penelope lifted the glass case protecting the chalice. She set it aside and, with a soft smile, nodded for me to proceed. I held up the blade and, with a quick motion, brought it down against my right palm—just the tip—and watched as a thin weal of blood welled up. As the crimson tears trailed down my flesh, I held my hand over the chalice and watched as the droplets began to fall into the ever-churning mix.

As they blended in with the kaleidoscope of liquid, a cold wind surrounded me and I found myself standing between the worlds—in the center of a misty web. Gossamer strings radiated out, the threads scintillating with sparkles of light. There, guarding a portal in the web, stood Penelope in all her radiant and gory glory. She smiled fully.

"Welcome to the entrance to the Veil, Kerris Fellwater, spirit shaman of Whisper Hollow. Welcome to the gateway that guards the world of spirit. Here, the dead come who have been prepared for their journey. Here, I escort them over to the Veil, where they rest before moving on. I hold them as well as I can, and when they break free and return to your world, it is your task to round them up and drive them back to me." Her voice resonated against the webs, singing rich and low. Here, she was vibrant and powerful, no specter in the shadows.

"What happened to you? How did you become the Gatekeeper?" I didn't mean to be rude, but the questions rolled off my tongue. Chagrined, I ducked my head. "I don't mean to be nosy—there's just so much I don't know because my grandmother died before she could teach me."

She laughed. "No offense taken. There are many things I can see from where I stand, Kerris, and I know—I see—that no offense was meant." She waved her hand and a bench appeared. "Sit and listen. This is part of your training."

I sat, wondering if Peggin and Bryan were okay. Were they seeing this? Or had I vanished along with Penelope? Were they hunting for me now?

"I was murdered when I was young. I was murdered for reasons that so disrupted the balance that the Phantom Queen bade me stay at the gate until the balance one day is righted. Then I may rest, as another takes my place. There will always be Gatekeepers, there will always be guardians; we each take our turn for a differing reason. I bear the scars of my death for all to see, that they might know death has come to visit them in my visage, and that none can evade the Veil. Together, you and I and the lament singer—we keep the balance of spirits in check."

"How will you contact me if you need me?" I wasn't sure about opening my front door to find Penelope ringing the bell at four in the morning.

She laughed. "I see your thoughts, Kerris. No, I will not appear on your doorstep. Have no fear, you will not fail to hear me when I have need for your services."

I nodded. "I came tonight to introduce myself, but also to ask you a question. You said you can see my thoughts—do you know what I want to ask you?"

Pausing, she closed her eyes and the entrance of the Veil flared to life. Then we were standing back in the mausoleum and Bryan and Peggin rushed forward to my side, skirting Penelope as best as they could. Penelope motioned to the plinth holding the chalice. In front of it, a mist appeared, and then in the midst of it, a scene. A steep ravine, alongside a narrow road, led down to a creek at the distant bottom. The scene swooped down into the thicket near the side of the water. And there, a faint glow caught my attention. I squinted, leaning forward, and saw a mound of moss-covered dirt. Then the scene swept up again to the top of the ravine, where a tree overlooked the edge.

Peggin gasped at the same time I recognized what tree it was. "The Tree of Skulls," she whispered from behind me.

I nodded. I knew where that tree was, and *what* it was—a terrifying reminder of the cruelty of people, and the violence within the soul of a man who had gone so far beyond the boundaries of humanity that he had forfeited all rights to the claim.

"The Tree of Skulls," I echoed back. And then the Crow Man's words came filtering back. *She waits in the ravine, for you to find her. Screaming skulls still lurk beneath long roots that dig deep into the ground.* "Is that . . . where . . ."

"Go. Seek. You will find what you look for. When you do, we can set her to rest." With that, Penelope faded away.

I raised my other hand to her, feeling oddly sad to see her go. All the fear I'd had of meeting her had drained away, and now I wanted to know more about her—to talk to her longer.

We hurried out to the parking lot, where I took the passenger seat, Peggin climbed in back, and Bryan began to drive. As we sped through the evening, passing a few cars, we were silent. I was so wound up inside that I had no clue what to say, and Peggin and Bryan seemed to pick up my mood.

We drove north on Bramblewood Way until it forked into Crescent Drive. Taking a left, we skirted the edge of Bramblewood Thicket until we came to the turn onto Whisper Hollow Way. Bryan took another left, and then, a few minutes later, a left onto Peninsula Drive. Ten minutes later, we eased into a turnout leading to the Tree of Skulls.

I stared at the trail that led into the woods. Beside the trail head, a large information board, erected by the city council, related the history of this place, and of the Tree of Skulls. I stared at the wooden structure. So much death. So much destruction took place here.

Bryan edged forward, resting his arm around my waist. "Are you sure you're up to this?"

I nodded. "I have to . . . this is too important to walk away from. Maybe . . . I'll finally get some closure. The past is coming back to haunt me, and I have to be prepared."

Peggin was holding my bag of tools. "I brought this, in case you need it."

Flashing her a grateful smile, I turned to the trail. "I guess there's nothing left to do but go in." Bryan offered to take the lead, but I shook my head. This was my job now—this was my fight. The moment we stepped onto the path, out of the parking area, I realized I couldn't see a damned thing. "Flashlight, anybody?"

"Got it." Bryan pulled out a flashlight and aimed it in front of me, so that we could all see the path.

The trail wound through the woodland, into the depths of the undergrowth. Here the forest was thick, dense with huckleberry and bracken, with fern and brambles and tall stands of skunk cabbage. The peninsula was a temperate rain forest, one of only a few in the North American hemisphere, and—in the depths of the Olympic Peninsula—there were places where it rained an average of 140 inches per year. Though we weren't in the Hoh rain forest proper, we were right in the shadow of it, and our forest mirrored its mother.

Conifers towered in the night sky, silent sentinels watching over the land. Red cedar, spruce, Douglas fir, and hemlock—they watched over the land, dripping with moss. Long veils of it trailed off the branches, creating beards of green on the ancient fathers of the forest. The trunks were covered with the soft mossy growths, and mushrooms jutted out from the sides of the trees. The scent was old and decaying, yet vibrant with life. When they toppled—from age or lightning strike or windstorm—they turned into nurselogs, providing a home for wildlife and insects as they decayed.

To the sides of the trail, waist-high ferns created a carpet of delicate fronds, lacy, and yet the leaves could be sharp when you brushed against them. Interspersed among the ferns were the huckleberry bushes—they were almost bare for the season, losing their leaves—and salmon berries, and brambles from the ever-present blackberries that were all so endemic no one would ever be able to root them out. Salal, and Oregon grape with its glossy leaves, edged the trail, the evergreen bushes remaining vibrant even into the winter months.

I hoped we could avoid the stinging nettle—of all the plants in the forest, it was the most aggressive around here.

While poison ivy and poison oak were common enough, stinging nettle was by far one of the most unwelcome visitors in the forest. The species found in the Pacific Northwest had nasty stinging hairs and hurt like hell. While some people swore by it for herbal medicine, I wasn't about to give it a try. I had a strong allergic reaction to it, and the welts that rose from even lightly brushing the leaves were highly painful and unpleasant.

The trail itself was fairly even, though ridden with tree roots that crossed the path, and pebbles and a few rocks buried so firmly that there would be no getting them out. As I pushed forward into the woods, a sense of dread began to steal over me. We continued along for about fifteen minutes, moving deeper and deeper into the thicket, and then, as the pathway began to open up, I stopped. I was standing at the edge of a circular meadow—one that was overgrown but not horribly so. The city kept it up, after a fashion, because of what had happened here. We had arrived. And maybe now we would find out what happened to my mother.

A signboard loomed to my left side, and Bryan flashed the light on it.

TREE OF SKULLS MEMORIAL PARK

# CHAPTER 14

⌒

I n the center of the meadow, which was ringed with benches, stood an elderberry tree. Ancient and twisted, whether it had been planted or just sprung up on its own, I doubted anybody would ever know. It was old, very old, and the thick trunk was rife with limbs reaching out every which way, black against the stormy sky. A faint glow hummed from the core of the tree and I realized that I was seeing its spirit.

"Elderberry . . . sacred to the Dagda." Bryan let out a hushed breath.

"Dagda . . . Ivy said he's the consort to the Morrígan."

"So he is. This is a faerie tree, too. Never, ever cut wood from this tree."

I nodded. Even from here I could sense the power it held within its core. And . . . there was something more. I glanced around the clearing. Memorial markers were spaced evenly around the base of the trunk. As I glanced around the meadow, misty shapes wandered through the field. They wouldn't hurt us, not these spirits. For they were the Mournful dead who had been left here, to rot and hide in the soil beneath the tree.

"The tree is guarding the spirits."

"I believe it. No wonder Nels ended up strung up here."
Bryan shook his head. "Never mess with the elder spirits of
the world, be they tree or rock or water."

Thirteen women had died at the hands of Jericho Nels, a
serial killer. He had kidnapped the women, tortured and raped
them, and then decapitated them. After dumping their bodies
elsewhere, he brought their heads to the base of the tree and
buried them. Police discovered the grisly burial site when a
hiker stumbled over one of the skulls—his dog sniffed it out
and found it. Though police set up a stakeout, they weren't
able to catch Jericho. But one night, shortly after the heads
had been discovered, somehow the murderer ended up hanging from the tree. Jericho was found with thin branches
wrapped around his neck—coiling tight as if the tree had
come to life and strangled him. The police discovered evidence in his house to prove he had been the serial killer.
Common belief was that the spirits of his victims had wreaked
their revenge on him, but—staring at the tree—I thought
maybe the tree itself had played a part in his execution.

A few months later, the city had discussed cutting down
the tree, but town opinion overruled the idea, and so the entire
area was turned into a memorial park to commemorate the
murdered victims. The trunk, though, seemed to have faces
embedded in the gnarls and burls—thirteen of them, if you
counted. A few people came here to picnic or to walk in silence
and remember the women who had lost their lives, but like a
lot of areas around Whisper Hollow, the Tree of Skulls wasn't
exactly the most lighthearted of places for gatherings.

A sudden shimmer caught my eye. I turned to see a wolf
spirit standing there, near the back side of the meadow. He
whimpered, faintly, and turned to stare through the foliage.

"What is that?" Peggin took a step closer to me.

"I think . . ." I closed my eyes and reached out. There
was nothing dangerous about the spirit. In fact, it felt familiar. "I think we've got ourselves a guide."

Bryan slowly nodded. "Yes, he is . . . was . . . a shapeshifter. I recognize his nature."

"Do we follow him, then?" Peggin shivered. "I've never been out here at night and I'm not thrilled about the experience. Honestly, when I think about it, we live in the most dismal town."

"Not dismal, just haunted. And yes, we follow him. It will be all right." I reached up to clasp my grandmother's pentacle, which was hanging around my neck, and knew I was right. I started off, following the wolf spirit, Bryan behind me.

"Right. Haunted, then." Peggin hurried forward, trying to keep up with us. "Do you know who sent the wolf spirit?"

"I haven't stopped to think about it, actually. I guess Penelope. That stands to reason, doesn't it?"

Bryan shook his head. "I don't know, to be honest." He paused, staring at the edge of the meadow. "The ravine—the one she showed us."

I hushed. Slowly, making sure we weren't dangerously close to tripping over any sudden drop-offs near the mouth of the ravine, I inched forward until I was standing right next to the wolf spirit. He looked up at me, his eyes soft and glowing, and nudged my hand. I felt only a soft wind against the back of my fingers, but it was enough to sense a deep, caring energy behind the touch. The wolf was a friend—whoever he was. He began to pick his way down the side of the bluff, glancing over his shoulder, inviting us to follow.

"Whatever he's showing us is at the bottom. The mound by the creek—there's something there that he wants to see." I contemplated the descent. In the dark it was almost impossible to see how stable the footing would be. "Just how easy is it going to be to get down there?"

Bryan knelt, testing the edge. "With all the rain, it could be dangerous. Let me go first. Peggin—you stay up here and keep an eye out. You have your phone?"

She nodded. "Yeah, though I'm not keen on staying alone in the dark. I've got protection against human miscreants, but not all that much against the ghostly kind." She opened her purse and pulled out something I never expected her to be holding—a handgun.

"What the hell? When did you start packing?" The Peggin I had known was an anti-gun crusader.

"When I got mugged a few years back. I never told you because I didn't want you to worry about me. A girl has to learn how to take care of herself, so I took shooting classes and bought myself a gun. I'm a damned good aim, if I say so myself." She sounded absolutely proud of herself.

I stared at the weapon in her hands. It looked so out of place, but then Peggin was never one to take anything lying down and if somebody had actually managed to mug her, they'd better not try again. She'd find one way or another to put a stop to it. "What kind is that?"

"Nine-millimeter Sig Sauer. I like the heft it has in my hands." She made sure the safety was on, then turned her back to the ravine. "I'll keep watch. But be as quick as you can. I'm not afraid of human freak shows, but this meadow . . . it reeks of death and decay. Nels saw to that years ago."

Bryan was staring at her with an amused expression playing over his face. "We'll be quick. Kerris, let me start down. Is there a stick around here you can use to balance yourself with?"

I nodded—finding a loose walking stick in these parts was as easy as finding a patch of mold. It simply was part and parcel of the general area. I nosed around in the nearby bushes and a moment later had found a sturdy enough branch that would help me tap my way down the side of the ravine.

Bryan started out, one foot at a time, and I followed him cautiously, trying to stay in the trail of his footsteps. He used the close-growing trees to balance himself, testing each step as he went. The wolf spirit slowly inched down in front of him, occasionally looking back to make sure we were following. He seemed to be sniffing out the best route for us to take. I used one hand to brace against the tree trunks, and with the other I carried the stick, using it to tap in front of me and make certain I didn't land in any spot that might twist my ankle.

We worked our way down, slowly, Bryan flashing the light as he went, first in front of him, then behind to light my way while he paused for me to catch up. And so we went, slowly, pushing through the undergrowth. I wasn't used to tromping around the woods—I was used to city streets, and while I'd had my fill of the concrete maze that Seattle had been, I also wasn't exactly in the greatest shape to tackle a hike like this in the dark. I made up my mind to find a gym and start training tomorrow. Some time on the treadmill wouldn't kill me, and it could only help me run faster when a ghost or toxic mist decided to head my way.

"This isn't my idea of a good time," I said, leaning against a rather large fir to catch my breath.

Bryan laughed. "Mine either—don't worry, I won't drag you out hiking on a date."

"And I won't make you come shopping with me unless you want to . . ." I huffed my way through a particularly treacherous patch of slick undergrowth, almost going down. Slamming into the tree next to me was the only thing that kept me from faceplanting on the ground. "How much longer till we hit the bottom? The ravine didn't look this steep at the top."

"I like to shop as long as it's in a bookstore, and we're almost there, I think. Are you okay?" He flashed the light on me. "You're bleeding."

I touched my forehead where I'd scraped along the bark of the trunk. "I'm okay—it's just a surface wound." At that moment, he stepped to the side and held out his hand. I reached for it and two steps later, I was on the flat surface of the ground, next to a small creek running through the narrow ravine. I looked up as he flashed the light toward the top. It didn't look all that high, but it had proven steeper than I had first thought.

The wolf spirit nosed around and then, just a few feet away, stopped and whined, pawing at the ground at the base of a small bush. There was the mound we had seen. A funny sensation formed in my stomach and I suddenly wanted to be anywhere but here—even back with Penelope. Even fighting the Shadow Man. There was something here I didn't want to see, and a sharp pang of fear stabbed me in the gut.

Bryan glanced at the wolf spirit, then at me as he knelt down beside the mound of dirt. "I should have brought something to dig with," he said. But the wolf spirit made digging motions and Bryan snapped his fingers. "Of course. Kerris, hold the light."

He handed me the flashlight and transformed into his wolf shape. I couldn't take my eyes off the riveting white coat that fluttered in the wind. He was as beautiful in animal form as he was in human, and I wanted to kneel down and wrap my arms around him, to burrow my head in that soft, plush fur.

But he set to digging then, furious and fast, his front feet kicking dirt out behind him. Another few moments and he stopped, backing away. With a whimper, he looked up at me and I could see the anxiety in those brilliant eyes of his. I flashed the light to the hole and my heart skipped a beat. Bones . . . there were bones in the hole beneath the mound. An arm was protruding—the left hand jogged loose by Bryan's digging. I walked past him as he shifted back into two-legged form and knelt down by the skeleton. As I slowly reached for the hand, the light caught hold of something glittering.

On the ring finger was a ring—what looked to be an intricately filigreed rose gold band, wrapped around a center diamond that had to be a half carat in size. I softly reached out and touched the metal. *Avery's ring.* This was the ring my father had given my mother. That he had asked her to marry him with. And that meant . . .

"Tamil." My voice caught in my throat. "This is my mother, isn't it?" I turned to the wolf spirit. He whined, and then he transformed, too, like Bryan had, into a man standing tall and proud. I recognized him from the photograph my grandmother had given me. Avery—the wolf spirit was Avery.

"You're my father, aren't you? And you were Tamil's shapeshifter—you were her mate."

He nodded and then sadly looked at the skeleton, and in the blink of an eye, he vanished, and Bryan and I were alone with the remains of my mother.

*   *   *

It was a blur from there. Somehow, Bryan got me back up the ravine and bundled into the car with Peggin. He called the police and we sat there, waiting, till the squad car rolled in. A woman, Hispanic and pretty, with a no-nonsense manner, had arrived, along with a tall all-American jock-boy type. I recognized both of them from high school, though I wouldn't have been able to pin names on them if they hadn't introduced themselves. Sophia Castillo—no wonder I hadn't recognized the name. Her maiden name had been Lopez. And Frank O'Conner, her sergeant. He had been a couple of years behind me in school.

We told them what happened. Here, in Whisper Hollow, there was no hemming and hawing over ghosts or telling them that I was the spirit shaman or that we had been to meet Penelope. They knew. A number of people tried to ignore the things that went on, but the cops knew on an all-too-intimate basis that Whisper Hollow held dark secrets.

Sophia radioed in for a crew. "You say you think this is your mother?"

"I'm sure of it. The ring on her finger—my grandmother, Ivy Primrose described it to me. She gave it to her son Avery, to give to my mother." I stopped, turning to Bryan, suddenly realizing just what this meant. "That means Avery must be dead, too. If his spirit guided us to her, then he has to be dead."

Sophia jotted that down, too. "Didn't your father go missing a few years before your mother? But I thought I remember you telling me he was on a secret mission for the government."

"Children's tales . . . what my grandmother told me to keep me from feeling abandoned. Ivy told me the truth. Avery vanished. My grandfather had told me that my father abandoned my mother when he found out she was pregnant. I guess he didn't go far." I stared at the trailhead. "The Tree of Skulls . . . the serial killer who murdered all those women . . ."

"He died long before your mother was born. He was found hanging on the tree in . . ." Sophia glanced back at Frank. "What was it, Frank?"

"I think it was 1956."

"Right—back in fifty-six. Jericho Nels couldn't have killed your mother because she wasn't even born yet." She brushed back a stray hair that had fallen out of the sleek ponytail she wore. She was a short woman, far shorter than I was, but she looked sturdy and serene, good qualities to have for a chief of police. "I'm sorry to ask you this, but do you have any idea of who might have wanted to hurt your mother? I know you were only three, but . . ."

I held her gaze, feeling some spark of kinship. She policed the streets and I was here to police the spiritual byways. "Yeah, I think so. Check into my grandfather Duvall's goings-on. He knew about this. In fact, I have something at the house you're going to want to check out. I was going to contact you about it but haven't had the chance yet." I told her about the trunk and the key in my grandfather's dresser. "I suspect Duvall might have killed her and I think he had help."

Sophia's eyes flared but she remained silent, simply wrote down what I told her. After a few minutes, the coroner and search-and-rescue crew got there. "I have to go get the guys organized. If you want to stick around, you're welcome to, but it's probably going to take the rest of the night. We have to move slowly. I think you should go home and rest. I'll call you in the morning when we know more."

I nodded. While I wanted to stay, the concept of sitting in the car in the pouring rain, waiting for them to dig up my mother's remains, felt all too grisly. I was tired. I was cold. And I felt numb all over again. I thanked her.

"I think I will go home. Please do call me first thing tomorrow. I'd say nice to meet you again, but the circumstances . . ."

She let out a soft, low laugh that made me want to hear it again. "No problem, Kerris. Bryan, get her home and see that she has a drink and some food. Even though you didn't expect to ever see her again, finding what are likely your mother's remains is bound to hit you on a gut level. Go home, Kerris. Rest. Eat. And sleep."

As we drove off, Bryan navigating while I rested in the

passenger's seat, I glanced out the window. There, watching over the activity, was the spirit of my father—in wolf form—standing guard over his love one last time.

Peggin hugged me as she stood next to her car. "Are you sure you don't need me to come in? I can stay."

I shook my head. "No, I'll call you tomorrow. You have work and I don't want you to be late. It's late enough as it is. Text me when you make it home, though. I know you don't live far, but I want to make certain you're okay."

She nodded, then—with a wave to Bryan—slid into her car and took off. Bryan walked me inside, taking my key from me to unlock the door. I was grateful we'd left the lights on—I didn't want the Ankou having any chance of returning and harming the cats when I wasn't around.

Exhausted, feeling grimy and soaked, I stood in the middle of the living room. I had always thought that once I found out what happened to my mother, I'd have closure. That I'd be able to move on, to shut the door on the past, but all it had done was to bring up more questions than I had answers for. But now, I felt numb. I wasn't sure if I wanted to cry or just to sleep.

Bryan pressed against my back and wrapped his arms around my shoulders, embracing me as he leaned down to kiss the top of my head. "You need a shower. You need a hot shower and some food and something warm to drink."

"Yeah, but I'm just so . . ."

"I know. I know how you feel. Come, let me help you."

He took my hand and led me into the bedroom. I was grateful that I had managed to make the bed and tidy up earlier. The new comforter gave a whole new feel to the room, and without my grandparents' things, it was beginning to feel like my own home. Bryan made sure the bathroom light was on, then returned to where I was standing in the middle of the room. He took my purse and the tool bag from me and set them on the vanity. Then he reached for my coat and peeled it off me. I let him, enjoying the sense of having someone take care of me. He grasped my left arm, raised it out to the side and over my head, then did the same with my right.

I felt my pulse quicken as he moved around in front of me and took hold of my sweater, slowly lifting it over my breasts. My skin prickled as the material—sodden and wet—pulled away from my flesh. My bra was plastered to my body as well, and he quietly moved to the back, unhooking it and then sliding first one strap down my arm, then the other. I shivered as his hand brushed across my breasts when he drew the bra away from my body, setting them to bounce free. My nipples stiffened, hardening as he reached out and lightly stroked them with his fingers.

"Stand still," he said. The command in his voice caught me by surprise, but I obeyed—I wanted to obey. To find out where he would take me next. "Raise your arms a little."

He reached around my waist from behind and undid the buttons on my jeans. Then, crossing to my front, he knelt and unzipped my boots, sliding them off as I lifted first my left foot, then my right. I watched him, shivering. Bryan glanced up at me, raised one eyebrow, and held his finger up to his lips. He slowly reached up, then began working my jeans down my legs. The tips of his fingers grazed my thighs and I shifted, gasping.

"I said to hold still, love." He helped me out of my jeans, one leg at a time, then tossed them aside. With one quick motion, he slid his hands under my panties and pulled them down my legs. I closed my eyes, almost embarrassed and yet so turned on I could barely stand it. He was staring at my crotch, then leaned forward to press a gentle kiss against my lower stomach. I wanted to move, to pull him up to me, but his words echoed in my head and I kept still as ice.

Bryan stood, walking around me, assessing me. "You have no idea how beautiful you are, do you, Kerris? Breathtaking. You have an inner glow that lights up your face and body." At that he stood back and held out his hand. "Time for a shower to warm you up."

I slipped my fingers into his and let him draw me into

the bathroom, where he turned on the shower and motioned for me to test the water. "Is that warm enough for you?"

I held my hand under the spray. The water cascaded over my knuckles, warm and inviting. Turning back to Bryan, I saw that he was stripping. He held my gaze as he yanked his shirt over his head, dropping it to the floor. The light of the bathroom shone through the rising mist from the hot shower, reflecting on his chest. His shoulders were broad, and he was muscled and strong. I liked that he had chest hair—not an overgrown amount, but enough to feel like I was snuggling against a man. Six-pack abs rippled out, narrowing into a tight waistline. A smile began to steal across my lips as I watched him reach for his belt buckle.

"You like to watch me?" The corners of his lips tilted into a teasing grin.

"I think I could get used to this, yes." My heart began to pound as he kicked his jeans off, revealing a pair of black Puma leisure briefs. The waistband rode low on his hips, covering what needed to be covered without the bulkiness of boxers. And yet they weren't cheesy—nothing about Bryan had struck me as tacky or cheesy or anything but complex and slightly exotic.

I couldn't tear my gaze away as he slipped his fingers beneath the waistband of his briefs and began to slide them down over his hips. As he tossed them on top of his jeans and straightened up, I restrained a whistle. But . . . *Oh Mama*, I was a lucky woman. Bryan was ready, erect and strong.

"In the shower, woman. Now." He pointed to the shower stall and I stepped in, with him following me. I started to say something but he murmured "hush" and spun me around so that he was behind me and I was facing the spray of lovely, soothing warm water. The chill began to seep out of my bones and the images of the past few hours started to fade in intensity as he reached around me for the shower gel. The next moment, I felt him lathering my back.

His hands were strong, but not rough, as he soaped up my back, sliding over my skin with a firm touch. I leaned against the side of the walk-in shower, resting my head against the wall, as he pushed close, his hands traveling down my body to sweep over the curve of my ass. He knelt, running the lather down first one leg, then the other, then came up between them with his fingers, teasing me— massaging my inner thighs, but never quite reaching their goal. I moaned as his hand cupped me, his arm sliding between my legs as he soaped my pubic hair.

"I'm glad you don't shave it all off. I want a woman who *feels* like a grown woman." His voice was thick and hoarse. But before I could squirm under his touch, he was standing again, pouring more gel into his hands. He turned me around, pushing me back against the shower wall. I was beginning to pant, breathing heavily as he rubbed the gel into a lather and began to massage my breasts.

The water was beating down on us, hot and steamy. My hair was plastered to my skin, to my face, as I let out a short cry when he pinched my nipple. Another moment and he took hold of the hand shower and unhooked it from the wall. He held it up to my breasts and turned it on, so that the spray of water hit me full force, stinging a little but also enlivening me. I gasped again, as he brought it down, grinning, to between my legs.

"Open them, love." He arched one eyebrow, cocking his head as I obeyed, standing spread-eagle. "Now put your hands on my shoulders."

I did, holding tight as he brought the hand spray down. The water pulsed against me, a wash of sensation dragging me under. He circled it, pressing it close to my body so the continual throbbing of the droplets against my sex made me ache. I tried to push hard against it, but he used his strength to keep me from pressing too close.

"Not yet . . . not yet." Laughing, he closed in, fastening his mouth against mine while he kept the body spray in place, driving me further under the wave of desire that threatened to overwhelm me. His kiss wasn't gentle this time, but demanding. I wrapped my arms around his neck, and he lifted me off the ground, bracing me against the wall.

Then the body spray stopped and the shower head took

over again, pulsating down on us full force as I wrapped my legs around his waist. With one finger, he encircled my clit, as his tongue probed between my lips, meeting my own. Just as I thought he was going to enter me, he pulled back, leaning against the wall with his hands, bearing down on me.

I opened my mouth but before I could ask why he had stopped, he sat me down on the built-in bench and pressed against me, his mouth gaining purchase on my breast. As he sucked, his tongue circling round and round the nipple, driving me into an aching mass of knots, he cupped the other breast with his free hand, massaging, pressing, kneading it hard enough to almost hurt.

I slid my hands around his back, stroking the broad muscles, wanting relief, feeling raw and exposed, and like a bomb, the fuse was burning but no explosion. Caught in the energy, I lunged forward and caught his shoulder, licking the fresh, clean skin and then biting him—not enough to draw blood but enough to make him growl. He brought his head up, gazing at me, and his eyes were clear crystal now, ringed with black—the way they had been when he was in wolf form. He let out a low snarl, but it was a challenge, love-play, not a warning.

"I'll meet your challenge and raise the ante." I pushed him back, so that he was on the floor of the shower. All the while the water was pouring down on us, a shower of warm rain. I straddled his calves. Then, leaning forward, I inched up his body, my breasts rubbing against him, till I was face-to-face with his cock.

He was strong, and wide, and I longed to feel that girth inside me, expanding me wide, stretching me out. I reached out and stroked the length of him with my fingers, grasping the head firmly. He gasped and propped himself up on his elbows, the water streaming down his face.

"I want you," I whispered. "I want you so bad I'm jumping out of my skin. But I need . . ." Damn it, how had we not thought of this in the beginning?

But he just nodded and within seconds was on his feet, stretching out his hand to help me up. Without a word, he

turned off the water and stepped out of the shower. He pulled
a bath sheet off the towel rack and wrapped me in it, then
bent over to retrieve something from the pocket of his jeans.
He held up two condoms, winking at me. I laughed, flushed
and hungry for him, my nerves on fire to the point of where
it felt like I'd burst if I didn't come.

I led him into my grandparents' bedroom. My bedroom
now, I thought. And what better way to christen it than . . .
I finished toweling my hair, then crawled onto the bed and
pushed down the comforter. As I stretched back on my side,
propping my head up with my hand, Bryan stood by the side
of the bed, his gaze running up and down my body.

I blushed. I was hardly model material, but the look in his
eyes said that to him, I was beautiful. I could read it as clearly
as I could read the book sitting on the nightstand. Never
wavering, he leaned down, put one knee on the bed, and began
to crawl toward me, a feral and passionate light flickering in
his eyes. Responding to the energy, I shivered, rolling onto
my hands and knees. He circled me, his face inches from
mine, the muscles of his arms rippling under his weight.

"You know that once I take you, you're *mine*? You know
that you will belong to me, and I to you. If we mate . . . once
we mate . . . our pact is binding, daughter of the Phantom
Queen. Shapeshifters mate for life, unless something horrible happens." His words sounded like a ritual, like a test.

My breasts rose and fell slowly as I felt him circling me
with his power, weaving a tapestry of magic around me. *The
magic of mating, the magic of the dead, the magic of those
who would guard against it, the magic of those who guarded
the guardians.* He was my sentinel, he was my protector. He
was my warrior, my soldier, a son of the Great Mother Shapeshifter.

"And you will be mine. Can you live with this? Can you
take on your duties and guard me?" Again, the words felt
like they were coming from some ancient rite, from days
long past and times that most thought long-buried, but which
were still as strong and vibrant and filled with life as the
most brilliant rainbow, as the most powerful storm.

"I will guard you, Kerris Fellwater, and love you, and make love to you. I will be your champion and your sentinel." And then, as he lunged for me, I felt my strength rise up and I met him midpoint, pushing him back, ripping one of the condoms out of his hand. I tore the package open with my teeth and, with firm fingers, slid it over the head of his erect penis, rolling it down, teasing as I went.

"You want my lips? You want me to taste you?"

He nodded. "Suck me, woman, suck me hard." And then he was on his back and I was sprawled out alongside him, my lips pressed against his cock, letting him force them open as he thrust up to meet me. I tightened them around the head, forming a seal as I worked the underside of the tip with my tongue. He moaned, fisting my hair in his hands as he shifted his hips. He thrust as I bobbed my head up and down, sliding my lips around the shaft of his cock, keeping the suction tight as I teased him with my tongue. His girth spread my lips into a perfect O and a warm flush rose up between my legs as I ached to take him inside me.

"Enough . . . or I'll come." He pulled away gently, groaning as he slid out of my mouth.

I was back on my hands and knees. "Now what?" I challenged him.

He answered by flipping me onto my back, where he slid between my legs, his breath warm against my sex. I cried out when he suddenly dipped, his tongue stroking my clit, worrying it round and round. He reached up, took hold of my hands as I reached for his head, and held them firmly to the bed at my sides. As he stroked me with his tongue, harder and faster, thought began to recede in the wash of the waves moving over me. He was grunting now, sucking and teething at me, nibbling to the point of pain and then pulling back to give me relief.

I let out a sharp cry as he sucked harder, almost biting me. The pressure was to a point where I could bear it no longer, and I arched my back as the dam broke and the cascade of release thundered through my body, a wave of loss and fear, of desire and hunger, of pain and joy all rolled into one massive tsunami. At first, it drove me under and I felt like I was choking, then I was suddenly riding atop it, watching from the crest as this new life I had entered took full hold. I gasped as Bryan was suddenly rising over me, and then with one sharp, dark thrust, he drove himself into me, plunging so deep and so hard that I once again succumbed to the rhythm our bodies made together.

"Come with me . . . come with me . . ." He was holding me down, his hands forcing my arms over my head, as he moved inside me, driving deeper and deeper with every swivel of his hips. His body hot against mine, his lips fastened to mine, he owned me—body and heart and soul— and for the first time in my life, I felt absolutely safe. As he leaned his head back, straining as a long, low growl echoed from the back of his throat, I surrendered to him, surrendered to the orgasm. Rising high over the scene, I capitulated to the reality that had become my life, and to the shapeshifter who had so quickly won my heart.

# CHAPTER 15

———

Morning came early, with the ring of my cell phone at six A.M. I blinked, wondering why I couldn't easily reach for the nightstand, and then realized that Bryan's arm was draped over my waist, holding me down. His soft breathing was comforting, and the smell of sex was heavy on the sheets, teasing me to stay beneath the covers, curled in the niche of his arms. But the night's events flashed through my mind and a swell of sadness filled my chest as I realized that there was no doubt left—my mother was dead.

The jangle of my phone startled me into action. My ring tone was "#1 Crush" by Garbage and I kept the volume turned up. I stretched my arm out, fighting the covers. Gabby popped out from beneath the sheet next to me. No wonder I'd been so warm, tucked between a fluffy Maine Coon and Bryan's heat. I managed to just barely touch the edge of the phone and coax it over to where I could wrap my fingers around it. I quickly tapped Answer before I even had managed to look at the caller ID.

"Kerris?" Ellia was on the line. "We're going to need you tonight. The Lady claimed someone this morning."

Fuck. Just what we needed. I eased Bryan's arm off my waist and pushed myself to a sitting position, sliding out from beneath the sheets. Shivering, as my nipples stiffened in the cool air, I moved into the bathroom so I wouldn't wake Bryan.

"Who? Anybody we know? And did they recover the victim?" It could be anybody, really. The Lady of the Lake took them all—young and old, male and female, healthy and sick. She was capricious, and she held on to the bodies as long as she could.

"No, but Pastor Jim saw her go in." She sighed. "Search and rescue are looking for the car, but you know the lake and you know the Lady. He recognized who it was, though— Tawny Marple. She was on her way to work, I think, and she just cut through the guardrail. Pastor Jim was down at the campground leading a tai chi class when he saw her plunge off the curve. He was able to confirm that she was alone in the car. That is, unless there was somebody asleep in the back. They checked with her husband and he said she'd headed out to work by herself. This was one of the few days she had to go in early, and so he volunteered to drop the kids of at school, thank heavens. He's devastated, to say the least."

I quickly ran through what I could remember from Lila's journal. "We'll need to start the ritual tonight, won't we? To ensure that she sleeps?"

"Yes. We have to go out to the point where she drove off the road into the water and begin the rites. We won't actually conclude the ceremony until later. We send her through the Veil after her memorial service, once her memory is laid to rest. If they can't find her body by then, we'll have to take a few other measures, so you'll need to bone up on whatever your grandmother did, because I know the songs she asked me to play in those circumstances, but I have no real clue of the process involved in her rituals. I'll be over around ten tonight, if you don't mind driving us. It's better if we do this in the dark."

The dark. Lovely, but it was part and parcel of what I had been born into. "I'm bringing Bryan. You know . . . Well, we'll talk later."

"I know. I knew who he was at the hospital. He will need to come with us as much as possible. He's your guardian and trust me, girl, you will need guarding." She paused. "Is it true? About your mother?"

I didn't want to answer, but finally— "Yes. We found her last night. She was buried in a ravine behind the Tree of Skulls. She was wearing the ring that Ivy gave to Avery. And . . . Avery . . . we saw his spirit there, guarding over her remains. So we're pretty sure he's dead. Please don't tell Ivy until I'm able to. I want to be the one to break it to her."

Ellia let out a soft sigh. "That's probably best. But this opens up a lot of questions . . ."

"I know, and we're on it. Sophia and her crew said they'd be searching for his body, too—they're looking around there because if whoever killed Avery also killed my mother, chances are the bodies were dumped near one another." I paused for a moment, thinking about the tangle we were in. "I think . . . well, I'll talk to you tonight. There's a lot I need to tell you, and a lot I need to ask you, but better we talk in person than over the phone."

"I've called an emergency meeting of the Crescent Moon Society. You and Bryan will also need to attend. I know it's on short notice, but we have to convene and discuss what's going on. We'll meet tomorrow night at eight P.M. At Niles Vandyke's garage."

I let out a long sigh. "I'll take a nap at some point today. And I'll tell Bryan. We'll be there." With that, I said a quiet good-bye and hung up.

I started to jump in the shower, but a sound from the bedroom made me peek out. There, sitting up in bed, was Bryan. His eyes were sparkling and he let out a low laugh.

"Before you get any ideas of lathering up, get your pretty ass back here in bed with me. I think last night deserves an encore, don't you?"

My body on sudden alert, I grinned back at him. "Yes sir, whatever you say. And for the record, yes, an encore is in order." The news about Tawny and the meeting could wait.

With that, I dove under the covers with him, and we discovered that we were as good together in the morning light as when we were exhausted, under the shadow of the night sky.

By the time we were clean and dressed, I had already decided what I wanted to do next. But first I put in a call to Sophia to see if the coroner had any answers. It was only seven A.M., but she was at her desk.

"I'm sorry, Kerris, but yes, we did a rush job—called in dental records in the middle of the night, given the circumstances. We've verified that the remains are those of your mother. Though it's hard to tell what killed her . . ."

"I'll bring down that jacket today. My guess is she was shot or something. There's blood all over it." I frowned. "What happens next?" I was used to dealing with people after they'd died, not their mortal remains.

"We'll examine the jacket, but I think we can release her remains to you. We may never know exactly how she died, but one thing's for sure—she didn't bury herself at the base of that tree. Which means, at the very least, someone covered up her death, whether it was accidental or deliberate. Speaking of which, we're hunting out in the woods to see if we can find . . . hold on . . . Frank just came in."

She put me on hold for a moment. "We found another body. Male. He was buried two trees over. I think . . . no, I can't make a call yet, not even tentative. But I will say this much: I want to pull your father's dental records and check for a match. And, Kerris, whatever the case, we have confirmed that this man's death was a homicide. He was bludgeoned from behind, enough to crush his skull."

I stared bleakly at the table. Sophia might not be able to confirm his identity yet, but I knew precisely who it was. In one fell swoop, they had confirmed I was an orphan. "Let me talk to Ivy. I'll do that first thing here."

"All right. Ask her to come down to the station, please. If we can verify where Avery went and who he was seeing the day he vanished, it might help us sort out this mess. I'm sorry, Kerris. It's bad enough you came home due to your grandparents dying, but now, your mother."

I let out a shaky breath. "Yeah, but I have the feeling it's going to get worse before it gets any better. Okay, Sophia. Thank you for letting me know. I'll talk to you later." And with that, I hung up and turned to Bryan, who was now busy at the stove, making pancakes.

"They found another body. A man. Murder victim. I know it's Avery. I know it's my father."

He nodded me over to his side, and I bleakly leaned against his shoulder as he stirred the batter. "What do you need to do?"

"I need to talk to Ivy as soon as we're done with breakfast. They might not have confirmed his identity yet, but I know it's him. And they want to talk to her, to try to place his whereabouts the day he vanished. Who he was with, that sort of thing. Oh, and Ellia called before you were awake. The Lady's claimed another victim. We have to visit the place where the car went over the guardrail tonight, in order to start the rites. That means that I devote some time this afternoon to read up in my grandmother's journal on what exactly it is I'm supposed to do." I turned to him. "You need to come with us—if you are truly going to be my guardian. Oh, by the way. Tomorrow night we have a meeting with the Crescent Moon Society."

"I can do that."

"And lastly . . ." I paused. Men generally shied away from the words I was about to say, but in our circumstance, I felt we needed to clarify where we stood. "We . . . I . . . need to talk about us."

"I told you last night, if we mated, you're mine. I'm your guardian and protector. I'm your mate. I thought that was settled." His eyes crinkled and I melted, just a little. Even neat and tidy, he looked just tousled enough that I wanted to reach up and bite his lip. I settled for reaching out and stroking my fingers down the back of his shirt.

"You're so yummy." I licked my lips, then pulled my hand away.

"You're pretty delicious yourself. How many pancakes do you want?"

"Three. I'm not used to men who can handle me seeing ghosts, let alone doing what I'm destined to do."

"Don't forget, I have my own destiny and it aligns with yours."

"True." I paused, thinking. "Why didn't you say something about being my guardian that first night when you ran in front of my car? Did you know about it then?"

"I told you about the dream I had, so yes, I knew." He poured more batter in the skillet and waited, spatula at the ready. "I didn't mention it because I wanted you to find out who I was. Saying, 'I'm your shapeshifter guardian and potentially your mate' when we first met might just have sounded a shade too close to creepy-stalker-dude." He laughed as he flipped the hotcakes.

I snorted. "Yeah, that's true enough. And I probably would have run like hell."

"Hell, I would have if I were you. I also knew that while shapeshifters are commonly chosen mates for the spirit shamans they protect, it doesn't always follow. And who was to say if we'd hit it off? I already went through one arranged marriage; I wasn't about to commit to another."

"Good point. I'd never want you to feel I expected you to be with me this way unless you wanted to. Being my guardian, if that's all you wanted, would be enough." Though in my heart, I knew it wouldn't be that easy. Not now, not after I'd been in his arms.

He paused. "The truth is, it would be my duty to protect you regardless of my feelings for you. But I had no clue if I'd want to share your bed. I'm no horndog. I really thought the decision would take longer, but, Kerris, even that first day when I pissed you off, I knew that I wanted to be with you." The tone in his voice was strained, a taut wire about ready to spring. "Now, I can't imagine it not working out this way."

He meant what he said. I could feel his hunger for me, his desire to be near me, and it was as great as my own. As the feeling settled in, I realized that I'd never, ever had anyone to protect me. I wasn't sure how it made me feel, either. Though there was a little part of me so used to making my own way that the thought of having a *guardian* chafed. I could take care of myself. I must have looked uncomfortable, because he picked up on it.

"Darling, having a guardian isn't like having a keeper. I'm not here to protect you from every scrape and bruise. I'm backup—I'm here to jump in if you need my help. I'm here to guard you so you can do your job right. I'm not here to turn you into the helpless little woman or the damsel in distress. You and I, along with Ellia, we all work as a team."

Nodding, I considered what he said. The truth was that I wasn't in Kansas anymore, my cats weren't named Toto, and this wasn't a fairy tale where happy endings were guaranteed. I was walking in dangerous territory. With the discovery of my mother's body, the danger had crossed from the spirit realm over to the physical. *Somebody* had put her in the ground, and while I knew that my grandfather had played a part in that, I was also smart enough to know that he probably had help. And that *help* might still be alive and kicking even though my grandfather was dead. If so, then whoever had helped him dispose of my mother wouldn't want to be found out.

I let out a soft sigh. "Thank you. Thank you for being here, for being who you are. Thank you for taking up the job as my protector. I really don't know what to expect, but I feel this thundercloud growing around me, and I'm waiting for the storm to break. It's nice to have someone I can trust. Two people, actually. I have Peggin, too." I still didn't know what to think about Ellia and Oriel and Ivy—they were on my side, it seemed, but something held me back.

He nodded, serious. "The post and duties of a spirit shaman go back long before anyone came to America, you know. The history goes back to the Morrígan herself. Other cultures have their own versions. My line comes from the Phantom

Queen, too. She's the Great Mother Shapeshifter to us, and most Celtic shapeshifters are descended from her spirit."

"You said most shapeshifters mate for life. What about Katrina?"

"When I was married to Katrina, I knew something wasn't right, but as I said before, I did my best to make it work. But in my heart I knew that something was going to happen. She wasn't the right one, though I gave the marriage everything I had. I just didn't expect her to die. I thought she'd leave me, or something like that." He flipped the pancakes onto two plates, added bacon, and handed me one.

An edge in his voice made me think he was harboring some sort of guilt. As I buttered my pancakes and doused them in a healthy dose of maple syrup, I asked, "Do you blame yourself for Katrina's death?"

That stopped him cold. He stood behind his chair, holding his breakfast like he didn't know what to do next. After a moment, he slowly set his dish down and then, still looking uncertain, slid into his chair. Picking up his knife, he stared at the tub of butter.

"Honestly? I think I do. I'm the one who got her pregnant. And yes, I know she wanted children, but . . . she was pregnant with *my* child. I don't blame our daughter, though I probably don't see her as often as I should, but . . . I guess mostly, I blame myself because secretly, I was a little relieved. Not that she was dead," he hurried to say. "But that the marriage was over."

I carefully kept my voice neutral, trying not to allow any nuance to color it. "Death is . . . often a tidy way to resolve something, regardless of how sad we may be. I was able to come home because my grandfather died. Would I have ever wished it on him? At the time, no. Now, maybe I have a different answer. But it afforded me the chance to return to Whisper Hollow."

Bryan nodded. "You understand. I cared about Katrina. I never would have wished pain or any suffering on her, but it freed me from having to deal with a divorce or anything messy, or causing a major falling-out with her family."

"Do they still keep in contact with you?" I forked a mouthful of the hotcakes, closing my eyes as I bit into their melty goodness. I preferred waffles, but Bryan sure knew his way around a kitchen, that much was for certain.

"No, they talk to Juliana quite a bit—she's their blood, too. They don't have much to say to me." He cast off the topic with a shrug. "But back to the matter at hand. I met you, and realized that we were meant to be together. I could feel the sparks from the beginning. I just had to let you make the decision about how much you wanted me in your life. As guardian . . . or as guardian and friend . . . or guardian and lover."

"Well, I think we've established which it is. This is new for me, too. I've had a lot of dates, a number of lovers, but I never really was close to any of them. There was always something holding me back. Whether it was the ghost of his mother warning me her son was pond scum, or the fact that he lived in his parents' basement and had no intention of making his way on his own. One after another, the parade of bad dates led me to eventually stop trying. For a while I wondered if it was me, but then I looked at the playing field and thought, no—when the toys are defective, I'm not the one with the problem other than that I tended to attract them."

I grimaced, remembering one particularly bad date, where the man had bluntly told me during dinner that I owed him a blow job to earn my pizza. That had been the last time I bothered going out.

"What are you thinking about?" Bryan laughed. "You're smirking in a most peculiar way."

I snorted and told him about the aborted date.

His eyes grew wide and he started to cough. "The guy actually said that?"

"Yep . . ." I put on my best swagga-voice. *"You know, girl, most chicks I go out with now offer to go Dutch, but I'd rather take it in trade. Your pretty pink lips on my dick. Suck me dry and we'll call it even."*

Bryan sprayed his coffee through his nose. "You have *got* to be kidding."

"I wish. But yeah, so I haven't dated much the past couple of years." I leaned back, finishing the last bite of my breakfast. "This was good." I wanted to forget about everything that had gone on the past couple of days and just go hibernate in the bedroom with him, but we both had things to do. I glanced at the clock. "I'd better go talk to Ivy, as much as I don't want to."

But the phone rang before I could say a word. I glanced at the caller ID. Aidan. Hurrying to answer, I almost spilled the last of my juice. "Hello? Aidan?"

"Kerris, I'm just settling a few last-minute details. I'll be in Whisper Hollow tonight, around eleven. Are you still living in your grandmother's house?"

"Yes, I'll see you then. If I'm not back, then just wait for me." I paused, then said, "Please, be careful." As I hung up, I turned to Bryan. "My grandfather—my real grandfather—is coming back to Whisper Hollow. Maybe now I'll find out why Lila married Duvall and threw Aidan over."

"Just make certain he's safe. I'll be here, with you." Bryan headed to the door. "I've got work to do, too. So, tonight, then? I'll see you here about nine?"

I held his gaze. "Make it eight and we can have an encore of the encore."

With a lascivious grin, he nodded. "Eight, then. And I'll bring takeout."

With that, he was out the door, as I carried the plates to the sink.

Before heading over to Ivy's—she said she could see me at ten thirty—I decided to tackle my grandfather's office. So far, I'd been putting it off, but I had come up with an idea, and to do that, I thought that it would be better if I could make at least a general pass through the desk and see what I could uncover before heading out for the day.

The bookshelves were packed. I had to hand it to Duvall—he owned just about every classic written and they looked well read. After a quick perusal, I focused on his desk and filing cabinet. The desk was a large, heavy oak design, and his leather chair was the epitome of old money. A drafting table stood next to one window, and I closed my eyes for a moment, remembering him as he sat on the high stool in front of it, designing his plans. His buildings had been in high demand, he was good at what he did, and he had never been lacking for work.

As I turned on the banker's lamp, I stared at the tidy desktop. Everything in its place. A large blotter covered one half of the desk, and to the left of that—a laptop. Curious, I opened it up and pressed the power button. As the screen flickered to life, a password prompt came up. I had no clue what to type in, so I just left it for now. Maybe I could find a list of his passwords somewhere, or maybe I could find someone to hack into it. I had the feeling he had plenty to hide, and obviously he didn't want my grandmother getting into it. Just as she had hidden her tools and journal from him.

I turned my attention to the drawers. Pens, Post-it notes, office supplies of one type or another . . . the usual things you'd expect to find filled the top three drawers. The bottom left drawer was locked, however. There had been a key in the center drawer, so I tried it, and bingo—the left drawer opened to reveal a handgun in a holster. I cautiously withdrew it. I knew how to use a gun, but I also knew enough to respect them. As I withdrew it from the holster, I saw that it wasn't loaded. A magazine was near where the gun had been, and it did have bullets in it. The gun looked clean, though. I had a feeling Duvall hadn't just left it there to mildew. He'd used it, whether in target practice or something more sinister. I made sure the safety was on and packed it up along with the ammo to drop off at the police station; maybe they could match it to the bullet hole in Tamil's jacket.

There wasn't much else in the drawer, so I turned to the right bottom drawer. It, too, was locked, but the same key didn't open it. There weren't any other keys in the other drawers, so I had to assume that my grandfather either hid it or kept it with him, and if he had kept it with him, it was probably at the bottom of the lake.

I jiggled the drawer, wondering if I could pick the thing. I had never formally learned how to pick a lock, but hell, it couldn't be that hard, could it? I dashed into the kitchen, found a couple of knives and a screwdriver, and returned to the den. There, after a bit of maneuvering and finally out-right bludgeoning, I managed to pop open the drawer.

Inside, a row of hanging files held several folders. As I began going through them, I noticed that several were old and dusty, while others were fairly new. I glanced at the tabs. They were neatly labeled, several with names I didn't recognize. As I peeked in the files, I saw they were some-thing to do with his business. I set those aside. But behind those were three thick binders, each labeled *Cú Chulainn's Hounds*. One was labeled *Meetings*, one *Members*. The third was labeled *Information*.

*Bingo!*

I settled into his chair and opened the first binder. Mem-ber lists, each dated with a year, went back to 1875—though the older reports looked like they had been photocopied and typed. I doubted they were the original lists. There was a section that appeared to be dossiers on various members, and a section for "members emeritus" . . . which I had the distinct feeling meant they had died, not resigned. This was one group that I'd lay odds on was nigh impossible to leave on a friendly basis.

The *Meetings* binder contained memos detailing minutes of various meetings. It was jammed and appeared to go back to 1872—just like the member lists. Again, probably second-generation photocopies. As for the third binder, it was stuffed with notes and newspaper clippings. There was no way in hell I could get through this before I left to visit Ivy.

I pushed the binders to the side. Along with my grand-mother's diaries, I had more than enough to read for several weeks. Then I returned to the drawer. One last notebook caught my eye. It was an expense ledger. I opened it and saw a listing of names that looked familiar . . . a quick cross-check proved me right. They were all members of the Cú Chulainn group. Every page was for a different month, and it looked like this ledger had been started about seven years ago, from the date on the first page. I flipped to the second to last, dated September 30. Each name was listed with an amount next to it. Each column had a place for a check mark, and all the names had been checked. The last page was written out for October 31, and all the names were there, along with the amounts, but no checks. They hadn't had their meeting yet.

October 31. That was coming up in a week or so. And that meant the group was going to remember about these binders and want them back, and I didn't want them to find them. I was surprised they hadn't broken in to get them yet, but ten to one, the thought had escaped their notice. But come their next meeting, it sure as hell wouldn't.

I glanced around, trying to figure out where I could hide them where they wouldn't be found. Then it hit me. *My grandmother's secret room.* I glanced back in the ledger to make sure of something, then ran the binders and the ledger upstairs and tucked them neatly out of sight.

That done, I shrugged into my jacket. It was time to hit the road.

After a quick stop at the police station, where I dropped off Tamil's jacket, showing Sophia the bullet hole, and the gun I had found, and picked up my mother's ring, I stood in front of Ivy's door. Hesitating before ringing the bell, I ran through ways to start the conversation.

Ivy must have been waiting because she opened the door before I could gather my thoughts. She took one look at my face and bustled me inside. "What's happened?"

I worried my lip, not knowing how to put it. I was usually a little too blunt, a little too direct, but I'd never been in this sort of situation before and I wasn't sure how to handle it. Finally, I reached for her hand and pressed the ring into her palm.

She looked at it for a moment, her eyes growing wide, and then wordlessly, she opened her arms. I moved into her embrace, resting my head against her shoulder.

"I'm sorry," I whispered. "We found my mother, and I think we found Avery's body, too."

Ivy pressed a soft kiss on my forehead. She let out a long breath and stood back, a sad smile on her face. "I've been both hoping for and dreading this day. Come in, tell me what happened."

Over coffee, I ran down the events. "They aren't sure yet if it's Avery—it might not be, but Sophia promised to call me as soon as she knows. She'll probably call you, too. I asked her to let me warn you first, to prepare you."

She paused for a moment, gazing out the window. Then—"I think you're right. My Avery has been found. He's coming home at last." She held the ring up to the light. I had stopped at the jewelry store and had it cleaned before bringing it back, not wanting the dirt that had clung to it all those years to be a silent reminder. "This is yours, my dear. I want you to have it. Your mother would have passed it down to you if she had lived." I started to shake my head, but Ivy pushed the ring across the table. "I mean it. And someday, when we have more time, I will tell you about Avery's grandmother. She was a pistol, she was."

Her cell rang, and she glanced at it, then looked back at me. "Sophia." She stood up and moved to the kitchen window with her phone, staring out into her backyard.

I held up the ring. It fit perfectly as I slid it onto my right-hand ring finger. As I studied the sparkling stone, not wanting to intrude on Ivy's conversation, her murmured voice rose and fell, and I knew that we had been right. I wasn't trying to eavesdrop but, even in the big old country kitchen, it was impossible not to hear what she was saying.

"Yes, she's here right now and she warned me that this might be coming. I'll come in right away. Is there any way we might be able to figure out who killed him? I know it's a cold case—an old one—but . . ." A pause, then— "I understand. Thank you. Yes, I'll make arrangements and have them ready when you release his remains." Another moment. "Thanks, Sophia. At least my boy's come home to rest."

As she turned back to the table, I looked up to see the

tears in her eyes and I knew exactly how she felt. It was one thing to suspect someone you loved might be dead; it was another to have it confirmed. And yet . . . there was a sense of closure when you found out that someone didn't abandon you, or run away, but had been forcefully taken.

"Murder. He was murdered. A crushing blow to the head. With a case this old, it's highly unlikely they'll find out for sure, but . . ." She slowly returned to her seat. "Whoever killed your mother probably killed my Avery, too. Why else would they be buried so close together?" She paused. Then, "Can you talk to their spirits? Can you find out who did this? You saw Avery in his shifter form. If we had a séance, could you contact both of them? Maybe find out the truth?"

That was one question I always dreaded hearing. I wasn't a medium—I was a spirit shaman. While I could speak with ghosts, it wasn't my place to call them out of their graves. Of course, neither Avery nor Tamil was resting. But regardless, talking to spirits didn't always work like people thought it did. Invoking the spirits wasn't the same thing as picking up the phone and calling for a delivery. And once you invoked the dead, getting rid of them was no simple matter.

"Let me try a few other things first. I have a couple leads I want to check out. Ones that might actually tie into some of the worries Ellia, Oriel, and you have about the escalating spiritual activity around the town." I thought about telling her Aidan was returning to town, but decided to wait for a bit. I needed to talk to him first—get a good gauge on his personality.

I glanced at the clock. It was eleven A.M., and time for me to put the first part of my idea into action. "Why don't you go talk to Sophia. I'm going to head out for a bit. But I'll keep you in the loop. I don't mean to sound so nebulous, but I just don't want to cause any fallout until I know if I'm on the right track."

She nodded. "I trust you. You're Lila's granddaughter, and you have a good head on your shoulders. Meanwhile, I'll do as you suggest." She pushed back her chair. "Kerris, what do you think about burying your mother and Avery in adjoining graves? They loved each other so much."

I smiled at that. "I think . . . they would like that. But my mother will be buried in a simple box. She spent so much time in the bare ground . . . I don't want to preserve her remains forever—she needs to go back to the earth for good, but this time, remembered."

Ivy nodded. "That works for me. I'll have to call Roger, to tell him. We haven't talked in years. All right, I'll see you later—at the Crescent Moon Society's meeting tomorrow night, if not before. And love, I'm sorry. I lost a son, but in one swoop, you lost your mother and father." She hugged me again, and then I set out.

# CHAPTER 16

⟋

The Peninsula Hotel was on Whistle Hollow Way N, shortly after it intersected Cairn Street—the street leading into town from the highway. Easy access for tourists, for one thing. The hotel was also across from the thicket where we had found Tamil and Avery's bodies. I gazed at the thick copse . . . the Tree of Skulls had poisoned the land there, but it was a good tourist attraction, even if a gory one, and it made sense to build the hotel near one of the more notorious murder sites in the area.

The hotel itself was a three-story building, modern enough to attract those angling for a little luxury, and large enough to accommodate a small conference and plenty of tourists in summer. I pulled into the lot, parking close to the front door. There were a few scattered cars around, but this late in the season there wouldn't be too many tourists touring the peninsula. As I pushed through the doors, I ran through my plans. Granted, they weren't the best-laid ones, but at this point, I just wanted to meet the man who had palled around with my grandfather and get a feel for him.

The Peninsula Hotel was even nicer inside than out. Not

five-star, but definitely not your freeway-exit penny-saver hotel. I headed over to the lobby desk. A man in his fifties stood behind the counter, and I laid my odds it was Leon Edgewater, Heathrow's son.

He glanced up at me briefly and did a double take. "May I help you?"

I wondered what had caused the reaction. "Hi, I'm Kerris Fellwater. I was wondering if I could talk to Heathrow Edgewater, the owner of the hotel? He knew my grandfather, Duvall."

Again, a long blink, and then Leon slowly set down his pen. "Let me see if he's available." He turned and exited through a door behind him.

I glanced around the lobby. The hotel was clean and neat. If I had just been passing through, it would seem a welcoming stop. A moment later, the door opened again and this time an older version of Leon walked up to the desk. He cocked his head, staring at me, a cold smile on his face. I had the distinct feeling that I was in the presence of a snake or some such creature whom I shouldn't turn my back on.

"Welcome to the Peninsula Hotel. So, you're Duvall's granddaughter?" The voice didn't lend me any sense of security, either. In fact, as he spoke, a chill washed over me. Heathrow was a short, lean man, but he wore his suit and tie well, and looked all too precise and tidy. He was the sort of man who let no detail escape his attention.

*Listen to what he says but listen more to what is said below the surface . . .*

The whisper sounded like the Crow Man, and I had to stop myself from nodding in agreement. Heathrow Edgewater wasn't to be trusted, and I needed to keep my wits about me while talking to him.

I forced a smile to my lips. "Yes, I'm just back in town. I'm just trying to piece together the jumble my grandparents left for me. In doing so, I found your name, along with several others, in a ledger on my grandfather's desk. I wasn't sure if he owed you any money, or had any business dealings with you that I should know about." I knew I was playing with fire, but I had to gauge his reaction.

His eyes narrowed and I noticed a stiffening around his shoulders. It was then that I heard something—a soft whisper—and I glanced to his right shoulder where a mist was forming. He seemed unaware of it, same as his son. Leon was ostensibly poring over some form or other, but I could tell he was actually listening very closely to the conversation.

I tried to watch the mist without being obvious. This was the way it usually worked for me. I'd meet someone, and then if there was a spirit tied to them, I'd see the spirit. If they had something to tell me, they'd start jabbering in my ears.

"Ledger? What kind of ledger?" Eyes glittering, he leaned across the counter, giving me better access to see whoever it was trying to materialize behind him.

"Oh, just some accounting ledger. Looks like my grand-father made a series of small loans or something to a number of people. The ledger goes back a long ways, but I flipped to the end and saw your name, along with a number of others, and an amount listed next to each, unchecked for October. I was driving past the hotel and thought I'd duck in to ask about it." I tried to sound offhand, though I wasn't all that good at bluffing.

Meanwhile, the spirit took shape behind his shoulder. I almost lost it when I realized that my mother was standing there. She held her fingers to her lips but then jerked her head toward Heathrow. I forced myself to stand still and not react.

Heathrow let out a soft sound, almost a grunt. "Bowling lodge fees. Just bring me the ledger and I'll take over. I'm sorry about your grandparents, Kerris. Their loss is a real blow to the community." He rested his hands on the counter. "So, you've moved back to stay?"

The question was casual; the intent behind it was not. He was fishing.

I nodded. "Now that Lila's dead, it's up to me to take over as spirit shaman."

Leon was staring at my hand, and Tamil's spirit franti-cally pointed toward her right ring finger, then to me. I suddenly remembered I was wearing her ring and quickly turned my hand to hide it before he could see it. If he had helped my grandfather murder my mother, I didn't want to chance him remembering the ring on her finger. "So nice to meet you. I'll run the ledger over later. I left it at a friend's by accident this morning, so I'll have to pick it up."

As he slowly raised his eyes to meet mine, I could tell the wheels were turning. He glanced over his shoulder, in the direction my mother was standing, and I held my breath but then he looked back at me and I relaxed. With a little luck, he was headblind and wouldn't take notice of any sign that she was watching over his shoulder.

"You wouldn't happen to know if there were any other . . . lodge documents along with that ledger, would you? Your grandfather was the president and he kept tabs on the group. I should really get them all from you so we can keep track."

"No, I didn't find any. Maybe he had them with him when the car went in the lake? They haven't found his body, you know, though my grandmother's washed up."

Again, a pause, and I began to get uncomfortable.

Finally, he gave me a faint sneer. "Perhaps so. Duvall had a habit of misplacing things, including his common sense at times." Before I could ask what he meant, he cleared his throat and leaned forward, too close for comfort. "I have to get back to work. Bring the ledger over as soon as you can and I'll take care of it. Nothing for you to worry your pretty little head over." He held out his hand.

I stared at it, debating. If I shook his hand, I chanced him seeing the ring, but I couldn't very well refuse. Quickly, using my thumb, I spun it around so that the diamond was facing my palm and all you could see was a rose gold band. I very lightly took his hand, then released it quickly so he wouldn't feel the stone pressing against his flesh. His fingers were cool and clammy. I wanted to wipe away the feel but forced myself to keep my hands away from the legs of my jeans. At that, Heathrow turned and headed back through the door, and the figure of my mother vanished.

Leon nodded good-bye, and I forced myself to calmly

walk out of the lobby. The moment I was out of sight of the huge lobby windows, I ran to my car and slid behind the wheel, locking the door. I pulled out my phone and dialed Bryan. He picked up immediately.

"I have a bad feeling. I just did something that may have been very stupid. Maybe it's just nerves, but . . . Are you home right now?"

"Yes, I generally work from home most days." A note of concern crept into his voice. "What's going on?"

"Can you go next door and keep an eye on the house? There's a spare key, hidden in a secret recess along the back wall near the second outlet down. I'll tell you when I get there, but I think I just may have triggered someone into wanting to break into my house."

"On my way," was all he said before hanging up.

I rested my head against the steering wheel. Why hadn't I thought through the possible ramifications before I stuck my nose in things? Then again, at least I knew for certain Heathrow was in on whatever had happened to my mother. Putting the car into drive, I headed out of the parking lot and home to tell Bryan what I had found out.

Peggin managed to get off work an hour early—apparently flu season was hitting late and Corbin had an easy day of appointments. She, Bryan, and I huddled around the kitchen table over an early dinner that Bryan had ordered.

The binders and ledger were piled to one side. Nobody had shown up, so my fears of someone breaking into my house had faded. At least for now. I patted the top binder. "We need to do a fuckton of research on these."

"I can help. I had a slow day at work, so I spent some time surfing the Net." Peggin pulled out her iPad. "I found a treasure trove of information on Cú Chulainn's Hounds. Turns out, Cú Chulainn is a folk figure in Celtic folklore."

"That's right." Bryan let out a snort. "He was quite the hero. He was also a fool."

"Why so?" I wasn't all that well versed on my Celtic legend and lore.

"Because he had a falling-out with the Morrígan." Bryan arranged the Chinese takeout containers. "I hope you like everything."

"Mmm . . . potstickers!" Peggin wrinkled her nose. "Love them!" As I carried the plates to the table, she continued. "Cú Chulainn was a major player, a major hunk, a warrior unparalleled, and was part of the Red Branch—an elite group of knights." She set her iPad on the table and began to sort through her notes.

"My grandmother mentioned them several times. I skimmed through her Shadow Journal this afternoon and to be honest, she seemed scared as hell of these guys." While Bryan and I watched the house, I had read my way through half the book. *Speed reading for the win, again.* Not only had I managed to find the ritual I needed to perform tonight, but I had also discovered that Lila was seriously worried about Magda and the Hounds.

"At one point, the Morrígan offered herself to Cú Chulainn and he denied her. She offered him help, and he rebuffed that, too. Long story short, after that, she considered him her enemy and vice versa. She did her best to hinder him in battle. One of the Bean Nighe predicted his death at the end, and Morrígan literally crowed over his corpse, settling on it when she was in the shape of a crow."

"And Cú Chulainn's Hounds?" This was sounding very much like a long-standing feud.

"The name actually comes from him killing a guard dog belonging to Culann—a blacksmith. Cú Chulainn offered himself as a replacement for the hound until a new guard dog could be reared, and that's how he got his name. Cú Chulainn means *Culann's hound.*" Peggin sat back. "And that's the name his followers chose for themselves. Just like the Morrígan has had the spirit shamans, Cú Chulainn has his Hounds. When he died, they believe his spirit went on to become a god of sorts. They are as much a death cult as the spirit shamans are."

I groaned. Blood feuds were not on my must-do list, but apparently one had been dropped in my lap anyway. "And I suppose they make it their mission to thwart the spirit shamans out of misguided loyalty to Cú Chulainn."

"You got it, chickie." Peggin shook her head. "I couldn't find out much more about them, except they aren't as powerful as spirit shamans, they tend to be human as far as I can tell, and they congregate in good-ole-boy clubs, though some women are known to join them. Usually the women have some sort of magical power."

I frowned as I scanned the names on the member list. True enough, most of them were men. Except Magda, and a scarce woman here or there.

"Why would Magda belong, though? Her daughters are a lament singer and a Gatekeeper. Wouldn't that make her a daughter of the Morrígan, too, since the powers pass down through the maternal side? None of this makes sense. I wish Mae—my great-grandmother—were alive. Maybe she could fill in the blanks."

"Well, we know that Magda killed Penelope. Could she be a rogue lament singer who turned her back on the Morrígan? Are you sure the lament singers are born into a family like spirit shamans?" Bryan frowned. "Shapeshifters for the Morrígan are always born of an Irish family; in fact, there are three clans of us dedicated to her service. But not everybody born into our clans and family is destined to be a guardian."

"Just as there are three lines dedicated to spirit shamans. Does that mean there are three families born into the service of lament singing? Nine is a sacred number, and so is three—three times three. And if so, then how is the Volkov family part of that, given their last name is anything but Irish?" I worried over the pieces, but then it clicked. "Last name wouldn't matter! If the blood comes through the mother, then she could have married anybody anywhere, as far as I know. So that wouldn't matter."

"*Volkov . . . Volkov . . .* that means something in Russian, I'm sure of it." Bryan leaned forward.

Peggin's fingers flew over her iPad. "Here it is. Volkov—it

is Russian and it derives its origins from the word *volk* . . . or wolf." She hunted a little more, then shook her head. "That's all I've got."

"Tonight, I'm pushing Ellia to tell us everything she knows. She's hiding something." I frowned. "And that's only going to lead to somebody getting killed." With a sigh, I glanced at the clock. It was almost five thirty. "Pass me the egg rolls, please."

Peggin flipped her iPad closed. She leaned back, playing with the hem of her dress. Black polka dots on white, it cinched her waist while flowing out into that retro-style skirt she liked so much.

I rubbed my temples. I had the beginnings of a headache but didn't want to take any aspirin because I wasn't sure how meds would affect the ritual I had to do. "Peggin, can you stay here this evening while we meet Ellia? I'm worried about Leon or Heathrow breaking in, and you have a gun, which would be very effective against human intruders. Also, Aidan will be showing up around eleven and if we're not back by then, I'd like to have someone here to meet him."

She snorted. "I'd like to see someone get through me and Molly." At my look, she shrugged. "So, I named my gun. She's Molly, like a gangster's moll?"

At that, Bryan broke out laughing. "You're perfect, Peggin. Never change."

She winked at him. "Anything for you, honey chile. And say, if either of you knows anybody single and sane, I'd be up for a blind date. I broke up with a guy three months ago and haven't had an evening out in ages. At least, not one that ended in a good-night kiss."

Bryan cleared his throat. "I know somebody and I think you'd get along great, but you have to be open-minded."

"Oh, that sets this up to be *oh-so-good*. Um . . . just who do you have in mind, do I know him, and is he a serial killer in the making? If the latter is yes, I'll pass. And if he's a mama's boy, I'll pass, too." Peggin liked her men like her coffee—strong, energetic, and with a kick.

"I don't know. Not at all. And not even close." Bryan

hesitated, enough for me to know that whoever he was about to mention was going to elicit a reaction. I was right.

She grumbled for a moment. "All right, already. Spill his name."

Said very flat, with a hint of *don't hit me*—"Dr. Divine."

Peggin inclined her head, just enough to stare at him over the tops of her glasses. "You did *not* say the name I thought you said. Did you?"

"I told you that you need an open mind." He shrugged. "I think you'd hit it off."

I hadn't met—or even heard of—Dr. Divine. "So, what am I missing here?"

Bryan sidled me a glance, begging me to shut up, but I wasn't about to see my best friend thrown to the wolves. So to speak.

"Seriously, who is he?"

Peggin coughed. "An artist. We think he may be human, but the votes aren't in on that yet."

Bryan snorted again. "He's human, all right, though he does seem to have a curious ability. But he's really quite shy beneath the butt-length cornrows and the goggles."

"*Goggles?* Really?" I turned to Peggin. "Who the hell is he talking about?"

She rolled her eyes. "As he said, Dr. Divine is an artist. He sculpts and paints. He moved to Whisper Hollow about six years ago. Dude came in on a visit and just never left. He bought that huge old house on the lakefront that used to belong to the Carters before the granddaughter moved away. Every now and then, one of his creations gets away from him. Don't ask how—nobody knows. But when he builds something, or paints something, now and then it takes a notion to go galli-vanting around town. His creations take on a life of their own."

I nodded. *Of course* Whisper Hollow would have an artist whose art came to life. That seemed only too fitting. "But . . . *goggles*?"

"He's very steampunk. Wears a top hat, goggles, and an ankle-length duster that looks like something out of the *Wild*

*Wild West* movie. Belts with gears and gadgets attached to them . . . who knows what else. I've never gotten a good look at his face, though."

"I have. Good-looking guy." Bryan was making a serious plea here. "Don't be too quick to prejudice yourself against him. He's brilliant and he lives all wrapped up in that mind, but he's very kind, really, when you get to know him, and he's funny and interesting. And he has good table manners."

"You sound like you've had him over to dinner." It suddenly occurred to me that Bryan's acquaintances would include a number of people I'd never met.

"I have. He's human, all right, but he just has a gift—or a curse, at times—with his art."

Peggin sighed. "Fine. I'll give him a chance. But if he gets weird on me, I'm blaming you. *Weird* being relative, of course." She stood, stretching. "I need to go home and feed Folly and Frith before I guard your house. I also want to make sure Molly is cleaned and ready to go, and I want to get out of these clothes if there's even a remote chance the bad guys are going to show up." She giggled. "I feel stupid using that term, but I guess that's really what they are."

As she headed out the door, she glanced back at Bryan. "Dr. Divine. *Really?*" At his nod, she shrugged. "Okay, I'll give him a fair shake. Set us up, maestro. I'll be back in an hour or so." And with that, she was out the door.

After she left, I turned to Bryan. "You promised an encore of this morning. I know it's been a weird day, but I'm hungry for you."

He met my gaze. "Come here, wench." He held out his arms and I snuggled into them. He was warm against my body and smelled of all things dark and delicious. As I burrowed my face into his sweater, he let out a soft sound and leaned down, sweeping me up into his arms.

As he swung into the hallway, carrying me back toward the bedroom, he hit the switch to flood the hall with light.

"We don't want to be interrupted by your friend the Shadow Man."

Hell, I'd almost forgotten about that. "I need to turn on the lights in the rooms so he can't get in." I couldn't keep the lights blazing all day, every day, but until I figured out a permanent way of keeping him out, I was afraid to let the cats go into any room that didn't have some semblance of light in it.

"Here." Bryan stopped at the bed, then gently set me down on it. "I'll go. You just get out of those clothes."

I reminded him to make sure the light was on in the attic, the pantry, and the secret room. With a salacious grin that made me want him that much more, he took off.

Sitting on the edge of the bed, I slipped out of my clothes, setting them aside neatly. I didn't like mess or clutter. It wasn't conducive to a clear mind. I opened the dresser to fetch one of my black nightgowns with sheer panels interspersed with the satin, and while I was at it, I prepared a couple of condoms, setting them on the nightstand, open and ready for use. Sliding it over my head, I gasped as the lace brushed against my nipples, making them harden and ache.

With a soft sigh, I ran my hands down the sides of my hips, feeling the moist heat rise between my legs. Yes, I wanted Bryan and I wanted him now. The thought of his chest against mine, of his firm hands holding me down, of his body pressed against mine made me hungry to the point where I whimpered. I'd always loved sex, even when I wasn't with a regular partner, but now I realized he set me to craving it. To craving *him*.

Pulling back the covers, I bounced on the bed, eager for him to return. I gave myself a very light spritz of one of my favorite perfumes and finally leaned back against the headboard. Another moment, and I was getting antsy, and a little nervous. Was he okay? Had the Ankou been lying in wait? I frowned, wondering how long he had been gone. It couldn't have been that long, could it? I glanced at the clock. Five minutes? Ten?

But then, just as the butterflies were hitting hard, he

popped back around the corner. "We don't have long. Peggin will be back in less than an hour. But I stopped to feed the cats. I don't know when you give them their dinner, but they were complaining loud and clear, so I thought I'd take care of them first."

And with that sentence, he won over another part of my heart. I slipped out of bed as he began to remove his shirt and pants, and walked over to him, stopping his hand. "Just . . . quiet. This time, you be quiet." As he stared at me, a quizzical expression on his face, I began to unbutton his shirt, easing it off his shoulders and arms. I held my finger to my lips, then pressed my mouth to his chest, leaving a trail of kisses down the center of his six-pack, heading toward his belt as he let out a satisfied moan.

At his belt, I paused as I stared at the silver buckle. A silver wolf's head, fierce and daunting. I glanced up. "According to legend, werewolves can't touch silver."

"I'm not a werewolf. I'm a shapeshifter—vastly different thing." He lifted my chin. "I'm *your* shapeshifter."

"*Mine*," I whispered, as I slowly undid his belt and pulled it through the loops, dropping it to the side. His jeans were taut, straining to contain him. I could see the hardness against the front fly, and I took my time, teasing as I slowly unzipped him. As the waist opened, the front of his briefs were stretching to cover his erection and I leaned forward, pressing a kiss against the soft material. Bryan gasped, his hand bracing himself against the bedpost. With one quick tug, I pulled down his jeans. He had already taken off his boots while he was turning on the lights, and so I slid the jeans over his feet and dropped them to the side. Then I slid my fingers under the waistband of his briefs and tugged them down, too, watching as his hard, stiff cock bounced lightly as the material slipped over it. That elicited an even louder groan.

Laughing, I tossed his underwear to the side and then decided to get up close and personal. As I rolled the condom over his penis, I traced the veins, starting at the balls, and followed the engorged shaft up its length. Even through the latex, his flesh was warm and pulsing beneath my tongue.

He let out a grunt, then fisted my hair with his free hand, holding my head as I fit my lips to the head of his penis and tightened them, forming a lovely suction as I slid my lips down his length. With one hand, I held him firm. With my other, I braced myself by wrapping my arm around his legs.

"Kerris . . . don't stop . . . don't stop." He leaned his head back, and I flickered my gaze up his perfect chest as I felt his ass muscles tighten. He thrust into my mouth, though gently—not hard enough to hurt—and I rode his cock with my lips, bobbing up and down, forcing him deep as I relaxed my throat muscles enough to take him up to the hilt. He was wide, and fully engorged, and the pulse of his blood pounded even through the condom. Another moment, and he pulled away, his eyes wild and feral.

He grabbed me up, tossing me on the bed, and I landed with a laugh. I slid one of the spaghetti straps of my night-gown down, exposing my breast, and began to brush the nipple, rubbing around and round, gliding over the areola, then cupped my breast, stroking the taut flesh. My breasts were large and full and he stared at them like a hungry man staring at dinner.

"You want them?" I taunted him, and he was suddenly against me, pressing me back against the pillows, his lips teething against my nipple, sucking deep as he caressed the arc of my breast. His touch was electric, a shock wave rippling through me, and I let out a gasp as the moist heat between my thighs became a raging fire. I struggled to pull up my night-gown and suddenly it was around my waist, and his hand was between my legs as he stoked the flames, his fingers brushing my clit, sliding inside me to spur on the hunger.

He brought his fingers up to his lips and slowly, as I watched, licked them. "I love your taste, I love the scent of you, the feel of you. Your cream is salty and sweet, like caramel, and it drives me wild."

"What are you going to do to me?" I whispered low, wanting to hear the words, wanting to know what he was thinking.

"I'm going to fuck you so deep, so hard that you scream

my name and only my name. I'm going to ram my cock in up to the hilt, drive it home to the center core of you so you forget everyone and everything else. I'm going to slide my finger up your ass and watch you squirm and scream for more. By the time I'm done, you'll be so wrung out, you won't remember your own name." His eyes were feral now, a wild light racing through them, and the sound of my heart racing matched the need and ache in his voice. "You want me, Kerris? Tell me you want me."

A wave of pain rushed over me—the pain of needing someone so much you can't stand it. I wanted him in me, wanted him to take me, claim me, own me for his woman. "Yes, I want you. Please, please fuck me."

With a rough laugh, he pinched my clit just enough to send me spiraling into orgasm, then replaced the condom with a new one, fire burning in his gaze.

I let out a scream, unable to keep my pleasure silent, as he was suddenly inside me, driving deep, plunging with a fierceness that made every fiber of me cry out in delight. I laughed, unable to hold back as he thrust again and again, the friction of his girth sending a ripple through my body. I came again, and he suddenly withdrew and flipped me over, coming in from behind. As he held tight to my hips, gaining even better purchase to leverage against my body, the tension began to build again and I suddenly felt his fingers as he reached down between my legs to massage my clitoris as his penis drove deep into my pussy. On fire, I came yet again, and as I climaxed, he carefully worked one finger into my ass, deep enough to make me moan.

"Do you want me there? Do you want all of me there?" His voice was rough and harsh with the crazed hunger that was fueling us both.

Aching, but wanting more—wanting him to explore every inch of my body—I nodded, almost crying. "Yes, please . . . yes."

He slid out of my pussy, and I heard something. I glanced around to see him lubing up the condom with gel. Another moment and he had hold of my hips and I braced, gritting my teeth as he began to work the head of his penis into my ass. Slowly, not in any rush, he inched it forward, holding me steady when I began to squirm. He eased it in as he grunted low with pleasure.

Every inch of my body was feeling stretched, and I was ready for the pain, but none came as he gently eased into me until suddenly, he was full in my ass, up to the hilt, his balls bouncing against the back of my legs. With a slow sigh, he eased back and then gave one long, sliding thrust, and then another, and another until I couldn't help it, but had to reach down, to rub my clit furiously as the tension built again. I moaned, falling into the sex haze, feeling the tension mount again, driving me up until there was nowhere to go.

Forced into a corner, the ache grew and then, with one last long plunge into my ass, Bryan let go. He cried out so loud that it echoed through the room. His pleasure mingled with mine and I pinched my clit hard, and once more, the orgasm raced through my body, shaking me to the core as I tumbled into the darkness of pleasure, coming harder than I'd ever come in my life.

# CHAPTER 17

━━━❦━━━

W e were back in the kitchen five minutes before Peggin arrived, gun in hand and dressed for business. She promptly took control of the remote, the living room, and the fridge, and—after warning her not to turn off any of the lights or night lights—Bryan and I headed toward my car.

"Hold on one sec. I'll be right back." Bryan dashed toward his house as I warmed the car.

In Lila's Shadow Journal, she had detailed the preliminary ritual for someone who had been taken by the Lady, when their body hadn't surfaced. Apparently, this was common enough, and it was also common knowledge that if the Lady of Crescent Lake claimed you, chances were your family would never see your remains again. I had everything I needed in the doctor's bag.

When Bryan reappeared, he was carrying a sheathed short sword.

I stared at the weapon as he climbed in the front seat. "You know how to use that?"

"Yes. Remember, I was born before modern weapons. I learned how to fire a rifle, sure . . . and a revolver, but I also

learned how to use one of these. I can gut an opponent before
he knows what's happening." The cool tone in his voice
made me shiver.

Softly— "Have you ever?"

A slight nod. "Yes. I've had more than one occasion to
bring this out." He paused. "After seeing my father murdered,
I swore no one would ever take me by surprise. No one would
ever hurt another person I loved. And I've made it my business
through the years to learn every method I could for preventing
that. Kerris, I'm a natural-born marksman, with both bow
and gun; I can wield a blade, I can use my body to take down
a man twice my size without a blink. If anybody's cut out to
be your guardian, that would be me." He leaned down and
pressed a gentle kiss to the top of my head.

There was nothing else to say. I kept quiet until we
reached Ellia's. She was waiting out in the street for us, violin
in hand. How the woman braved the chill nights, I did not
understand, but she seemed unfazed by the cold weather.

As she settled in the backseat, she paused, then let out a
little laugh. "You two have chosen to become a mated pair,
then?"

I blinked. "How did you know?"

"The energy around you is thick as thieves. Thick as my
grandmother's gravy was. And believe me, that was a gravy
you could stand your spoon up in." She settled back in the seat.

I decided it was time to address my concerns. I couldn't
have the question lingering over us, or I would never be able
to work with her at the level of trust required for our interaction. "Ellia, I need to know this, and I need the truth. Your
mother—Magda. What's her story? Why would she be part
of a club that is dedicated to an enemy of the Morrígan?"

She let out a sharp breath. "You know, then . . ."

"I know she belongs to Cú Chulainn's Hounds. I know
they consider themselves enemies of the Morrígan, and
therefore of me. I know my grandfather belonged to it, and
so did—do—the men he hung out with. And your mother
belongs to it, as well." I suddenly realized that my voice had
risen. I was angry. I wanted to know who had killed my

mother and father. And I wanted to know why Ellia's mother was aligned with the enemy. As I heard my thoughts, I cringed. I had enemies now. Scary, murderous enemies.

Ellia cleared her throat. "All right, I'll tell you what I know. I would have tomorrow night at the meeting, anyway. You'll learn a lot more there."

Feeling slightly mollified, I let my breath out slowly. "All right. I'm ready."

She deflated then, and I could hear the pain enter her voice, like when you rip open a scab you thought you'd finally forgotten and been able to tuck into the past. "Magda—my mother—joined the group many years ago. So many that I lost count. While she's not devoted to their particular cause, she is devoted to their general nature. I told you that there are spirit shamans worldwide, by different names, serving different gods?"

"Right."

"In Russia—I'm no more Irish than I am a potato—they are called дух мастер . . . *spirit masters*, roughly translated. The goddess who rules over them is Morena. She's very much like the Morrígan. One of her nemeses is Baba Volkov—Mother Wolf Witch, a dark crone from the forest who possesses great power over the shadows. She can summon the dead and make them do her bidding, but not like you. She doesn't drive them back to the grave. She enslaves them. She can create form out of shadow. She is a dangerous enemy, and all the women in our family have been pledged to her service and that's where we got our last name. My mother is a powerful witch, dedicated to Baba Volkov."

I caught my breath. "So . . . she would befriend an enemy of the Morrígan because the Morrígan is much like her own deity's enemy. But, how then did you become a lament singer?"

Ellia paused, then nodded. "I don't really know how it happened, but I was born with the ability. I was also born with the dark magic of Baba Volkov. My mother was furious when she found out that I wanted to sing the dead to sleep instead of learn how to use them. By the time I was thirteen, I had become a prodigy on the violin. Mother said it was time for me to set that aside and begin learning the craft of my ancestors."

*Oh, this couldn't have a happy ending.*

"I refused. I insisted I was going to become a lament singer—I told her my hands were filled with music. She . . . she said that if I insisted on cavorting with the dead instead of using their powers, my hands would be filled with madness, as well. She grabbed my hands and there was a searing pain. To this day I can still remember the agony. And after that, any time I touched anybody, it sent them into a dark pit of aching madness. The day after she cursed me, I put on my first pair of gloves. I found out what happened when I touched my dog."

Her voice filled with pain and I wished I'd never asked her; even though we needed to know, it wasn't worth putting someone through this kind of memory.

I sighed. "I thought maybe it was a power that went with that of lament singing."

"No. My mother cursed me to drive anyone to madness if I touched them with my hands. I can touch them with my lips, with any part of my body except my fingers, and nothing happens. But if I shake hands, stroke a face . . . pet a dog . . . without my gloves? They are consigned to agony. And I cannot live with myself if I were to do that, so that's why I always wear gloves. Except . . . I cannot wear them when I play, so I never get near enough to touch someone during those times. The only thing I've felt under my fingers since I was thirteen is the feel of a bow, and of material." Tears trailed down her cheeks. "Magda killed Penelope, my sister. I barely knew who she was before she was found dead, and a horrendous death it was, too. But Magda didn't count on Penelope becoming a Gatekeeper."

"Why did she kill your sister?"

"Because she, too, refused to learn the art of Baba Volkov. We both failed our mother's wishes . . . and so she set out to destroy us."

As I took a right onto Hydrangea Way, and then another right onto Whipwillow Lane, I thought over what she had told us. Magda had chosen to focus her anger where she could do the most damage and get back at her wayward daughters at the same time. Morena, Morrígan, I doubted whether the names made a difference. It was the energy behind the name that counted.

"In your mother's eyes, you both betrayed her and went over to the enemy, then."

"That's about right."

"How old is your mother?"

"How old is Magda?" Ellia paused. "She was born in 1900, so she's almost one hundred and fifteen years old."

"That's what the records say. But she's human, isn't she? Aren't you? Not a shapeshifter like Bryan?"

Ellia shrugged, leaning forward to peer over my shoulder. "Not all humans are of the same stock. My lineage goes back for hundreds of years and is steeped in magic and sorcery. The legends I grew up on were gruesome and dark, and Baba Volkov a harsh taskmistress. The spells her followers—including my family—work with are dangerous and incredibly powerful."

"That would answer where some of the magic is coming from, like the toxic mist in my garden." I told Ellia what had happened the night before.

"Yes, that would be right up her alley. My mother could toss off a mist like that without even a moment's notice. And she would have no compunction about doing so."

Bryan cleared his throat. "Most people don't realize that there are differing lineages of humanity, and nobody has clocked every single strand of DNA on this planet. And the life spans? Those born of magical blood tend to live longer and heal faster. Kerris, your grandmother Lila would have probably lived strong into her fifteenth decade, had she not been killed. Her mother . . . I'm not sure how your great-grandmother died, but chances are, it wasn't natural."

"Mae supposedly died of a heart attack, when she was in perfect health." I blinked. I was heading into uncharted territory here.

"My mother could engineer a heart attack, as well."

"Or my grandfather could have colluded with Doc

Benson to take her out. I wouldn't be surprised by anything at this point." I let out a long sigh. "But I no more believe Mae died a natural death than I believe Whisper Hollow is the sunshine capital of the world."

As I veered onto Snowstar Avenue, we were nearing the place where Tawny was seen going off the road. She had plunged into the water right before the bridge that ran over Juniper Creek, which flowed into the lake. The road was very, very close to the lakeshore there, and it was easy to swerve too close to the guardrails. And if the Lady was calling? *Through them.*

"So, Magda saw hooking up with Cú Chulainn's Hounds as a way to get back at you and your sister. At all of us who walk this path. She's on a vendetta."

Ellia pointed to a turnout ahead. "Park there." As I pulled over, she continued. "Yes, but there's more to it than that. Whisper Hollow never really welcomed her in. She fits the energy of this place, of these woods. Baba Volkov would be as much at home up on Timber Peak as she was in the forests of Russia, but there, people respect her as well as fear her. Here? In town, Magda was laughed at for her folkish ways, and while there are a few other Slavic and Russian families here, the Irish tend to rule Whisper Hollow." A faint laughter filled her voice. "But you're right on one thing. The use of the word *vendetta*? Most appropriate for Magda's nature. She never gives up a grudge. Our family still holds blood feuds against others from the old country that have been waged for centuries. Magda hated this town when I was young, and so I wouldn't limit her designs on revenge to just the spirit shamans."

I glanced over at her. "You said a force was coming out of the woods, aimed at the town. You were referring to her, weren't you?"

"Yes. My mother and her followers. I have no doubt that she's made Cú Chulainn's Hounds reliant on her by now.

Another thought crossed my mind. "You said she can work with shadows? Create beings out of them?"

"If you're thinking she's responsible for the Shadow Man

in your house, you may be right." Ellia shrugged. "She's capable of that and so much more. Now I wish I had learned about some of my heritage, because I might be better suited to help us against her. But I have no Shadow Journals to read up on, unfortunately."

"Magda can probably perform the rites to summon the Ankou. I'm sure the Hounds have provided her with plenty of options. I wonder, though, if Cú Chulainn's Hounds know how she feels about the town itself? If not, they might see her as a power supply without realizing they are also in danger. Which means she could manipulate them into actions that were far beyond what they originally planned."

Ellia readied her violin and then climbed out of the back-seat as we slipped out of the front. "Magda is a master of manipulation. I know they have no clue of just what she's up to. If so, she'd be off their rolls and quite possibly dead, if they could manage it."

"Do you know how she got involved with them in the first place?"

Ellia remained silent. "You'll find out that at the meeting. I'd rather not go over it twice. Come now, we have to prepare the ritual."

By the tone of her voice, I realized I would get no further until the meeting, so I opened my bag and pulled out my wand. I also had prepared a packet of Follow Me powder, which I found in the secret room. "I'm ready. I memorized what I'm supposed to do, but this is the first time I'll have tried out one of her rituals, so be . . . prepared, I guess. I have no idea what's supposed to happen."

Ellia laughed. "Well, I know this much: After we perform the ritual, we should see a fog rise from the lake—a glowing fog—where Tawny's car was last seen. It will shimmer and then head for the graveyard. We drive back to the cemetery then, and finish binding the spirit within the confines. Then, when they perform the memorial service, regardless of whether the body has been recovered, we will ease Tawny into the Veil. Penelope will take over then."

"Right. Force her out of the water here, then bind her in the graveyard." The thought made me sad. It felt almost like we were jailers, which was technically the truth.

We got down to business, with Bryan keeping watch. The edge leading down to the water was too steep to descend, and there was no good trail nearby, so we'd have to do all of this from above. Which was just as well. I didn't fancy trying to navigate my way through the brush down to the lakeside in the dark, especially with the Lady so active. I had the feeling we hadn't seen the last of her trolling for victims for this year.

Bryan guarded against oncoming cars, using a flare to warn people around the area where we had parked. It was dark enough that an oncoming car might not see us and pull into the turnoff, shoving my own SUV into the drink. And I really, really didn't want to be explaining that one to the insurance company.

Ellia took off her gloves, pocketing them. I stared at her hands. They were creamy white in the night, and I suddenly wanted to take them in mine, to squeeze them and let her fingers know that something other than the bow and the cloth existed. But I held myself back.

She caught my gaze and I swear, she knew what I was thinking, because she gave me a sad, soft smile before lifting her violin to fit it under her chin. Closing her eyes, she took a deep breath and began to play—softly at first, coaxing a haunting trill of notes out of the instrument, a melancholy hymn to the lost. The music cascaded up and overflowed the edge of the cliff, fluttering down, tumbling like autumn leaves toward the dark surface of the lake below.

I raised my wand, instinct taking over and putting into place the steps I had so painstakingly memorized. Holding the wand aloft, I stared at the silver shaft, and a brilliant light began to sparkle within the crystal atop the end—it was like a beacon, a calling card.

"Tawny Marple, I call you forth from the arms of the Lady. Come to me, come out of the depths, away from your body. The Lady may claim your remains, but I claim your soul and waken you with the kiss of music and magic, with the call of the Morrígan! Come and follow me, back to the valley of the dead, where you will rest even if your body should never be found."

As my voice fell away, the light from the crystal shot down, turning into the shape of a sparkling crow made up of a thousand pinpoints of light. The brilliant bird landed on the wind-churned waves of the lake. The energy of Ellia's music rolled in behind it to circle an area on the water's surface, the notes creating a web to catch the fog that began to rise from the spot. The mist glowed, sparkling and beautiful, a pale violet, and the notes of Ellia's song forced it to follow the crow into the air, where both hovered, glimmering in the night sky. Mesmerized, I watched, catching my breath as I realized Tawny's spirit was in that fog—I could see her, a vague form, confused and searching.

"Follow me, Tawny Marple. Follow me." I whispered the last, and Ellia let loose with one final sweep of her bow. The crow vanished as the fog rose to the level of the road and began heading west, toward the cemetery. "And now, we get a move on."

Bryan put out the flare as we stowed our gear and returned to the car. He drove so I could focus. None of us spoke on the way, Ellia and I keeping hold of the ritual, of the energy that surrounded us and reached out to control Tawny's spirit that floated on ahead of us.

Once we reached the cemetery, Ellia and I tumbled out, and without a word, she took up her violin again. The crow reappeared and landed on the roof of Penelope's tomb. Together Ellia and I swept the spirit toward the mausoleum with our magic. Penelope was waiting for us at the edge of the doorstep. She opened her arms and the mist, with Tawny's spirit in it, surrounded her. Penelope closed her eyes, laughing low and soft, and as she brought her hands together in front, the mist vanished and she let out a long, slow sigh.

"She is locked here, within the graveyard. I will watch after her until the service is performed and you sing her into the Veil. You have done well, Kerris." But then—as she was beginning to turn, to go back into the mausoleum—a noise startled us all. Penelope froze, her back stiffening. She seemed taller, more regal than she had before as she called out, "What are you doing in my realm? You know that I do not tolerate your kind."

I whirled, just in time to see a figure on the outskirts of the graveyard. It was dark and shadowed. *One of the Ankou.*

Instinctively, I reached for my dagger, but the blade was back in the car.

"I imagine that he's after you." Penelope's voice was calm, emotionless, but she leaned forward. "There is dark magic afloat through the Veil lately, magic that knows neither balance nor respect."

Ellia inhaled sharply. "Mother. She's messing with the dead."

"Yes, it's from Magda. The Ankou stinks of her meddling." Penelope moved forward, between us, and it felt like a rush of wind roared past. She held up her hand and a dark crow suddenly swooped down, low over her shoulder. But it was no ordinary crow, nor did it belong to the Crow Man. No, this bird was skeletal in nature, flying on bone wings. It swooped toward the Ankou, shrieking, and the Shadow Person fell back, moving away as the bird swiftly pursued it.

"Then you agree that Magda has the power to summon them?" I turned to Penelope, a ripple of fear racing down my spine. We had to find her and put a stop to her attacks before they grew worse. But she wasn't dead—I couldn't just drive her into the Veil for Penelope to deal with. And you couldn't put someone in jail for disrupting the spirit world.

"Oh, she's behind this, no doubt. And I can do nothing to her, even though she's the one who stripped away my life." She turned. "You should talk to Veronica, but let me contact her first. She has been in a mood lately, and I will summon you when it is safe to meet with her. It may take some time, so be patient." Penelope sighed, the sound of the wind rustling through dried corn husks and old papers flowing out with her breath. And with that, she ducked into her tomb again.

* * *

When we arrived back at the house, it was ten minutes till eleven. Peggin was sprawled out on the sofa, watching *A Letter to Three Wives*, an old movie from 1949. She had always been a sucker for the glamour girls like Bette Davis and Marilyn Monroe, and the dapper stars like Cary Grant and Laurence Olivier.

"Has Aidan arrived yet?"

She shook her head. "No, but he called the house and left a message that he'll be here soon. So, how did it go?" She set the bowl of popcorn aside but didn't stand up, as she was playing cushion to Daphne and Agent H, who were snoring on her lap and across her legs. Gabby was sprawled on the floor playing with a catnip mouse.

"We were able to guide Tawny into the cemetery. Once the service is performed, we'll guide her into the Veil and Penelope can take over from there." I rubbed my head, tired. "Bryan convinced me we should take the ledger and binders with us to the meeting tomorrow night. I guess I should leave them hidden till then."

Peggin shifted, tumbling the cats onto the sofa. "That's a good idea. A lot can happen in twenty-four hours." She started to gather her things together.

"So, where's the meeting tomorrow night?" Bryan dropped into a chair, looking just about as tired as I was.

"Niles's garage, of all places." Niles Vandyke was from my high school class and, apparently, he'd managed to open a garage. He was a genius with motors and engines, and from what Peggin had told me, he washed up pretty good under all that oil and grease.

"Niles . . . yes. I've always wondered about him. It seemed odd to me that he would be content with the small-town life, but I guess he has more going on beneath that muscled exterior than I thought." Bryan grinned. "He makes all the women swoon, I gather."

Peggin laughed. "Yes, yes he does. Hunky, inked, and a wicked sense of humor. I dated him for a few months, but

I'm afraid he's looking for a woman who's a little less edgy than me. But we're good friends now."

Leaning back in the chair, I closed my eyes and let my mind drift. I was tired, so very tired, and all I wanted was to fall into bed for a long night's sleep. But the doorbell roused me from my impending nap.

I jumped up. Bryan motioned for me to wait until he had my back—after the past few days, who knew who was going to be on the other side—and then I flipped on the porch light and peered through the peephole. Aidan—he looked a lot like his picture in the locket. I opened the door.

But it wasn't a ghost or more toxic mist waiting for me. Aidan was burly, wearing weathered jeans and a button-down shirt under a Windbreaker. His hair skimmed his shoulders, and even though he looked around his midforties, the look in his eyes was far older. I ushered him in.

I wasn't sure what to say. In one week, I'd met my paternal grandmother and my maternal grandfather and they were both shapeshifters.

But Aidan solved the awkward problem by breaking into a wide smile and holding out his arms. "My granddaughter."

The warmth in his voice was so infectious that I couldn't help but move into his embrace and give him a big hug. He felt warm and snuggly and cuddly, like a big teddy bear. When he let go and stood back, holding me by the shoulders to look me up and down, the oddity of him seeming so young fell away. He *felt* like a grandpa.

"Aidan . . . come in. Meet Bryan Tierney—"

As Aidan turned to Bryan, he paused, then held out his hand. "Blood recognizes blood. Which clan?"

Bryan inclined his head. "Originally Ó Tighearnaigh of Brega. And you?"

"The Corcoran clan comes from the MacCorcráins clan of Leinster. So, do you stand guard over my granddaughter?" Aidan glanced at me and I blushed.

At that point, both Peggin—who was watching from the sofa—and I were mesmerized as Bryan went down on one knee and lowered his head.

"By my blood and clan, I pledge my life in her service. I will guard against the powers that seek to harm her." He glanced up at Aidan. "With your grace, Lord Corcoran."

My grandfather made some sign over him—I couldn't tell what it was, but it was deliberate and had to have some meaning. His voice grave, he said, "You have my grace and my trust, Tierney. You have pledged on your blood to protect my own. Let your blood be spilled if there is need." And with that, he reached down and offered his hand to Bryan, pulling him back to his feet.

They both turned to me. By now, Peggin had crept up behind me, and we both stared at them. I had no clue of what to say, but Peggin was never at a loss for words.

"What the hell was *that*?"

Bryan and Aidan began to laugh. Aidan shook his head. "Girls, clan recognizes clan. I spotted him for a shapeshifter first thing. But if two guardians meet, it's a little more complicated. Not to mention I wanted to make certain he was here for your benefit and not some other reason." Arms at his side, he gave a half bow to Peggin. "My granddaughter is remiss in her manners. I am Lord Aidan Corcoran. And who might you be?"

I blushed. "I'm sorry—I was just so taken aback. This is Peggin Sanderson, my best friend."

Peggin raised one eyebrow, grinning, but held out her hand. "Lord Corcoran, my pleasure."

He took her hand and raised it to his lips. "No, the pleasure is mine. And a beautiful friend you are." But his eyes were serious and he turned back to me. "We need to talk. And we need to talk now. Is this house secure?"

"Secure in what way?"

"It's not being monitored, is it? Bugged?"

I frowned. Now we were talking spy movies? "I have no clue. That never occurred to me. Who would want to bug my house?"

"Anybody who didn't want you back in Whisper Hollow. There are magical ways of doing it, but the old-fashioned kind is so much simpler and easier to install." And then he looked around and his shoulders slumped. "I haven't seen

this house since I was eighteen. Since I left town. Lila . . .
I can't believe she's dead."

The catch in his voice stabbed me in the heart. He still
loved her. Beneath that gruff exterior, I could still hear the
love in his voice. I escorted him to sit down.

"When was the last time you saw my grandmother?"

Aidan held my gaze. "When she came to visit me in
Seattle. In late September, it was, 1973." A pause, then—
"Please, you really should be sure nobody is listening in. I
have equipment that can pinpoint just about any sort of electronic surveillance devices around."

"Go ahead, then." I was curious now. The house had been
left empty after my grandparents' deaths; someone could have
gotten in and planted a bug, though why they would want to
still confounded me. But then, considering the ledgers I had
hidden in the secret room, it wasn't all that far outside the realm
of possibility. Cú Chulainn's Hounds weren't going to want that
information in the hands of the Crescent Moon Society.

Aidan ran out to his car, a huge old pickup truck, and
returned with both a suitcase and a messenger bag. He
extracted what looked like a miniature walkie-talkie from
the bag, except that it had several buttons and a line of lights
on it. He flipped it on and the lights remained a steady green.
As he swept it around the room, he visibly tensed. The lights
began to flicker from green to red.

Aidan held his finger to his lips and began to sweep
around the room. I stared at the device, flabbergasted. What
the hell? Duvall was aligned with the Hounds. Why would
they have bugged his office?

The lights held a steady red near the landline. Aidan
picked up the phone and turned it over. Pulling out a pock-
etknife, he settled himself at the desk. He opened the knife
to the screwdriver function and began unscrewing the bottom of the phone. Another minute and he pointed to a small
black nodule that was tucked inside the case. It had been
taped there and obviously wasn't part of the phone. Aidan
cut the tape holding it in place, and then, setting it on the
ground, drove his heel down. He was wearing cowboy boots,

and he twisted his foot, smashing the bug into bits and pieces. The lights on the device turned back to green.

I knelt to clean up the mess before the cats got into it, still wondering who had put the bug in place. I didn't want to bring up the subject of Cú Chulainn's Hounds just yet— but would they have really bugged the home of their president? But then . . . Lila was here. Duvall wasn't the only one who used the phone.

Aidan glanced at me. "I can tell you don't know what to think, Kerris. But let's finish sweeping the house first before we talk this over."

We checked out all the other rooms and found nothing. I wasn't about to reveal the secret room to him, though. Grandfather or not, I wanted to keep some secrets for myself.

When we were back downstairs, I turned to him. "Okay, before we go any further, I want to know something. I know this is a painful subject. I can tell you still miss Lila after all these years. But why did she send you away? What did Duvall hold over her head that made it possible for him to force her to marry him?"

Aidan settled into a chair as Peggin emerged from the kitchen, carrying a tray. She had made a pot of tea and set out an assortment of cookies. She poured, while Bryan jumped up to help her hand out the cups. I was grateful when I saw she had opted for a raspberry lemon tea rather than caffeine. I was just about wrung out and my nerves were shot.

Clearing his throat, Aidan took a sip of the tea. "I was born in 1736, Kerris. I came here, to the United States, in 1922—my clan sent me. From the beginning, my parents knew I was to guard a spirit shaman, but it would not be till later in life. When I arrived in Whisper Hollow, I could still pass for a teenager and so I enrolled in high school. I met Lila when she was fifteen, and we began dating. Trust me, I never touched her in any untoward way, not until she made the first move—and then it was just kissing. I told her I wanted to save myself for marriage because while I fell, and fell hard, I wasn't about to take advantage of a woman who wasn't of full consent by the law of the land."

I realized he thought I might be uncomfortable with the idea of a man who was over two hundred years old making goo-goo eyes at my underage grandmother. "I'm dating a man who was born in 1872. I think age gaps kind of go out the window at this point, as long as you weren't feeling up a young teen."

He ducked his head, smiling. "I just wanted you to know that I always treated your grandmother with utmost respect."

"I believe you." And I did.

"She knew who I was, by the way. She knew right away—the first day we met, she looked at me and said, 'You're my guardian, Aidan Corcoran, and I'm going to marry you one day.' And I did not argue with her."

I laughed, then. I could imagine Lila doing just that. "I wish I had known her before Duvall. I saw glimpses of the girl you're talking about, but he changed her."

Aiden's look darkened. "Duvall did at that. He was always a dark soul. He was two years older than she was, and until I came around, she said he paid little attention to her. But after we started to date, Duvall was always hanging around the outskirts, watching. When we got engaged—she was seventeen—things grew worse. He was constantly trying to get her to go out with him. I wanted to beat him senseless, but Lila begged me not to. She was scared because Duvall and his friends had joined the Cú Chulainn's Hounds. You know who they are? I'm not sure how much your grandmother had a chance to tell you."

"Not as much as I wished. I left home when I was eighteen and only now returned. Grandmother left me her Shadow Journal, but there's so much I don't know yet. And yes, I know of the Hounds."

"Well, things grew more tense, and then one day, I was out for a walk in Bramblewood Thicket. A group jumped me—Duvall and several of his friends—and beat me a good one. As strong as shapeshifters are, there's a limit to how many opponents we can fight off. But I managed to break free and, in the scuffle, I slammed one of them hard and he landed against a tree trunk. I don't even remember his name; he wasn't from Whisper Hollow."

Bryan growled. "Not good."

"Not good is right." Aidan frowned, then let out a long sigh. "He hit hard, and broke his neck. Duvall just laughed. He told me that if I didn't leave town, he'd tell the police that I had murdered his buddy."

"But you were the victim—" It seemed hard to believe that the police wouldn't take that into account, but then I stopped. I had only to look so far as the news to see that this happened on a regular basis. Someone portrayed as a thug when they were, in fact, in the wrong place at the wrong time.

"The chief of police at that time was a friend of Duvall's family. My blood was on the body—I had been cut and had bled all over him when I was fighting. I was an outsider, and Duvall and his friends had the Hounds to back him, and the members of that group? They had clout in this town and in other towns."

"What happened? Did you leave?"

"No, I decided to tough it out. I was determined to find a way around it, but they began to threaten Lila. One of his buddies had taken pictures of me attacking the man, then of the body. They sent copies of them to Lila and told her that if she didn't agree to marry Duvall and send me packing, they'd turn everything over to the cops. They would tell them that she knew about it, and that I'd hang and her family would be dragged into a major scandal."

"Blackmail. And given the high placement of some of the Hounds, they probably could have managed to implicate her somehow." Peggin was sitting cross-legged on the sofa. She reached for another cookie. "What did she do?"

"She confronted me and I told her the truth." He shrugged. "I told her I'd face whatever they threw at me, that somehow I'd prove my innocence, but she was afraid for my life and she was afraid for her family. She ordered me to leave. I begged her to reconsider, but she said she couldn't live with herself if something happened to me. We fought for three days about it, and finally, I realized she wasn't going to back down. I left, though I sent her my address and kept in touch with her secretly."

"And she gave in to their demands and married Duvall."
I mulled over the story. "So what happened in 1973 that
she . . ." I didn't know how to say *My grandmother paid a
booty call to you*, so I just left the sentence unfinished.

"We had been writing for years—she had a post office
box that Duvall didn't know about, and I wrote to her, never
signing my letters and never putting a return address on
them. She was desperately unhappy, and at one point, I told
her to take a trip to Seattle—we would meet. Her mother
knew, I think. Mae was sharp as a tack. So Lila showed up,
and . . . well . . . all the old feelings were still there. She was
unhappy because she couldn't get pregnant. We slept
together—it was the best weekend of my life—and then she
went home. A few months after that, I got a letter. She was
pregnant, with my child. After Tamil was born, I got one
last letter. I had sent a locket for the baby."

"I found it. That's how I recognized you tonight." I
smiled softly, thinking about the rocky road my grandmother had walked.

"Lila wrote to me saying it was too dangerous to keep in
contact. She told me she'd always love me, but she didn't
dare let Duvall find out Tamil wasn't his child. She was
afraid he'd take it out on the baby if he did. And that was
the last I ever heard from her."

I stared out the window at the dark night. But Duvall *had*
found out—he had known since the beginning. And, for whatever reason, he had eventually done just what Lila feared he
might—only years later. Why, I didn't yet know, but the fact
was, my grandfather had known he was sterile and he'd never
told my grandmother. So when she showed up pregnant, the
question was: Did he know who the father was? And if so,
why had he taken so long to avenge himself?

# CHAPTER 18

Peggin took off for home, and Bryan stayed over that night. I put Aidan in the guest room. By the time he was done with his story, I was too exhausted to do anything but retreat to bed. The next day, Aidan would keep a low profile—he would be too recognizable to a number of people who might still remember him.

Bryan and I were up at dawn—he had a busy day ahead of him before we headed to the meeting that night. "I'll grab a bite at home. I have food that needs to be eaten. Call me if you need me. I'll be back at around five or six." He gave me a hurried kiss and then headed out the back door toward his house. After he left, I fed the cats and made myself some toast and eggs for breakfast before settling in with Lila's journal at the table.

Half an hour later, around seven A.M., Sophia called. She had plenty of news.

"I just got off the phone with Ivy. We're certain the remains are those of your father. I'm so sorry, Kerris. I also had

ballistics look at your mother's jacket. The hole? Matches the
bullets that belong to your grandfather's gun. While we can't
be absolutely certain, I'm willing to state that evidence points
to the gun in the office being the likely weapon that fired the
bullet through the jacket. We've sent the blood on the jacket
and bone scrapings from your mother's remains out for DNA
analysis. This will take some time, but I'm betting there's a
match, given what you've told me. While we're going on cir-
cumstantial evidence, my guess is that your grandfather did
have something to do with your mother's death."

I wondered whether to tell her that Duvall hadn't been a
blood relative, but then decided that could wait till later.
"What will happen if it's a match?"

"We'll close her case with him listed as the likely suspect.
You need to make arrangements, by the way, for her remains."

"I will." I frowned. The fact still remained that I knew
Duvall hadn't been acting alone. "What if I suspect he had
help and that the person I think was involved is still alive?"

"The problem is, do you have any proof?"

That stopped me. The fact was, I had nothing to link
Heathrow to my mother's death other than her spirit showing
up pointing fingers when I'd been talking to him. And that
wasn't admissible in court. "No, to be honest, I don't."

"Then there wouldn't be much we could do about it. We
have to have something to go on in order to investigate,
especially when we're potentially exposing a living person
to a murder accusation." She sighed. "Look, you find me
some evidence that I can act on, and I promise you, I'll move
on it. But until then, my hands are tied."

I cleared my throat. "All right. I'll see what I can do."

"Just don't put yourself—or anybody else—in danger."
She paused. "Talk to Frank and Gareth tonight. Don't ask
questions of me, just do it. You know what I'm referring to."
And with that, she ended the call.

My grandfather was still asleep, so I went back to my
studies. Luckily, my photographic memory would help me
with the rituals I had to learn. The journal was filled with
them, along with notations for every time Lila had been

called out to calm the dead, which seemed to have increased in frequency as the years went on. In fact, the last two years were packed with more and more cases of the dead crossing back from the Veil.

By the time Aidan appeared in the kitchen, I was almost done. I still didn't know any more about what was going on—except that Lila had suspected Magda of stirring up the spirits not only in the graveyard but in the forest. She had also expressed concern that as the power structure of the town changed, Magda's personal influence was growing while the Hounds were actually waning. And she considered Magda a far worse threat than the Hounds. I set aside the book and looked up at my grandfather.

He was eyeing the espresso machine with a smile. "Your grandmother loved her caffeine."

"And you?"

"Like a fish to water. May I?" He moved to make himself a drink and I nodded. As he deftly handled the machine, I opened the refrigerator.

"What do you want for breakfast?"

"Oh, eggs would be good, and toast. I can fend for myself, Kerris. You don't have to wait on me."

But I didn't mind. Over the past few days I had discovered that I liked having people around me. I had been such a loner in Seattle that I'd forgotten how social I could be. "Not a problem. How many eggs and how do you want them?"

"Three, scrambled is fine." He pulled himself a couple of shots and added hot water for an Americano. As he settled himself at the table, he added, "You have yourself a fine man in Bryan. I'm so glad he's here for you."

I cracked the eggs into a dish, whipping them with a fork as the pan heated, and popped a couple of slices of bread into the toaster. "Tell me more about you. I am so new to this. Bryan changes into a wolf. What about you?"

"My clan? The Corcorans are lion shifters. Kings of the jungle, kings of the shapeshifters." His eyes twinkled. "I so wish I could have met my girl. Do you remember her, Kerris? Tell me what happened to my daughter."

As I finished cooking his eggs, I told him everything I had found out. "Duvall killed her, but I know he had help. And I know who helped him. I just don't know how to prove it. I also think that he killed my father. The question is, why did he wait so long to kill my mother? If he wanted revenge, wouldn't it have been worse to do it while she was a baby? That would have destroyed Lila."

"That's a good question. Tell you what, my dear. I'll go out today and scout around. I promise to keep a low profile. You tell me where you found their bodies and I'll see what I can find out."

"Are you sure it's safe?" I set the plate of food in front of him. "What if somebody recognizes you?"

"Nobody will see me. I'm not going to hang around the center of town." He wouldn't hear of me coming with him, so I told him where we had discovered Tamil's grave, and I gave him a spare key.

"Just be careful, all right? By the way, can I tell Ellia and Ivy you're here?"

He gave me a short nod. "Yes, you can at that. I would like to see them again, if they're willing. I want them to know why I left. Why your grandmother married Duvall. They were always on my side and I wish to thank them."

After he ate and had taken off, I decided to try out one of the rituals I had found in Lila's journal. She had spelled out a rite to prevent the Ankou from entering the house, though she had also upped the ante through having Ivy enchant some of my toys. I spent the rest of the morning drawing the Runes of the Void onto every entrance in the house, following her instructions. As the energy sank into the walls of the house, a deep peace settled around me. She had recommended strengthening them every month, and so I marked my calendar so I wouldn't forget.

By then, it was afternoon, so I headed outside to the garden in back. The house sat on a half acre, and the backyard was a tangle of overgrown foliage. I had no clue why Lila had let it go, but after the mist had crept through, I didn't have any intention of leaving it to rack and ruin. The less clutter, the less chance for something to sneak in.

I found the pruning shears and a saw and shovel and hoe, and under the drizzly day, I got to work. My breath coalesced into white puffs—it was downright chilly—but I worked away for several hours, taking my nervous energy out on the undergrowth. By the time it was almost four, I had cut away most of the debris and hauled it over to a pile in the corner. The rosebushes had been in need of a good pruning, as had the butterfly bushes; I cut the wisteria back from where it was threatening to wind over to the house and then weeded the flower beds. It would take me several sessions, but by the time I was done for the day, the backyard looked a hundred times better.

Pausing by the kitchen door, I pulled off my muddy sneakers, thinking that it would have been nice to have a back porch right about now. I shrugged off my jacket and fixed myself another latte. Daphne came in, meowing for petting, and soon I had all three cats perched on the table for a grooming session.

It was four P.M., and I hadn't heard from Aidan. I was starting to get worried when his truck pulled into the driveway and he hopped out. He struck a fine figure, all right, and I shook my head, thinking that he was actually my grandfather. It was going to take some getting used to—with Ivy and him.

*And what about Bryan?* The thought raced unbidden through my head. *What about when you start to age and he doesn't? What are you going to do then?* I tried to shake it away, but a niggle of worry had settled in.

Aidan rang the bell and I answered. "You have a key, you don't have to ring the bell."

"It's not my house, and you were home. I wasn't about to intrude. If your car had been gone and nobody answered, I would have let myself in." He was soaked, and it was obvious he had been out prowling through the woods.

"Let me make you some coffee. You look soaked through. Do you want a towel?"

He held up his hand. "Another Americano, three shots, please. Thank you. And, if you don't mind, a sandwich or something would do nicely. I'll get the towel. I know where the bathroom is."

By the time I fixed his coffee and made him a thick turkey sandwich, he was back, looking a lot drier. He had changed his clothes and toweled off his hair. He settled in at the table and glanced out the window. It was almost dark, but he squinted through the glass.

"Looks like you were busy out there."

"Yeah, I had to get things in order. Lila loved her gardens. It was hard to see them so overgrown. So . . . find out anything?"

"Nothing around the graves. But I revisited several old haunts. Lila was right. The energy is shifting. The woods have become far more dangerous. There are creatures roaming out there who have no good in their hearts, and I'm pretty sure that last time I was here, they were sleeping. Magda is waking them." He took a long sip of his coffee and smacked his lips in a satisfied way. Leaning back, he played with his coffee cup. "What are you planning to do next? I fear for your safety."

"Well, I found a ritual to guard against the Ankou. The house should be safe enough from them for now. I am meeting with the Crescent Moon Society tonight. I thought I might ask them for help."

"That's not a bad idea, but I'm going to warn you about something. If they're the same as they were before I left, they'll have more than enough internal politics to make things sticky. Mae and Lila used to complain about the bureaucracy even then."

"Point noted." Lovely. Why was it that any group deciding to form itself into an organization seemed to create its own mass of red tape? "I'll keep my eyes open. You do know that if I tell Ellia and Ivy about you, the CMS is going to find out?"

He shrugged. "Maybe it's better that way. But be careful, Kerris. Treachery is sometimes found under the guise of friendship, and people who love you can let you down, even if they don't mean to." Glancing out the window, he nodded. "Here comes your guardian. You should get ready for your meeting tonight. Show up neat and composed. You have a better chance of impressing them and not getting pushed to the side than if you show up looking like you just came tromping out of the woods, and your time in the garden has given you just that look, my dear." And with that, he insisted on greeting Bryan and making dinner while I went in to take a shower.

The drive to the garage took exactly seven minutes, and as we pulled in, I noticed the cars parked along the side. Bryan hoisted the binders and ledger as I opened the door and slid out. The garage seemed empty, though the lights were on, but a man was sitting inside, waiting for us.

"Wait here." He spoke into a cell phone.

A moment later, Ellia appeared from a door to the back and motioned for us to follow her. We passed into the hallway leading to the office and restroom, but Ellia stopped in front of the janitor's closet. She held her finger to her lips and opened the door, shooing us into the tiny room. The floor was concrete, with a pink and blue design in the center of it that looked like tile to me. Once we were inside, she closed the door and turned to the back wall, where there was a row of coat hooks. As we watched, she pressed the second one from the left and a panel opened up to a hidden staircase. "Be cautious, there are railings but it's steep."

She led the way down, and we descended the spiral staircase. We must have gone down forty steps before we reached the bottom of the chamber, which opened into a large room with two doors, one on either side. And there, watching us, was Michael Brannon, the owner of the Broom & Thistle. He was holding a long sword, the edge of which glistened with a razor-sharp glint.

Ellia nodded to him. "We're here."

"You're late—but you're the last, so get a move on. I'll

be right behind." He was brusque, and gave me a look that made me think, as I had in his shop, that he wasn't all that keen on my presence.

Ellia swept past him, motioning for us to follow. "Come, we don't want to disrupt things any more than they already are."

She led us to the room on the right side of the chamber. I half expected some secret knock, but she just opened the door and filed through. Bryan and I followed.

The room was smaller than the main chamber, with a long rectangular conference table in the center. Around the table were several people whom I recognized, and some I didn't. I knew Oriel, Ellia, and Ivy. I recognized Frank O'Conner from the police station. Michael Brannon, of course. Trevor Riversong was there. But the others, I wasn't sure of.

A woman, tall and thin, looking very much the rich-bitch soccer mom, stood up and held out her hand. "Kerris Fellwater. Welcome to the Crescent Moon Society. I'm Starlight Williams, and I'm the president."

As she spoke, Ellia took a chair and pointed Bryan and me to the two adjoining. "I'm sorry we're late."

"Let's get things moving, then. I know we all have busy evenings. Kerris, Bryan, you know Ellia, Oriel, and Ivy. And Michael, Frank, and Trevor said they've met you. Everyone else, please introduce yourselves."

They went down the row, each giving their name and a brief introduction, starting with Niles Vandyke, the owner of the garage. He was heavily tattooed and gorgeous, just as Peggin had said. Then, Gareth Zimmer, a hulky biker who looked like he could just as easily gut a person as a fish.

Tonya Pajari was a fortune-teller. Her husband, Nathan, sat beside her—an ex-military man. Clinton Brady, owner of the Fogwhistle Pub, who looked like another old biker. Nadia Freemont, owner of the Mossy Rock Steakhouse. And last, Prague Helgath, owner of the Herb & Essence, who looked so Goth that he could easily pass for a vampire.

As I gazed at the faces, a few of them began to come

back to me. Besides Michael, Starlight and Tonya were around my age, and I vaguely remembered them from high school. Frank and Trevor were a bit younger. Nadia, Niles, Prague, and Nathan were all in their mid- to late forties, I would guess. Oriel and Gareth looked about the same age. And then Clinton, Ivy, and Ellia were in Lila's age group, though Ivy didn't look it at all.

Starlight picked up a judge's gavel and rapped on the table. "If you had trained under Lila, you'd already be a member. As it is, allow me to explain who we are and what we do."

I detected a note of disapproval in that prim little voice of hers and gave her a long, icy look.

She rapidly cleared her throat. "Yes, well, simply put, the Crescent Moon Society was formed back in 1936, when your great-grandmother first took up her post here as spirit shaman. At first, we were an adjunct group, dedicated to backing her up with whatever she needed, and to counter an organization bent on pushing the spirit shamans out of Whisper Hollow."

"Cú Chulainn's Hounds."

"You know of them?" Surprise, and a hint of wariness. And, next to her, I could see the misty form of an older woman, looking a lot like Starlight, shaking her head. The spirit looked vaguely disappointed and turned to me.

*My daughter, the prig. But she's trustworthy.*

I smiled softly at Starlight's mother but said nothing, simply inclined my head gently. Moving my gaze back to Starlight herself, I patted the binders. "Yeah, and more about that in a minute. I have some valuable information for you. But first, finish telling me about the Crescent Moon Society."

Starlight frowned. I had the feeling she had rehearsed her speech down to the last nuance in tone, and my interruption had thrown her off balance.

After a pause, she continued. "As more issues came to light, having little to do with the spirits who walk here, we increased our scope in order to take on cases that law enforcement cannot handle. We focus on the other entities that make the forest here their home."

I nodded. "That's pretty much how I figured it worked. Okay, now let me say a few things. You all know that I ran off when I was young. You know why? Duvall was a bastard—a vicious old man. And I have also found out, as you surely know, that he belonged to the Hounds. What you may not know is that he was president of it—or something like that—and that he had a treasure trove of information on them. Which I am prepared to hand over to you as long as I am totally kept in the loop." I shoved the binders and the ledger forward.

The collective gasp from the group told me that they in no way expected this. Ellia smiled softly, as did Ivy, who gave me a *good-going* nod.

I pushed myself to a standing position. "Furthermore, I refuse to be treated like a traitor because I had to get away from Duvall. For one thing, evidence proves he's not really my grandfather. And, as Frank has no doubt told you, we just found my mother's remains—and I'm pretty sure Duvall had a hand in killing her. I also expect that one of his buddies is involved. We also found my father's remains. I intend to ferret out his killer, as well."

The gasp turned into silence as all eyes focused on me.

Starlight chewed on her lip, then let out a little huff. I could see the wheels turning in her head as she frantically tried to regroup. "We have to walk softly, Kerris. There are too many powers at work here to charge in and send things spinning. I can't let you go off half-cocked."

"Half-cocked? I've got Ankou invading my house, a toxic mist tried to kill me, and I'm trying to sort out why Duvall wanted my mother dead. Hell, I wonder why he even wanted to marry Lila in the first place. He drove off Aidan—I know you have heard about him." I had already decided to keep the fact that he was in my house under my hat. I didn't like Starlight, and I wasn't sure how much I liked the Society as a whole. They rubbed me the wrong way.

Gareth spoke up. "Duvall was a danger to many people, but he's dead now. I think we can take this on more directly now, Starlight."

"Duvall was not the only power player in this town! He

is *not* the only danger. There are other powers at work, far more deadly than he was." Starlight turned on him, her eyes flashing. A sudden flicker of the lights startled me, but nobody else except Bryan seemed surprised.

"Maybe so, but we can serve him up as a sacrifice. We can use him to play on them—get them to think that we're pinning everything on him." The scarred biker barked out a sarcastic laugh. "Duvall's dead. Unless he decides to rise—and Kerris here can take care of that. We can make him a scapegoat and throw them off track about how much we know."

"What the hell are you all talking about?" I was getting pissed off by now as I realized with growing apprehension that the Crescent Moon Society was determined to play the puppet master. "My grandfather and his cronies murdered my mother and father. I want to know why, and I want them brought to justice."

Oriel cleared her throat. "We can answer the *why*—or at least I think we can."

I stayed standing, so tense I could barely breathe. Had Oriel just admitted that they knew Duvall had murdered my mother and yet done nothing about it? "Are you saying that you know he killed my mother? That you've known she was dead all along and you didn't tell me *anything*?"

"No." Oriel gave me that cat-and-canary smile again. "I'm saying we *suspected* she was dead. We knew Duvall had something to do with her disappearance, but we didn't know he had actually killed her. But . . . I suppose you might as well know the truth before you go opening a can of worms that we can't slam the lid back on."

Slowly, I sat back down. Bryan reached for my hand and squeezed it. He was just as angry as I was—I could feel his emotions as clearly as I could feel my own. "Then tell me. Now."

Without waiting for a go-ahead, Oriel let out a long breath. "Your grandfather murdered your mother because he believed a prophecy that Magda told him. She had a vision that together, Lila, Tamil, and you would have the force to bring down Cú Chulainn's Hounds. He believed it would take all three of you, so he removed Tamil from the equation, hoping to nix the chance."

I gasped. "When did he find this out? And how?"

"He believed it before he ever married your grandmother. We know this for a fact—one of the Hounds told us after he managed to extricate himself from the group."

That would account for my grandfather marrying Lila. If he believed he was sterile, then she would never bear a daughter and the prophecy would be canceled out without any further ado. But he hadn't counted on Lila getting pregnant. "What happened? Tell me more about the prophecy."

"Duvall and the Hounds got their wires crossed. The prophecy was corrupt. The truth is, Kerris, that the one destined to take down Cú Chulainn's Hounds—at least the branch here— is *you*. And that's why we let you run away. We wanted you out of his reach until we could safely bring you back."

And with that, the room once again fell very, very quiet.

"What are you saying?" That was the last thing I'd expected to hear. "That he killed my mother because of a *mistake*? And why did he wait so long?"

Starlight rapped her gavel. "Let's have some order—"

"Shut up." I turned to her. "Just shut the fuck up."

"There's no need for—"

"Starlight, back off. Kerris, calm down." Oriel shuffled in her seat and I thought I smelled a whiff of orange and gardenia wafting by from her position. She rubbed her head and the cryptic smile fell away, for once, making her look older and world-weary. "Kerris, this goes back a long way. Ellia, you don't know about this either—it happened long before my time, but I was left holding the information. Now it's time to bring it out in the open."

Starlight stiffened. "You've been withholding information from the Society?"

"Everybody withholds information from the Society at one point or another. We each have to bide our time till it feels right. I kept my hat on this until now because the signs were not in place." She was sounding more cryptic by the minute, and everybody in the room seemed restless.

"What is it?" I leaned forward. Her energy flared and a woman appeared by her side.

I jerked. I knew who it was, though I'd never met her. But I had seen photographs. My great-grandmother Mae caught my gaze and nodded with a gentle smile, then placed her hands soothingly on Oriel's shoulders. Oriel didn't seem to notice, but she took a deep breath and let it out slowly, visibly relaxing. I wanted to talk to Mae, to ask her some questions, but now wasn't the time or place. The fact that she was soothing Oriel spoke a thousand words, though.

I forced myself to ease back. "What is it, Oriel? Tell me, please."

Ellia, taking my cue, nodded. "Yes, we need to hear now."

Oriel bit her lip, then once more straightened her shoulders. "Here it is, then. Mae told this to my mother, Trudy, the keeper of the boardinghouse before I took over." She turned to me. "Trudy held my place. She was . . . she guarded Whisper Hollow like I do."

I nodded, beginning to see that there was a web of protectors strung throughout our little town. "I understand . . . I'm still not sure what you do, but I'm sure I'll learn. Go on."

"Back when Mae first arrived, Magda worked with the Crescent Moon Society."

"That can't be—" Ellia started to say, but Oriel held up her hand.

"But it is. And in 1939, the Society hatched what they thought would be a foolproof plan but ended up backfiring in a horrible way. They decided to infiltrate Cú Chulainn's Hounds, to learn everything they could about the organization."

"Oh, no." Ellia paled. "They didn't . . . ?"

"Yes, they did. They sent Magda in undercover. She was the only one the Hounds would conceivably believe would be willing to join up with them. Magda's heritage made it all too plausible."

"Baba Volkov . . ." Ellia frowned.

"Precisely. Mae argued against it, but she was overruled. Until then, Magda fought the way in which her family brought her up. Oh, she was a wild card—that's why Mae didn't trust the plan. But the Society thought it would work, and Magda wanted to be appreciated. So she sought out the Hounds, told them about her heritage, and they admitted her to their ranks. Then, everything fell apart."

"Power . . . she loved power and she longed to be accepted." Ellia's whisper echoed through the room.

Oriel nodded. "Precisely. Once in their ranks, they treated her with the respect the town never gave her. By the time Mae was pregnant with Lila, Magda became the very force Mae feared she would. She told the Hounds everything she knew about the Society and gave them a terrible edge. When Penelope refused to join the Hounds and learn the dark magic of her ancestors, Magda killed her. And when you came along, Ellia, she cursed you for not following her demands."

Ellia slowly nodded. "I never knew who my father was; Magda never told me. Was it someone from the Hounds? Do you know?"

"No, I don't. It could be one of the Hounds, or perhaps someone else. Penelope had a different father than you, you know. He died early on, when your sister was eight. He was an older man, and had come from the old country along with Magda." Oriel's gaze darted from Ellia to me. "When your grandmother was ten, Magda had a vision. She told the Hounds that together, Lila, her daughter, and her granddaughter would overthrow them. As I said, we found all of this out when one of their members broke ranks and came to the CMS, looking for help to get away from Whisper Hollow while he was still alive."

"Did they ever try to kill Lila? To stop the potential destruction of their group? It seems like a natural thought . . ." I was beginning to realize how deep, and how dangerous, the politics behind the spirit shamans and the Hounds were.

"There were a couple of times that might have been close calls. But back then, they were still afraid of Mae. I think they decided to take care of the issue through subterfuge. They engineered the marriage between Lila and Duvall, though I'm not sure what they intended to come from that." Oriel shrugged.

I gave her a long look. "I know why. Duvall was sterile. I found proof positive that he couldn't father children. They thought that Lila would never get pregnant and that would end the prophecy right there. But they didn't count on one thing—Lila stepping out on Duvall."

Gareth cleared his throat. "Then who fathered Tamil?"

It was now or never. As much as I wasn't sure what to think about the group, I decided that I'd stand a better chance with them at my back. "My grandfather is Aidan, Lila's guardian whom she drove out of town. He's sitting in my house right now."

And with that, the room erupted in a rush of surprised voices.

# CHAPTER 19

❧

Of course, that opened me up to tell them everything that I had done and found out since I'd been home. When I finished, Starlight wasn't the only one with her mouth hanging open.

Since nobody else was jumping into the conversation, I decided I would. "So, if it was going to take my grandmother, my mother, and me to stop them, does that mean there's no chance now?"

Oriel shook her head slowly. "Not at all. I'm sorry—processing all of this is going to take some time. But, Kerris, here's the thing. As I said, Magda's vision was wrong. We've done plenty of scrying on the subject, and we discovered that she missed her mark. She got her wires crossed. It's not the three of you needed to take them down . . . it's the fiftieth generation in your line. And that . . ."

"Is me. I'm the fiftieth generation." My voice was soft as I remembered the inscription in Lila's journal.

*I leave this journal to my granddaughter, Kerris, since my daughter, Tamil, the forty-ninth generation, has*

*vanished. Take up your post and keep it sacred and
honor your word and work.*

"How did she make that mistake, and are you sure?"

"The man who came over to us? He brought the original
text that she wrote down while in trance. Ellia translated it
for us. Magda's translation had mixed up a few words. The
original specifically refers to you. You and your guardian."

"Mother's English was never very good and she was
resistant to learning," Ellia interjected.

"The question is, then . . . do the Hounds know this? Do
they think they're safe?"

"I think . . . they must have an inkling that they were
wrong. The fact that Magda sent an Ankou to your house
tells me she's wary of you. So we can't go on faith that they
are sitting pretty, feeling safe." Ivy pushed herself up from
her chair and paced around the room. "I'm uneasy for
another reason. Word's out that Tamil's remains have been
found. According to Kerris, Heathrow was in on her murder.
He's going to wonder . . . and he's going to worry just how
much Kerris knows. They know she's the spirit shaman, so
why wouldn't they think she talked to her mother's spirit
and found out he was in on it? The statute of limitations
doesn't run out on murder. He's going to worry that he left
some clue behind that will tie him to the act."

"Meaning that he'll be after me." The look he had given
me when I left the hotel had stuck. "He knows about the
ledger. I made a mistake, I admit it, by telling him. And
though I told him that I didn't find anything else, why should
he believe me? I'm a danger both to him personally and to
the Hounds now."

"And he might just take it into his own hands to dispatch
you. Hell, that would make him a hero among them. We
may not have to worry about the Hounds getting to you if
he does first." Bryan leaned forward, a stark look on his
face. "What can we do to ensure her safety? We have to take
Heathrow out of the equation."

"We can't do that," Starlight countered. "He's too well

known. We'll just have to hope for the best for now, and keep our eyes open."

I stared at her. "I fully intend to prove that he was responsible—along with Duvall—for my mother's death. I'm not about to let him slide on this."

She crossed her arms. "I'm afraid you don't have any choice. That's my decision. Nobody who belongs to this Society is going to help you there."

The room fell silent. I slowly rose to my feet, holding her gaze, wanting nothing more than to smack her a good one across the face. Shaking my head, I picked up the journals. "Then the Crescent Moon Society will have to do without my participation. And without these journals. Because I intend to avenge my mother and father, and if I have to do so without your blessing or help, I will. I'm here to take up my grandmother's post, and I'm not going to knuckle under to politics. Lila may have played the diplomacy game because she was married to Duvall, but you're going to find me far less tractable."

With that, I turned to Bryan. "We're leaving."

He jumped up and followed me as I headed for the door. Ellia and Ivy were trying to call me back, Starlight was sputtering, and either everybody else had gone suddenly mute or they were afraid of speaking out.

When I reached the door, I turned around. "Ellia, we have to work together. I expect you to do your job. The rest of you can go to hell."

Ivy jumped up. "Kerris—this is giving in to the Hounds. They'd love to see us rip the Society apart. Heathrow's just one cog in the wheel—"

"How can you stand there and say that when you know Duvall—and probably Heathrow—killed your son?" Fed up and furious, I slammed out the door and marched over to the staircase, Bryan on my heels. "I suppose you agree with them?"

He shook his head. "No, actually. The Crescent Moon Society could be a powerful force, but I have the feeling that their hands are tied."

"By Starlight." As I began the long haul upstairs, Bryan

followed me. A couple of moments later we were in the main shop and sweeping past the guard at the front. I didn't say a word to him, just slammed out the door and toward my car.

On the way home, I was still so angry I couldn't speak, so Bryan insisted on driving. But as we neared my house, my fury began to smooth out. I ignored the repeated calls from both Ellia and Ivy, letting them go directly to voice mail. As I leaned my head back against the headrest and closed my eyes, a sudden prickle ran up my arms, making the hair stand on end. I could almost hear someone calling my name. Without a second thought, I told Bryan, "Drive to the cemetery, please."

He said nothing but obeyed. As we pulled in, I motioned for him to take one of the side roads, and as we swung around to a back parking stall, I realized we were near the Pest House Cemetery. Bryan turned off the ignition and we sat there, listening to the silence.

"Is something wrong?"

"Yes, I can feel it—something's out of order. But if I sit here for a while, I'll figure out what." I stared at the gates leading into the remains of the Pest House. "My grandmother hated this part of the cemetery."

"What's a Pest House? I've never heard of them."

I regarded the overgrown wall that separated the older section. It was stone that was breaking down, covered with ivy and vines of all sorts. The gate across the walkway was iron, but it, too, was swathed in overgrowth. Behind the gate and wall stretched a wide swath of cemetery, and beyond that, the remains of a broken-down building. Large and dark, it loomed in the night with an unhealthy light surrounding it. I knew that few people could see that light—it was the energy of the dead that inhabited the area—but it told me all I needed to know. Magda might have dark magic, but there were darker forces than she, and some of them could be found beyond these gates.

"Back before the turn of the nineteenth century, some areas kept buildings where they . . . well, bluntly put, where the doctors would lock up seriously ill people. TB, cholera, typhus, whatever the disease . . . if it could kill and was contagious, the patient was sent to the pest house until they recovered—which seldom happened—or died. Thousands of people died in these houses. Mostly, they were left there without any care, often without enough food, water, or blankets. The pest houses were also known as fever sheds. The ghosts around these areas are angry and often violent, just like they are around the old asylums."

Bryan stared into the darkness, the only illumination coming from the dim lamplights that lined the walkways. "People—and I include my own in this—have a way of being cruel to those in need. So, then, this is a dangerous area."

"Yes. And the way to Veronica's lair is through the Pest House Cemetery. She's got it tucked away in back, against the bluff that rises up to overlook the lake." I frowned, trying to figure out what had drawn me to the graveyard. "Somebody's up and walking. I can feel it."

"Shouldn't you call Ellia?"

I didn't want to, not after the meeting. But she was my lament singer, and I knew better than to let myself have a temper tantrum. With an exaggerated sigh, I pulled out my phone and gave her a call. She answered on the first ring.

"Ellia, I'm at the cemetery. Somebody's walking tonight. I'm not sure who, but I can feel them as sure as I can feel my own heart beating." I didn't ask if she could come over. It was her job and I expected her not to let the mess with the CMS get in the way.

"Are you sure? Did Penelope contact you?"

I frowned. "No, but . . . just come."

"I'll be there shortly. I'm on my way home now, so I'll just detour and meet you there. Where are you?"

"Near the entrance to the Pest House. Whatever is running around, it's hanging out near here." I suddenly realized that my bag of tools was at home. "I don't have my things with me. Can you stop at the house and ask Aidan to let you take them? I'll call him to let you know you're on the way."

"Almost there."

Even as she spoke, I saw a blur race past. "Hold on." I

tossed my phone on the seat as I jumped out of the car. Bryan was on my heels.

"Kerris, wait up! Kerris . . ."

I went racing through the grass, finally skidding to a halt in a clearing fifty yards away. Bryan caught up to me as I stood in the middle of the grass, looking this way and that for whatever it was that I had felt. The next moment, a dark shadow blurred out from the trees, making a beeline directly for me. It slammed into me, knocking me down, and I realized it was one of the Ankou. Maybe not *my* Shadow Man, but one like him.

Bryan immediately shifted to wolf form and lunged forward, growling. The shadow darted away from him as I rolled to my feet and came around, a little bruised but no worse for wear. It hadn't managed to grab hold of me.

I didn't have my tools, but instinctively, I raised my hand, bringing it down with full intent, drawing the Runes of the Void with large sweeps through the air. I focused all my strength to channel the power that was rising within me, and then I sent it out into the runes and pushed them toward the Ankou.

They lunged forward, sparking, and hit the Shadow Man straight in the chest, and he screamed as black smoke began to pour out of his head. A moment later he vanished. I dropped to the ground, sitting in the sodden grass, panting.

Bryan shifted back and knelt beside me. "Are you okay?"

I nodded. "Yeah, but . . ." Something was wrong. That was too easy.

My head suddenly cleared, and I realized that whatever I had been chasing, it wasn't nearly as strong as the Ankou I'd met in my house. In fact, I wasn't sure if that *was* an Ankou. And come to think of it, how did I know he was here? Penelope said she would come to me if there was a problem, but I would think that she would announce herself instead of just feed me the information.

"Something's wrong, Bryan." At that moment, I realized that I was hearing something from the truck. It was my ring tone. I hurried back to the car and grabbed my phone. Ellia. "Hello?"

"Kerris, you need to get home now. Don't ask why . . . just get here as fast as you can. Leave whatever's in the cemetery. We'll get to it later." And with that, she hung up.

Panic can either freeze you or spur you into action. For me, the worry in her voice translated to worry over my cats. "Home. Now!" I jumped in the car. Bryan had the keys and he was in the driver's seat before I could even think of repeating myself. He gunned the engine and we sped out of the cemetery, back to my house. Even though I lived only a block or so away, the entire trip a numb refrain echoed through my mind. *Please let them be okay . . . please let them be okay . . .*

When we arrived at the house, I was already opening the door before Bryan brought the car to a stop. I raced inside. The living room was a mess, and the kitchen no better. Ellia was standing there, waiting for me.

"The cats are okay," she said before I could ask. "I found them—they were all hiding under the bed, terrified. But they're okay."

"Thank God . . . but . . ." I glanced around. The house felt empty. Very slowly, I turned back to Ellia. "Where's Aidan? His truck is still outside."

She shook her head and held out a note. "I found this."

Gingerly, I took the paper. The handwriting was all too human. *Your one chance to save the shapeshifter: Bring the ledger and the binders to 3364 Timber Peak Drive to make the exchange. Come alone and be there in one hour, or I will kill him.*

Bryan shook his head. "You aren't going alone. It's going to take you half an hour to get out there. They don't want you having any time to contact the police."

"It's Heathrow. He's the only one I know who knew I had the ledger . . . except for the members of the Crescent Moon Society." I paused. "They knew about Aidan—"

"No, Kerris. Don't get all paranoid. I know those people. As stiff a stick as Starlight has up her ass, she's not in Cú Chulainn's corner. Every one of them can be trusted." Ellia patted my hand. "You have no choice but to take the kidnapper what he wants."

"I wish I had time to photocopy the binders." I turned to Bryan. "I can't chance them seeing you with me. Aidan's life depends on it."

He cocked his head, his expression dark and feral. "Don't worry about that. I'll be there and they'll never know. I won't be in the car." He took the note and scanned it again. "Got it. I'll meet you there." And he took off out the door before I could ask what he was planning.

Ellia was talking on the phone as I turned around. She finished. "I asked Peggin and Ivy to come over and stay."

"You can't bring the Crescent Moon Society in on this. They'd want me to ignore it, to give them the binders and let Aidan pay the price." I was ready to fight on this one, but the lament singer just shook her head.

"No, my dear. I'm not going to suggest that you let them harm Aidan. But you should know that not every member agreed with Starlight. Oriel, Ivy, and I are on your side. As are Gareth and Clinton. I don't know about the others, but you have us to stand behind you."

I glanced around the room. "I don't know what to do. Surely Heathrow isn't going to let me walk out of there with Aidan, not in one piece. I don't trust the Hounds any more than I trusted Duvall."

Ellia righted a small table that had been turned over. "I don't think the Hounds are behind this, Kerris. Heathrow's looking for glory and what better way than to secure their information? That would move him up the ladder in the organization, or at least I think he believes it will. He's not going to want to share the spotlight until he has the goods to prove his worth. But how did he know Aidan was here?"

I frowned . . . then I knew. "The phone. I called Aidan from the house phone. There was a bug on the landline—Aidan found it last night."

"Then Heathrow must have been keeping a watch on you as well, to know when Aidan got here. What happened out in the cemetery?"

I told her, including the fact that something had seemed off. "It was almost like . . ."

"A distraction, to keep you from coming home until he had time to overpower Aidan. My guess is that Heathrow somehow knew you were headed back early and he did what he could to run interference. Kerris, do you have Aidan's security monitor—the one he found the bug with?" Ellia glanced at the clock. "Hurry, if you do."

I nodded and dashed upstairs to the guest room. It, too, had been trashed, but the bug zapper was there. I grabbed it up and raced back down the stairs. "Here."

"Let's go check your car." She bustled me out the door and we went over the CR-V. As Peggin drove up and joined us, we found two devices. I held my finger to my lips and pointed at them. Peggin knelt down as Ellia flashed the light so we could see them more clearly. After a moment, Peggin pried them off and then, walking across the street, she set them down and stomped on them. That would be enough to smash anything, given that she was wearing pumps with solid brass heels on them. When she returned, she had a crease in her brow.

"One was a bug like last night. One was a GPS. Heathrow was tracking you."

"Damn it. Well, that means he was able to tell when I left the meeting tonight—"

"And waylay you because you were arriving home too quickly. You said the Shadow Person seemed too weak? Chances are it was nothing more than a Taunt."

I stared at her. "What's a Taunt?"

"It's a magical construct—not all that hard to create. Or to have someone else create for you. Taunts are easy enough to conjure up, for anybody who knows low-level magic. They're good at appearing like Ankou until you actually take them on. A Taunt is similar to a spirit-golem, but it's weak and easily dispelled. And now, you'd better go, if you expect to meet Heathrow on time. I don't doubt he'll kill Aidan if you don't show up, Kerris. But Bryan will be there. Trust in him."

I nodded. That's what I was supposed to do, wasn't it? Trust in my guardian? Trying to weather a brave face, I slid the binders into my CR-V and then gave Peggin a quick kiss. "Watch my babies for me."

"No problem there. I've got Molly with me." She patted her purse. "Now get out there. Ellia will fill me in." She pushed me toward the car and tossed me my purse and keys. She also had brought out my bag, and now she tucked it in the back. As I took the note from Ellia so I wouldn't forget the address, I climbed into the driver's seat and, fastening my seat belt, took off.

Part of me wanted to call Sophia. Police backup would be nice. But just the explanation alone would take me forever to get through. As I sped along the road, I punched the address into my GPS. It came on, giving me the turns and twists to make. I didn't want to think about the fact that I was going to meet the man I suspected of helping Duvall kill my mother. It seemed entirely stupid and foolhardy, but Aidan's life was at stake and I had inadvertently opened him up to danger by contacting him. I wasn't going to let him down.

Timber Peak Drive headed up into the mountains, up into Timber Peak, which was a bluff before the land swept down to meet the Strait of Juan de Fuca. Compared to the Olympics, or the Cascades, it was a day hike, but if you weren't used to the topography around the area, it was fore-boding and steep. Loggers had ruled these woods for so many years it was hard to count, but now Timber Peak was protected, off-limits to logging and deforestation. It was also a gold mine for hauntings and ghosts.

The drive was an easy grade at first but shortly steepened. I wasn't far into the forest when the town dropped away and only scattered farms lined the sides of the road. Another five minutes, and my turnoff was coming straight ahead. I won-dered who owned the land that Heathrow wanted me to meet him on, but then decided it didn't really matter. Friend or foe, it didn't matter. My only hope was that if it was an innocent bystander, they wouldn't know what was going down and wouldn't get hurt.

I eased onto the dirt driveway leading off the road and followed it back among the trees. It led into a dark, wooded area, and then through to a clearing where a house sat, and an old mobile home beyond that. The house was a ranch style. The lights were on and the front door was open, which didn't bode well for whoever lived here. The mobile home looked dilapidated and empty, but there was a Mercedes-Benz near it. A big old truck sat off to one side. There were no other vehicles in sight.

I turned off the car and waited, staring at the house, but there was no movement from inside. Quietly, I slipped out of the car, thinking about Peggin and her gun. I wished that I'd had the foresight to arm myself, but though I could use a gun, I was by no means an expert.

*Don't know how to use a gun properly? Fucking don't buy one.*

One of my baristas at Zigfree's had been a top-notch shot, and he told us over and over that in the hands of an amateur, guns were a bad, bad choice.

I finally pulled out my crowbar and slid the dagger—still sheathed—out of my bag and into my pocket. Nothing else wanted to come with me, so I locked the car and made a dash for the house, hoping to avoid notice for the time being. I left the books in the car. Heathrow wanted the binders? He could come out to my car, along with Aidan, to get them.

As I approached the house, I saw that not only was the front door open, but something was blocking the entrance. I moved toward it and saw a body sprawled half in, half out of the doorway. The victim was male, and he looked to be in his sixties. He was a large man, wearing coveralls and cowboy boots. Blood blossomed across the front of his chest, the stain spreading to cover most of his torso. The smell of gunpowder filled the air.

Wincing, I debated whether to call Sophia. Finally, I decided that it could wait. He was dead and he wasn't going anywhere. I'd call her after we were done with this. I made a quick sweep through the house. *Nothing.* Nobody was here, so that meant . . . the mobile home.

I slipped back out to the front yard and approached the structure, crowbar in hand. It was pitch dark and I considered hauling out a flashlight, but the fact that Heathrow had used a gun to dispatch the owner of the house—I assumed it was the owner—told me he was willing to put distance between him and his victims. It also told me that it was likely he wasn't planning on letting either Aidan or me out of here alive.

The mobile home was propped up on blocks, with a precarious set of steps up to the front door. A massive huckleberry bush sat to one side. As I passed a stand of fern surrounding a cedar, a movement caught my eye coming from behind the tree. To my surprise, a misty figure popped into view in front of me. Dressed in a pair of overalls, wearing a cowboy hat, a man stood there, husky and looking mildly confused. His torso was bloody, the stain emanating from his heart, and I could see what looked like a bullet hole in the middle of his chest. I caught my breath as he slowly moved toward me. The owner.

"What happened?" His voice was mere whispers on the wind, but to me, it was loud and clear. "I'm not sure what to do next."

Dealings with the newly dead could be problematic, but maybe I could get right on top of this and turn it to my advantage. The thought occurred to me that we might be able to strike a bargain.

"I can help you if you help me," I whispered. Ghosts didn't need loud chatter; they could hear loud and clear even with a whisper, if the person speaking focused on them enough. "I can free you, if you'll help me in return. The man who hurt you is in this trailer. He has another man with him. I need to know where they are."

The farmer stared at me, then with a soft nod, turned and pointed toward the mobile home. "He's there. The two of them."

I sucked in a deep breath. "Is there a way to get in there without being seen by them? Where are they?"

The farmer nodded and turned back to the tree, motioning for me to follow him through the brush and around the side of the trailer. I tried to move carefully and quietly. It was pitch dark, but the glow of the spirit was helping light my way, though I almost turned my ankle several times on a wayward rock. We were to the right side of the mobile home within minutes, and then around the back. A door to the right, near the end, provided a second entrance.

"Are they on the other side?" I whispered.

He nodded.

"Can you make sure for me?"

Without a sound, the farmer disappeared. I waited, not wanting to move till I was certain. As I stood there, I sensed someone near me. Forcing myself to keep silent, I turned, praying I wouldn't be facing Heathrow, but there, to my delight, stood Bryan in wolf form. He had arrived before me. I knelt down and wrapped my arms around his neck, burying my face in the silken fur that covered his body. He whimpered softly and nosed my face, giving me one long lick.

The next moment, the farmer was back. He pointed toward the door again.

"It's safe for me to go in there?"

He nodded. I paused, remembering the Taunt. If Heathrow could conjure up a Taunt . . . but no. Spirits were far different than Taunts or constructs. I was a spirit shaman and I could figure out what was real and what wasn't when it came to ghosts. The farmer was no illusion. He was a very real ghost who had, until recently, been very much alive.

I turned to Bryan. "I have to go in. You cover the front, will you?"

He whimpered again and I could tell he clearly didn't want me to endanger myself. "This is something I have to do. Aidan is in danger because of me. I owe it to him to go in there and save his ass. He wouldn't be in trouble if I hadn't called him."

Bryan paused, then turned and loped around the side of the trailer. The farmer was watching us closely, looking just as confused as before. I had another idea.

"You can be seen when you want to be seen. The man who hurt you? I want you to go in there and show yourself to him. Scare him. Pretend to be a Haunt."

Whether he understood me would be another matter. The

newly dead were often terribly confused, especially when they were victims of violent crimes. But the farmer caught a glint in his eye that looked almost like a smile and vanished. A moment later I heard a loud cry from inside the trailer. I yanked open the door and raced inside.

There, in the faint glow of the light, I saw Heathrow, waving a gun at the ghost. Behind him, trussed up in handcuffs and a ball gag, was Aidan, looking worse for wear. The farmer vanished as soon as I came inside—not what I'd had in mind, but sometimes ghosts took things literally. He had shown himself to Heathrow, and in his confused state, that sealed the bargain.

Heathrow turned, training the gun on me. "I see you finally got your ass out here. No more tricks now. You try something like that again and I'll kill both you and the shapeshifter. Where are the binders and that ledger?"

"In my truck." I eased my way over to where I could see the front door, trying to keep myself from focusing on it. No use giving away Bryan's position. "Heathrow, you can't get away with this. The farmer's dead. You're going to be tied to his death even if you kill Aidan and me."

"One death . . . three . . . five . . . what difference does it make? And if you're all dead, who's going to be able to pin it on me? I know you saw your mother's ghost when you were at my hotel. I knew then that you had put two and two together. But a ghost can't testify in court."

The shock must have shown on my face. "You knew she was there?"

"She's trailed me for years, the little bitch. Ever since Duvall and I dragged her out in the woods and killed her. Not only spirit shamans can see the dead, Kerris. That's where you made your mistake. In assuming that nobody else but you can talk to ghosts."

A thud hit the bottom of my stomach. "Why didn't you just ask Duvall where the binders were?"

"Duvall? That old fool was going to sell us out. He was going to tell the Crescent Moon Society all about Tamil and Avery, and he was going to hand over everything on the

Hounds to your people. He didn't know that I had bugged his house. The minute I knew he was terminal, I knew we might have a problem on our hands. But the Hounds won't listen to me. *Heathrow, you're just a hotel owner. You're just a simple businessman. Just follow orders, Heathrow.* Well, I'll show them I'm a whole lot smarter than most of their Ivy League degrees now."

I stared at him. So Duvall had been going to confess. And given my grandmother's cryptic messages in her letter, he had told Grandma Lila all about it. "What made you suspect Duvall of turncoating?"

"I've seen it before. Impending mortality can play strange tricks on a conscience. He was a strong old bastard, but Lila got to him. You think he didn't love her, don't you? But he did. Duvall was obsessed with her from the start, and that only made things easier to engineer. But at the end? I had to do something to protect myself. His testimony could have sent me to jail for life. I may be old, but I'm not willing to live out the rest of my days in jail. Damned fool . . . a change of heart wouldn't do him any good in the afterlife, but he didn't see it that way." Heathrow laughed, rough and harsh.

"Why? Please, just tell me why you killed Tamil and Avery." I had to keep him talking.

"Avery would have protected your mother. He was her guardian, so he had to go. And don't think that Duvall didn't try several times before, but somebody kept thwarting his attempts to kill Tamil. Your grandmother just thought Tamil was accident prone. It's like she had some fucking fairy godmother watching over her."

*She did*, I thought. *Two of them. Ivy and Ellia.*

"It took us years to get the job done, and then only to find out that fool hag had given us the wrong prediction. For years, we thought with your mother gone, there would be no way for you and your grandmother to take down Cú Chulainn's Hounds. But Magda screwed up. My son figured that one out—he took Russian in college. When he read the original prophecy, he realized that Magda had mistranslated what she had seen. You, Kerris—*you're* the enemy of the

Hounds. They know it, and once I take care of you, I'm going straight to the top. They think I'm a hanger-on. Duvall got all the credit for everything, but it's my turn now. I'm going to take the lead."

With that, he brought the gun to bear. I sucked in a deep breath. If I jumped to the side, would he still be able to hit me? There was no place to hide. "Let me say good-bye to my grandfather, at least."

With a snort, Heathrow shook his head. "You can say good-bye when you're both dead."

At that moment, the front door splintered open and Bryan—still in wolf form—burst through. In one leap, he was on Heathrow, taking him down. Behind him, Ellia rushed in, followed by Ivy. Bryan was snapping, biting at Heathrow, but the older man managed to bring the gun up and fire off a shot. Bryan whimpered and rolled to the side, blood spreading across the brilliant white fur.

I screamed and lurched forward as Heathrow shot again— this time at me. The bullet grazed my shoulder but didn't hit square on. The burn echoed through my body but I ignored it, falling to my knees by Bryan's side. At that point, I heard a loud scream—this time Heathrow's.

Turning, I saw Ellia pressed against him, her bare hands clasping his face. He struggled to free himself, but Ivy managed to hold him still as she pried the gun out of his hand. Ellia continued her hold, her hands trembling as the faint odor of burning flesh rose from Heathrow's face. He screamed again as his eyes rolled back in his head, and then he fell to the ground.

The lament singer followed, her hands still pressed against his face as he went into convulsions. A dark look filled her eyes as she pressed her fingers tight to his temples. Heathrow shuddered, arching his back as foam poured out of his mouth, and then—his body going totally stiff—he relaxed and collapsed.

# CHAPTER 20

---

"B ryan! Bryan, are you all right? Bryan . . . please, please be okay." I brushed through his fur to look for the wound. It was in his thigh, and I pressed my hands against the blood, trying to stanch it. "What can we do? I don't know how bad it is! He's not in his human form."

"We have to call Corbin," Ivy said. She pushed me aside. *"Charm, charm, mute the harm, still the blood, slow the flood . . ."* As she brushed her hands over the wound, the bleeding slowed to a trickle. "He should make it till we can get him to help, but I don't want to move him. Call Peggin, tell her to send Corbin out here. Then call Sophia and have her get a couple of ambulances out here, along with the coroner. Tell her we're going to need Gareth and Frank."

Frantic, not wanting to leave his side, it took everything I had to obey her. I pulled out my cell phone and called Peggin. "Don't ask why. Just get Corbin out here now. You still have the address?"

She said nothing but, "Yes, hang up and I'll call him."

I put in a second call to Sophia. After I got off the phone,

I turned back to find Bryan breathing softly. "He's still in his wolf form . . . is that good or bad?"

"Good, actually." Ivy smiled at me. "Dear, we shapeshifters heal better when we're in our natural forms—and our natural forms are not human. He's safer like this." She looked over at Ellia, who had put on her gloves and freed Aidan from his bonds. Ellia was sitting on the bed, where Aidan had been, staring at Heathrow's prone figure.

"Is . . . is Heathrow dead?" I didn't know whether I hoped for a yes or a no.

"No," Ellia said. "But he's trapped in his mind. He'll exist in agony forever." She looked faint and I realized how hard it must be for her to face her own powers. She caught my look and shrugged. "I couldn't let him shoot you. I had to do something. This . . . these"—she held out her hands—"are my only weapons. My mother cursed me. This time, that curse was a blessing." But her voice was trembling.

"You saved me. You saved Bryan from getting shot again. You saved Aidan." I paused, then whispered, "I had no idea he could see spirits. He knew all along my mother was there, telling me about him."

Ivy lifted me to my feet and pushed me into a chair. Aidan was there, rubbing his wrists. He looked bruised up and groggy. Red weals marked where the too-tight handcuffs had bound him. "He took me by surprise. I opened the door to find the gun pointed in my face and the next thing I knew, he stabbed me with a needle. Some sort of sedative. Bryan—are you sure he's all right?"

As if responding to his name, a quiet whimper came from the wolf on the floor. Ivy knelt down again by his side to calm him. "I think he'll be okay. My spell countered the bleeding. If the doctor gets here in time . . ."

I hugged myself. I was cold and all I wanted to do was curl up beside Bryan and hold him, but I didn't want to take a chance on disturbing what Ivy had done. I turned to Heathrow. He was in a fetal position now, rocking on the floor, murmuring in what sounded like another language. Every few seconds he'd let out a cry, or a shriek, and then go back to rocking.

Ellia stood and pushed open the front door. "I'll wait outside for the others." She vanished into the darkness.

"It's going to take her a while to recover from this. The only other times she's ever deliberately used her curse against anyone . . . it took her a long time to face the damage she can do. Even though she had no choice, it still hit her hard. Ellia's nature isn't geared toward deliberately harming people." Ivy glanced over at Aidan. "Outside, when she realized what was going on, she stripped off her gloves and I knew what she was going to do. She told me to stand back and then . . . well . . ."

"Will he ever come out of it?" I nodded to Heathrow.

"She took him so deep, I doubt it. He's locked in his mind, in a place of fire and madness that will never end, not until he dies, and I don't know if that will even break the curse. That's how her hands work. She drags people into a world where nothing else exists but the pain she inflicts on them. Her touch consigns them to hell, Kerris. Literally, Ellia's hands are . . . hell on earth." Ivy gave a soft shake of the head. "He deserved it, though. We were close enough to hear what he was saying."

At that moment, voices from outside echoed through the night and Corbin came bustling into the room. He took one look at Bryan and then knelt beside the wolf, smoothing the fur back.

"Um . . . that's not an average wolf, Corbin—" I started to say, but he waved me off.

"I know how to treat shapeshifters, girl. Remember, this is Whisper Hollow. Now back off and let me attend to your boyfriend." He glanced over his shoulder. "He'll live, so you calm yourself and go outside for now. Sophia is there and she has questions for you."

As I stepped outside, I saw a blur of activity going on. Sophia had arrived, along with two ambulances and Jonah Westwood, the undertaker. I stuck my hands in my pockets and reluctantly headed over to her, wondering how to explain everything that had happened. But I noticed that Gareth was standing beside her, along with Frank, and no other cops.

"Kerris . . ." She gave me the once-over. "Are you all right?"

The burning graze on my arm flared again. "I caught a bullet on the wing, but it just grazed my arm. I guess I should get it looked at, but . . . yeah, I'm okay." I had no clue where to start, but she held up one hand.

"We've got time to sort out things. I gather Heathrow's inside?"

I nodded. "He confessed to helping Duvall kill my mother. Duvall wasn't my grandfather. My real grandfather's inside there. Heathrow kidnapped him and was going to kill both of us. He also killed the farmer."

"Do you know why?"

"Yeah, I know." I glanced at Frank and Gareth. "I have something he wanted, and he saw this as a chance to get rid of me and to gain . . . popularity among his crowd. Apparently Duvall was going to confess everything the day that the Lady took him and Lila. Heathrow knew about it. I think . . . I think he somehow had something to do with the Lady taking them, but can't prove that."

Gareth motioned for me to be quiet. "We need to keep this on the down low, Castillo. We don't want the Hounds to know any more than we can help."

"Fix it, then." She shoved her gun back in her holster. "I'm not on duty tonight—officially. Figure out the story and get back to me. Frank, you help him. I wasn't here. You can tell Jonah . . . Corbin will take care of the medics." She turned away, then—with one last look at me—said, "Get your arm looked at. You can't take chances with wounds like that. Officially? Your grandfather killed your mother. That's what will *go* on the books and that's what *stays* on the books. Officially? Duvall was your grandfather. Aidan can be your uncle or whatever you want, but keep his real nature out of the gossip mill. The Hounds will use everything they can against you and this town. As to your father . . . well . . . cold case. I'm sorry but that's the way it has to be."

I sucked in a deep breath of the cold night air. "I understand. I'm beginning to see the way things work around here." I turned to Gareth. "You want me to run down what happened?"

He nodded. "Yep . . . then I'll get back to you with the *real* story. One word, Kerris. You may not like Starlight, but she helps keep this town together, just like Oriel does . . . just like you will. Deal with her. We can usually get her to come around. For now, there are bigger fish to fry than personal grudge matches within the Crescent Moon Society. You're part of it whether you like it or not. You don't have an option. Understand?" But his look was kind under the gruff exterior.

I gave him a firm nod. "Got it. My friend Peggin—she has to know about this . . . And my grandfather—Aidan."

"Then they have to join the Society. I'll get everyone to agree. Leave that to me. Now, excuse me. I have a jigsaw puzzle to put together." And with that, he turned back to the scene and headed over to talk to the coroner.

Ellia was sitting on one of the nurselogs so common through the area. The fallen tree trunk was a good twenty feet long and covered with moss, bracken, and brown toadstools. I joined her.

"I don't think I expected anything like this when I came home to Whisper Hollow."

"I don't think *anybody* knows what to expect. This town has a soul, Kerris—it's alive and vibrant and has a will of its own formed from the forest and the ocean and the mountains. We're allowed to live here, but Whisper Hollow? The town controls the way things go. Maybe now that you've had such a rough introduction, you can settle into doing what you're here to do."

I nodded. "But . . . the Hounds are out there . . ."

"I know."

"And your mother."

"And my mother." She let out a slow sigh. "But . . . Magda's been part of this town for decades. She won't be going anywhere soon. With Heathrow vanishing—and trust me, he'll just vanish as if he never lived here—they'll be cautious for a while. They won't know what happened. He obviously wanted to surprise them, so they don't really have all the facts. Not yet. And by the time they do manage to put it all together, we'll be waiting for them. Because you're here now, and you and Bryan are the answer to destroying the Hounds."

I stared into the darkness, feeling the weight of destiny settle on my shoulders. This was why I had run away from Whisper Hollow, and this was why I had run back to Whisper Hollow. And now that I was here . . . life was about to get real.

Bryan and I were standing in the backyard, near the fence that divided his estate from mine. His thigh was bandaged beneath his jeans, but he would live and recover. My arm was sore, but it had escaped except for a nasty graze.

I stared out into the mists. Heathrow had been carted off to a private asylum. Aidan was inside, waiting for me with Peggin. Ivy was also there, and Ellia, too. Her curse had saved my life this time, but it was only a matter of time until the Hounds took aim at me again. We had a lot of work to do, and fast.

Sliding into Bryan's arms, I leaned my face against his chest. "I was so frightened when I saw Heathrow shoot you. I thought . . ." I stopped, not wanting to say the words. They were too frightening, even now. The thought of losing him struck fear deep in the pit of my stomach. I gazed up at him as he leaned down to kiss my forehead.

"Kerris Fellwater, I'm not going anywhere. I'm your guardian. I'll protect you till the end of time. Till we both pass through to the Veil, and beyond." He paused, then brushed a strand of hair away from my face. "I love you. You know that, don't you? You're my mate. You're my match."

I pressed against him, wanting to crawl inside his skin. I had never said those three words to any man in my life. But now, I pressed my face against his chest and murmured, "I love you, Bryan Tierney. You're my guardian, my mate, and my match."

"Then that settles that. Now come, we have work to do."
And with one more kiss, he led me inside.

One week later, we gathered in the cemetery on a wild
windswept night, Ellia, Bryan, and I. Peggin stood
nearby, as did Aidan. Somehow, our triad had expanded to
include them. Ellia was unusually quiet. The memory of sending Heathrow into an unending agony of madness would
weigh heavy on her for a long time, but she made no mention
of it. But, having seen the power she held in her hands, I could
only wonder about her mother and just how strong Magda
was, and how powerful Baba Volkov and her followers must
be. Dark magic, indeed, and dark hexes, aimed at me. At all
of Whisper Hollow.

Ellia fitted her violin under her chin as Bryan took up
his post, guarding and watching. We were standing beside
a freshly dug grave. The marker simply read, *Robert Walters, Son of the Sacred Land.* No one had come to his
funeral. No one knew he had been murdered except the few
who had been out on his land. Everybody else thought Bob
Walters had a heart attack. He had no next of kin to notify,
and Gareth and Frank had done an excellent job of covering
all the bases.

I gave Ellia a long look and she smiled at me, nodding as
she struck a chord. The lilting notes that filtered out trickled
down to surround the grave. I held up my wand, summoning
the farmer's spirit to rise and walk with us. He stood there,
between the lament singer and me, looking bewildered.

Then as I stepped forward, he smiled and held out his
hand.

*You promised.*

*I did, and I'm here to help you. Follow me . . . follow the
music.*

I led him through the cemetery as Ellia played the path
ahead. Bryan swung in behind, as did Peggin and Aidan.
We were a solemn procession, the slow march leading
toward Penelope's tomb. As we neared the door, it swung

open and the Gatekeeper stepped out, her long dress flowing in the wild wind that surrounded us. A gust swept past, chilling me to the bone, carrying Ellia's notes high and aloft to spin out over the town and remind the people of Whisper Hollow that the dead were walking.

"Welcome to the Veil, Robert Walters. Take my hand, love, and join my dark kingdom." Penelope held out her hand. The nails protruding from her flesh glistened under the lights of the walkway; the dried blood pooling around them shimmered like jewels.

The farmer stared at her, a look of fear and dismay crossing his face, but as she clasped his hand, it fell away to be replaced by a dream-filled smile and he murmured a soft thank-you. Penelope turned to me, the coy smile on her face twinkling under the wild wind.

"They all fall in love with me, Kerris. Death is a temptress, she's a dark mistress, and the Morrígan rides high on the mourning winds. And so we begin our journey together, you and I. There will be many more nights like this, and many more spirits. You need to corral Betty and Tommy soon; they're getting too big for their gravestones, so to speak."

I laughed then. "Teenagers are always full of themselves."

"Yes, but most teenagers aren't Haunts and can't wreak the havoc that pair can." And with that, she turned back to Robert and led him into the tomb. The door swept shut behind her and Robert Walters vanished into the Veil with the Gatekeeper of the dead.

I turned back to the others. "And that ends that . . ."

But it wasn't true and I knew it. It wasn't over by any means. I had found the answer to my mother's disappearance, and to my father's . . . but Penelope was right: The journey was just beginning. The Hounds were out there, waiting and planning. Magda was aiming her sights on the town. And the Lady lurked hungry in her murky waters.

"What are you thinking?" Bryan whispered.

"Dark thoughts for a dark night." I gave him a soft smile, grateful to have him by my side. Seattle seemed a world away—a lifetime ago. Whisper Hollow was my home now and forever, and the cemetery my office. As we returned to the grave, I scooped up a jar full of dirt and labeled it *Robert Walters, October 23, 2015*. The first jar with my handwriting to take its place in the hidden room.

And then Ellia pushed aside her gloom and began a merry jig, and, remembering my childhood, I let go and danced through the graveyard, grabbing Peggin's hand as we spun in circles, whirling through the gravestones. Ellia stepped up the music, her notes trilling through the headstones. Bryan and Aidan stood, laughing and clapping as the wind caught up the music and our voices with a swirl of autumn leaves and tossed them all to ride the haunted night.

# THE PLAYLIST

I write to music quite often, and each book will have a playlist that fits the mood of the book. For *Autumn Thorns*, this is the list of songs I listened to:

**A.J. Roach:** "Devil May Dance"

**Android Lust:** "Saint Over," "Here and Now"

**The Black Angels:** "Don't Play with Guns," "Holland," "Indigo Meadow," "Young Men Dead," "Bad Vibrations," "Black Isn't Black"

**Black Rebel Motorcycle Club:** "Feel It Now"

**Bob Seger:** "Old Time Rock & Roll"

**Broken Bells:** "The Ghost Inside"

**Buffalo Springfield:** "For What It's Worth"

**Celtic Woman:** "Scarborough Fair"

**Clannad:** "Newgrange"

**Crazy Town:** "Butterfly"

**Damh the Bard:** "Gently Johnny," "Obsession," "Willow's Song," "The Wicker Man," "Morrighan," "The Cauldron Born," "Cloak of Feathers"

**David Bowie:** "Unwashed and Somewhat Slightly Dazed," "Fame"

**Death Cab for Cutie:** "I Will Possess Your Heart"

**Dizzi:** "Dizzi Jig," "Dance of the Unicorns"

**Donovan:** "Hurdy Gurdy Man," "Season of the Witch"

**Eastern Sun:** "Beautiful Being (Original Edit)"

**Eels:** "Souljacker, Part I"

**Fatboy Slim:** "Praise You"

**Faun:** "Tanz mit mir," "The Market Song," "Hymn to Pan"

**The Feeling:** "Sewn"

**Flight of the Hawk:** "Bones"

**Garbage:** "#1 Crush," "Queer," "Only Happy When It Rains," "Push It," "Not Your Kind of People," "Bleed Like Me," "I Think I'm Paranoid"

**Gary Numan:** "Dead Heaven," "Splinter," "Here in the Black," "When the Sky Bleeds," "He Will Come," "Petals," "The Angel Wars," "Down in the Park"

**Godsmack:** "Voodoo"

**Gotye:** "Somebody That I Used to Know"

**Heathen Kings:** "Rambling Sailor," "Rolling of the Stones"

**Huldrelokkk:** "Trolldans"

**In Strict Confidence:** "Silver Bullets," "Snow White," "Tiefer"

**Jessica Bates:** "The Hanging Tree"

**Lady Gaga:** "Teeth," "I Like It Rough"

**Ladytron:** "Black Cat," "I'm Not Scared," "Ghosts"

**Lenny Kravitz:** "American Woman"

**Lord of the Lost:** "Sex on Legs"

**Loreena McKennitt:** "All Souls Night," "The Mummer's Dance," "The Mystic's Dream"

**Low:** "Half-Light"

**Mark Lanegan:** "Phantasmagoria Blues," "Gray Goes Black," "Wedding Dress," "Riot in My House," "The Gravedigger's Song," "Methamphetamine Blues"

**Matt Corby:** "Breathe"

**M.I.A.:** "Bad Girls"

**Morcheeba:** "Even Though (Acoustic)"

**Nick Cave and the Bad Seeds:** "Red Right Hand"

**Nirvana:** "Plateau," "Lake of Fire," "Where Did You Sleep Last Night?" "Heart-Shaped Box"

**Opeth:** "Death Whispered a Lullaby," "Hope Leaves," "To Rid the Disease"

**The Pierces:** "Secret"

**P. J. Harvey:** "In the Dark Places," "The Words That Maketh Murder," "Good Fortune," "The Colour of the Earth," "Let England Shake," "Bitter Branches"

**Rachel Diggs:** "Hands of Time"

**The Screaming Trees:** "Where the Twain Shall Meet," "All I Know," "Dime Western"

**Sweet Talk Radio:** "We All Fall Down"

**Syntax:** "Pride"

**Tamaryn:** "While You're Sleeping," "I'm Dreaming"

**Tom Petty and the Heartbreakers:** "Mary Jane's Last Dance"

**The Verve:** "Bittersweet Symphony"
**Voltaire:** "Brains!"
**Voxhaul Broadcast:** "You Are the Wilderness"
**Warchild:** "Ash"
**Zero 7:** "In the Waiting Line"

In the sleepy town of Whisper Hollow,
spirits walk among the living, secrets don't stay buried,
and the lake won't give up her dead . . .

Look out for the second book in the
enthralling Whisper Hollow series

# DREAMING DEATH

Coming soon from

headline
ETERNAL

# headline
## ETERNAL

# FIND YOUR HEART'S DESIRE...